Forever and Back

ASHLEY MANLEY

WILDFLOWER
BOOKS

Copyright © 2025 by Ashley Manley.

All rights reserved.

No part of this publication may be reproduced, distributed, or transmitted in any form or by any means, including photocopying, recording, or other electronic or mechanical methods, without the prior written permission of the publisher, except as permitted by U.S. copyright law.

This is a work of fiction. Names, characters, places, and incidents either are the product of the author's imagination or are use fictitiously and any resemblance to actual persons (living or deceased), places, buildings, and products is entirely coincidental.

Identifiers:

979-8-9899682-6-8 (paperback) | 979-8-9899682-7-5 (eBook)

Cover by Elise Stamm, Blue Heron Graphic Design

Interior graphics from iStock

First edition: April 2025 | Wildflower Books LLC

Editors:

Victoria Straw (developmental)

Kaitlin Slowik (copyedit)

Melissa Smith (proofread)

Dear Reader,

I've said it before and I'll say it again, thank you so much for picking my book to read out of the eleventy bajillion there are in the world. I hope you fall in love with June and her house of chaos as much as I did as I was writing. Please know, June's story is about the difficult parts of marriage and motherhood/pregnancy and also contains explicit language and on page romance. If you would like to skip the romance scenes, these are included in chapters sixteen, seventeen, twenty-seven, thirty-one, and thirty-three (go June!)

Thanks for being here.
Xo, Ashley

To the moms.
The ones who struggle and the ones who don't. To the ones who nursed for years and the ones who gave bottles on day one. To the moms who birthed at home in bathtubs and the ones who screamed for the epidural from a hospital bed. To the gentle moms, the tired moms, the stressed-AF moms, and the happy moms. To the ones who feed seaweed snacks and the ones who feed fruit snacks. To the ones who have lost, wept, and somehow kept going. Through car lines, through grocery store aisles, and through endless loads of laundry.
To the moms of angels and rainbows.
To my mom, my mother-in-law, and the women who have mothered me in between.
Most importantly, to the moms who love, in whatever color of the rainbow, to forever and back.

ONE

Spaghetti night is my own personal hell, yet here we are again. Because it's easy. Because everyone will eat it. Because the thought of thinking of something different makes my eye twitch.

"Boys! Lyra!" I shout over my shoulder as I set bowls on the dinged-up kitchen table. "Dinner!"

When the twins appear—seemingly out of nowhere—I nearly drop the pot of pasta. "Hank! God! Get that plastic bag off your brother's head!"

Hank frowns as Tyrus pulls the bag off his head and climbs into his chair, revealing a tiny-toothed smile. "I was seeing how long I could hold my breath."

There's no time for a safety lecture before they both start shoveling sauce-covered noodles into their mouths.

"Where's Dad?" Lyra asks, seventeen-year-old vibe of nonchalance as she strolls into the room and drops into a seat at the table. The bright green lace of her bra pops against her skin as the oversized neck of her dusty grey T-shirt slides down her shoulder.

I do not say the sarcastic *great question* that stabs at the tip of my tongue. Instead, I ignore her. *If you can't say anything nice, don't say anything at all.*

I wince when the dog barks, a booming sound that nearly rattles the walls of the small house. Thor, our godforsaken bullmastiff, prances into the room—claws tapping against the wood floor at a cadence that scrapes at my sanity—until he reaches the table.

He sits, drools, and whimpers as he eyes the food.

"Ty, Hank . . . gross," Lyra says, scrunching her gold-hoop pierced nose as she looks at her twin brothers, already elbow deep in their dinner. Literally.

"Boys, slow down," I tell them, trying not to focus on how much of their meal is missing their mouths. *Positive moms focus on positive points.*

The phone vibrates in my back pocket.

I don't need to read it to know what it says, but I do anyway. Because apparently, I like high blood pressure.

Camp: *won the softball game grabbing dinner and beer with the guys tell the kids good night for me*

Camp is late—again.

Camp is off having fun while I'm dying in the trenches of the dinnertime war zone—again.

Camp texts like a Neanderthal with no regard for punctuation marks—again.

I slide my phone back into my pocket without responding to him and force a smile. "Your dad has a softball game."

Lyra grins. "Living his best life, as usual."

A bitter taste fills my mouth as I try not to glare at her. Lyra is whip-smart, top of her class, and, much to my fucking chagrin, her dad's biggest fan.

"Sure," I mutter, glancing at the clock as I scoop spaghetti in my own bowl, swallowing every annoyed thing I want to shout.

Because why wouldn't he join a recreational softball team on top of the baseball team he coaches and the full-time job he has as the athletic director and the planning of the new sports complex and all the team sports events he goes to because he's supportive and can't say no to anyone except his own wife?

"Is that gluten-free?" she asks.

I shake my head, pointing to the pot with the less flexible, more mushy-looking pasta. "That one."

"What's gluten?" Hank asks, the marinara sauce covering the corners of his mouth the perfect match to the wild red hair and freckles that cover his four-year-old face.

"Looks like glue," Tyrus observes from next to him around his own spaghetti-filled cheeks, identical freckle-smattered nose scrunching.

I chuckle. "I don't think it's glue, Ty."

"It's healthy," Lyra says, defending her current dietary trend as she swirls a mass of glue-pasta onto her fork, hair falling in her face—currently dyed pink. "That stuff you're putting in your mouth is toxic." She widens her eyes for dramatic effect; they ignore her, shoveling more *toxic food* into their mouths.

"Ms. Mitchell put a note in your folders, boys," I say, situating myself in my chair, positioning my own bowl of spaghetti in front of me, eyebrows raised. "You got red cards today."

Ms. Mitchell's approach to teaching preschool errs on the side of terrifying with a discipline system that doubles as a barometer of parental capabilities: green means good mom, yellow means less-good mom, and red means I suck.

"She doesn't like us," Hank whines, noodles plastered to his chin. "She says our red hair makes us mean."

I scoff. "She does not."

"Does too!" Ty shouts, meat sauce spitting out of his mouth like a volcanic eruption across the table. "She's only nice to the girls! They never go to time-out!"

I sigh. "You know that's not—"

"I have a scholarship essay to write tonight," Lyra says, oblivious to the boys' shouting.

"Need help?" I ask her as the boys continue to shout their grievances. "After dinner I can—"

"Meh. I'll wait for Dad," she says over the boys' shouts, twirling spaghetti onto her fork. "It's about chasing your dreams, and, I mean, duh, that's, like, Dad's expertise, right?"

I drop my fork on reflex, every molecule in my body taken aback.

My face must show everything I'm thinking, because she adds, "No offense, Mom, it's just, you know . . . Dad chased big dreams, and you were happy with this." The boys take this opportunity to have a race to see who can finish their spaghetti first, red noodles being shoveled into their mouths at warp speed as Thor's dinosaur-sized brown head squeezes its way onto the table between them, lapping up the food that misses their mouths. Lyra's face twists as if she's witnessing life's worst-case scenario being played out in front of her. "You know, just being a mom. Simple." I try to make an agreeing noise, but there's not enough momentum in my body to will it out of my mouth before she continues. "Don't get me wrong, someone has to do it—all this—but Dad . . . he's just out there doing it, you know? Making a difference and creating a legacy." She shrugs. "Plus, he went to App State, so . . ."

My jaw drops. "I went to Appalachian State University, too, you know. And had a 4.0 GPA. And got a degree!"

She laughs, like I've said something silly. "I know, Mom, but you know, it's Dad. He, like, went *went* to App. What was your degree even in?" She squints, but her tone is rhetorical. She doesn't care. "Either way, I'll wait for Dad."

I nod about thirty-two times as the boys holler and the dog whimpers. "Right."

I smile through the searing pain that burns through my body. Like my heart is pumping lethal chemicals through my veins. As if she didn't just say the most insulting thing I've ever heard in my life. As if she didn't just let me know that nobody sees the real me. The living, breathing thing that lingers in a dark cage beneath my bones; a silent being that only I know exists. Invisible.

"Let's do Today's Best," I say, mostly to distract myself from the fact I wish the floor would open up and swallow me whole.

I listened to a podcast once that said having kids reflect on their day and talk about the best parts promoted compassion and increased likelihood of healthy relationships long-term. Out of my own inadequacies, one of our many podcast-inspired practices was born.

"I did the monkey bars at school today," Ty says, proud.

I smile. "That's ama—"

"You cheated! I saw you standing on Rhett's shoulders!" Hank argues, outraged his brother would even claim such a thing.

"Did not!"

"Did so!"

"Boys!" I snap, taking a breath to level out. "Either way, Ty, that's amazing. Hank, your turn."

When he says, "I did the monkey bars," another argument ensues, Lyra telling them both to shut up, neither of them listening.

The dog barks.

Ty starts crying because Hank pinches him.

"Hank, don't do that. That's not nice," I say as Ty climbs onto my lap, smearing the spaghetti sauce from his face to my shirt—the only white one I own—as he cries.

Lyra eats two bowls of pasta, then tells me she doesn't like that brand.

"I'll buy a different type next time," I tell her, forcing a smile. "Today's Best, Ly?"

Hank's spaghetti spills on the floor. I want to yell, but I stay quiet. Blindly reaching for a useful piece of advice in the doldrums of my mind.

Kids can't self-regulate if parents don't demonstrate self-regulation.

3-2-1.

3-2-1.

I do a mental countdown. Keep myself in check.

"Hmm." Lyra seems oblivious to the chaos, which only fuels the feeling of insanity that's thrumming through my body. "Oh, I know!" She perks up, starting a story about something that happened in science lab. I force a smile, but mentally I check out.

Ty's milk spills. I calmly get a paper towel. Keep my cool even though I'm a pot of water sitting over a roaring flame, the boil consuming my body.

The dog barks.

A phone rings—Lyra's. She stands, mutters, "God, this place is a circus," then drops her dirty bowl in the sink and disappears down the hall into her bedroom. Her door clicks closed.

The room starts to spin. The whole house.

The dog barks again.

It's not so different than any other night, but I feel like I'm about to die. Like a plastic bag is over *my* head.

Where the hell is Camp?

Jamming my palms into my eyes, I force myself to take a deep breath. Then another.

Since the day I sat on an off-kilter toilet lid, fresh out of college but still working as a waitress, and saw that positive pregnancy test, I was in it. I may have never wanted to be a mother, may have never held a baby in my life, but damn if I wasn't going to be the best one this world had ever seen.

Now, sitting in the middle of this disaster—this loud, thankless, exhausting disaster—I feel every shortcoming in my life. A simple truth sinks deeper into me with every strangling breath: I suck. At all of it. A mom that can't control her kids. A wife whose husband doesn't show up to dinner. A once-ambitious girl turned forty-year-old worn-down hag.

Reality threatens to swallow me whole.

In a haze of mayhem, dinner ends, and I get the boys clean, in pajamas, and tucked into bed.

Now I face the war zone of a kitchen. Multiple dirty pots for multiple kinds of pasta. Slobbery sauce smeared on the table and floor.

3-2-1.

3-2-1.

Pushing the earbuds into my ears, I cue up the next podcast from *The Perfect Mom*. While I've been listening to podcasts nearly a decade, I found this one after the boys unexpectedly came along and connected to it right away. Abbigail, the host, started it as a "one-stop shop to fix all your parenting woes," interviewing a different expert in their field every week, gaining millions of listeners. Social proof she was on to something. I've been hanging on to every word since the first episode.

I had been a young mom with Lyra, but suddenly, with the boys, I became the old mom. Everything felt different this time. Every day happening with quicksand beneath my feet and a vise around my chest. Camp focused more time on work; I was drowning. Babies, a tween, a dog the size of a Shetland pony . . . it was overwhelming. The advice that played in my ears helped me regain control. Solidified the ground beneath me and deepened my breaths.

Experts, guiding me to be better than I was. Than I *am*. Sometimes even solving problems I don't know I'm having.

I turn up the volume and reach my hands into the soapy water.

THE PERFECT MOM PODCAST WITH ABBIGAIL BUCHANAN

EPISODE 208: The Plight of the Stay-at-Home Mom with guest Dr. Lisa Cowart

Abbigail: Alright, mamas, we have special guest Dr. Lisa Cowart here to talk about her new book, *The Plight of the Homemaker*. Welcome to the show, Doctor.

Dr. Cowart: Thanks for having me, Abbigail.

Abbigail: Let's get right to it, shall we? Tell us about your book. What inspired you to write it, and what do you want all those perfect mama listeners to take away from it?

Dr. Cowart: That's such a great question.

In her brief pause, I snort a small laugh. Is that really a *great question*?

Dr. Cowart: I was a stay-at-home mom for years but felt like I was just in a hamster wheel, you know? Like I did the same thing over and over and over and over. And everyone around me seemed so fulfilled. My kids won awards, and my husband got promoted at work, and they were all celebrated, while there I was, riding on their coattails . . . a doctor, for God's sake! Then, I found out the whole time I was working so hard to make everyone happy, my husband, along with pursuing whatever dreams he wanted, was also having an affair.

Abbigail: Gosh, that must have been hard.

Dr. Cowart: The hardest. And us wives—we want to believe our husbands love us, don't want to see what they are doing—but it's part of the plight I discuss in my book, which you can purchase at my website, doctorlisacowart-dot-com. We are so closed off in our own bubbles of chaos, we forget that everyone else out in the world is exposed to so many choices. People. Sure, Stan, as you'll read about in my book, left me for a younger version—a working woman, as you'll read in my book—but you know what? It was the shove I needed. Getting out of my marriage opened my eyes to everything I'd given up. How wrong I had it. I leaned on my psychology background and looked into what happened—how I got it so wrong. I went through studies—conducted my own—and found the biggest problem is women who choose to stay home and raise babies are simultaneously handing over their happiness to others without even knowing it. They take care of others to the point of draining their own happiness tanks! Think of any stay-at-home mom you know, Abbigail . . .

When she pauses, I still, mid-drying of a pot, eyes pinging around the room as if a hidden camera is watching me die a death of domestic duties.

Dr. Cowart: Do they pursue their own interests outside of their family? Are they taken seriously? Do their kids and spouse even know them? Do they even know themselves? Do they take an active role in making choices for their own life?

She pauses, dramatic and all knowing, as the word *no* fills my skull like a balloon.

Dr. Cowart: If the answer is no, they need to shake it up.

Abbigail: Shake it up?

Dr. Cowart: Rediscover themselves. Remove the bruised fruit. If a woman is slaving away at home, not being appreciated, while her husband—for example—is out having beer with friends, or golfing, or getting into another woman's bed . . . where's the justice? The balance?! One person can't always sacrifice. And these women, home and working hard to raise kids the best they can but not being supported by a spouse, their ability to parent suffers with that.

Abbigail: So you're saying that if the women listening aren't being supported by their husbands, they'll never be the moms they want to be?

Dr. Cowart: You are exactly right. Not just want to be, need to be. And studies show—all included in my book—that children raised in homes by mothers who aren't respected and fulfilled are more likely to grow up lacking the ability to set and achieve long-term goals.

At this, my eyes bug out of my head.

Abbigail: So unfulfilled women should what—leave their husbands? Go to work?

Dr. Cowart: Let me ask it to you this way: Is it fair that men get to chase their dreams while women don't?

Abbigail: Hmm. I definitely see what you're saying. But what about the mamas out there listening that are skeptical of this. Who think "I like staying home and taking care of my family. This is advice from a woman scorned"?

Dr. Cowart: I can see how people think my husband walking out on me for a younger version and posting photos of their European vacation all over the internet would make them think that, but it's simply not true. I'm happy in my life—single and independent and navigating the narcissists of modern dating—and presenting this information, all in my book, from a completely unbiased and healed perspective. I harbor no ill will toward my ex leaving me high and dry. None. Without him shattering my life into a million pieces I wouldn't be where I am now. I'm saying, if you have even the slightest feelings of being unappreciated, the slightest inkling that your husband isn't around enough because he's selfishly pursuing his own interests . . . feel like you're failing because you are being swallowed in the daily grind. The fun sponge while your spouse gets to be the hero . . . maybe you don't know what's best. Take it from me, things are never what they seem. For every person sacrificing, there is someone who isn't. Who never will.

She pauses, dramatic silence hanging in my earbuds, anticipation squeezing my throat.

Dr. Cowart: At the end of the day, you have to ask yourself: Is your marriage a source of life or the demise of it? Is your husband supporting you or standing in your way? Is he really trying or just making excuses?

Abbigail: Wow . . . that's wow. Okay, mamas, on that explosive note, we will break with a word from our sponsors. We'll be back in a minute.

I pop the earbuds out of my ears. Stare at the soap. The small house we live in. The snoring dog on the floor. The door my husband still hasn't walked through.

All I can think . . . *how the hell did I get here?*

Two

It's nine thirty when Camp finds me glaring at myself in the bathroom mirror, anti-wrinkle patch stuck to my forehead.

After I cleaned up the spilled drinks and spaghetti.

After I did the dishes.

After I read bedtime stories and filled water cups four thousand times.

After he played a softball game and had beers and burgers with his friends.

He strolls in—filthy cleats leaving a trail of clay through the house—without a care in the world and an easy lopsided smile on his lips. I'm not someone I'd consider as having a short temper, but the sight of him—relaxed, unaffected, handsome despite the ridiculous mustache that covers his upper lip like a 1970s porn star—has me twitching.

Dr. Cowart's words from the podcast become lyrics to an annoying song that's stuck in my head.

Is it fair that men get to chase their dreams while women don't? For every person sacrificing, there is someone who isn't. Who never will.

I take him in, this man who had big dreams he chased and caught. Who gets to float around life doing whatever he wants. I want to scream. Maybe even use violence. Fine, I'm self-aware enough to know that if there were no consequences, I'd punch Camp "The Slinger" Cannon right in his goddamn face.

I must be a good actress because he coolly says, "Hey, J." His thick southern accent that once felt like warm honey dripping all over me now hits my eardrums like nails on a chalkboard.

He kisses my temple, slightest hint of beer on his breath. An IPA. Local. I don't have to ask. After twenty-five years together, there are no mysteries.

He smiles at my reflection in the gold-brushed framed mirror that covers the white-tiled walls before stepping aside to start the shower and toe off his clay-caked cleats. In the middle of the bathroom floor. That I'll eventually move to the front door. After sweeping up the mess they made without him even noticing.

I clear my throat. "Hey." Then, like someone else is controlling my mouth: "You had beer."

His eyes narrow as he unties his pants—some sort of athletic jogger with burnt-orange streaks of clay across them.

"Yeah. I texted you after the game. We had burgers at the brewery." He chuckles, pants slipping to the ground. "We were just about to leave and in walked Dani, so we had one more with her."

"Dani?" I frown. "What was she doing there?"

My voice is clipped but he doesn't react—he never reacts—only shrugs as he peels his clothes off.

"Coincidence, I guess."

Fat chance.

Dani is the girls' softball coach with dewy skin and muscular thighs. Always where Camp is. Gushing. And giggling. Camp isn't even funny. And there's her hair, chestnut brown with the swish and bounce shampoo commercials are made of.

He reaches into the stream of water to check the temperature, then steps in, oblivious to my glowering as he stands in the glass-walled shower.

"We had spaghetti, and it was a disaster," I say, mostly to myself, slight echo in the room.

"Ah," he says, a layer of fog forming on the glass as he squirts shampoo into his palm, tilting his head into the water. "That's no fun."

He massages shampoo into his shaggy blond hair, eyes closed as he faces the spray of the faucet. Steam fills the bathroom, water drips down his toned body, and an itch forms beneath my skin. Every inch of him triggers a memory.

The boomerang-shaped birthmark on his ribs, and his familiar *To forever and back* when I used to trace it.

The tan lines across his biceps from hours upon hours spent on baseball fields.

The slopes of his muscles from a life dedicated to movement.

The bump on his nose, a reminder of the night we almost weren't.

His body, a timeline of us, unnerves me.

It's taken years for me to get to this point—years of giving him the opportunity to show up and him not—but now that I'm here, there's no coming back. Now that I'm here, I see he's been living, and I haven't.

With every drop of water that streams down his body, the things I once loved about him I begin to hate. Resentment stacks up inside me like bricks of a building.

I look from him in the shower—without a care in the world—to my own face in the mirror.

My now overly moisturized skin, a vain attempt at maintaining some kind of youth, is framed by penny-red hair that hangs down my back and eyebrows that have no actual shape. I'm a stranger. Dr. Cowart's words the only truth I know.

Here I am, forty, an age when I always thought I'd be so sure of who I was and what I wanted, completely lost. A frayed rope one thread away from snapping. The girl who was once the best at everything she did, now failing miserably. No career. No direction. I'm a bus driver, chef, and maid—all without a title or paycheck. All without an ounce of appreciation from anyone else. A former wannabe photographer without a lick to show for it. I'm nothing. A dud.

The black sky against everyone else's bright stars.

Or, according to Lyra, *simple*.

Every time a human was plucked from my uterus, I lost a piece of myself, no doubt scrambled up in the weird and bloody mess of afterbirth. Maybe that's why celebrities eat the stuff. A futile attempt at retaining their identities.

The strange thing is, I didn't see it happen. Somewhere between peanut butter sandwiches, loads of laundry, and committee meetings at the school, I began to vanish. A silent thief stealing away my pieces without my permission as the years passed by. Camp has emerged from the over two decades since high school larger-than-life while I'm a shaved-away version of my previous self with a soft belly and stretch marks.

There's no laughing.

No flirting.

No intentional time together.

Assigned roommates who tolerate each other.

His life is work and baseball; mine is kids and keeping a house I never wanted to live in.

This realization—the fact this is who we've become, who *I've* become—makes pressure swirl in my gut. There's an urgency, a desperation, pulsating through me as Camp pushes the shower door open and hooks a towel around his perfectly unchanged waist.

I can't do this anymore.

Dr. Cowart was right. It's not just about me. The implications for the kids if I stay in this are dire.

Is your marriage a source of life or the demise of it?

I square my sleepshirt-covered shoulders to him. "I'm done."

He steps around me to the sink, taking his razor from a drawer, and snorts a laugh. "With what? Spaghetti?"

Typical Camp response. *Idiot.*

"You. Us. Being alone all the damn time."

His chin pulls back as he puts a layer of shaving cream on—careful to avoid his mustache. Almost dismissive. Any other day, his silence would shut me up. Would be enough to make me want to avoid the argument. But today? Today I was called simple, and I will not willingly go back into my cage. For once, I want the argument.

"And you wear your cleats inside."

He sweeps the razor down his jaw, eyes in the reflection flicking quickly to mine.

"And you're always late. Always with the team or-or-or at work. And I'm here. Cleaning. Picking up your shoes. Picking up the dog shit."

My own eyes widen along with his at my uncouth use of *shit*. I pause, but only long enough to get enough oxygen in my lungs to keep going. Voice firming with conviction with every spoken word.

"And I'm going to be honest, it doesn't feel like you even like me. What do we do together? Anything?"

For the first time in years, I'm shouting at him.

"You go out on Tuesdays—all game days—and that's not even mentioning the team you coach, or the other games you're obligated to attend as the athletic director. And the sponsor dinners! You laugh and drink beer with the team and your friends and coaches, and I'm here making dinner and doing homework. Putting out never-ending fires with the boys—sometimes literally. Repeating bedtime routines over and over and over while my skin starts to sag from my bones. Life passing me by. I'm nobody. Because I gave it all to you. To the kids. But-but-but—"

He sets the razor down, half of his face still covered in thick white foam. Expression unreadable as his head turns from looking at reflection me to real me.

"I can't do this anymore, Camp. I won't. I refuse."

Eyebrows pinched, one palm resting on the counter, the other hanging by his side, his half-shaved chin pulls back.

"Are you about to start your period?"

His question nearly knocks the wind out of me.

"No, Camp," I say through gritted teeth. "I'm not about to *start my period*."

"Where is this comin' from then?" He takes another swipe of the razor down his face. "You know I've been crazy at work."

I bark out an unexpected laugh that shocks me as much as it does him.

"Do you hear yourself? You've been playing softball tonight. With grown men. Not getting paid!"

His mouth drops. Stunned.

"Do you know how many dinners you've made it home for in the last month?" I pause but don't need to; he knows the answer just as well as I do. "Two. Both Sundays." My hands fly into the air. "At your parents' house!"

"I invited you to come to the game tonight, you always like talkin' to—what's Johnny's wife's name?"

He squints at his reflection as he thinks. Like that's what matters right now.

"I don't want to go to your stupid softball game, Camp!" He blinks, says nothing. "We have kids. With homework. And bedtimes. We all don't get to float around living our best lives every damn night."

We stare at each other, tension thick. My breaths match the cadence of my pounding heart: so fast it's like I've been running nonstop for the last seventeen years.

He rubs his index finger across the bump on his nose and looks away, studying something on the counter that doesn't matter, before looking back at me. For the first time since I've started talking, his face says he's listening.

"I don't do anythin' around here because you've already done it, J. How was I supposed to know . . . ?"

I scoff. "Really, Camp? How were you supposed to know that I needed you to come home?" *Unbelievable.* "Every week?!"

"You know how those refs are!" He holds up his palms, defensive. "They sit over at Liberty Tap and lose track of time. We never start on time!" he cries. "And you know how busy things are right now at work. Baseball season is in full swing with a crazy schedule. And we're wrappin' up basketball playoffs. But the sports complex is almost done, and the board is—"

"You staying for one more beer with *Dani* has nothing to do with the refs sitting at Liberty Tap!" I snap.

"Dani?" His half-shaved jaw goes slack. "Are you kiddin' me right now?"

I cross my arms, heart pounding against my throat.

"I'm done." I hear the words before it registers I've said them. "I'm done letting you live a life you want because I don't have one at all."

He scoffs. Says nothing.

He doesn't get it. I would laugh if I didn't think it would make me cry.

In college I had a photography teacher that said a good photographer takes a picture, a great photographer tells a story. I don't know why I think of him right now, but I do. Clear as day, I see Professor Glenn standing in front of a classroom in his daily uniform of khaki-colored clothes and floppy hat with a dinged-up Canon slung around his neck, like he was moments away from leaving for an African safari.

He didn't just look at photos, he studied them. Scrutinized every line. He'd stare at an image and hum and nod.

I imagine a photo being captured of Camp and I in this bathroom. Him perfect, me lost. Him aging like a barrel of fine wine, me a bushel of rotten apples. Him living, me not. Him. Me. Him. Me.

And then I know, clear as a photo with a new lens, this scene tells one story: We're over.

I've heard right before a person dies, life flashes before their eyes.

And while I don't think I'm about to die, in the seconds I take to work up the nerve to say what I need to say, I see it all. *Our* life.

The first time we kissed.

High school graduation.

The college parties.

The new baby.
The small wedding.
The sleepless nights.
The deep loss.
The drifting apart.
The unseeing.
The quiet.
So.
Much.
Quiet.

Then, the words I never dreamed: "I want a divorce."

A breath gushes out of him, and his eyes go wide. "A divorce?!"

I swallow, unsure if I can repeat it. I nod, pause, then add, "Would we even be married if I didn't get pregnant with Lyra?"

His expression crashes, palms gripping the edge of the vanity as he hinges at the waist. We're quiet, breathing, letting the question float like fog in the small bathroom.

Upright again, he picks up the razor, drags the final line down his jaw, a small dot of blood bursting at the surface before he rinses his face. The whole act takes less than a minute but lasts a decade.

He looks at me—so much unexpected hurt in his eyes it sends a stab of guilt into my chest.

"I would have asked, but judgin' by the question, I'm guessin' you wouldn't have said yes."

He bends over, scoops up his cleats, and walks out of the bathroom, leaving me alone with the pile of clay in the middle of the floor.

No fighting.

No promising me things will get better.

When I tell my husband our marriage is over, he walks away.

Alone in the bathroom, hands trembling, I yank the drawer open and pull a pair of scissors out, doing the only thing I know to do. In four angry snips, I cut a jagged line of bangs across my wrinkle patch–covered forehead. Locks of my red hair fall down the front of my face before scattering across the tiled floor.

I refuse to cry the tears burning behind my eyes.

I sniff, wipe my nose with the back of my hand.

When I leave the bathroom, I don't clean the mess. The strands of my hair sit in a pile next to the clay from his shoes.

It's all still there when I walk in the next morning.

Three

Standing over him, I study his face. Bulbus nose, spotty skin. Harold Griffin, ninety-seven years old. I can't decide if this is a really long time or just a blink. Even with eyebrows so thick and wiry they basically form a single overgrown caterpillar across his forehead, he looks peaceful.

I take a seat in the floral wingback chair and read the paper in my hands.

Happily married sixty-eight years.

I scoff.

"I don't know how you did it, Harold."

I close my eyes and drop my head back before letting my next words come out the way they always do when I'm here: in an unfiltered stream of consciousness.

"I listened to a podcast. I'm getting a divorce." I let the words echo in the sterile room of concrete floors and stainless-steel equipment. "I'm not getting a divorce because of the podcast," I clarify.

"Not really. It just made me see what I haven't been able to. I told my husband last night. He just doesn't see me. I don't even know if he realizes what I've done so he can be who he is. I'm nothing. *Nothing!*" Anger thrums in my chest as my voice rises. "I drive kids around and wipe butts, and they don't care about any of it. Volunteer at the school. For them! Nobody thanks me. Nobody says, *Good work, June, let's have a luncheon in your honor!* Hell, nobody even takes their shoes off at the front door! Like, how many times do I need to ask?!" I huff out a breath and lower my voice. "Your wife probably never felt like that. You're the kind of man that listens, I bet." I look down at the paper. "You wear a lot of tweed; men in tweed always listen. Camp wears athletic clothes and either cleats or something called barefoot shoes..."

I imagine Camp's feet, and a fresh shot of anger gushes through me.

"And you know, Harold, this isn't what I wanted, but it's what has to happen. It's either him or me—and what? I'm supposed to just choose him, forever? I'm supposed to be some kind of unappreciated maid that does *nothing* with her life?" I scoff. "And don't even get me started on the sex."

I drop my head back and stare at the ceiling, snorting a kind of unamused laugh, like this whole thing is hilarious.

"I don't know how you were doing it for sixty-eight years, but did it ever feel like a chore?"

I roll my eyes; of course Harold never felt like that. He's a man.

"It doesn't matter what you think, all I know is it feels like one to me. He's the only man I've ever been with, and now it feels like a duty more than anything enjoyable. Sometimes I make mental grocery lists while he does what he needs to do . . ." My voice trails off with that confession. "You know, he's the only man I've ever been with. I've seen one penis in real life!"

I wince at the shouted *penis* that echoes in the room, once again lowering my voice.

"Everything is just so . . . stale. And predictable. And the fact he doesn't make any effort outside of the bedroom, I mean, what am I supposed to do with that? Just supposed to say, 'I ran around like a chicken with my head cut off all day while you threw a baseball with your buddies but, hey! let's jump into bed'?!" I shake my head. "I just can't. I'm not wired like that, Harold. It's all connected . . .

"Either way, I know you had sixty-eight years of marriage in you, but I don't. And that doesn't make me a bad person—or-or—selfish or weak or whatever your generation would call it. Some marriages aren't made to last, Harold." And with that declaration, I jam my palms into my eyes, nearly giving myself a paper cut with Harold's now crumpled memorial bulletin.

Yes, I'm talking to a dead man.

Again.

But they seem to be the only ones that get it. My mother is off living her best retired life with my dad in their Winnebago, my brothers only live a couple towns away but are men with lives of their own, Camp doesn't listen to me, and my best friend, the whole reason I'm in this room and didn't completely hate the idea of returning to Ledger in the first place, is my person, but she doesn't know—she can't. She's never been married, doesn't have kids, and has no clue what it's like to live a life shoved in a box. Not when she lives by her own rules, wild and free.

A tap on the glass window pulls me from my thoughts, and there she is, Scotty, standing in the jade-green-painted witnessing room. She points to her watch with a lift of her chin before holding up a hand with wiggling fingers. My five-minute warning.

I nod, blow out a breath, and look back at the tweed-covered Harold lying quietly in his box.

"I have to find a job now, I guess. I have a college degree that I've never used, and my resume might as well be a black hole, so this should be interesting. But my teenage daughter looks at me like I'm a wet rag, so maybe if she sees me working, she'll change her opinion of me."

I lift my chin, feeling a bit more confident in my decision.

"Now that I think of it, she *needs* me to do this. To leave my marriage and be independent so she knows how to do the same thing."

I nod, smile, and for the first time think that this is what I should have done all along.

I stand up, sniff, and put Harold's crumpled memorial bulletin in my purse.

"Thank you, Harold. I hope you rest in peace . . . you probably need it after sixty-eight years of marriage."

Steps a little lighter than when I entered, I walk to the witnessing room where Scotty's waiting and looking like an eternal badass. My best friend since we were kids, she owns the town crematorium,

Happy Endings. She's wearing her typical work uniform of black heels, fitted dress pants that cost more than my entire wardrobe, a blazer, red, and a band T-shirt. Today it's Elvis.

In the background, "Blue Suede Shoes" plays softly through a speaker.

She doesn't look at me as I open the door, picking at a well-manicured fingernail from her spot on the leather sofa, as her wavy bob sits wildly perfect around her face.

"Wanna talk about it?" she asks, like she always does after I visit for one of my sessions, eyeing me skeptically. "Or your new haircut?"

What had Lyra said this morning when she saw me . . . ? Oh, yes: *What happened to your face?*

I shrug. "Camp and I are getting a divorce."

"What the fuck, Joo?!" The words fly out of her mouth as she pounces to a stand, making me wince. "Who did he screw because I will slash that bitch's tires and cremate her vagina."

"Jesus, Scotty. Don't be so dramatic."

I drop into one of the chairs and pluck a tissue out of the box to blow my nose.

"How do you stay in business with a mouth like that? Harold's wife will probably have a heart attack if she hears you."

"It's part of my business model," she deadpans, slowly lowering back to her seat. "Now what the hell is going on?"

I sigh, heavy. When Scotty texted me this morning that she had someone to see me, I almost didn't come because I wasn't ready to face her.

"I don't know, Scotty. He was late again, and Lyra called me simple and-and-and I listened to a podcast about how—" She groans. "This is why I didn't want to tell you. I don't need your podcast tirade today. And Harold made me realize that—"

Scotty barks out a laugh. "Harold made you realize? Joo, he's dead, you know that, right? Like, I'm minutes away from bringing his family into this room and them looking through that window and watching him burn to ashes."

The expression on her face tells me she does not agree with any of my life choices.

Which is why I listen to podcasts and talk to the Harolds of the world and not her.

I huff out a breath. "You wouldn't understand. You aren't married. It's . . . complicated. Like you look at this person and think 'is this all there is . . . forever?' and finally, I asked myself that too many times and I just have to see. See if there's a way to live a life where I'm doing something that matters and get my kids to, I don't know . . . Lyra doesn't even want me helping her because Camp is so much better."

Her eyebrows pinch. "One, I've been married."

I snort a soft laugh. "I'm sure that weekend in Vegas gave you all the monotonous marriage feels." I rest my head on the back of the sofa. Stare at the ceiling. "I'm failing. At everything. The girl that once conquered anything she ever took on is a shitty mom, unwanted wife, and complete dud."

"God, do you hear yourself?" she groans. "Do you think anyone thinks they are doing it right? Even those dick feathers on your podcasts?" I shoot her a glare; she ignores it. "Just because I don't have kids doesn't mean I don't recognize how hard it must be. But nobody is perfect, Joo—nobody can be everything. Not even you. Especially not at all of this. Life is supposed to be messy. This just feels so . . . extreme. Divorce? You and Camp are fixtures in Ledger. Like, there's me and you." In her pause, I chuckle softly. "And there's that big ice cream cone at Cone Heads, the lake, and then there's you two. It's just . . . wrong."

"Maybe you should marry him," I mutter, not looking at her.

"You're so fucking dramatic, Joo. I love you, but seriously."

I glare at her, every piece of our history connecting us like links in a chain. She moved to town with a life so different from mine. A dad that couldn't stay away from the bottle, a brother that couldn't stay out of trouble, and a mom that never showed up where she needed to. Compared to my life of doting parents, Taco Tuesdays, and two brothers who threw a football in the front yard, we couldn't have been more different. And somehow, we became best friends. Sisters that neither of us had.

The day I told her in Mrs. Nettle's English class I had a crush on Camp, she passed him a note that said: *Hey Camp, your name is stupid, but my friend thinks you're hot. Ask her out or I'll knee your nuts.*

I wanted to kill her as much as I loved her for having more guts than I ever would.

He read it, turned and looked at me—burning in my own humility—and smiled his lopsided smile, braces just removed from his teeth, and that was it.

She was there for the beginning, and now she's here for the end.

I don't argue with her, though. I stay silent, studying the shelf of urns—locally made by a potter a few towns over. Wondering how bodies and life can burn down and fit in one of them when it's all over. I take a breath. Another. Silence our conversation until I'm ready to say something.

"I followed him to college, Scott. Put my dreams aside so he could chase his on the pitcher's mound. Moved back here when those dreams fell through. What? I'm supposed to do that the rest of my life? Just let Camp be Camp while I hang out like his shadow and pick up his damn cleats?"

Her eyes widen and mine close.

"You know, there might be a middle ground. You being more of you without quitting him. Your podcasts . . ." I shoot her a withering glare, and she holds up her palms before continuing. "Hear me out. Your podcasts . . . might not be . . . awful." Her lips twist like it's an effort to say the words, and I groan until she speaks over me. "But they don't know you and Camp. They aren't the end-all. I'm just asking you to really think about this. Sometimes the people that drive us the craziest are who we need the most."

I say nothing. Reeling. Staring at the ceiling.

I knew she would do this. Try to convince me to stay. Take Camp's side. Ironic coming from the woman who's pathologically unattached to anything.

I didn't mean to start talking to her bodies; it just happened. I'd had a bad day, one of the worst, and when I came to see her, she was on the phone. While I waited, I saw the door to the cremation room open with a cardboard casket waiting inside. I just wandered in, not planning on starting some weird therapy-with-dead-bodies situation, and the words flew out of my mouth as soon as I looked in the box. It was a woman in her seventies, I remember, and despite how thin she was she looked tough. She was in a powder blue pantsuit and had pearls around her neck. *She's about to turn to ashes*, I had thought, *maybe she'll take my heartache with her.*

And now, all these years later, I keep coming back. Sometimes I text Scotty and ask, others she texts me. On the days she does, it's like she can feel a shift in the atmosphere and knows that I need the release. Knows I've become a kite in a hurricane.

Papers shuffle, heels click across the floor, and the couch shifts when she sits next to me, pulling me into a hug. Home in my best friend's arms, I nearly come apart. The closest I've come since my bathroom divorce declaration.

"If this is really what you need, fuck those cleats, Joo," she whispers into my hair.

It's a line stupid enough it makes me laugh and wrap my arms around her, being all of who we are: bad words and hard truths.

We pull apart, and she hands me a certificate, Resort 765—the fanciest hotel in town that I've never once stepped foot in—written in gold across the top.

I blink.

"The owner gave it to me after his mom's send-off," Scotty says, using her token phrase for the cremation: *send-off*. "You need it more than I do." She squeezes my arms. "Go. Clear your head. Take a day for yourself. Buy some clothes that aren't also from a grocery store."

I snort.

"I'm serious. I get that Camp hasn't been the most attentive, but you've gotta be responsible for you too. Get a tattoo to go with those badass bangs. Go skinny-dipping in that fancy-ass pool they keep tucked in those trees at the spa. *Something*. Have fun; you need it."

I chuckle softly. "Thanks, Scotty. For this. And Harold."

She smiles, and we stand at the same time the door opens. An elderly woman shuffles in with a blue cardigan and the assistance of a cane in one hand and a younger woman on her other arm.

Scotty greets them with a kind smile, less severe tone than usual. "Hi, Mrs. Griffin. Abby. Right this way."

Harold's wife smiles, eyes slightly wet, hands trembling as she takes in Scotty's shirt. "Oh, Harold loved Elvis. He'd like you."

Scotty shoots me a wink as she leads Harold's widow and, whom I assume to be daughter, to the window to see his tweed-covered body in his casket, all lined up to roll into the cremation machine.

As I slip out the door, I hear Scotty ask, "Do you want to go in and see him, Mrs. Griffin?"

The air, a mix of the fleeting coolness of winter and the pending warmth of summer, blows across my skin. Even in town, it smells sweet.

In the minivan, my phone dings with missed messages from Camp.

Camp: *Sorry J I had to leave early for a meeting but I want to talk about this please tonight*

I roll my eyes.

Camp: *Please J*

3-2-1.

3-2-1.

My stomach ties knot upon knot as I reread his words. It would be so easy to write okay. My thumbs hover over the keys, but instead of responding, I scroll to the other missed message, one from the boys' preschool teacher.

Ms. Mitchell: *Tyrus just pulled a lighter out of his backpack—did you know he had this? I'm quite sure I shouldn't have to tell you it's irresponsible parenting to allow four-year-olds to play with fire. We will meet after school.*

Shit.

Add irresponsible to my list of parental shortcomings.

To Ms. Mitchell, I respond: *No, I'm sorry. I'll talk to him. I'll be there.*

To Camp: *I'm telling the kids at dinner tonight. With or without you.*

Camp: *Ill be there*

I almost laugh. If he was *there*, we might not be in this situation.

I sit in the minivan, my own personal asylum on wheels, without turning it on. Willing my heart rate to lower. Thoughts volleying between *I have to do this* and *What am I doing?*

Through the windshield, the buildings of Main Street in Ledger run parallel to one another with faded bricks, paint-peeled facades, and one lone, oversized ice cream cone. The town moves like a secret against the rolling slopes of the Blue Ridge Mountains in the backdrop. It's the same as it was when I was a kid. The changes here happen like they do in all small southern towns: So nuanced and slow they aren't noticeable until someone points them out.

The street I walked with Scotty when we got ice cream every summer.

The street I walked holding Camp's hand every Friday night in high school.

The big mural on the side of the brick building that welcomes everyone to town: Ledger, North Carolina, Life on the Ledge.

A bitter laugh escapes me—I've never felt so *on the ledge* in my life.

With a deep breath, ignoring everything that's churning with the familiarity of it all, I turn the key and point my minivan toward the lashing that awaits me with Ms. Mitchell.

Four

The chair is too small for an adult body, and the way Ms. Mitchell glares across her large desk leads me to believe it's an interrogation tactic by design. That's working.

I remember as a kid thinking how cute she was when I saw her on the playground or reading a book in the library, but adulthood has revealed that's a lie. The way she glares, reprimands, and passive aggressively lets me know how terrible my children and I are, leads me to believe she's a beast in a skin suit. White hair, plump waist, floral prints, thick glasses, and too much perfume I would bet money hide fangs and scales.

Clearing my throat, I shift my knees that are bent nearly at eye level. "Ms. Mitchell, I'm so sorry about the lighter, I've talked to the boys about fire safety, but clearly we need to revisit it. I'm not sure—"

She holds up her hand, silencing me, the boys shrinking in their seats on either side of me. Her eyes, so dark they're nearly black, turn to slits. "This cannot continue. These *children* are a disruption." She pauses, long and weighted enough it makes me squirm. "Tell me, Ms. Cannon, do you even believe in discipline?"

My jaw drops, bristled. "Of course we *believe* in discipline."

Her expression is one of skepticism as her lips twitch between a pout and frown. "It goes without saying, but your husband's celebrity status will get them nowhere in here."

"Celebrity status?" I ask, voice barely above a whisper.

"I don't care about baseball!" she barks, making me jump. Her alabaster cheeks turn fire-engine red.

"Camp?" I ask, confused. "I don't think . . ."

"That's evident," she says, "and genetic." Her eyes cut to Ty, then Hank, mouth twisting in disgust.

"I don't thi—believe that their dad playing major league baseball fifteen years ago really has anything to do with the lighter, Mrs.—Ms.—ma'am," I say, stuttering. Her eyes narrow further. If she can still see out of the slits, I'd be impressed if I wasn't also trying not to piss myself. "Sure, Hank is named after Hank Aaron and Ty after Tyrus Cobb, but, I mean, they don't even like baseball, so . . ." I look at the boys with my lie, and they slink farther down their chairs. Kid-sized sandbags with scared eyes.

She cocks her head to the side, smooths a palm over her coif of white hair, and studies me like I'm a strange animal. When she stands, towering over the three of us further, her entire outfit is revealed—a frilly dress making her look like an angry Mother Goose. "I'm retiring this year, and your boys will not be the ones to break me. They are just like their father was. I've seen it all before—unruly right out of the gate made worse by weak parenting which leads to a life of crime."

Weak parenting?

My eyes widen as her words assault me like a karate chop to the throat. I stare at her. Anger overshadowed by my own incompetence that's on full display. "They're only four, life of crime seems a bit extreme." With a weak laugh, I hug my purse to my chest before her glare kills the sound on my lips. "But yes, I see what you're saying. Camp was probably difficult when he was their age. It could be genetic—I read an article about that once, I think. Or heard a doctor talk about it . . . We'll try harder. Right, boys?"

They don't respond.

She bites her lipstick-laden lips between her teeth, chin whisker catching the light from the window. Her silence becomes a suffocating life force in the classroom of tiny furniture and alphabet letter cards.

Not sure what to do, sweat beading in my eyebrows, I stand, motioning for the boys to do the same. "Okay then," I say, taking a step back. She hasn't aged much since I was in preschool, and I'm not sure if that's a compliment, insult, or evidence of her evil powers.

"Parenting takes work," she says, hands settling on her round hips. "I advise you to try it."

My muttered, "Yes, ma'am," barely makes it out of my mouth as we stand, scramble out the door, and silently speedwalk down the hall until we get to the doors and burst outside.

Hank and Ty, paler than usual, stare at me, eyes big and on the brink of gushing tears.

I kneel next to them, heart pounding in my chest. "Okay, so first, let's all just agree that woman is scary. Possibly with some lineage to Hitler."

This softens their faces enough to hold off tears but not to the point of smiles. "But you have to listen. No more lighters. That's dangerous."

"But, Mama, she—"

I hold up my hand. "I don't care. You must listen. She's your teacher and wants what's best for you." *Maybe.* "And she'd probably be a lot nicer if you weren't, you know, trying to commit arson."

They both nod, gazes at the ground, and scuff their feet across the sidewalk.

"Now, let's go to the library, shall we?" I say with forced cheer. "Hopefully the librarian won't be so terrifying."

Story time at the library is like a recurring nightmare that I voluntarily show up for.

First, there are the other moms, all younger than me by roughly a decade. Not only do they point out the fact I'm of a *mature age*, but they also constantly refer to their kids as their best friends. Who wants to be best friends with a four-year-old? They are the epitome of emotional time bombs and bring absolutely nothing to the friendship table.

Of course, I don't say that. I smile and nod. And agree.

Spending time with moms of similar-aged kids helps women build confidence and a sense of community, better aligning us with the way nature designed us to parent.

Then there's the librarian, Librarian Alice as she likes to be called, who reads with a high-pitched voice and too-big smile that makes me want to rip my fingernails out.

Yet, I continue to show up every week. For the sake of child development best practices. For the sake of literacy. For the sake of being a good mom even though I was just called weak by someone that specializes in educating the youth of our nation.

"Did you see that study about the harmful effects of red dye? I know your generation never gave that a second thought, right?" Mom One asks Mom Two and I as she pulls a boob out to nurse her nearly two-year-old kid; my chest tightens. Like her being some kind of long-haul milk producer needs to be showcased. She catches me staring and smiles. "Breast is best!"

I smile and nod then avert my gaze to another kid who is pulling seaweed snacks out of her purse, chomping on it like it's the best thing he's ever eaten.

I bought them for the boys once. They gagged and fed them to Thor. Who immediately puked them out onto the rug.

That I had to scrub.

Which stained anyway.

I stay silent, busying myself with a board book that I don't care about as we sit on a brightly colored rug filled with numbers and letters.

"The red dye—I did!" Mom Two gasps. "June?"

"Oh gosh, yes. Tragic," I reply, nodding with so much enthusiasm it brings my whole body into the mix like an outdated dance move.

"You know, when I was reading—oh, hon." Mom Two turns her attention to the toddler throwing trucks on the floor and screaming like a demon. "Let's think about our actions, Dyllan. My ears *hurt*"—she speaks slow and dramatic as she points to her ears, big frown on her face—"when you do *that*, and it makes me *so* sad. I don't like it when my best friend hurts trucks *and* ears and"—she points to her chest, eyes wide and serious, voice now somewhere between a whisper and a cry—"*my* heart breaks when *your* beautiful heart acts like that."

The kid blinks, screams louder, then stops abruptly when another kid shows him a dinosaur from a nearby basket, distracting him to silence.

She beams. "Isn't gentle parenting just the best?"

I resist the urge to laugh in this woman's face and call her a fuckwad. Instead, I mentally flip through my Rolodex of studied and stored parenting techniques, and reply with, "It is. It's always worked so well with my boys." I lie. My kids are gunslingers of the Wild West; there's no "gentle" parenting with them. I need zip ties and a cattle prod to get them to listen.

As if timed by the universe to make me look like the mother of the year, Hank steps up to me, ripped page of a book in his hand, proud smile on his face. "I found a picture of Hank Aaron in the baseball book to take to Dad."

He destroyed library property, and my pulse rams against my sinuses.

"I love that you're so thoughtful," I say, voice tight, putting the paper in my purse along with the fruit snacks I don't want anyone to know I feed my kids. Out of the corner of my eye, Ty is climbing onto the top of the bookshelf, books falling as he steps on each shelf. Instinct tells me to hook an arm around his waist, tell him to knock it the hell off, and flee this building like there's a live bomb inside. *Never stifle adventurous curiosity.* Instead, I hear my mouth say, "I love how adventurous you are, Ty. Make safe choices when you climb."

Mom One and Mom Two put hands to their chests, like it's the most endearing thing they've ever seen, and start talking about which Montessori school they will be sending their kids to in the fall.

The ear-piercing voice of the librarian is a welcome reprieve when she calls the kids to the circle, reading *Chicka Chicka Boom Boom*. I smile, clap at all the right times, but inside, every repressed thought and word zooms around my chest like an angry swarm of hornets.

This is my life.

Sitting with women I don't want to talk to about parenting techniques I can't make work with kids that don't listen to me, hiding snacks in a purse because they aren't healthy enough after a meeting with some version of Satan in a grandma suit who told me I'm a *weak parent*, as a husband I have lives some fun life of kids' games, and my teenage daughter thinks I'm a complete loser.

What. The. Fuck.

As sure as Librarian Alice has a voice high-pitched enough to communicate with birds, I know it's true. I'm failing. If I wasn't sure this new start was what I needed, I know it is now as I watch the letter P walk up a coconut tree in the colorful pages of a children's book—everyone smiling around the room except me. My legs are restless, like I need to run twelve miles to get all the energy that's bouncing through me out.

"The End," Librarian Alice says, smile wide, clothes bright, cheeks rosy. Living her best librarian life.

I clap the loudest—I need to get out of here.

Boys' hands in mine, I beeline to the door, dragging them behind me.

"Bye, June!" Mom One calls. "See you next week? Love the haircut, by the way!"

Over my shoulder, she's eagerly sitting on the rug, smiling in her gauzy shirt and flowy pants. I open my mouth, desperately wishing for once I could be my true self and scream, "hasta la vista, bitches!" but I don't. I can't. The boys need this. Books, Librarian Alice, story time, moms that feed their kids seaweed.

There's no such thing as too much positive exposure when it comes to raising happy kids.

I reply the only way I know how: "See you next week!"

FIVE

IT TOOK ALL OF ten seconds of me googling how to get a divorce to have my dreams shattered: The state of North Carolina requires a year of separation before filing. At the computer, I swore under my breath and flipped the screen the middle finger as I printed the forms. While it isn't ideal, sometime after being yelled at by a preschool teacher and driven to the brink of my sanity at the library, I convince myself this time would be a good thing. I haven't had a job outside of the house since before Lyra was born, so I'd have to get a job and somewhere to live. Ledger is a small town; I could do this. A year is the perfect amount of time for me to come up with a plan. Find a career. A place to live. I never understood why Camp had insisted on buying his parents' old house anyway. He just did it one day—announced it, like he'd done something so noble.

"*It's more than it's worth, Camp . . . why would we do this?*" I asked, stunned as he handed me the keys.

His smile faltered, but just for a split second. *"I had a good life here, J . . . I wanted to surprise you. My old room could be Lyra's."* He beamed, thick drawl stretching out his words, proud smile forcing my doubts into a box and slamming the lid closed. I never imagined us living in Ledger, much less living in his parents' old house in Ledger, but after all he had lost, I couldn't fight him on this. Everything changed when I got pregnant. When his shoulder shredded and he was cut from the team. His dreams changed, so mine would too.

I looked around the house again—small and dated with wallpaper, shag carpet, and wood paneling—and fought like hell to keep the tears I wanted to cry from falling. Camp had made nearly a million dollars in his few short years playing baseball, and this is where it got us. Overpaying—significantly—for a house that needed a gut job.

"You're not happy," he said, shoulders slumping, eyes worried.

I forced a smile, bouncing Lyra in my arms. *"I'm so happy,"* I lied. *"I'm just wondering what we're going to do about this carpeting."*

Then he laughed, relieved, and hugged me so tightly it was like his life depended on it.

I had thought it would be a starter house, but we're still here.

Now is my chance to find something *I* want.

Step out of the shadow of Camp Cannon and be fully June. Independent woman, thriving career of something, good mom, and living in a house *I* pick out.

Now, staring at the faces of three kids over plates of tacos to the tune of the dog's claws tapping against the floor as he circles the table like a hungry shark, I don't know about this. *Kids, your dad and I are separating.* It's only seven words, but each one feels bigger than the last. Like they aren't in my lexicon.

And, of course, even though Camp told me he would be here, he's nowhere to be found.

Ty bites a chip, sending cheese onto the table and floor and the dog wastes no time licking up the scraps. All I can think: *Camp gets that damn dog in the divorce.*

"Today's Best, Mama?" Hank asks between bites of his taco that's dripping ground beef and cheese out of one end while he bites the other.

"Today's Best . . ." I tap my chin.

"I'll go first!" Ty interrupts. "How loud Ms. Mitchell screamed when I showed everyone how I could use a lighter." He smiles, proud, and I shoot him a glare that he doesn't seem to notice. Like he wasn't just as scared shitless as I was sitting in those too-small chairs just hours ago.

I press my lips in a tight line while Hank laughs, and Lyra rolls her eyes and scoops sour cream onto her tortilla. "Grow up, Ty. You're so weird."

"Well, Ty, I think that will be your last time making Ms. Mitchell scream like that, correct?" I raise my eyebrows, and he shrinks in his seat. "Hank, your turn. Today's Best, kiddo."

Hank sits thoughtfully. "Well . . ."

And there, in the pensive silence of Hank and the loud crunching of teeth and tacos around the table, the door swings open, and in walks Camp.

"Hey—sorry I'm late," he says, almost breathless as he drops his bag at the front door and pets the dog on the head. His eyes meet mine before dropping them to Thor. "Hey, Dogg-o!" he says in a high-pitched voice, instantly shredding my nerves.

I focus on making a taco, like it's the most interesting food I'll ever create. "What are you doing here?" I ask.

"Eatin'," he says, dropping into a seat.

"Eating?" I ask, pinching my eyebrows.

He looks at the table, sweeps his hand through the air at the food. "Eatin'."

I pause, knowing I should stop, but something in me pushes out, "You're late."

Lyra laughs. "Dad has better things to do than be on time for dinner, right, Dad?" I flick my eyes to her, and dammit, she means it. "He had a big meeting with the architects for the new complex."

Internally, I roll my eyes so hard they nearly detach from whatever tendons hold them in place. Externally, I smile. "Good for him."

Camp grabs a taco shell and stares at me so long it's as if he's trying to send a telepathic message I'm not interested in receiving, then starts to fix his plate.

Hank shares his Today's Best: He made something out of clay in art.

"Lyra, what's yours?" Camp asks before biting into his taco.

"Umm . . ." She wipes her mouth with a napkin, sudden splash of pink covering her cheeks. "I dunno. Nick and I hung out after school today . . ." She clears her throat. "That was fun, I guess."

"Nick?" I ask, perking up at the mention of a boy's name. "Are you two a thing?"

She scoffs. "A thing?"

I shrug. "You know, dating? Why does nobody ever date anymore?"

"You're so old, Mom," she says with a slight groan, rolling her eyes. Camp chuckles, looking at me like, *duh*. "People don't date, they hang out. It's casual."

Casual.

"I like Nick," Camp chimes in between bites. "He's a helluva center fielder too."

They break off into conversation about baseball, Lyra more enthralled in the sport than I've ever seen, meaning she *like* likes Nick and hanging out possibly means making out. Or more. Which means I need to talk to her about that. *Does she need to be on birth control?*

And a new truth crystalizes as I watch her and her dad talk: She's not talking to me about it. I flip through the encyclopedia of reasons in my mind. I know it's not because I'm not around . . . because I'm always around. She doesn't trust me? She's not comfortable with me?

Panic sets in. I'm failing again. The daughter I've spent seventeen years trying to do right by is shutting me out.

This will change. When she sees me—working or independent or something. Shit. *Something.*

Spiraling in my thoughts, desperation tightening the skin around my bones, I clear my throat. "I'll go next," I say, nobody listening. Anxiety gripping my chest, everyone continues to talk around me. Oblivious to my voice. "Y'all, listen . . ."

Nothing.

Chatter.

Laughing.

The dog barks.

I poke my arm to make sure I actually exist.

Finally, I shout: "I said I'll go next!"

The table falls silent this time, all eyes instantly on me, curious shades of green and brown—even Thor's black—staring. I clear my throat, lower my voice. "Right." I hesitate, but only long enough to catch the subtle shake of Camp's head which propels me forward. "So your dad and I have decided that—"

"*Ohmygod*!" Lyra quasi-shouts, smacking her hand on the table, stealing my spotlight. "I forgot to tell you about Kimber!" Her brown eyes go wide at the mention of her best friend.

"Kimber? Is she okay?"

"Mom, *no*. Her parents are getting a divorce!"

Maybe it's the word—divorce—hearing it come out of my daughter's mouth. Maybe it's the fact it's Lynn and Dean, people we know and see. Hell, I was just with Lynn last week at the prom committee meeting and she never said a word. Actually, what she said was: *"We should go with the theme* Kickin' It Old School. *The gym is done after this year and, gosh, June, won't it remind you of our prom? I can't imagine Dean and I ever young enough!"* Then she laughed.

More than all that, it's the tone Lyra has, which is half disbelief, half disgust. Whatever it is, knowing that I was about to use the same word to her sinks my guts.

"Really?" Camp asks, shifting in his seat, light brown eyes cutting from her to me. Nervous energy whipping off him like tentacles of a jellyfish.

"Right?" Lyra continues, tucking her pink hair behind her ears. "Like, she had no idea this was even going to happen. Like, totally blindsided." She scoops salsa onto a chip and takes a loud bite, talking around crunches. "Like, so blindsided, she thinks she's going to be a lesbian now."

I choke on my water.

"What's a lesbian?" Hank asked.

Camp chokes on his water.

"A girl that dates another girl," Lyra explains, matter-of-fact.

"I don't think that's how it works, Ly," I say when I don't die from shock.

Her eyes narrow, biting another chip. "You don't think that's what a lesbian is?"

"I don't think that's how you *become* a lesbian."

She laughs. "No offense, Mom, but what do you know about sexuality?"

My jaw drops, Camp chokes again, and Ty asks, "What's sexuality?"

"It's wha—"

"Not important!" I shout, cutting Lyra off. "It doesn't matter what anything is or isn't or who marries who. Or whom. However you say it." I take a breath. Trying to regain control of the situation. "I'm sorry Kimber's parents are divorcing. Lynn and Dean always seemed so happy, but I guess you never know when things aren't working. That's hard, but you know, marriage is hard, and people change and, you know, sometimes things don't work out because one person might feel like they can't be who they want to be or something. But, yeah, I guess that would be complicated for a kid to understand."

My gaze hooks to Camp's; he wipes his mouth with a napkin.

Lyra shrugs. "A promise is a promise, right? I mean you can't just break it. What's the point of taking a vow if you aren't really someone that believes in, you know, a vow?" Another chip.

Crunch.

Crunch.

Crunch.

Hank throws an entire taco on the floor, and I don't bat an eye as Thor inhales it.

Another truth bomb in the never-ending bombardment of them today: I'm screwed. I can't win. The game is rigged and it's not in my favor.

My marriage isn't working, but if I leave, I'm a quitter. If I stay, I'm a dud.

This time, it's Camp that speaks. "Lyra, your mom and I decided—"

"No!" I shout—again—this time with palms slamming onto the table, causing yet another stunned silence to fall. Thor cocks his head to one side.

If my daughter is becoming a lesbian, it's going to be on her own accord, dammit.

"Sorry. I just really wanted to be the one to tell her, honey." Camp's eyes narrow, gaze dropping to the fingers I've wrapped around his forearm. "Your dad is going to go with you on your field trip in a couple weeks. The one about career exploration." Lyra's nose scrunches and confusion fills her face. "I went to the last one and he wants to be more involved. So I told him, *'You know . . . honey . . . that's a good idea.'*" I clear my throat. "So, yeah, that was my Today's Best. Dad on a field trip that doesn't involve baseball, can you imagine?" I laugh robotically. "But, you know, father-daughter bonding and all . . ."

"Okay," she drawls out, somewhat skeptical, before she takes another bite of taco.

The dog's tail thumps relentlessly against the floor.

Thump.

Thump.

Thump.

After eons, Camp says, "That's my Today's Best too. Can't wait, Ly."

"Ty took a lighter to school today and got in trouble, Daddy," Hank says, snickering.

"I hope you brought marshmallows to roast too," Camp teases. "Ms. Mitchell is probably so grumpy because she doesn't have snacks."

The boys laugh. Everyone laughs.

Everyone but me.

I stand up from the table, walk to the fridge, and take a slug of rosé straight from the bottle.

"Are we done gettin' a divorce?" Camp asks, pulling the blankets back from his side of the bed.

I glare at him from where I'm sitting, pausing mid-rub of lotion on my legs. "No, Camp, we aren't *done* getting a divorce. We have to wait. Were you not listening to Lyra?" I demand. "Divorce is basically an atomic bomb on the teenage psyche. Of all the mistakes I've made, I can't do that."

He stills, holding a pillow.

"So, I was thinking, we'll just fake it. We'll put on a show of a happy marriage—she graduates in three months—actually, I counted, it's seventy-five days—and then it will be summer, where she'll be distracted and getting ready for college. She'll be looking forward to living on her own. Our marital status won't matter that much, not really. And the boys will be fine. They're young enough. And, you know, Ty is trying to burn the school down, so he has bigger fish to fry." I'm not sure if I'm trying to be funny, but neither of us laugh. "I've been acting happy for years anyway, this won't be that much different."

Camp drops the pillow he's holding on the floor and rubs a finger down his nose. "So let me get this straight." He squeezes his eyes shut before opening them again with a long exhale. "You don't want to be married to me—because you believe you've sacrificed your life for me and I've done nothin' in return"—I open my mouth to interrupt, but he holds up a palm to silence me—"and because you're worried Lyra won't recover from this fact, we're going to fake a happy marriage—"

"For seventy-five days," I amend.

He blows out a frustrated breath, gritting his teeth. "Fine—for seventy-five days—until she graduates, when we will drop the bombshell on her that it's all been a lie and we're gettin' a divorce?"

I huff out a breath. "Don't say it like I'm ridiculous, Camp. You know just as well as I do this marriage isn't working. We aren't happy. And, since you were shockingly sitting at the same table I was at dinner tonight, you heard Lyra as well as I did. I won't destroy her months before she leaves. I refuse."

He scoffs but says nothing as he goes to the closet and pulls out several extra blankets and drops them on the floor next to the bed.

"What are you doing?" I demand.

"I'm not sleepin' in a bed with a woman that doesn't want me."

I consider his words, watching him make a floor bed.

"We need rules. Guidelines or something."

He shakes his head with an incredulous laugh when he drops to the floor. "What the hell kind of rules could this require?"

"Shhh!" I hiss. "They could be right outside the door. *Listening!*" I pause to regroup, now sitting cross-legged on the bed. "Okay, okay. Let me think." I chew my thumbnail, wracking my brain for how this can work. "Okay, nothing crazy. Just-just-just, we need to be genuine. Nice. No fights in front of them or arguing.

North Carolina requires a year of separation; I have a paper—it's already filled out in the drawer of your nightstand. All you have to do is sign." His head jerks around, and he stares at the small table like it's just arrived from space. "Anyway, what about sex?"

"Sex?"

"Don't repeat me, Camp. I said sex. I don't think we should have sex with other people."

His eyes get somehow wider than before. "The hell? Is that what this is about? Is there someone else?"

My spine straightens in offense. "I won't even dignify that with an answer. I'm just saying in case someone else comes up, we live in way too small of a town to date other people without the kids finding out . . ."

He pummels a fist into a pillow before dropping his head into it, fingers running down the crooked line of his nose. "Fine."

"Fine," I echo.

A loud silence presses on my eardrums.

"And no kissing." His head shoots up and he gapes at me from where he sits on the floor, starting to argue when I talk over him. "I mean me, not other people. But probably not other people." He starts to argue again; I keep talking. "Oh, don't act like that's such a big deal, Camp. We barely touch anyway. Hell, you barely batted an eye last night when I told you I wanted a divorce." He starts arguing; I ignore him. "But it will confuse things. Complicate them. Just-just-just—we can be affectionate without being intimate. To keep things simple."

He sighs, heavy, and drags a hand down his face. "Do I get a say in any of this?"

I almost laugh. How many times have I ever had a say? Camp just thinks of things and does them, telling me after—or never thinking to tell me at all. I've spent our entire marriage in his wake, every movement dependent on what he'd already decided to do.

"You've had a say in everything else."

We stare at each other until my eyes start to burn, but I refuse to look away. Finally, he does. When he turns off the lamp, for the first time in years, my husband and I sleep in two separate beds.

Six

Over the next few days, absolutely nothing changes. My fake happy marriage is exactly the same as my real unhappy marriage.

Camp is blissfully absent while I am a complete lunatic.

Camp coaches baseball every afternoon and plays softball with his friends—I run around like a lunatic.

Camp sleeps on the floor, the lull of his breathing letting me know that he is completely unaffected by our arrangement—I stare at the ceiling and let my thoughts spiral. Like a lunatic.

I drive the boys to preschool, listening to them scream the same words over and over.

I offer to help Lyra organize scholarship applications; she repeatedly declines in the name of *waiting for Dad*.

I show up to the high school prom committee meetings, making endless to-do lists of materials and vendors and fabric colors and finger foods.

I feed the dog.

Camp goes on his morning run before I'm up, showers while I make breakfast, and leaves while I get the boys ready for school.

He makes no attempt to change anything. And, though my decision has been made, I expected . . . something. A fight? Some sort of remorse? Whatever I'm looking for, there's none. He could be happy as much as devastated and I'd never know the difference.

The few minutes a day I do see him, I want to slap his stupid face.

Of course, I don't. Instead, I play nice and try to hide the fact I *want* to slap his stupid face.

As annoying as he is, I tell myself it's not that bad. Tolerable. We don't touch. Outside of our conversations in front of the kids, we barely talk. It's not ideal, but it's manageable. It's only a few more months. Seventy-one days, to be exact.

On Friday morning, the house is quiet, everyone else at school and work, and I go into the closet in the garage and pull out the tub labeled June's Photography Stuff. Across the scratched-up, crayon-colored kitchen table, I unpack my camera, lenses, and now expired rolls of film. Paraphernalia of a life not lived. So many stories I was going to collect with this gear, but all it collected was dust. Seventeen years sitting on a shelf, doing nothing. Like me.

It's weird now, looking at the equipment—just glass and plastic—and the flood of memories it holds. Mental snapshots of who I was, who I thought I'd be.

Who I never became.

Now here we sit, me with crisis bangs and not a damn clue.

Thor's blocky head lands on the edge of the table, slobber clinging to his jowls as he eyes the gear like it's the juicy rotisserie chicken of his dreams.

"Don't even think about it," I mutter, not bothering to look at him when he whimpers.

I need a plan. Some way to use this stuff to make money.

My dad's voice from twenty-two years ago blasts in my ears.

"The hell you plan to do with that degree?" he asked, baffled. *"Visual Arts?!"*

When I grinned, he frowned. *"Make things people like to look at. Tell stories."*

His frown deepened.

My dad was an accountant, and more than once, he showed me how the numbers of being a photographer would never add up.

Now, staring at my gear, needing a plan to support myself, I wish I'd listened to him.

I'd taken my first photography class in high school and fell in love with it. To be able to capture a moment and freeze it forever felt like something of a superpower. At a time when digital wasn't really a thing, I printed every picture I took, driving my parents crazy with the albums. I gifted photos to everyone for every occasion. Stuck them to lockers, in greeting cards, on refrigerators and car windshields.

Some of my favorite memories were in that class. A room I felt entirely myself with people who were creatively themselves. Molly Burchfield always photographed flowers at her family farm. Kip Johnson took photos of animals—dead or alive—from his tree stand during hunting season. And Reed Simmons . . . I squeeze my eyes shut on the thought of the name, the blurred image of his eighteen-year-old face. He became my best friend in the class, and then . . . and then.

But me? I was drawn to snapshots of everyday details. I loved them. The spray-painted stop sign. Empty beer bottles in a field. Flip-flops on the shore of the lake. Confetti on the ground after a party. Hands wrapped around waffle cones, covered in sticky streams of melting ice cream. I couldn't get enough of them. They told entire stories without saying a single word.

As much as I knew these snapshots of life weren't going to get me taken seriously, I fought it. Told anyone that would listen in my first college classes I was shooting weird things in the name of fine art.

I won a competition, a photo of an on-campus concert where the band was in focus but everyone dancing in the field was blurred with motion, and it was put on the front page of the Appalachian State student newspaper. One image was picked to hang in the library—a shot of students covering the courtyard with books and blankets, some throwing frisbees. But it wasn't straightforward; I shot it through a prism, making the image mirrored and fractured. Distorted to a point it straddled abstract and perfect reality.

Finally, it happened. Carving my own way came to a record-screeching halt by way of red-penned margin notes in a collection submission. "Tell a Story" was the assignment.

So I did.

I told the tale of a baseball game tailgate party. I shot details. Keg beer spraying into a Solo Cup. Burgers grilling. Face paint. The bare chest of a girl who drunkenly flashed me when I pointed my camera at her.

Then came the words of the note: *There's a point in every creative's life where they have to decide if they are shooting for themselves or for others; one choice will make a career more difficult, but not impossible. Choose wisely and with eyes wide open.*

Translation: Make pictures that will make people smile when they are tucked under windshields, or make pictures that will make money. I hated the note, considered ignoring it, but knew deep in my bones that wasn't who I was. I had always been good at everything I did—grades, sports, photography—but it wasn't by paving my own way. I've never been one to trust my own instincts. Instead, I lean on experts. Those who had proven what to do by already doing it.

I knew if I wanted to make photography a career, I needed to push aside what I wanted—what I felt in my bones—to be the kind of photographer that the world wanted. There was no future in a photo of a random lamp and slice of watermelon sitting on the side of the road or too up-close shots of familiar faces. No value in getting experimental with draping pieces of fabric over the lens or refracting light with a prism. Silly snapshots and intentionally weird images would get me nowhere. Landscape photography would.

A new dream was hatched. I shed the silly creative skin of my youth and grew into something more mature. I bought every book created by Irma London—the biggest female name in landscape photography at the time—and studied her work. I threw myself into my new plan: Camp would play baseball, and I'd see the world and photograph it. Little details were garbage; big pictures were golden. Breath-stealing vistas would be my new passion.

I chased that. I waited tables to make ends meet and photographed every landscape I could . . . until I got pregnant.

The abrupt end of my story sends a heavy breath gushing out of me. I refocus on the pile of equipment.

Thumb pressed between my eyebrows, I squeeze my eyes shut, willing inspiration to appear from years and years of making art that I'd hidden away.

It doesn't matter where I've been or what I've loved, I need money. A job. A way to provide some sort of stable life for myself. My kids.

Think, June.

There's family photography . . . *no*. Over my dead body am I going to spend my days photographing other families when I'm failing my own.

Wedding photography? *Pass*. My marriage is ending, love is dead.

Which brings me back to my plan B dream: landscape photography. In college, the path I'd planned led to me photographing remote landscapes, filling pages that inspired others to travel. And, aside from the fact that I don't know if people even still read magazines, that's not happening. I'm stuck in Ledger.

My phone vibrates with a text.

Camp: *Mornin darlin I left my practice bag in the bedroom if you have time can you drop it by the school I'd love to see you.*

I grind my teeth. *Darlin'?*

I've seen Camp play this game when we've argued. Turn diabetically sweet when I'm feeling anything but.

Well, two can play this game of pretend, asshole.

Me: *Sure, honey. I'd love to.*

"There she is!"

Camp's words startle me to a stop as I pass an open door to a conference room. Instead of the grimace I want to make at the severe odor of fresh paint and new carpeting and the blindingly white walls—I fake a too-big smile.

He stands, smug, holding court from the head of a long, rectangular table, one ankle crossed over the other as he leans a hip casually against the edge. In a hunter-green Ledger High School Lake Trout polo shirt, khaki-colored golf pants, and shoes that look like every toe has a spot, he grins, extending his arms out to me.

"I was just sayin'," he continues, southern drawl thick and the opposite of charming as I step into the room and give a small wave to the familiar faces of coaches, board members, and Dani who all smile politely in return. "I wish my amazin' wife would be here to see this. And there you are. Showin' up like a boomerang. To forever and back." His reference causes confused expressions to form on some of the faces in the room, but I glare. He grins wider. "This is what the printed maps of the complex will look like."

He points to the screen behind him.

While most schools, especially in towns as small as ours, have busted-brick gyms and just-good-enough fields, Camp's five state championships coaching the baseball team in the last decade put Ledger on the map, helping secure funding for the beast that's being projected onto the wall. In the center of the map—where we are—is a large building with a gymnasium, locker rooms, conference rooms, a small banquet hall, and offices, Camp's as athletic director included. Outside, the baseball, softball, football, and soccer fields surround the building, gravel paths connecting them to one another.

It was his wins that led to the funding, and, working closely with architects and builders, he's been part of every step. The complex won't just be for the kids of Ledger to play at; the goal is to host tournaments and become an athletic destination for the region.

"Impressive," I say, hating that it really is. Then, because I can't not, I add, "Good thing I have everything under control at home so you can spend so much time working on this."

He brings a hand to his chest, overzealous look of relief on his face. "Can y'all believe what a perfect and supportive wife God gave me? What did I do to deserve such a woman?" Without warning, he pulls me in for a too-long hug that makes me grunt.

"What the hell are you doing, Camp?" I hiss in his ear as every eye in the room looks at us, a few of them chuckling.

"Pretendin', of course," he whispers, squeezing me tighter until I wriggle myself free, glaring at him before giving a tight smile to the rest of the room and taking a step back toward the door.

"Well, I'll leave y'all to it." I pin Camp with another wasted glare, lifting his bag toward him. "I jus—"

"Nonsense, we were just wrappin' up." He lifts his chin toward the room, a silent yet charming, *meeting over*.

Jack, Camp's assistant baseball coach, steps next to us. In his early thirties, Jack has boy-next-door good looks with shaggy brown hair that always hangs from under his ball cap and a friendly smile.

"June," he drawls, giving me a half hug. "Good to see ya."

Before I can respond, Dani's with us, across from me, the four of us forming a kind of circle.

"Hi, June," she chirps. "Isn't the complex great?" Her bouncy youth makes me feel like a crypt keeper. She probably shits fairy dust. "Jack—and Camp, of course," she says as she giggles, a breathless sound, and her cheeks go pink before she continues, "have been working so hard to get it all finished for the dedication. All those late nights will be worth it, right?"

Her bright eyes go from me, to Camp, to Jack, and something—not jealousy—bangs against my sternum.

"Of course," I say, involuntarily grabbing Camp's hand with mine, interlacing our fingers with a squeeze. Her gaze follows the movement, something flittering across her face. *Ha!* I lean against him, sweeten my voice and stare at him with doe eyes. "But, you know, what's a few late nights in the scheme of a lifetime of happy moments together?"

"It's all for you, baby cakes," he says, smooth, dropping my hand to wrap his arm around my waist. I swallow the vomit that threatens to shoot out of my mouth.

"You two are so cute," Dani says with a grin. "Aren't they, Jack?"

Jack snorts a laugh, adjusts his ball cap. "Cute is the last word I'm using to describe that mustache."

They laugh; my blood boils.

"Ha! Yes. Very cute we are," I say, brushing a hand across my bangs as I step out of Camp's arm and toward the door. "I should get going."

"See ya at dinner, J."

Over my dead body.

Since the taco dinner debacle earlier in the week, he hasn't been home.

"Right, well, I doubt that. We have to eat early tonight because Lyra has . . ." I wrack my brain. "Homework." I wince. "Yes, Lyra has so much homework that we need to eat early—at four thirty—so I know that won't—"

"Sounds great, I've been meanin' to start eatin' dinner at four thirty." He turns to Jack. "You good with runnin' practice today?"

Jack nods.

My jaw drops.

Hell freezes over.

With a wink and the slightest of twitches of his mustache, he turns his back to me, jumping into conversation with Dani and Jack, letting me know with his silence and charm, *meeting over.*

Seven

In the parking lot, in my minivan, facing a beautiful building that my husband helped design, I scream until my throat hurts.

Eight

Driving toward home, I cue up a podcast.

THE PERFECT MOM PODCAST WITH ABBIGAIL BUCHANAN

EPISODE 209: Finding Your Confidence with fashion expert Mara Weekly

Abbigail: Okay, perfect mamas, I'm excited about today's episode. Today we have Mara Weekly who will be talking to us about feeling desirable again and giving our wardrobes a boost. I don't know about you, but for me, my fashion took a nosedive when I had babies.[Chuckles.] Mara, is this something that you see frequently?

Mara: Absolutely, Abbigail. Thanks so much for having me. So, what I notice most is a lot of moms accidentally let themselves go at first. You know, we're tired, and our bodies are different. The last thing we want to do is put buttons around the belly that just had a baby, right? [Laughter in agreement.] But then what happens, at least what I see, is a sort of guilt associated with getting dressed up. Maybe some moms feel bad for not making income, so they don't want to spend money on themselves. Or they think, I'm a mom now, I can't wear trendy clothes, I need to look like a mom. Always in leggings and some loose-fitting shirt. We adopt, what I like to call, unfashion.

At her words, I frown, looking down at my own black leggings and baggy chambray shirt as I sit at a red light. A gold-star standard of unfashion.

Abbigail: You are so right, Mara. I know for me, too, a lot of times I'll ask, "What do I need nice clothes for if they are just going to get ruined by kids anyway?" [More laughter in agreement.]

Mara: And that's valid, but my argument would be, even if the clothes might get messy, how do they make you feel the rest of the day? Is there a way to combine them: be fashionable and confident *and* functional for your lifestyle? And I don't think I'd be on your show if I didn't say yes!

Abbigail: What do you say to the mamas that just don't know where to start? Like, they are listening to this as they do dishes or drive around in their minivans and think—I have no style and no clue how to fix that.

Mara: I got you, girlfriends! [Chuckles.] In all seriousness, there are a couple hard and fast rules I give to all the mamas I work with when we get started on revamping their wardrobes.

One, color is your friend—dare to be bold!

[Abbigail gasps.]

I know, I know, this probably made a few of you turn the podcast off, but I'm here to help—promise! Women tend to hide behind blacks, greys, and tans, so getting away from those can be a freeing thing. We don't need to look like we are going to a funeral or in some kind of depressing uniform every day of our lives. So, unless it's a little black dress you are wearing on a date night, ditch it. It might even be making you look more tired than you already are. Do not be afraid to buy a hot-pink shirt or a bright-blue skirt!

Abbigail: Okay, I'm glad this isn't video because I'm definitely wearing a black shirt right now.

Mara: I won't turn you into the fashion police. [Chuckles.] Okay, and the second thing I tell women, don't be afraid to show some skin. We've been conditioned to believe that because we have children, because we aren't twenty-three and our bodies are different, we need to dress in burlap sacks, but it's just not true. You have my permission to wear the cheeky swimsuit, show off some cleavage . . . whatever you like about your body, don't be afraid to show it off. And if you're self-conscious, do it anyway. When you go shopping, use it as a time to reinvent yourself. Be someone different. Bolder. Brighter. Better! You are great as you are, of course, but give yourself a chance to be You 2.0!

Abbigail asks a follow-up question, but the words of the podcast fall on deaf ears as I slam my brakes at the sign that comes into view.

Ledger Art House is written in a contemporary black font against the whitewashed brick building on Main Street.

An art gallery? In Ledger?

"When the hell did this show up?" I mutter to the windshield, a truck honking at me as it drives around where I've stopped.

I ignore it, parking haphazardly along the street, craning my neck around my steering wheel to get a closer look.

Large canvases fill the front windows, and a woman with a dark pixie cut, white flowy blouse, and gauzy pants emerges from the propped-open glass door and sets a chalkboard sign on the sidewalk.

Now Open, Featuring North Carolina Local Artists.

I slip out of the van, floating to the windows like a moth to a flame, unsure if I even turned the ignition off.

In one window there are black-and-white photographs of women, nude, but not showing too much, and double exposed. The edges soft and the silhouettes filled with landscapes. The title, WOMEN OF THE EARTH, is written on a large placard.

In the other window: paintings. Vibrant and loud, they are mostly covered with flowers and what looks to be Lake Ledger.

The color alone makes them stunning, but it's the textures that hold my attention. The paint is thick, almost globs, sticking off the canvas in piles of oranges and purples and yellows, bringing the petals to life. Calling to my fingertips to touch them.

The woman with the sign is next to me, patting the side of her dark pixie cut which I now notice has hints of silver. I study her, guessing she's in her sixties, and oddly familiar, but not enough for me to place her.

With a tight smile, she gives a curt, "Afternoon," then squats to rewrite something on the sign with a piece of chalk before dusting her hands.

"Afternoon," I parrot, gaze returning to the pieces in the windows.

"Are you in the market?"

I look at her.

"For art?" She points to the paintings in the window.

I laugh softly, still dazed there's an art gallery in Ledger. "Sorry. Not really, just looking. They're beautiful. The photographs too."

She smiles again, softer this time. "Ah, yes. Come in then, we have more."

I smooth my hands on my quasi-wrinkled shirt, my mom-chic fashion, or, as Mara from the podcast called it, unfashion, and follow the woman's gentle, leather-flat footsteps into the gallery.

Inside, the creamy walls are covered in art of various mediums. Watercolors of downtown Ledger and the lake, abstract sculptures on podiums, asymmetrical wooden bowls, textured paintings, and, of course, photographs. Even the furniture—several pieces of live edge wooden tables—are labeled as being made by local regional artists.

We stop in front of a landscape photo. A black-and-white image of the Blue Ridge Mountains, showcasing the familiar scene in an artistic way. High contrast, grainy, and raw. A modern Ansel Adams.

"It's beautiful," I tell her. "The composition of this seems straightforward, but the photographer made it interesting. The lines of the mountains pulling the eye to the horizon and textures of the fog . . . the depth of field is shallower than I'd expect, but it works brilliantly."

"You know photography," the woman says, seemingly shocked.

"I do—did," I clarify, stepping to another photograph.

She follows. "You either know it or you don't, there's no 'did.' It's like a bicycle. You can or you can't."

I laugh under my breath. "It's been a while. I raise you a maybe."

She makes a sound—half puff of breath, half laugh—and folds her elegant arms across her chest as we study the next photo, another landscape, as familiar as the woman next to me but still I can't place it . . .

"I'm Irma—"

"London!" I blurt, recognition clicking into place as I shoot my hand out toward her. "You're Irma freaking London! World traveller and landscape photographer! Youngest woman to win a Pulitzer in photography." Gushing, I have no shame. "Holy shit!"

Her eyes widen but dance, and another soft laugh puffs out of her as she extends her hand. "Yes, that's me, I suppose."

I shake her hand, soft beneath mine, disbelieving laugh bubbling out of me. "Sorry. It's just that—wow. I'm June. Cannon. Gosh, I studied your work in college." I gush, starstruck. "I wanted to be you when I grew up."

She chuckles. "I'm flattered." She runs her fingertips through her short hair, then adds, "I think."

"Why are you here? In Ledger?" I ask, looking around the room, at the landscape photos I now very much recognize as hers, dumbfounded. "You-you-you've seen the world."

"Ah," she says with a wry smile, as if I've revealed something to her with my observation. "Ledger is part of the world, too, June Cannon."

I try not to stare at her, at this queen of her craft, and reach through the cobwebs of my memory to try to make sense of why she's here. She's a North Carolina native, that much I remember. Charlotte born, I think. But the places she's been. Remote islands in the Pacific, quaint villages in the Alps, fjords of Scandinavia. I can't wrap my brain around getting all that but choosing to have a gallery here.

As if she's reading my thoughts, she studies me, slender face cocking slightly to the side as a slight smirk pulls at her lips. She has a secret that I want to know, and she sees it.

With a nod, I force myself to stop staring at her—at Irma freaking London—and return my attention back to the art, now beside one of the pieces from the same collection of photographs in the front window. A woman's body fills the frame, seated but facing away. The lines of her are obvious, curved and soft, but the inside is more abstract, filled with ripples of water. Subtle compared to the edges. The title: *Woman of the Water*. Next to it, a similar image, except inside the woman, there's a rocky coastline.

"So this is your gallery?" I ask as we wander around, giddy smile plastered on my face. "I recognize the landscape pieces now that I know who you are."

"It is," she says. "This is my gallery—and back here," she says as she leads us down a short hall, to a large open room, "is a shared space for creatives. That corner is for the mess makers." She points to an area with drop cloths, small tables, paint splatters, and a utility sink. "And over here we have a setup for photographers. Mostly portrait work." I nod, studying it all. Bathed in natural light, a few stools sit in the corner, and a neutral-toned backdrop hangs down the exposed brick wall. It's perfect.

"I love this." Translation: I can't believe this.

Out of the room, she—Irma freaking London—follows a few steps behind me. Commenting on the pieces in my silence. She tells me about local artists I didn't know existed though I've nearly lived here my whole life. We stop at a table covered with art books, and I pick one up to thumb through. None of the images register in my brain, but I do it for no reason other than not wanting to leave her. This room. The idea that this life could have existed for me in some alternative universe.

"We have a wall that needs to be filled. If you know anyone . . ." she says, one eyebrow arched.

"I—"

The rumbly roar of a motorcycle fills the air, stealing both my words and our attention. A man on a Harley parks on the street, pushing the kickstand down with a booted foot before slinging his other leg around to stand. Helmet off his head, his eyes meet mine and send a surge of shock straight to my belly. In worn jeans, a faded T-shirt, and a black leather jacket, a blast from the past—twenty-two years older, yet still very much the same—strolls into the gallery with a laugh and a deep, "Well if it isn't our little Ledger sweetheart, June Downing."

My grin turns to an unexpected laugh as he wraps me in a hug, his body much broader now than it was in high school. A gangly boy replaced by a man. He lifts me off the ground like I'm a child.

"It's June Cannon now, thank you very much, Reed Simmons," I say, unexpected weakness in my voice as we pull apart and I take him in.

Different than he was when we were teenagers, new lines and edges with the vibe of James Dean and the scent of cloves and soap.

But his bottom lip? Still full, pouty, and highlighted by a faded white scar. His hair? Still dark, thick, and something between windblown and styled.

Reed Simmons, the only other man I've kissed on this planet, stands in an art gallery with me. In Ledger. Looking like *that*.

Instantly, I'm self-conscious. Smoothing my hair. Wishing the bang situation wouldn't have happened. Or wardrobe situation. Or the fifteen pounds I've gained since I last knew him.

"Ah, yes. How could anyone forget that June married the famous baseball player?" he asks, teasing me as he folds his arms across his chest. Though his tone lacks heat, my face warms like it's been blasted by a blowtorch hearing the truth of my life being said aloud.

"You two know each other?" Irma asks, reminding me she's there.

"We went to high school together," Reed says, looking from me to her to me again. I fidget with the hem of my shirt. "Not sure what she's told you, but June here is a helluva photographer."

"Not true." I laugh, nervous. "I'm just looking. And you, Mr. Simmons? Are you in the market for art all the way from wherever it is you went after we graduated?"

He laughs, easy, scratching his scruff-covered jaw, blue eyes dancing. "I went everywhere, but my dad passed last month . . . I'm here sorting his estate for a few months."

A look passes between him and Irma.

"Don't be modest, Reed," she interjects. "He's the gallery's first visiting artist too. WOMEN OF THE EARTH." She gestures to the wall of double-exposed women. "That's him."

At this, my jaw drops, eyes bouncing around the canvases like a bouncy ball. "*You* shot those?"

He grins, sheepish, and shoves his hands in his pockets. "Guilty."

"These are gorgeous," I say, moving toward them again. Seeing them differently. Seeing *him* differently.

Our gazes hook, hold, and then the gallery phone rings, slicing the moment.

"I should go," I tell Irma.

"Bring me your work," she calls over her shoulder as she moves toward the ringing phone. "If he says you're a photographer, you are."

Then she's gone, into an office, and I'm awkward, looking at Reed in all his bad-boy, artistic Reedness.

My, "Sorry about your dad," comes at the same time as his, "I'll walk you out."

When we get to my minivan, lame next to his motorcycle, I fumble with my keys.

"I never would have predicted the girl that drove a cherry-red convertible in high school would drive a minivan, Junie." He grins, leaning easy against the side of it.

I laugh under my breath. "Yeah, well, would you believe it if I said me neither?"

I fumble to get the door open, my heart pounding in my tonsils, looking him over one last time and letting our history gush through me like floodwaters through a broken dam. All the *what ifs*.

"How do you know Irma London?" I ask.

He smiles, but it doesn't meet his eyes. "She was a friend of my dad's."

I nod, wanting to ask a million more questions but don't.

"Maybe I'll see you before you leave," I say as I drop into the driver's seat.

"Maybe you will," he says with a wink and a smirk, revealing a brand-new truth I didn't need to know: Grown-man Reed looks sexy as hell when he winks and smirks, and it dries my mouth.

I clear my throat. Twice.

All I can say is: "Right."

He knocks his knuckles against the roof of the minivan before stepping away. "Give my best to Camp."

I snort a laugh as I shake my head. He knows damn well I will *not* be doing that.

It takes a full block of driving before I can breathe again.

Irma London.

Reed Simmons.

What the actual hell?

At the next light, heart still hammering in my chest from the unlikely scenario that just played out, the open sign at a local boutique has me slamming on the brakes. Again.

Reinvent yourself. Don't be afraid of color. Show some skin.

Another honk—this time a fellow mom in a minivan shaking an angry hand at me as she circles around where I've stopped.

I give an apologetic wave and turn into the parking lot.

With just enough time before I have to get the boys, I will myself into the shop and buy every item of clothing I can that isn't black and shows more skin than I've shown in years. I don't think, I just buy, not wanting to talk myself out of whatever this is.

An embarrassing number of bags in hand and money spent later, I hurry across town, pick Hank and Ty up from preschool—complete with a fifteen-minute lecture from Ms. Mitchell on how they taught the entire class to make spitballs, and now the wall is covered—and make a four thirty spite dinner of meatloaf just to prove a point.

For the first time in years, Camp is right on time.

Nine

"How's it work?" Ty asks, eyeing the canister of film as I load it into the camera.

"Well," I start, pulling it into the winder and cranking the arm. "This film is covered with special chemicals, and when the light hits it, it saves the picture." I smile at him, closing the back of the camera. "Then, it goes into more chemicals, and the pictures stay on the film and can be printed out."

Strike one! An umpire calls from the background at the same time Hank climbs on my lap. "What are you going to take pictures of?"

I adjust his boney behind on my lap as Ty brings the camera up to his face, little green eye peering through the viewfinder.

"Hmm." I look around, the scene of a bunch of high schoolers on a Saturday morning baseball field is about as far from the wild landscapes I once planned on photographing as it can get.

"Get Daddy," Hank says, pointing to Camp where he's coaching third base.

Hinged at the waist, hands on his knees, iridescent-lensed sunglasses on his face to hide his expression, he looks toward the batter who scrubs his cleats in the clay, orange clouds puffing up around home plate. Camp lifts a hand, scrubs his knuckles across his mustache three times, slides a palm down the opposite arm, claps twice, then nods. The batter responds by lifting his chin and squaring up to home plate, bat pulled back, jaw set.

I click the shutter, Camp oblivious, his intense gaze going from pitcher to batter.

I take four photos of him in a row: Serious as he watches the pitch. Standing upright when the bat connects with the ball. Watching the ball fly over center field. His head back, mid-laugh, when the ball soars over the fence.

When the crowd cheers, I laugh, watching Camp through my viewfinder as the batter rounds third and gives him a high five. For a split second, I'm a seventeen-year-old girl watching a boy live his dream.

"Can I see the picture now?" Hank asks, tugging at the camera from my hands and my attention from the field.

I show him the back of the camera—the solid piece of black plastic a far cry from the modern screens of digital age—with a dramatic frown. "This is old school, kid, you gotta wait for the good stuff."

As opposite from exotic or exciting as it can get, I lean into a morning of photographing nothing special. Getting to know my camera again. Light. Shadows. Lines. Remembering what it means to compose something ordinary and make it look extraordinary.

I shoot Lyra standing with her friends, laughing as they look at their phones and take selfies. I take photos of the boys, right before I drag them out from under the bleachers where they are eating all the popcorn off the ground. I photograph the crowd, making them blurry, clearing the details but somehow making the image sharper. More real. It could be a story about no one as much as one about anyone.

When the game is over and the boys chase Camp to the locker room, I load another roll of film and wander around alone, capturing details. The light hitting the chain-link fence, cleats in the dugout, the empty bleachers. The scoreboard. The bases. The umpire pulling his vest off. The smudged lines in the clay.

Then, somehow, I'm on the other fields, photographing the soccer goals, a rogue softball, the tackling dummies and practice football jerseys piled up.

"June!" a deep voice calls in unison with a high-pitched, "Mama!"

Coming out of the locker room, Camp and the boys move toward me in the parking lot, and I drop my camera in my purse.

"What were you doin' out here?" Camp asks, pulling his sunglasses off as he falls into step next to me.

"She was taking pictures," Hank says, making Camp's eyebrows shoot up and my throat pinch.

I shift my weight between my feet, not wanting to discuss it. Almost embarrassed. "Just playing, you know. It's nothing."

Camp grins. "It's not *nothing*, J. You always loved it so much, I never understood why you stopped."

My jaw drops straight to the asphalt beneath my Birkenstocks, and I look at him—so much genuine sincerity on his face—a deluge of thoughts blowing through me.

Starting with: Are you fucking kidding me? Can he not see that I was forced to choose between him and the kids and everything else? Surely, he's not that naïve. Hell, given our current situation, maybe he *is* that naïve.

"I was just playing," I say, blinking away from his gaze. "Boys, you ready to go? Lyra's riding with friends, and I know your dad has stuff with the coaches, so—"

"He's coming with us," Hank interrupts.

"What?"

No.

No.

"He's coming with us," Ty repeats, shoving a handful of rocks into his pocket.

I pin Camp with a glare, which he meets with a smug smile. "I said to the coaches, 'We spend too many Saturdays together, we should take today off.' So I planned a picnic."

"You planned a picnic." I set my purse in the passenger seat of the van and cross my arms over my chest.

"I planned a picnic," he echoes, amused.

I huff out a breath. "I heard you, Camp," I say through gritted teeth, moving my mouth like a bad ventriloquist. "Why did you do that?"

"Because I love my wife and am happily married." He blinks, as if it's entirely insane that I'm mad. As if us pretending to be happily married meant we need to do all of this. Together. Like a real happily married couple.

Pockets full of God knows what, the boys slide the back door of the minivan open and climb into their booster seats while Camp and I have a silent argument with our eyes. My narrowing, nostril flaring, head tilting battle only finds a ceasefire from the roar of a motorcycle.

Reed.

Fingers lifting off one handle in a half wave at the stop sign and a lift of his chin, I return the wave with a too-big smile in his direction before he drives away.

"Friend of yours?" Camp asks, opening the door to his truck that's parked next to me.

"Reed Simmons," I say, letting the name steal all the oxygen off planet Earth and cause Camp's expression to falter exactly the way I hoped it would. *Take that, you smug sonofabitch.* "He sends his best." I smile sweetly as I drop into the seat of my minivan. "Let's go on a picnic, *honey.*"

I'm a spiteful bitch. I know this because when the picnic is a disaster it warms my cold heart like summer asphalt on bare feet. In this moment of Lyra looking at Camp in outrage over a picnic table while mosquitoes nibble on our skin, I've never been so elated. I've never loved bugs and bad food more.

"Dad, this isn't gluten-free bread!" Lyra cries, looking at the sandwich like it's about to bite her.

I swat a bug on my arm, blood bursting on my skin with the kill, and press my lips between my teeth.

Camp's eyes narrow, looking at the bread like he's trying to will it to turn into something else. Something gluten-free.

"Gluten-free . . . ?" He runs a hand through the long hair on the top of his head. "No, I don't think so . . ."

She huffs out a breath, pulling the bread off her ham and cheese. "Mom, why didn't you tell him?"

I scoff. "Don't pin this on me, Ly. Your dad did all this."

"Why are there seeds in the crust?" Ty asks, leaning toward his paper plate until his nose hits the sandwich and he sniffs.

"You think that's weird," Hank chimes in. "The cheese has holes." He presents the table with a piece of Swiss cheese. "And it smells weird."

"Okay, okay, okay. The sandwiches aren't a hit." Camp scrubs his knuckles across his mustache. "I brought more."

Out of the cooler, Camp pulls a container of raw broccoli, a bag of apples, and, my personal favorite, a jar of pickled beets from the local farm stand. At the kids' puckered faces, I can't contain my joy and bark out a laugh.

"What's wrong with all this?" he cries. "I know you guys like apples . . ."

Lyra snorts a laugh and grabs an apple. "Sure, Dad."

The boys each grab apples and hand them to me, making my eyes go to Camp. "Did you bring a knife?"

"A knife?"

"Yes, *honey*, a knife. To cut the apples. Ty won't eat them whole, and Hank doesn't eat the skin."

He nods, squinting into the cooler, again, as if he's hoping it's a kind of magician's hat that will make cutlery and new ingredients appear.

"I did *not* bring a knife," he says, hands going to his hips.

"Who are the beets for? Gross," Lyra asks around a bite of her apple.

"Your mom. She loves them." He looks at me, shoulders slumping slightly. "At least, she used to."

And I see it there, something Camp never feels: defeat. And dammit, as much as I love watching him fail, love seeing him live my life and struggle through it, his gesture makes my cold heart warm just enough for me to notice. Because it's Camp, and I do love those stupid beets. And even more, he's trying. For what feels like the first time in over a decade, maybe more, my husband is making an effort off of the baseball field.

I could say I don't. Could make him look like a fool in front of our kids and remind him of all the reasons our marriage isn't working, and yet . . .

"I do love those beets," I say with a grin, swatting a buzzing mosquito away from my face. "Here." I lean over the table and rearrange the nearly inedible ingredients, making a sandwich for Hank of all bread and ham, Ty gets plain cheese, and Lyra has ham and cheese roll-ups. I twist the lid off the beets, putting one on each kids' plate, along with the broccoli—which I serve with a look that says *you will eat this, and you will like it*. Out of my purse, I pull out my camera, set it on the table, and find the utility knife I keep for emergencies—mostly when the boys tie something to something else that shouldn't be tied together—and slice the apples, peeling the skin for Hank.

As they eat, without complaints this time, I pop a beet in my mouth with a satisfied moan. Camp nudges me with his elbow from next to me, amused look on his face as I bring a napkin to my mouth, chuckling around my chews.

"Thanks for savin' me," he says, low enough the kids can't hear over their too-loud conversation. "How did you know how to do all that?"

"We eat dinner every night, Camp." One simple statement summarizes everything he's missed.

He looks at me, his mouth open slightly, but says nothing.

"Mom, when did you get this camera?" Lyra asks.

"College," I say with a smile, picking it up. "I wanted to be a photographer. Digital was just coming out, but I couldn't shake the magical pull of film. The mystery of shooting something and having to wait to see what you made." I pull it up to my face and fill the frame with Lyra's beautiful face—pink hair pulled into messy pigtails—and capture the moment. "See, now you'll have no idea if you have broccoli between your teeth until this gets developed."

"Hey!" she cries, running her tongue over her teeth. "Can I try?"

I pass her the camera, showing her the buttons and settings. She points the lens at me then lowers it, waving a hand through the air. "With Dad."

"Right, of course." I flick my eyes to him, scooting closer on the bench.

His arm reaches around my waist, pulling me to him, and my head drops onto his shoulder. For one click of the shutter, I feel how well we used to fit together.

When she pulls the camera away from her face, she grins. "Guess you'll have to wait and see if you have beet juice on your face until the film's developed."

"Ha. Ha," I say, throwing a napkin at her as I sit up straight. Camp's palm moves from my waist to the small of my back where it lingers. Where I notice.

"Why did you quit?" she asks, pointing the camera at the boys who now have broccoli shoved up their nostrils. When she pushes the button, nothing happens. The film is out.

"Hm." I fish another roll from my purse and reload the camera as I try to figure out how to answer her in a way that doesn't sound depressing. "I got busy with you. Life is . . . busy."

Camp's hand drops from my back, silence hanging for a beat.

"Well, judgin' by how bad the rest of my food choices were"—he swats a mosquito on his neck—"and how awful these bugs are, I'm guessin' my only chance of redemption is ice cream on the way home."

When the kids cheer, I start stacking paper plates and sweeping crumbs into a pile.

Lyra helps repack the cooler as Camp walks the boys to the minivan, wrestling with them the whole way, causing giggly screams to cut through the park.

"That a new shirt?" Lyra asks, eyeing the bright yellow fabric.

I tug at the hem, which barely brushes the top of my jeans. "Um. Yeah. I got it yesterday. I don't know—maybe it's silly." I tug the hem again, suddenly self-conscious. "I just liked the color—thought it was a little different than my usual. I might return it—"

"Why? I love it. That color looks great on you." She gives a wry smile. "I might have to steal it."

I puff out a laugh, staring at her as she finishes clearing the table, her confidence the opposite of mine.

"Dad sucks at packing lunch."

"Hm," I agree with a small smile, watching as he makes faces to the boys in the back of the minivan. "That he does."

"Even with the bad food and bugs"—she shrugs—"this was fun."

I nod but don't say anything, because she's right . . . this was fun. I wonder if someday she'll also realize it was fake.

"You stopped photography because of Lyra?"

Camp's voice from the floor in the darkness of our bedroom startles me. I roll to the edge of the bed and look down to where he's lying. With one arm crooked behind his head, the other palm resting on his chest, he looks up at me. The streetlight through the window illuminates his face just enough for me to make out his features. The bump on his nose, the bristles of his mustache, the unfair smoothness of his skin.

"I guess." I pause, wondering if we've never had this conversation. How we've never had this conversation. "I don't think it was as cause and effect as that though. Not as definitive. I had a baby, I was too tired to think about it, and we were living with my parents, which..."

A breath wooshes out of me with the recollection of that time. Camp was off trying to make it in the world of baseball, and I was alone with a baby. Our bank account was made up of more dreams than dollars, and my mom welcomed me and Lyra into my old bedroom with open arms. What I didn't account for was that my parents would drive me crazy. Between their weird routines and seeming rediscovered sex life, it was the last place I wanted to be. Photography was the last thing on my mind. "I was trying to survive; you were trying to figure out baseball . . . I just kind of forgot about it. I thought I would do it when you figured out your career, but then . . ." My voice trails off with that, and he sits up.

"Then what, June?" he asks, propping himself up on a forearm. "Because I didn't play baseball you couldn't do what you wanted?"

And just like that, I relive it all like it's in real time.

I got pregnant with Lyra, had a baby, and got tired. Camp was chasing his dreams of playing in the majors, so I waited. Waited to see what he was going to do—who he was going to be—before

I decided what I wanted. Then came the injury. And though the recovery was slow, I was so sure he was going to recover. We both knew it. His big break was coming.

Then the phone call. I'll never forget it. He was at spring training, and I was in the tiny apartment we finally rented to escape my ever-humping parents. Lyra was sick, wouldn't stop crying. I felt like I hadn't slept in days. "How's the arm, Camp?" I asked between her screams.

He didn't answer me. "What's going on there?"

I said something to Lyra, trying to soothe her, both of us yawning. Both of us feeling so damn defeated. "She's sick, can't shake the fever. It's fine."

Then he paused, long and weighted, as if he was trying to work up the courage to tell me the bad news. "They don't think my arm is going to get better, J, they aren't extending my contract." His voice caught, and my throat, nose, and eyes all burned like they'd been stuffed with hot coals. My heart shattered to smithereens for him. "But the year I had in the majors made us enough money, financially we are fine. You can stay home with Lyra, and I'll come back there—we can buy my parents' house, it'll be perfect for us—and there's a position at the high school. It's mine if I want it. It's all going to be okay."

And there, while Camp confessed his baseball career was over, I refused to speak up about anything else. To tell him I didn't want to live in Ledger or his parents' old house or spend my whole life pouring into other people's cups. It was what he wanted, and I would do it. For him. For us. Even as Lyra screamed in my face,

I believed I'd figure it out. How hard would it be? My mom had done it. Stayed home, raised three kids. She seemed to come out of it mostly unscathed.

I went from chasing dreams to chasing kids and started shoving things in a box, never telling Camp what I really thought about anything. No matter how hard. Ever. Because: *I could do this. I could do this. I could . . .*

"June?" Camp's voice brings me back to the present. A dark bedroom and separate beds.

My eyebrows pinch and I lift my head off the bed. "No, I didn't say that. It's not about what you did or didn't do, Camp. It's-it's"—I pause, letting out a long exhale—"it's that your dream was shattered when you were injured, and you seemed so happy with me being able to stay home with Lyra. I wanted to be good for you, for her. Then the next few years . . ."

I look at him, our shared history connecting us like ends of a complex spiderweb.

"The next few years," he echoes. Saying it all. The hard and the ugly. The pieces of life people sweep under the rug.

I drop my head to the mattress, turning my own gaze to the ceiling. Quiet.

Same ceiling; separate beds.

"Lyra called me simple."

"June, that's not—"

"Don't, Camp. Not now. We're beyond all the placating. I know I'm simple, especially to a teenager. It's hard to believe I ever was who I once was. But I feel it right now, hard, everything I never did." An unamused laugh rumbles in my chest followed by a thick silence that coats the room.

"How did you know Reed was in town?"

I roll on my side to face him again. "He came into an art gallery I went into. The Ledger Art House—it's new. He's a photographer of all things, in town because his dad died and has an installation there."

"Of course he does," he replies, bitter.

One heartbeat. Two. Twenty beats later, he speaks again.

"You should go take photos tomorrow, J. I don't have anywhere I need to be." His eyes meet mine, dark in the night. Crescent moons flickering up at me.

"You don't have to do this, Camp. Change who you are because we didn't work. I can figure this out a different way. Manage on my own."

He scoffs. "I'm your husband, you don't need to *manage*."

I want to tell him managing is all I've been doing for years, but instead, I say, "Only for seventy more days."

Another silence. My pulse thumps in my throat; my mind spins in a million directions.

"I didn't know you were unhappy."

Unhappy. It punches my chest.

I know I'm not living the life twenty-two-year-old me envisioned. Know I'm living in a town I thought I'd escape with a husband that doesn't feel like a partner . . . but unhappy? It's so . . . severe.

He doesn't say anything else, and, lost in my own head, neither do I.

Ten

Ledger, North Carolina is a tourist town. Which, to anyone from here, is laughable. There's nothing—a Main Street with a dozen or so businesses surrounded by quiet neighborhoods that lead to even quieter farms. But it's the lake that brings them in. Lake Ledger rests like a 765-acre jewel in the middle of the thick forests of the hills that lead to the steeper slopes of the Blue Ridge Mountains. To the people from Charlotte and even Atlanta, it's a getaway. A quiet place to unplug.

While most of the shoreline sits down at water level with a gentle slope, there's a long section that's bordered by a slick granite rock face that drops right to the water. At the top, a rock ledge. As if ordained by geographic destiny, the people that settled on the ledge, however many years ago, declared the town Ledger.

When I packed up my gear this morning, I convinced myself that I would wander the familiar landscape and feel inspired. Now, looking at the lake—pristine as it is—nothing.

Climbing the trail along a smooth rock face to a cliff that overlooks the lake, my gear shifts on my back, thighs screaming as I climb. And my lungs? They're one wheezy breath away from collapsing. This once familiar trail is where I have come to die.

Despite the spring breeze licking my skin, my shirt and backpack cling to me with sweat.

Finally, the summit, and I nearly collapse with relief.

I'm hungry, so I eat a granola bar—fine, I eat two granola bars—then make work of setting up my tripod and organizing my lenses.

Through the viewfinder, I see the familiar lake—the same but different. Boathouses on the water sheltering pontoon boats, skiffs, and a couple of Jet Skis. Kayaks are haphazardly scattered on beaches and one man is swimming, Olympian-esque with a swim cap and eager strokes that cut through the water. I pan my camera around to the trees hugging the shoreline. There's a deer. Three birds.

It's quiet.

My heart beats, soft and steady in the cage of my ribs.

I click the shutter.

Once.

Twice.

Framing the lake with the trees, the mountains claim the entirety of the skyline.

One shot with more lake than sky, the next with more sky than lake.

While my heart wasn't in landscape photography when I first made the switch, I fell in love with it when I figured out a sort of formula of composition and light. As a niche, it's reliable, patient, and, with the right light, predictable. The subject is completely compliant, standing still, and all the photographer has to do is look, frame, and click. Learn the rules and apply.

A high-pitched squeal cuts through the air, dragging my gaze to a sandy beach. A mom and two young kids sit on the shore, one of them screaming as he smacks his hands against the water.

The mom says something, her voice a muffled echo that I can't decipher from my distance. I pan my camera to them, a wide-angle lens making them small in the scheme of the bigness of the lake. Sticks in the water.

I take one shot of them, clean and in focus. And, while I know it won't be a keeper to anyone else, I take another and make it weird. Blurred with a sun flare. When the shutter clicks, there's an unnamable feeling in my belly.

I eye the beach. The perspective from there would offer a great shot of the rest of the lake and the floating dock in the middle.

I reload my gear into my bag, tripod strapped across the top, and hitch it onto my back.

The air, thick with fragrant pines and celery-green leaves exploding on the trees, is pure. I breathe just to smell it. There's a sharpness to it, something as familiar as it is new. Two hikers approach, I turn to let them pass, and it strikes me I haven't been out here in years. Camp and I used to always hike together, but that's been . . . years. Before the boys were born.

Why did we stop?

Baseball games. Kids. Sleep deprivation. Life.

Other than shuffling the kids around, talking to Scotty's bodies, and meetings for whatever school events are going on, I haven't been out of the house like this in years.

Approaching the bottom of the trail, stepping onto the sandy spot of the beach, I see that's how it happens. We always do something until we don't. We are who we are until we change. Life erodes us like the waters that formed this lake until we are a completely different shape. One day we hike together, the next we're strangers.

The two kids—babies really—are splashing at the edge of the water wearing T-shirts and soggy diapers. I wonder how many more times this will happen. How many more visits their mom will bring them here.

Down the sandy beach from them, I set up my tripod, screw my camera into the fitting on the top, adjust my settings, and frame the view. From here, with the angle of the sun, the water shows two scenes: one real, one reflective. Hills of trees pointing in both directions. One skyward, one to the depths of the lake. Lake Ledger is a mirror of itself.

I take a shot, tack sharp and perfect. And another.

I switch my lens, take one more.

Face behind the camera, something hits my leg. I look down—*mud?* Mud.

One of the babies, just over a year, has discovered me and has his mud-covered fingers wrapped around my jeans. With a mop of blond curls, gigantic blue eyes, and now only wearing a water-swollen diaper and amber beads around his neck, he's adorable. "Hey, little guy," I say in a soft voice. I smile, and he returns it, gummy and drooly.

"Oh my gosh, I'm so sorry!" The mom rushes over, hooks a hand around his wrist. "Henry, no!" she says, apologetic look in her eyes. "I didn't see him come over here. He loves strangers." She groans when her gaze drops. "Your jeans!"

I laugh softly and wave it off. "Don't worry about it."

She's younger than me, maybe thirty, but she's familiar. Not in that I know her, but that I've been her—maybe still am. When she smiles, it's tired, and the way I understand is visceral. Exhaustion, overwhelm, and loneliness all wrapped into one simple expression. I take in her leggings and oversized shirt and almost laugh. How I must look to everyone around me.

Unfashion, indeed.

I kneel and scoop up some of the mud around us, holding it out to Henry. "I have a few at home. I get it. They can be . . . unpredictable."

She laughs, relieved, and Henry pokes a finger into the watery sand in my hands.

"Cherish it before it's gone, right?" she says ironically with a shake of her head, adjusting the baby on her hip.

The cliché rips a roaring laugh straight from my chest. "If I had a dollar for every time someone said that to me in a grocery store as my boys were bringing down an entire shelf of food, I'd be rich!"

Next to me, she laughs, only when I stop, she doesn't. Her laugh turns to a shoulder-shaking sob. Tears fall down her face as an unkempt braid hangs sadly over one shoulder.

"I'm so sorry," she says, swatting at her cheeks. "I don't know why I'm crying."

I stay quiet, simply letting her tears fall as I crouch next to her son, mud in my hands. She might not know why she's crying, but even without knowing her, I most definitely do.

"My husband is military. Deployed." She sniffs, wiping her nose with the back of her hand. "And just, some days you know . . ." Another sniff. Another sob. "Some days are awful." She squeezes her eyes shut. "I'm sorry, I shouldn't have said that, I just mean—"

"That some days having your face screamed in after three hours of sleep doesn't feel all warm and fuzzy?" I fill in for her, knowing smile pulling at my lips.

She laughs, relieved, wiping her face again. "Yeah, something like that." Another sniff, then she studies the calm lake. "Does it get easier?"

"I wish I could say yes." Her expression crashes, like this is the worst news of her day. "But it gets different," I add. "The diapers go away. There's more sleep. But my boys are four . . . there's still a lot of mud." She smiles weakly at my words. "And my teenager"—my eyes widen—"that's a whole different ballgame."

Finally, she laughs—a true one—then looks at my camera.

"You a photographer?"

I make an acknowledging sound as I wipe my muddy hands on my jeans and stand. "I don't know. Maybe."

She nods, as if she understands what I'm saying even though it makes absolutely no sense.

"Anyway, sorry again. We have to get going. Thanks for . . . thanks."

I smile. "No problem."

She shuffles away, fumbling with diaper bags and babies, then disappears down the short trail that leads to the parking lot. It's not until the sound of her voice and car doors opening and closing fade that I turn back to my camera and the lake.

Alone again, I take a few more shots before pointing my camera toward the ground, taking a close-up of the shore. The blurry line where water meets land. The spot babies sit and toes tingle.

I sit, prying my shoes off, letting the water lap against my feet. The air is cool; the water is cold.

By summer, this small beach will be packed, and the lake will be covered in people, but now, it's just me, the birds, and a slight breeze.

My parents used to bring my brothers and me here. We'd rent a boat a couple times a year and spend entire Saturdays under the sun. In high school, my friends and I overtook this beach. Scotty and I in string bikinis and covered in tanning oil with boy bands playing on the stereo. And Camp and me . . . Camp and me. In canoes. On Jet Skis. In the bar that overlooks the water sharing French fries. I look across the shore, and when my eyes land on a small opening in the trees where we used to go camping, my chest hurts.

Like everything else in Ledger, this place holds a million stories, most of them tied to Camp.

The pinecone-sized lump in my throat is accompanied with a burn that pricks my eyes. Even alone with the expanse of the lake, in an instant, I'm trapped. Drowning above ground.

Clothes suddenly tight as skin, I jerk to a stand.

I can't breathe.

I tug at the neck of my shirt.

My heart pounds.

Every breath feels like it's through a cocktail straw.

I can't do this.

I can't sit here.

I just . . . can't.

I claw my jeans off.

Run into the water.

And despite the frigid pain, I dive under.

Underwater, ice-cold shock seizes my entire body for a split second wrapping me in painful aliveness.

At the surface, I gasp for air as I tread water.

And then, in the middle of a Sunday in April in a T-shirt and underwear, I swim, blue shirt swirling around me as my strokes cut through the water until I flip to float on my back.

Alone and freezing, a laugh bubbles out of me, echoing off the water like every mother's anthem.

It doesn't stop, the laugh, I can't stop, and it hurts. Burns. Because I'm not laughing. Like the woman that was just with me moments ago, the sound I make is pained. Face to sky, for the first time since I told Camp we were over, I let myself cry.

Tears for me, my marriage, and the life I thought I'd have fall into the water that surrounds me. The water that watched me grow up and fall in love is now the place I fall apart.

The wet shirt clings to my chest, dripping, as I load my gear into the back seat and move in some kind of post-cathartic cryfest haze. Someone could tell me I cried for twelve seconds or twelve hours and I'd believe them both.

"June?"

I turn. Confusion morphing to a muddled sort of embarrassed disbelief.

"Reed?" My gaze darts around. "What are you doing here?"

He holds up a camera bag as his eyes drop to my chest—my very cold, very wet, *very cold*—chest. My nipples, now some kind of weapons of mass destruction, point directly at his amused face. "Shooting." A smirk pulls at one side of his lips. "You?"

"Same," I croak, pulling my shirt from my chest with a loud *shleck*. To my dismay, it does nothing to hide my situation—to dull the headlights. With the grace of a forty-year-old, soaking-wet woman, I cross my arms over my chest, pretending it's fine. I'm fine. "And swimming. I was shooting"—I nod toward my gear—"and then had some kind of . . . swimming urge."

A breeze blows and freezes me to the bone while sending a fresh shot of heat up my neck. I don't dare move my arms for fear of a nipple poking out someone's eye. Reed's eye. Not that his eye and my nipples have anything to do with anything.

He leans against the minivan, dark hair tousled from his helmet. "Get any good shots?"

I clear my throat. "You know film, it doesn't tell you right away. But there's a good lab here in town, surprisingly. Even in this modern age of digital, Ledger still has a film lab. Probably is fitting. Slow, sleepy town and all. Maybe everyone uses film now that I think of it. But that will be a couple days, I guess and—"

"June." He laughs my name out, runs a hand through his hair and takes a step closer to me, bringing a wave of cloves and soap with him. Blue eyes, playful and sincere, latch onto mine. "Relax. It's just me."

"Sorry . . ." I say on an exhale. "I'm wet."

His eyebrows raise.

A laugh puffs out of me despite my skin melting off my bones. I tighten my grip around myself. "No. Right." *I want to die.* "I didn't expect to see anyone here is all. More shocking than the minivan I drive is that I now swim fully clothed. Ta-da! Adulthood!" I laugh at my expense; he shakes his head with a chuckle.

Please, God, let Reed Simmons be a serial killer and murder me right now.

Silence follows, two seconds or years; time is hard to measure in moments of self-destruction.

"Well." His tongue darts out and swipes his bottom lip before he taps his knuckles on the hood of the van and tilts his head. "Can't wait to see what you shot."

"Right."

With a smirk and a wink, he hoists his camera bag onto his shoulder, and he's gone. Leaving me cold and wet.

Eleven

"Anyone home?"

I'm quasi-dry when I walk in the door. Camp's truck absent from the driveway, house devoid of the usual noise the boys create on a constant loop. "Ly?"

It's quiet. I drop my camera bag at the door. Drop my keys onto the hook. Then I hear it: the unexpected laugh and low muffle of voices.

Quietly, I move toward the sounds. The hallway of the kids' bedrooms. Lyra's door is cracked, just enough for the waves of whispers to come out. Music. Giggles. Words. All of it soft.

"Ly, what's—" I push the door open and the sentence dies.

Lyra is in her bed. Without a shirt. With Nick. On top of her.

"Mom!" she shrieks, reaching for a blanket and wadding it at her chest. "I didn't know you were home." Her cheeks are red, lips swollen.

"Surprise. I live here now." I eye Nick, who stumbles from the bed and across the bedroom like Lyra's suddenly contagious. He adjusts his shirt, and I hate that I notice the tent that's pitched in his basketball shorts.

I'll be scrubbing that visual away later.

"Nick." I look at him, my eyebrows raised as I lean in the doorway.

"Ms. Cannon. Mrs. June. Mrs. June Cannon." He's terrified. *Good*. "Do I call you . . . ?" He blows out a shaky breath. "Coach is going to kill me," he mutters.

We are silent for one, two, three heartbeats, and I decide to put us all out of our misery.

"Nick, tell your parents I say hi."

He nods, relieved, and grabs his backpack that looks like it hasn't been opened. They might not *date* anymore, but it seems *studying* still means the same thing.

"See you tomorrow, L," he mumbles, looking at her briefly, hand poorly hiding the situation in his shorts as he moves toward the door. I turn to the side so he can pass, and he avoids eye contact. And, though it's low, I don't miss the apology he gives on his way by.

Poor kid.

The front door opens and closes, I look back to Lyra. Blanket still clutched against her chest where she lays on her bed, gaze on the ceiling.

I wrack my brain on what to do. I listened to a podcast once that said giving kids sexual freedom in their teenage years leads to a life of promiscuity. Then she rattled off a statistic, some insanely high number of adult prostitutes grow up in households where the parents allowed what she called "free love." But, looking at Lyra mortified and closed off in her bed, I hate that advice. For the first time ever, I feel the need to ignore an expert. I have no fucking clue what to do, but shaming her for what she's feeling and what's happened doesn't feel like the answer.

"So, this is awkward," I say, sitting on the edge of her bed and studying a bulletin board covered in pictures and random notes scribbled with inside jokes and sketches. Lyra in all her shades and phases filling the frames.

She scoffs, focusing on a loose thread in her blanket.

"Where's your dad?"

"Soccer coach got locked out of the locker room, he took the boys to get him out."

I nod. Of course. Duty calls and Camp is gone, once again leaving me to deal with all the hardest parts of being a parent. Alone.

I take a breath. Then another.

My mom did a lot of things right, but we never had open dialogue about sex. She knew school handled the basics and let me figure out the rest. I'm sure I could have gone to her with questions, but I never did. Never had to. Scotty taught me everything I never needed to know with vulgar detail and sometimes pictures.

For the first time as a mother, I want to do something different than the examples I've been shown. I want to talk to Lyra about this—want her to talk to me.

With a gentle tone I ask, "Have you had sex with him?"

Her eyes cut to mine for a split second before looking away as she hugs the blanket tighter to her chest.

What she doesn't say, I can see written all over her: They have not had sex.

"I lost my virginity to your dad in a tent by the lake," I blurt, half laughing at the confession.

"Mom! Gross!" she groans, finally keeping her eyes on me. "TMI."

I laugh, louder this time, and shrug.

"It hurt like hell, and I cried when I bled after," I tell her, remembering that night like it was yesterday instead of twenty-three years ago. "I thought I was going to have to go to the hospital and tell the doctor what happened. I knew my parents would kill me. And Camp. And—"

"Please. Stop," she groans again, but there's the slightest hint of an amused smile that pulls at her mouth and in turn lightens the mood.

Slightly.

We look at each other, not saying anything. Me understanding what she's feeling and hoping she knows.

I drop back onto her bed, lying next to her, and stare at the ceiling. The glow-in-the-dark stars Camp hung for her when she was little somehow still hanging on for dear life. We're quiet for the length of the entire next song that plays. A love ballad, of course. Lines crooning out about fast hearts and slow hands.

"How did you know?"

I turn to face her.

"With Dad. How did you know you were ready? That he was, you know, *the one*?"

My breath comes out in a soft *pah!* and I close my eyes, teleporting to a different time and place and reality. Of me and Camp, seventeen with our whole lives ahead of us. Our love the only thing that mattered. His lopsided grin, nose not yet broken. More gangly than the man he grew into. Cocky, but not as sure of himself.

Then there was me. Red hair like fire, camera slung over my shoulder, too much eyeliner and ridiculous Doc Martens on my feet. The first few months Camp and I dated I was convinced the only reason he was with me was because he was scared of Scotty.

Then, one day, I knew it was more. Camp just loved me. Every weird piece of me. And I knew he wouldn't hurt me. Not ever. Even if we weren't destined for forever, Camp would protect me.

And so, one night, camping with friends, we snuck into our tent pitched down by the lake, and it happened. We stripped each other down, clumsy hands and nervous mouths, and said yes to each other.

"Mom? What's wrong?"

Lyra's voice pulls me out of that tent and back to her bed.

"Huh?"

"You're crying," she says, voice laced with concern.

I swipe at my cheeks, feeling a moisture I didn't expect to find, and laugh as I swipe my hands across them. "Gosh, sorry. I don't know. I was thinking about your dad." I sniff. "I knew I was ready because it was him. Because he loved me, and I was never once worried he would hurt me. Even if we didn't last, I wasn't scared. I trusted him."

I find her hand and squeeze it in mine. "You're ready if you can talk about it with me. If you can tell me he makes you feel safe and beautiful, you're ready."

She grins. "You learn that in a podcast?"

"Actually, I came up with that line all by myself, thank you very much," I tell her with a light laugh.

I slip off the bed and move toward the door. At her desk, I stop, tossing her the T-shirt that's been draped over the chair.

"Mom?"

I still in the doorway, looking back at her. Hair newly purple, eyes bright, shirt bunched to her chest.

"Did you know you'd love Dad forever?"

The question burns my face the same way the water of the lake had.

Our marriage ending isn't about love; it's about more. Me needing more than he's willing to give, a point proven by Lyra being topless in her bed when he was supposed to be here. It's about him, over and over, choosing other people over me. Us.

"Camp Cannon is impossible not to love."

When she smiles, so do I. Because annoying as it is, it's as true as it is frustrating.

Twelve

Camp starts coming home, and it turns me into the very worst version of myself.

A month ago, this would have been cause for celebration and a ticker-tape parade, but now, just over a week since I told him I'm done, his presence tap dances across my last fucking nerve.

At first, it's subtle.

On Monday, he comes home as I'm serving dinner—toeing his cleats off at the door—and though I don't expect to see him, everything is normal. We sit around the table, talking about our day as the boys cause their usual crime scene with the food, and Lyra spills the high school tea. We do Today's Best. It's fine, friendly, and absolutely not out of the ordinary other than him being there.

I sleep in the bed; he sleeps on the floor.

Tuesday, his softball game night, he misses dinner, but instead of going out for his usual drinks after, he comes straight home.

"What are you doing here?" I demand, stunned as I wash the dishes, Lyra and Nick sitting at the table doing homework—where I can watch them—looking up at our exchange, confusion chasing across their faces at my tone.

"I live here," he drawls, toeing his cleats off at the door, smile on his face. "Hey, Nick. Ly."

"You live here?" I demand, cutting off their responded *heys.*

He sweeps his arm through the air. "Yes, *honey,* I live here."

I don't growl at him though this wild animal that's been unleashed inside of me desperately wants to.

Instead: "Right."

Lyra eyes me, gives Nick a look, and shrugs before going back to whatever math problem is on the page.

When he's next to me at the sink, my glare goes unnoticed.

Instead, he rolls up his sleeves, gently bumps me out of the way with his hip, and says, "I'll do these. You relax."

It's so infuriating—him and his athletic wear and crooked nose and sparkly brown eyes being in my space and helping—that instead of relaxing, I stomp to the bedroom and slam the door.

I sleep in the bed; he sleeps on the floor.

Wednesday, he has an away game. I revel in the time away from him, knowing his absence proves every point I've been trying to make.

When he comes home, it's late. I sleep in the bed; he sleeps on the floor.

So goes our week.

During the day, I sneak away to take photos as often as I can, but when the clock strikes four o'clock every afternoon, I can't pull my eyes away from the door. Wondering what's going to happen. If he's going to come home. If he's going to rub Thor's head with an annoying "Hey, Dogg-o!" and forget to take his cleats off. If he's going to be eating dinner.

The weekend comes, we watch his game Saturday morning, and he plans another stupid picnic for the afternoon.

He does a better job packing and it irks me. We're at a park with ducks we can feed, and it's fun and I hate it.

Sunday, I go take photos all day; he spends the day with the kids at his parents' house.

The whole time I'm shooting—at a state park over two hours away—I can't shake the annoyance that sticks to me like flypaper. Because—the nerve of this guy. Years of him being away, and now he just shows up so he can pretend to be something he isn't.

All day, I grunt and groan at nobody and smash the buttons on my camera too hard.

The next week comes, and it's with an insane weather front pushing through that's bringing record rain. As I stand folding laundry in the living room, rain pelting the roof so hard I wonder if it will cave in, Camp texts me: *hey honey buns games and practice cancelled all week looks like well have so much time together Ill get stuff for dinner if you dont have plans*

I don't respond. Instead, I throw the phone as hard as I can at the couch, groan so loudly Thor barks, then retrieve said phone and turn on a podcast.

THE PERFECT MOM PODCAST WITH AB-
BIGAIL BUCHANAN

EPISODE 261: The Importance of Follow-Through with family psychologist Dr. Jill Winthrow

Abbigail: Alright, perfect mamas, if you've ever been in a situation where you've made a threat and then haven't been able to follow through, today's show is for you. We have family psychologist, Dr. Winthrow today, and she has so many good pieces of advice on helping those of us that need a little motivation to stick to our guns, so to speak.

When they both chuckle and Dr. Winthrow introduces herself, it's hard for me to listen. Every drop of rain that spits against the window is the reminder I don't need that in mere hours, Camp will be here. Because he lives here.

I gag and turn up the podcast to drown my thoughts.

Abbigail: Okay, so a lot of this makes sense, but what about those moments where we tell our kids or our spouses our hard line, and then they make changes?

> Like we tell our teenagers, you know, because of your attitude you don't get to go to your friend's house on Friday, and then all of a sudden, the attitude drops and improves. Or we tell our spouses, I don't know, we're making some big change because we don't feel appreciated, and then they start appreciating. Short question long, [they both chuckle] if we say we are going to do something for some reason—some need we have that isn't being fulfilled—and they change that dynamic, is it still necessary to follow through?

I pause, holding the towel I'm folding in the air, and listen like my life depends on it.

> **Jill:** I absolutely see what you are saying, and I know this answer isn't going to be the most well-received, but, even if there's improvement, you have to stand your ground, or you are opening yourself up for constant manipulation. "Oh, Mom doesn't like this attitude, but I know if I change it for three days all is forgiven." Or, "My wife wants me to do more around the house, but if I wait until she's making threats and up my game for a week, we're all good." See what I mean? We aren't making lasting changes if we cave the moment the skies start to clear. By caving, you are saying a little bit today is better than a lot forever. It's big picture vs. little details in these situations.

Abbigail: And you're team big picture?

Jill: [Chuckles.] I am team big picture. Little details are important, those day-to-day things definitely matter, don't get me wrong, but when we lay down the law, we want big-picture changes. We are in this for the long game. Is a few good minutes today worth a lifetime of suffering?

Ha! I knew it!

Camp can come home, pretend to be here, but this is about big-picture changes. My eye is on the prize. The long game.

That's what I tell myself all day. All afternoon. As the rain falls in buckets, it becomes my mantra.

All the way until Camp walks through the door with groceries in hand and a smile on his rain-soaked face.

"Hey, J." He sets the bags on the counter, soaked from the rain, and shakes his head like a wet dog. "I got stuff to make pizzas."

I blink.

He pulls cheese, sauce, and toppings out of the bag. "You didn't respond earlier to my text, so I got stuff anyway. Thought it would be fun."

I blink again; he stills. "Or . . . not?"

I look from the ingredients to the too-eager look on his face, and dammit—it's not big picture, but the fact he planned a meal and bought the groceries to cook is too luxurious not to take advantage of.

"Fine," I finally say. "The kids will love it."

He smiles, relieved, and puts a hand on my back as he reaches around me with the other to pull wineglasses out of the cabinet.

"I bought a red, you want a glass?"

I nod, not liking how the moment makes me feel. Not liking him taking up so much space in the kitchen he's usually absent from.

"Boys! Ly!" he shouts, working the cork out of the bottle. "I got stuff for pizzas, but you freeloaders are doing the work!"

He pours the wine, hands me a glass, and grins.

The kids appear in the kitchen, and Camp puts them to work. Ingredients lined up, they assemble the pizzas.

More than once, I laugh.

More than once, Camp catches me looking at him a second longer than I should be.

More than once, I have to remind myself that this is about the long game—the big picture—and finding what makes *me* happy.

Every thought I have dances with its opposite.

It's real but it's fake.

It's fun but it's awful.

I want this forever, but I can't wait for it to end.

Then I remember: It's only been a couple weeks. The damage from the last few years can't be fixed with a couple picnics and wine.

At the same time, I know I made the same deal as him. So, while this won't last, I'll pretend that this is who we are. A happy couple that makes pizza in bare feet on rainy nights for fifty-four more days. I know it's not real, but the kids don't have to.

"More wine." I raise my glass to Camp, who obliges, leaning next to me at the counter as the kids sprawl across the living room floor and search for a movie.

He studies me, sets his wine down, and slips his fingers under the hem at the neck of my sweater. With a gentle motion, he glides his index and middle finger along the fabric. "I like this. It new?"

I clear my throat, the wine loosening me up enough I don't pull away from his touch.

"It is."

I look down, as if I need a reminder of what I'm wearing. It's a navy blue sweater, a little slouchy but cozy, with a deeper-than-usual neckline.

His fingers move like a slow zipper from my collarbone down toward the bottom of the V then back up—twice.

And it's just the effect of the wine, but I notice. My whole body does, turning into one of those electric balls at museums that makes hair stand on end.

"Hmm," he says under his breath, eyes climbing from my sweater to my face. "Looks good on you, J."

As far as compliments go, it's not special. Lame even. But when his gaze meets mine, heat crawls up my neck, and I drink the entire glass of wine I'm holding.

The jackass smirks. He sees his effect.

"You're an ass," I say, grabbing the bottle of wine and jerking the cork out with a loud *pop*. "Stop trying to get me drunk and take advantage of me."

He chuckles, tone playful. "Me? Nah . . . But I still know what makes you tick, J. And you do look damn good."

I stare at him; he does the same.

The timer on the oven goes off, making me jump and Camp call, "Pizza's ready!"

We eat, we laugh, we tuck the kids in. It's the same as always with one simple change: we.

Back in the kitchen, when the last dish is clean, I look at him as I dry the pan. "You don't have to do all this, you know."

His head tilts, eyebrows raised. "All this?"

"Be here. Buy groceries. Make pizza. I know the weather cancelled things, but I know you also have a lot going on . . ."

He turns the sink off and faces me, drying his hands with a towel. "I do have a lot goin' on, and it'll get busier—the comin' months until the complex is done and baseball season is over will get wild. But, just because I'm gone, J, doesn't mean I don't wish I wasn't. I've missed this. I *like* this."

His blond hair hangs across his forehead, and I have to grip the counter to physically keep myself from touching it. From feathering my fingers through it and letting myself trace the familiar lines of his jaw.

"Either way," I finally say, clearing my throat. "We agreed to being friendly in front of the kids, don't feel like you have to put on some big show like this every night."

He looks at me, warmth in his eyes going glacially cold.

"Good to know," he says, sharp edge to his voice as he tosses the dish towel on the counter. "Won't make that mistake again."

This time, he's the one that leaves me in the kitchen, slamming our bedroom door closed behind him.

When I work up the nerve to follow, he's already on the floor. For the first time in weeks, the bed I sleep in feels too big.

Thirteen

"You like these?" Irma asks, black-framed, rectangular glasses low on her nose as she looks from the photo she's holding to me. Her expression and tone skeptical.

It's been two weeks since I went to the lake. Two weeks of stealing away to photograph landscapes within a couple hours' drive of Ledger. After they were all developed, scans emailed to me, I printed and brought in the best ones. Mostly black and white—just like she does. There are only fifteen keepers of the dozen rolls I've shot, but they are crisp; perfect from any technical standard. Straight horizons and tack-sharp focus.

The rest I saved in a file titled *nonsense* on my computer and don't give them a second look. I've been out of the game a while, but I know how this works. People don't want messy details and abstract still-life images now any more than they did twenty years ago.

I swallow, smoothing my cream slacks. "Umm, yes?" I clear my throat, summoning confidence before repeating: "Yes."

"I see." She takes another photo out of the stack. "And what do you feel when you look at them?"

My eyes narrow. "Feel?"

She sets the photographs down, a black-and-white image of a rocky creek from a local state park on top, and pulls the glasses from her nose, letting them hang from a beaded chain around her neck. "*Feel*. Photographers never make images that pierce the soul if their own souls aren't pierced first."

I shift the weight between my legs, uncomfortable from her question or my shoes or both or neither.

"Umm." I shuffle through the photos, slipping one out of the stack from the day I went to the lake. "I feel peace," I start, the image in my hand taken from where I stood on the beach after the crying woman left. Water reflecting the scene like a mirror. "It was quiet this day, nobody there really, and it was peaceful . . ." My voice trails off as I look from the photograph, filled with flat water, tree-covered hills, and boathouses on the shore, to Irma's face, which is frowning.

"I see."

And, because her silence is a loud and deafening thing, I decide, like some insane person fresh out of the asylum, to fill the void to make her see what I see. What I *need* her to see.

"And, you know, I know these aren't anything new. Not fresh, or anything, but I worked with what I have. I mean, there are only so many ways to creatively photograph the landscapes of North

Carolina." I laugh; she doesn't. "Same vistas over and over. And it has been a long time, so these were just a test run. My plan"—I start stacking the photographs, placing them back in the portfolio I brought them in, hoping they catch on fire—"is to go farther. To see different places." She looks from the photos to me, skeptical.

"And how do you plan to do that?" she asks. "You have kids. A husband."

A lump seemingly made of barbed wire forms in my throat.

"I'm getting a-a-a—" I can barely swallow, much less finish that sentence. "A break."

She raises her eyebrows.

"Yes. From my marriage." I clear my throat. "And, once that happens, I can do more. I won't be so-so-so limited. I'll go out more. And see more. And photograph something more exciting than all this. And this town. Which, as I'm sure you'll agree, is the dullest place on Earth and, if anything, sucks any inspiration right out of the creative part of the brain." When my voice turns scratchy, her lips press together tightly.

Every godforsaken tick of the clock thuds against my eardrums with its relentless cadence and sends a dull pain fledging at my temples.

I swallow.

She's quiet.

I swallow again.

"You aren't a landscape photographer," she says in a matter-of-fact tone that turns my confidence to smoke.

"Not this landscape, no. But other landscapes—more exciting ones—that's where my heart is. If I—"

"It won't matter," she says sharply. "Your composition is perfect." She takes the portfolio from my hands and selects a shot of a waterfall. I used a slow shutter speed to capture the blur of the water, leaving everything else tack sharp. The lines draw the viewer in, directing the eye to where the water flows. "This photo is technically flawless, you did nothing wrong, but it looks like a stock photo. A Viagra ad."

"A Viagra ad . . . ?"

My image looks like a malfunctioning penis. Awesome.

"There's no passion." She puts the photo back in the portfolio. "What were you thinking of when you were shooting?"

"Thinking of . . . ?"

She huffs a frustrated breath. "Yes, June, thinking of? Stop repeating me, for God's sake. It's unnerving. What motivated you to take this photo? Why this spot? This waterfall? What does it mean to you?"

My thoughts scramble like eggs with the intensity of her gaze and rapid fire of her questioning. Despite the cool breeze blowing through the propped-open door of the gallery, my armpits are sweating.

"Just say it already. Don't filter yourself. This isn't a classroom, you won't fail." She's annoyed, arms crossed over her flowy top.

"I-I-I—" I look down at the photo, wanting something profound to come from my mouth, but instead: "I was thinking about how to take a photo that you would like. That would look like what you have here. That looks like you shot it. This spot was picked out of convenience and because it's pretty. It means nothing to me. Not really."

With my confession, I slump; she softens.

"Ah," she says, eyebrows arched high on her forehead. "You're one of those types."

"Those types . . . ?"

"The type that tries to be what everyone else wants." The look on her face is smug, as if she's just analyzed me like a photograph with all the details in perfect clarity. Like she knows me.

The brief second of feeling like she just ripped the skin right off of my skeleton quickly turns to anger. She doesn't know me. She has no clue what type I am. My nostrils flare. "No, that is not who I am." My voice wavers, making me wonder if that is who I am. *No.* "I just shot these to fill a portfolio in a rush. Once I have time—space—I can shoot new places and—"

She shakes her head, raises her hand, and cuts me off. "You don't need new places to take photos that feel like something."

"But maybe just not *these* landscapes," I argue, my desperate CPR on a future that's flatlining in a gallery at the hands of my hero. The one thing I was always good at, now another failure. I'm screwed. Starting over with nothing. Bad mom. Bad wife. Bad photographer. "You know, Ansel Adams was known for photographing the West, and you did so much of your iconic work in—"

"You're too old for me to coddle." *Ouch.* "You aren't Ansel Adams, and you aren't Irma *freaking* London. You aren't a landscape photographer." She pauses, letting the words hit with their intended severity before continuing. "Are you a photographer? Absolutely. But you haven't found your subject matter. Your muse. Or maybe you have, but you just don't see it. Or won't look for it."

In my silence she crosses the room, retrieves a leather book—a portfolio?—and hands it to me.

I blink at her.

"Open it," she commands.

I do. Shocked when I see what's inside: not a flawless landscape photo, but a snapshot. The woman I recognize as being Irma, though I know she's decades younger, with a man. He's as stunning as her. Long shaggy hair with loose curls, dark eyes, scruff-covered chin. Her face is pressed against his jaw, nose smooshed down as she smiles against his skin. He's grinning wide.

I lift my eyes to her, and she dips her chin; I flip the page.

On the back of the photo, a scribbled handwritten note: "lover, Argentina, 1997."

My eyes lift to hers, but her expression doesn't give anything away.

The next photo is her with a group of dark-skinned kids. Their hair is cut short, nearly shaved, and the beaded necklaces around their necks stand out against their bare chests as much as the bright white teeth of their smiles on their faces. Irma is in the middle, their arms wrapped around her neck in a hug. On the back: "kids, Namibia, 1999."

In our silence, I flip through the pages. Not a portfolio; an album. Her with old women. With farmers. More kids. Locations of various years and as many locations. In every single one, her smile is face splitting. On what feels to be the hundredth one that's noted lover, this time a woman, I look at her again, this time with raised eyebrows, and she gives me a knowing smile.

Irma has a weakness for hot men—and, if her labeling is correct, the occasional woman. Though, judging by how happy she is in every picture, maybe it's more of a penchant.

"I shot *for* them. Inspired by them. I met the people—some local, some like me, chasing a shot or a study or something else—*then* I picked up my camera. Channeled them. Tried to embody my time with them by capturing the landscapes in a way that felt like them."

She takes the album from me and points to the large canvas on the wall. It's a trail, shot in color, but the light is low, probably blue hour—the time just after golden hour when everything is bathed in warmth but just before night swallows day—and, even though it's beautiful, it's somber. "What do you feel when you look at this?"

My response is instant. "Sadness. Lonely."

She nods, staring at it. "I shot this right after the one that didn't love me back." Her voice catches on the words, surprising me. Irma London, award-winning, world-travelling photographer, knows heartbreak.

"I . . ." The roll of a motorcycle rips through the air and grabs my attention. It roars to a stop, the rider pulls off his helmet, blue eyes sparkling, and pushes the kickstand down. My throat pinches.

No.

On top of everything Irma just said, I can't deal with Reed Simmons right now.

I take my portfolio from her, the walls of the gallery closing in. My breaths are suddenly shallow, like poison ivy got shoved down my throat. All the photographs with *feeling* smothering me. Death by art. Reed's boots cross the sidewalk; dread swells.

"Well thank you for your time, Irma. I'll think about it." I clear my throat, my words coming out rushed. "What you said, I mean. I'll think about it all."

It's too late. He's here, I'm trapped.

"June." Reed grins, running a hand through his hair, smile slicing his scruff-covered jaw. He scans me in my cream-colored suit, approving look in his eyes. "Got those scans?"

Irma slides the portfolio out from under my arm and passes it to him before I can respond. "She shot these."

He thumbs through them, humming and nodding. "They're nice," he says when he gets to the last one, snapping the portfolio closed and handing it back to me.

"Nice?" I ask, bristled by the word.

He shrugs. "Nice. Safe."

Safe? Of course they're safe, it's a collection of limp dicks.

Irma makes a sound from next to me that I translate to *I told you*. I glare at her. Then Reed.

She gestures toward the wingback chairs at the front of the gallery, taking a seat as I do the same, Reed standing next to my chair, smelling like cloves and soap. Pissing me off. He's good; I'm not. He's living a dream; I'm not.

"A good landscape photographer makes the viewer either feel like they are there or wish they were. Yours do neither," she tells me, hands folded on her lap.

"I—"

"It's probably not her subject," Reed says, not letting me defend myself as he drives another nail into my heart and leans on the back of Irma's chair. Crossing one denim-covered leg over the other, he works his teeth over his full bottom lip, as if in deep thought about how shitty I am.

"That's what I told her," Irma responds, as if I'm not sitting there. As if my entire vision of my future isn't being torn to shreds. Again.

When I graduated, all I wanted was to be a photographer. I went to college and got a degree built on that truth. And now, these two people—professionals that I'll never be—are having a full-blown discussion on how that will never happen. Something about vision and passion being volleyed between the two as I sit in a pantsuit that cost too much money.

"I think that's a great plan. June, will that work with you?"

I shake my head. "Sorry—what?"

"You and Reed should get together, brainstorm. He can help you. God knows he never had a vision when he started shooting." She chuckles.

"I'm free tonight," he says, grinning. "That is, if Camp won't mind."

Since the demolition of my ego that started the second I walked into the gallery today, I force myself to square my shoulders and lift my chin. "What I do has nothing to do with Camp. I'm free."

"Then it's a date."

"No," I say, looking at him with conviction for the first time since he sauntered back into my life. "It's not."

Fourteen

With Camp at a coaches' meeting and whatever that entails after, Lyra offered to watch the boys while I have my not-date with Reed. When I came out of the bedroom in a pair of new jeans and burnt-orange shirt that slides off one shoulder, Lyra's eyebrows shot to the sky.

When she asked, "When did you get hot?" I nearly ran to the bedroom to put my legging-chambray-unfashion uniform back on. Instead, I laughed, muttered, "It's nothing," then scuttled out the door like a crab on crack.

Do Reed and I have a history? Yes. But I'm married—albeit fake happily—and I'm a lot of things, but even Reed and his unfairly bad-boy good looks and sexy photographs won't change that. This is a work meeting. And he is a line I won't cross.

Me trying my damnedest at looking like a sexpot is more about leveling the playing field. Between him and Camp looking like they've spent every day since high school bathing in a fountain of youth, I'm tired of walking around like everyone's grandma.

Regardless, I don't tell Camp about the meeting. Sure, he's been coming home for dinner more over the last two weeks, and our conversations have been polite—friendly, even—but what I do has nothing to do with him. I'm pursuing a career. A passion. It's none of his damn business.

I slide into the booth at Liberty Tap and scrub my palms down my jeans.

Reed's already across from me, waiting with a bottle of wine and two glasses. The same deadly degree of hotness as he has been, only tonight he's more polished. Hair more styled than windblown, jeans more clean than worn. Instead of a T-shirt, he's wearing a black long-sleeved button-down.

If I was describing him, I'd call him delicious.

"Reed," I say, tugging the shirt up my shoulder.

"June." His gaze follows the fabric as it slips back down.

He pours the wine, and I slip my portfolio and a small notebook out of my purse. He watches me, nervously fidgeting as I stack and restack the items before taking a too-big sip of wine.

"You look good."

I laugh. "Liar."

He shakes his head, scrubbing a hand down his day-old scruff, and grins. "So tell me what's happening."

I debate how to approach it. How honest to be, how open. The dead bodies and me—they're the only ones that know everything.

But, in this booth with this wine, my photography career—if that's even the word for it—on the line, I err on the side of honesty.

"Camp and I are over. Or will be—that's complicated." I pause, let the sentiment roll around my tongue and palate. When I decide I hate the flavor, I take another long sip of wine. "I put my camera away after college, when Lyra was born, and it got busy. Harder after . . ." My voice trails off with the bruised spots in between. "After moving back and all. But now . . . Now I have this chance, this second chance, I guess. And, well, Irma told me I suck. So . . ."

"She didn't say you suck."

My eyes narrow.

"Okay, fine, she kind of said you suck, but only with landscapes." I roll my eyes as he continues. "That doesn't mean it's over. It means you have to keep looking. Do you remember what I photographed in high school?"

I chuckle as I recall. "Cars."

He folds his arms on the table and leans forward. "Cars. Hell, I didn't even know I wanted to be a photographer, I just took the class because I had a crush on a girl with a fire in her eyes brighter than the hair on her head." He stops then, staring at me, and I shift in my seat, not ready for this conversation. He reads me well, because he pivots. "But I went out, did some living, kept picking up my camera." He leans back in his seat, takes a sip of wine, and tilts his head.

"What lights you on fire these days, June? Because, judging by your photos, it's not waterfalls and lakes."

As offended as I am, as mentally ransacked by the observations he and Irma made earlier in the gallery, I know he's not wrong. Even worse, I don't know the answer. I don't have a damn clue what lights me on fire.

"I don't know."

My confession fills the space between us until the waitress comes, takes our order—a salad for me, steak for him—and leaves.

"How did you start photographing the women?"

"A crazy ex-girlfriend."

I laugh, loud, considering his images. "Sounds interesting. Multiple personalities?"

"Maybe." He smiles. "Definitely crazy. She was beautiful, quiet, but then she had this other side of her. A storm rolling beneath her skin. So, I shot it, her profile layered with these intense and ominous clouds right before the sky opened up. And that was it. I felt it. A story I could tell. Feel in my gut. Showing all our layers." Another shrug. "I love it."

I nod, envious of his passion. "Are all the women people you've dated?"

He shakes his head. "No, only the first one. The rest I find randomly—or they find me. Sometimes they reach out on social media, tell me their story. Or we meet over coffee. Sometimes there's a vision—who they think they are inside—but sometimes I get to interpret it."

"That's beautiful. I'm happy for you."

He studies me. "I could photograph you."

I shift in my seat, twirl the stem of my wineglass. "I wouldn't be so interesting. My profile filled with . . . air?" I laugh, self-deprecating, hating the words—how fully they tell how little I've become.

He lifts one shoulder. "I don't know, I need more time."

"And then some."

The waiter arrives with our food, and the conversation turns to different topics. His dad passing from cancer. The age of my kids, his relationship status—divorced. Twice. He asks about my parents, who are currently spending six months a year travelling the country in a Winnebago. He even asks about Camp and his baseball career.

"He got injured pitching, needed surgery. He was healing, it looked good." I shrug. "But it wasn't good enough, I guess. They didn't extend the contract, and we ended up here. We bought his parents' house, they moved to the country. We raised Lyra, which was easy compared to the twins who spend their days trying to give their teacher a mental breakdown—Ms. Mitchell, remember her?"

He wipes his mouth with a napkin, laughing. "God, how old is that woman?"

"Right?" I laugh. "She's perpetually the same age and terrifying as hell."

It's easy, us talking and taking the trip down memory lane, his blue eyes watching me, sparkling like I'm interesting. Like I have something to say that isn't just *Do your homework* and *Time to eat*. Like I'm not just a mom, but a woman. Something other than the people I've made and the man I married.

"What should I do about these?" I ask after the waiter takes our empty plates, thumping the top of my closed portfolio.

"I'd photograph everything. You'll know when you find it. When you get *the* scan, you'll feel it change the rhythm of your heartbeat and rearrange your DNA. You'll find it, give it time."

I puff out a laugh, take a sip of wine. "You got all insightful, Reed Simmons."

He chuckles, pouring more wine into each of our glasses. A look at each other, a look away. An energy as nervous as it is tension filled.

"Do you ever think of that night?"

I knew the question was coming, but I choke anyway.

"It was a long time ago," I say as I wipe my chin covered in dribbled wine.

"I do."

And in an instant, I'm there. Graduation night, the party at the house on the lake. Camp went inside—a behemoth of a house owned by someone's uncle—to get us beer. Reed found me on a chair, alone, my toes in the sand. The air was cool, the cicadas were loud.

He sat next to me; we talked, I don't remember about what, and laughed. I was laughing hard when he kissed me. So abrupt, as if he couldn't not. Hands around my head, he pulled me in, tongue working its way through my lips and into my mouth. I wouldn't be able to admit it until later, but, for a split second, I kissed him back. Tasted Reed Simmons like a piece of hard candy.

Then I realized what I was doing, pushed him away from me. "I can't, Reed. Camp . . ." I said, panting. Panicking. Wanting to vomit over what I'd just done.

"You gonna chase Camp Cannon around for the rest of your life?" he asked, his eyes bright blue—intense—even in the dark.

Before I answered, before I said anything, Camp was there. He'd seen it all from where he was standing silently behind us.

He threw the two Solo Cups of cheap keg beer on the ground, foam spreading across the sand, then marched over to Reed and punched him in the face, busting his lip.

"She's too good for you," Reed yelled, wiping his lip, red streak of blood staining the back of his hand. There was no stopping what came next: Reed punched Camp in the face, a blow to his nose, breaking it with a crack.

"Fight!" a girl shrieked.

Camp hinged at the waist, hands cupping his nose, which was spitting blood as he spit curses. When he raised his head, ready to attack, more people were on the beach. They shouted a litany of swear words at each other, me screaming at them both. Shouts of *Stop!* on repeat.

Reed was dragged away by a group of boys.

I stayed with Camp.

Camp, the only boy I had ever had sex with, ever kissed until that very moment, looked at me like I had shattered his heart, and in turn, mine shattered. And he forgave me. As he cleaned himself up in the bathroom, changed his blood-covered shirt, I traced the boomerang-shaped birthmark on his ribs. "To forever and back," he said, lopsided smile on his battered face.

I cried. Hugged him too hard. And he hugged me back.

And that was it. Why Reed and Camp started hating each other twenty-two years ago.

"It doesn't matter now," I say, pulling myself off that lakeside beach and back to the booth.

"It does to me."

I say nothing, letting the words loom like a storm cloud.

Someone approaches the table, and still, we stare.

Until they speak. "Well now, Reed, I'd love to know what the fuck you are doin' with my wife."

Fifteen

"Camp," I say on an exhale. Instantly breathless at the sight of him, in his polo, athletic pants, and Ledger Lake Trout ballcap. Here. With Reed. With me *and* Reed. Realizing how bad this looks.

I fumble to slide out of my side of the booth, bumping the edge of the table, making my wineglass fall, last drops spilling across the table.

Much to my dismay, Reed follows suit, albeit smoother than me, sliding out of the booth until he's next to Camp. Then there's the staring, them at each other. A testosterone-fueled sizing up like two animals in the wild.

"Maybe if *your wife* was getting what she needed at home, she wouldn't be sitting here having wine with me." Reed delivers the words like a bat to a ball on a perfect pitch.

Camp growls, literally the first time I've ever heard him make a sound like some kind of beast, and steps toward him. Reed stands barely an inch taller than Camp, and with their proximity, the rim of his hat swipes across Reed's forehead.

"Okay, maybe let's not do this," I whisper, wrapping my fingers around Camp's bicep which he shakes off without looking at me. A family from the table nearby gives us their full attention. Forks down, eyes glued.

"Camp," I plead.

His fists clench and unclench by his side. "My *wife* gets exactly what she needs at home."

"Really?" Reed laughs, too loud to go unnoticed. More people looking. "Because the way she tells it . . ." He shakes his head, letting out a low whistle.

Another growl out of Camp.

"Are they gonna fight?" a kid asks from the table next to us.

"Couldn't get her twenty-two years ago, so this is what you do? Try to win her over with a bottle of wine?" Camp scoffs.

The owner, Matthew Dalton—who we also went to high school with—notices the commotion across the restaurant and starts lumbering toward us.

Reed. Smirks.

Dear God, please let lightning strike this building.

"I don't think I need the wine, Camp."

Another. Growl.

This can't be happening.

When Reed starts to roll up his sleeves, I wedge between them.

They don't react to me—their eyes locked on one another like I'm not even there.

"Guys. Stop this," I hiss, the restaurant eerily silent. "Everyone is watching."

Camp's chest, rising and falling in rapid fire, pushes against my back. "I don't give a fu—"

"We're done here," I snap, pushing one hand into Reed's chest and the other into Camp's. "We're leaving."

I fumble in my purse; Matthew is almost to our table, waving across the room to a male server.

Shit.

Camp's shout of, "Let's go for round two outside, asshole!" is met with my strained whisper of, "Camp, stop!"

I drop a wad of cash on the table.

Reed laughs. "So I can break your nose twice?"

"Enough!" I snap.

With an apologetic wave toward Matthew, the staff, and tight smile to anyone that looks at us, I bulldoze a shouting Camp. Around the tables. Out the door.

Down the street.

And into the bar next door where I shove him on a stool and order us two drinks: him a beer, me, tequila.

"Are you insane?" I demand. "That was the entire town witnessing your little temper tantrum!"

The bartender sets my tequila in front of me, lime wedge on the rim that I toss to the side before shooting it back and gagging loudly.

"Me?" he asks with an incredulous shout. "My wife goes on a date—with Reed Simmons—in public—and I'm insane?!"

The bartender looks up from where he's standing at a cooler, studying us a beat before pulling out a bottle of beer.

"Jesus, Camp. It wasn't a date," I hiss. "It was a work-dinner thing. And he ordered wine before I got there. And you—you came in like some sort of Tasmanian devil ready to tear the place down!"

He scoffs, opens his mouth to say something, then scoffs again before taking a too-big pull of his beer.

"Are you fucking him?"

I nearly fall over.

"Are you kidding me right now?" Now *I'm* shouting. The bartender snaps his head toward us, again, glares, then goes back to wiping the bar. "I can't even believe I'm dignifying this with an answer but no, Camp, I'm not—" I lower my voice to a whisper and say, "*fucking him.*"

Without breaking the lock of our eyes on one another, I spin the empty glass on the bar.

"Just so I'm clear," he says, popping his jaw back and forth. "We can't tell our kids that you want a divorce. I can't put my mouth on you if I want—can't even sleep in the damn bed with you—but you can go out on a date, with Reed Simmons, in the busiest restaurant in town, and make me look like a fool."

Shit.

"Camp, I didn't think of it like that, I swear. I went to that gallery today—with all the photos I've been shooting—and the owner basically told me they were bad. Then she suggested I get together with him—to brainstorm or something—and, I don't know, it was innocent, and nothing happened." I pause, Reed's face when he asked if I thought about that graduation night from twenty-two years ago flittering through my mind. "I didn't do this to hurt you, and I'm sorry if it did. We might be over, but I'd never do that. Never."

His eyes bounce between mine, as if he's rereading a transcript of what I've just said to check for accuracy and trying to decide if he believes me.

When he says, "I hate that fuckin' guy," I know he does, and despite the tension, I let out a small laugh.

"I know you do, *honey*."

Bringing his bottle up to his lips, he chuckles.

I prop my chin on my hand, facing him with a small smile on my lips, belly warm from adrenaline and tequila. "You were coming on pretty strong with all the wife-calling."

"You're still my wife."

I snort under my breath. "You sound jealous."

"I am."

My spine straightens as my arm drops to the bar and my hand smacks the top. "You aren't *jealous*, Camp. You haven't paid attention to me for years. You just don't want me with him."

He shakes his head.

"I don't want you with him." He takes a sip of beer, then adds, "Or anyone else."

I roll my eyes. "You know just as well as me that we haven't been good for a while. We've been fine. Existing. Is that really what you want? A life of stasis? And, you know, there's no romance—no passion. You never even touch me!"

He looks at me, heat consuming the brown of his eyes. In one swift move, Camp sets his beer on the bar, brings a palm to my knee, and slides it up my denim-covered thigh.

High.

Where he stops.

Squeezes.

Stays.

Face an inch from mine, his breath is warm against my lips. I don't breathe; I can't.

When he tightens his grip, blood rushes and muscles clench.

My pulse pounds in my ears and between my legs.

If he moved his hand . . .

Just.

A.

Little.

Higher . . .

"What I do and what I want to do are two very different things, *wife*."

His fingers move, enough to brush me. *There*. A skimming against the seam of my jeans. Lingering.

I open my mouth; his eyes drop to my lips.

My husband is looking at me like he wants to feast, and the way my whole body feels like it's been lit on fire makes me think I would very much enjoy that.

His lips pull to a smirk as he drags his palm back down my thigh and wraps his fingers around his bottle of beer.

Sonofabitch.

He's playing me. Pretending. Just like he was when we made pizza.

Beer to his lips, his body squares to the bar. Like I'm not sitting next to him stunned and covered in chills. Like my lower body isn't throbbing and swelling to the point of trying to rip out of my jeans.

"I don't know what that means," I say, my attempt at being haughty betrayed by the breathless sound of my voice.

"Of course you don't." He cuts his eyes to mine, and they rake down my body before snapping back up. "Years of me tryin' to peel your clothes off and kiss your skin only to be told that you're too tired. You have a headache. You've been touched too much already. Not tonight . . ." His voice trails off; he takes another pull of his beer. "I got tired of askin'. Of the excuses. Of the rejection." He shrugs, eyes now on the TV playing ESPN. He cracks the shell of a peanut, tosses the nuts into his mouth. "Doesn't mean I don't think about it. Or want it." He looks at me again, eyes dropping to my bare shoulder. "Or you."

I scoff. "That's ridiculous." I raise my empty glass toward the bartender who nods and grabs the bottle of tequila, strolling over to fill my glass. "I don't make excuses."

Camp looks at me, says nothing, expression annoyed as he turns to the bartender. "I'll have what she's havin'."

As the bartender pours drinks, I sift through the weeds of my mind to the last time Camp tried to touch me. It's been a while—months even. We were lying in bed, he traced the line of my hip, kissed my shoulder; I told him I was on my period, but it was a lie. It was still a week away. My stomach drops—I rejected him.

But then I remember the rest of the story.

He was late—missed dinner again. The sink wasn't working, and the boys had gotten a bad report from their teacher. And the dog . . . Thor had chewed my favorite sandals to smithereens. I may have rejected Camp, but he had unknowingly rejected me first.

I look at him and his familiar features that I fell in love with so many years ago. His chin, his eyes, the bump on his nose. He works to open another peanut, pops it into his mouth. I can't read him, not like I used to. *Does he want me?*

The bartender sets the tequila in front of him. Lime on the rim.

"It's hard to get hot and bothered when you don't come home until the day has already kicked my ass, Camp."

He scoffs. "It's *my* fault now?"

Even though he asks, we both know any response is moot. It will lead to an argument with no winner, only proving my point. This. *This* is why we can't be married. He doesn't see the whole picture. I've pushed him away . . . because he lets me. I've shut down . . . because he doesn't show up. I'm done because he stopped long before this.

I take a small sip of my tequila.

"What are you goin' to do?" he asks.

I blink.

"About the photos?"

"Ah." I spin my glass, study the gold liquid as it moves. "I don't know. Reed and Irma both said I'm not a landscape photographer. Said I'm good, just not good at that." I shrug. "So I guess I just need to lick my wounds with that one and figure out what comes next. After Lyra goes . . . I need a job."

He's quiet, and I wish I knew what he was thinking—desperately—but his expression is neutral. He looks unaffected as his tongue moves along the inside of his lower lip while he watches the TV behind the bar. Tequila and lime untouched in front of him, all these years later he's still so good looking it hurts.

I'm staring; he notices. I don't look away. I can't. I hate him but I love him, it's as simple as that.

He stands, drops cash on the bar, eyes staying on mine as he reaches across me for the . . . salt?

I still.

With his free hand, he grabs mine.

Bringing the inside of my wrist to his mouth, he pauses. I don't flinch.

He licks.

Camp Cannon licks my wrist.

Shakes the salt onto my skin.

Licks again.

Drops my hand.

Shoots his tequila.

Sucks the lime.

The only thing moving is the blood rushing through my veins.

He leans in, bringing his mouth to my ear. "You ever decide to crawl into Reed's bed, it'll be my tongue you're thinkin' of."

I don't take another breath until he's gone.

Sixteen

"Bye, y'all, have fun today." I wave at the boys in the back seat of Lyra's sedan as she backs out of the driveway. "And be good!"

Their shrieks and window slams in the back seat make her wince as she lifts her fingers off the steering wheel in a half wave. A smile tugs at my lips despite the dull hangover-induced headache that's throbbing at my temples. Between Irma's lack of regard for my ego, Reed's visit down memory lane, and Camp . . . *Camp.*

I rub my temples. A morning away from the hell of car line and Ms. Mitchell's withering glare is a gift.

I need a minute.

A deep breath.

A shower.

After the way Camp looked at me and touched me and *licked* me, probably a cold one.

I left the bar right after him, but he was already asleep on the floor when I got home because I sat in the driveway and stared at the house in the dark. Confused.

Nothing made sense.

After years of being together, the way Camp looked at me, the things he said, were uncharted territory. Heat that cooled long ago. Or so I thought.

And worse, I don't even know what's genuine. What's how he feels versus what's pretend. What's what he really wants versus him lashing out because it's Reed.

Thor's paws click against the wood floor on my heels, the sound broken up like morse code as he communicates with short taps and long whines. In the middle of the kitchen, on his haunches, he stares at me with his head tilted and drool dripping to the ground and bouncing up like disgusting slobbery yo-yos. I play a game where I pretend to make him wait for Camp to feed him, but when his whimpering reaches a crescendo, I swear under my breath, and relent, scooping food into his bowl. He inhales it like a canine vacuum cleaner and, despite how annoyed I am, I chuckle. *Stupid dog.*

I move on autopilot into my morning chores—folding towels from the dryer, picking up toy cars and Lyra's hair clips from the coffee table—and I hear the pipes in the old walls creak with Camp's post-run shower.

Taking a sip of my coffee—half milk, half coffee, one small squeeze of honey—something in the quiet air feels different. Delicate almost.

Setting my coffee down, I pick up my camera. Through the viewfinder, the frame is filled with jagged snake plants, worn jute rugs, Thor in all his sprawled-out glory, and picture books on every flat surface. But it's the light that makes it magic. The way it paints over all our stuff and makes it look like something valuable. Like it's coated in magic. Like the dust particles catching the light are really flecks of sparkly gems in the midst of a treasure trove of us.

As annoyed as I've been by this house—how we came to be in this house—in this moment I can't imagine living anywhere else.

I only take one photo before abandoning the camera for the stack of folded towels and head to the master bathroom. The door is cracked, a steamy haze lingering in the threshold.

"Fuck," I hear Camp say, voice low as I push the bathroom door open with my toe.

Eyebrows pinched, I open my mouth, but as the scene in front of me registers, I snap it closed.

Through the fogged-up glass wall of the shower, Camp stands, the familiar lines of his back toward me. His narrow waist. Toned ass and legs. Droplets of water dripping down him like rivers in a canyon. One palm is pressed against the opposite wall—fingers splayed against the white subway tiles—his head is bowed, forehead nearly touching the wall.

I take a quiet step closer; his eyes are closed.

"Now," he grits out, half groan, half grunt.

What the . . . ?

That's when I see it: his other hand.

The one wrapped around himself.

Moving.

Back and forth.

Fast.

I shouldn't, but I take another step forward, watching my husband, jaw set, shoulders wracked with tension, stroking himself.

He moves faster, muscles popping along his arms.

When his eyes open, I'm caught. Watching him. Unable to *stop* watching him.

But he doesn't stop either. And he doesn't take his eyes off me.

Not when I suck in a sharp breath.

Not when I drop the stack of towels I forgot I was holding onto the floor.

Not for the six more strokes it takes for him to finish.

Which he does.

Which I watch.

Entirely.

Our eyes stay hooked—heated and silent—until the garbage truck on the street makes its token *beep beep beep* and Thor lets out a deep bark at the sound.

Then I'm gone, stumbling out of the bathroom trying to process what I just witnessed, sprinting to my coffee like it will erase my thoughts and my memory like some kind of magical potion. I drink it in gulps, burning my tongue and singeing my throat. When I refill it, I chug it black, not even caring that the bitter flavor is scorching my tongue.

It does nothing to dampen the shock of seeing Camp when he walks out of the bedroom. His hair is still wet, and his skin is rosy from the shower or his hand or both.

"Hi," I say, awkward, grabbing a spray bottle of cleaner and misting the already-clean counter in a layer of moisture before scrubbing it with a rag; it's my only idea to escape the situation other than shoving my head into the garbage disposal.

"Hey," he says, pouring himself a cup of coffee, letting the silence hang a torturous beat. "Are you mad?" he asks, leaning next to me, watching as I scrub the clean counter.

"Mad?" I ask, flicking my eyes to his for a fraction of a second. "No. Why would I be? You have needs, I know that. I don't care. I don't think it's any of my business." Maybe it's the chugged caffeine hitting me all at once, but my mouth won't stop talking. Some sort of hidden talent for theatrics peeps through, because my voice fluctuates between extremely high-pitched and very deep. "If anything, you should be mad at me for intruding. You know, going all Peeping Tom on you or something. Like, hello, June! Take a social cue! Ha!" Camp's eyes widen. "Closed bathroom means do not enter." I laugh now, a scratchy, hacking sound. "I guess I just didn't know you did that. Not that it's my business. I'd never seen it before. With you. Or any man. So-so-so-so it was unexpected. But, of course, the frequency isn't my business. Unless you wanted to talk about it. How often, I mean. You do that. You know. In the shower. Alone. How often you . . . umm . . . you know, in the shower."

Finally, my voice box runs out of batteries, and I fill a glass with water and drink the entire thing before spraying another layer of cleaner on the counter. Camp sears the side of my face with his dark-eyed stare but stays quiet.

When I finish re-wiping the now cleanest kitchen in the Western Hemisphere, I let out a long exhale and fully face him. "I'll knock next time."

He smirks, taking a final sip of coffee—with an annoying slurp—and sets his empty mug in the sink. "We're married, do whatever you want."

Then, he leans in, straight toward my face, lips toward my lips.

He's going to kiss me.

I hold my breath, my palms wrap around the edge of the counter, and my back bends slightly. He follows suit, but instead of stopping his mouth at mine, his face slips around the side of my jaw, stilling when he's next to my ear. His breath, hot on my skin, his mustache, close enough to scrape against me, scratches chills that ripple across the entire right side of my body.

"And I do that every time I want somethin' I can't have."

I nod. Dumb, stunned, and . . . hot?

Then, like the emotional terrorist he is, he's gone. Grabbing his keys, petting the dog with a cool, "See ya later, Dogg-o," Camp Cannon strolls out of the house.

When I hear the truck start in the driveway, I have one thought: I hate that man.

Seventeen

I have never masturbated.

Until thirty-seven minutes ago, I assumed it was something people only did if they were single.

Which, I guess, by some criteria, Camp is. Even though we're married. Real but fake. Or fake but real.

Even though Camp and I have our issues, even though I know as sure as the sky is blue this marriage isn't working, watching him—hearing him—was one of the hottest things I've ever experienced.

I've read some of the smutty books Scotty reads. I know hot—but this was *hot*.

More shocking was when he strolled into the kitchen after—leaning in and getting all low-voiced and close—making heat pool like I'd dumped the entire pot of coffee in my underwear. Confusing me. And my vagina.

Either way, Camp jerking off in the shower revealed some kind of secret on what it means to be human. Like maybe the entire world knew it was okay to make yourself feel good, but nobody told me. Honestly, I'm kind of pissed that Scotty never told me about the regularity of people having sex with themselves. She's ground zero for all things taboo; if anyone knows this, it's her.

I've never considered myself a prude, at the same time, I became aware of my sexuality in my teenage years and Camp was there. We learned together. He taught me about my body, and I taught him about his.

On top of the visual I can't turn off, the need to know what he was thinking of has my imagination going wild. Was he thinking of someone he knows? Is it traditional sex that he imagines? Or a mouth? Or . . . ?

When my own legs squeeze together, I physically shake my head to pull myself out of the spiral.

Ultimately, it doesn't matter. There is no together. At least, not for much longer—only fifty more days. Who or what drives Camp to grab himself in the shower has nothing to do with me.

But my body doesn't care about any of these things. After last night and then this morning—logic is gone. As of this moment, I have one thought: If Camp gets to feel good, so do I.

And I won't feel bad about that. If I want a retaliatory orgasm, I'll have one. That I create.

I reach into the shower, spin the knob, and wait for the water to heat. I peel off my clothes, nervous when I step into the hot stream. My body trembles like I'm on a first date.

With myself.

I tilt my head toward the water, slicking my hair back.

I can do this.

I will.

Forcing my hand to move, I grab my chest with a squeeze. My breasts, nowhere near as perky as they once were, fill my palms. I fondle my fingers around my nipples.

I feel nothing close to pleasure.

Moving with a bit more aggression, my own skin feels completely awkward and the antithesis of good in my hands.

My frustrated groan echoes off the tile. It already takes an act of Congress for me to have an orgasm, why I think I can do this by myself is beyond me.

No.

Independent women act like independent women—I heard that on a podcast once.

I can do this.

Back to the tile, water bouncing around the walls and pinging against my skin, I bring my hand to my breast again—just the fingertips—tracing a line across my chest, down the curve of my waist, to the outer line of my hip. I hesitate, then move it inward. Across the firmness of my hip to the softness of my low belly.

Between my thighs.

Fumbling, I rake my teeth over my lower lip, water blasting my chest.

My body is foreign in my own hands, so I close my eyes and pretend they aren't mine.

Camp would make circles, use knuckles—*no*.

This is not about Camp.

My head drops back; I start moving my hand. Pressure and strokes. Faster then slower. Better not great. Closer but—

"June!" a voice shouts. "I forgot my ba—"

My eyes fly open—one hand on a breast, the other between my legs—and there's Camp, on the other side of the foggy glass, eyes dragging from my face to my hands.

"June." He repeats my name, a throaty sound like he's tasting all the letters. His eyes study my body like they've never seen it before as he moves toward the shower, stopping at the other side of the glass. And here we are: Him staring at me, stupefied, while I stand like a middle-aged, masturbating statue, humiliated.

I pinch my knees together.

"Uh . . . This isn't what it looks like," I lie, water spitting out of my mouth as I talk.

He nods, serious, brown eyes turning to black coals as a swallow drags down the column of his throat.

"Do you want me to leave?" he asks, eyes hooked with mine.

Yes; I say nothing, only moving to bring one arm to hide my chest while spreading the fingers of the hand between my legs to hide the space I was failing to please.

He wraps his fingers around the handle and opens the door.

Don't you dare; I say nothing.

Fully clothed, he steps in the shower, positioning himself in front of me, not flinching as the water pelts him.

Leave; I say nothing.

My mouth betrays me and will not tell him to get the hell out of here. Fully clothed and soaking wet, Camp stands so close to me his chest touches the forearm covering my chest as we breathe.

Water drips down his face and clings to his mustache before slipping to his lips.

Tension seizes me and my breathing becomes a ragged, wet kind of sound, similar to a fish out of water.

Arms hanging by his sides, he clenches and unclenches his fists, like he doesn't know what to do with his hands. *Welcome to the club.*

"Have you ever done this?" he asks, voice raspy and a new level of deep as water turns his blond hair brown before dripping down his face and clinging to his jaw.

"Y-yes," I lie.

His jaw pops, chin drops. He studies my naked body again before he lifts his head, eyes searching mine. "And?"

"And?" My toes curl against the tile floor as my fingernails dig into my own chest. I refuse to look away from him.

"And what do you do?"

Water from the tile bounces onto my skin; I open my mouth, but once again it betrays me because it says nothing.

At my silence, his eyes flare in a kind of understanding before a smirk tugs at his lips. The bastard knows I'm lying.

"Has it been so long you forgot?"

Son. Of. A. Bitch.

My eyes narrow. "No," I say, water clinging to my eyelashes. "I do this all the time. Alone." I pause, water pelting around us, then add, "Which was why I was surprised earlier when I-I-I saw you doing the same. Because I was glad for you. Because I always do this." And, for good measure: "Alone."

He doesn't bother hiding the smirk that's now permanently slanted across his face. "What. Do. You. Do?" he asks, punctuating each word, cool, calm, and smug as shit as water soaks him completely.

He doesn't think I can do it; I see it all over him. He's calling my bluff.

This idea alone—that Camp doesn't believe I can get my freak on with myself—pushes me forward.

I watched a movie once where a woman found herself in a particularly lonely situation in a bathroom. She used the: "Showerhead," I blurt through the spraying water, my own eyes widening as his eyebrows raise. "I use the showerhead."

He licks his lips, droplets covering the entirety of his mustache. "The showerhead?" he asks, skeptical.

I wipe water from my face then re-cover my chest, lifting my chin slightly. "The showerhead."

"Really?" he asks. "How?"

"How?"

"You heard me, J—how?"

Oh no.

I swallow.

His eyebrows raise, challenging me.

I have to do this.

I eye the showerhead for three pounding beats of my heart then reach a shaking arm overhead, my copper hair webbing across the fair skin of my chest and shoulders. He stands upright, watching me as I wrap my fingers around it and remove it from the holder.

Shaky in my hand, water stops raining from overhead and now ricochets around the stall, deflecting from the tile to us. I stare at the nozzle like it's a stick of dynamite and awkwardly try to re-hide myself with my arm and showerhead that's now spraying water directly at Camp's chest.

"Show me."

"I-I—" *can't do this*. I don't even know what to do. I look away from him, more humiliated than I was when he walked in and found me. I don't know what to do and he knows it.

Our silence seems eternal, and I'm so embarrassed I might cry. Or vomit down the drain. Or both.

"I bet I know," he says, making my head—slowly—turn toward him.

He wipes a hand down his face, clearing the water, and takes the showerhead from my hand.

I say nothing.

He points the stream of water against the forearm covering my chest, sliding it up and down the outside of my arm, from wrist to shoulder. "I bet you start somethin' like this." He smirks, but it's not smug. Not anymore. He's being gentle. "I bet you start like this to get relaxed."

As the warm stream pulsates against me and massages my skin, I look from him to my arm back to him.

I swallow; maybe nod, maybe not.

He drags the water across my arm and onto my chest. When I try to cover myself, he stops me. "No," he says, voice low as he shakes his head and moves my hands to my side. "I don't think you hide from yourself."

Water streams across my chest, fear and anticipation becoming a noose tight around my neck. He directs the water across every slope and curve of my breasts, my nipples tightening so severely I look to see if they're bleeding. "I bet you go here next." He moves from the peak of one breast to the other. "Like this?"

I swallow, force myself to nod.

My rapid-fire thoughts: *What is he doing? Should this be happening? Dear Camp, please fuck me.*

He moves down, pressure builds.

As he massages my belly, the room quiets with all the water pressing into my skin, and a small whimper escapes my lips.

I might orgasm before he touches me where I need it, and I do not want that to happen.

"And here?"

At my belly button, he yo-yos the showerhead down then up, down then up, going lower with every dip.

I watch him, and there's a tenderness in the way he looks and touches me. He's helping me. I see it in the way he moves, the way he watches me—he sees I can't do something and is showing me how.

"Yes," I manage. "And there."

He presses a palm against the tile, chest not touching mine, as we both look down to where he wedges the showerhead between my thighs and spreads my legs open. I fight it, but just barely.

"How'm I doin', J?" he asks, rubbing his nose against my jaw in a way that feels so sweet I almost cry. "This where you go?"

I nod—weak—before dropping my head back as the showerhead glides between my legs. Water shoots on me, in me, and makes an ache throb deep in my belly.

"Yes," I grunt, my back arching off the wall. "And there."

I hate that he's doing this, hate that I like it, hate that I never want it to stop.

"What are you thinkin'?" he asks as my body moves with less control between the tiled wall and him.

Our eyes lock; I cannot find the courage to tell him the truth. Cannot confess that he's giving me something I desperately need and can't give myself.

It's seconds like that—me silent, water shooting, pressure building, my body responding, him staring—until he finally leans in and brings his mouth to my ear.

"I was thinkin' of you, J," he rasps, every syllable sounding like sex and honey. "When you saw me—it was you. I was imaginin' me makin' *you* scream my name as I bent you over in this shower and slid inside of you."

Three.

Two.

One.

Blastoff!

That visual is all it takes.

Between the pulse of the water and the way Camp's words sing through me like a siren's call in this shower, pleasure wrecks every cell of my body, and I scream, loud.

My body convulses between the wet tile and his hard body. He doesn't move—not his body or the showerhead—as I whimper and writhe and wonder if I'm about to black out.

He leans in, pinning my hips to the wall as he keeps the showerhead wedged between my legs and relentlessly sprays me stupid. Just when I think I can't feel any better, Camp says, "Let it go, baby," and my bones melt. His *baby* turns me into a wet noodle against the wall, and sensitive pleasure begins to toe the line of pain across my whole body.

The showerhead drops and bangs against the wall with a loud *clack!* as it swings from its cord. Water once again sprays around the stall.

Fully clothed, fully hard, for the first time in years, I want my husband in a very dirty way.

His hips rock against mine; we stare. Panting, horny, and soaking wet.

"How did you know—how did you know . . . ?" I ask, mouth so close to his I feel his mustache on my lips when I talk. "I didn't know what to do."

"I know," he says, lifting his chin just enough I feel his mustache tickle my nose. "I know you."

I swallow, hating that he does.

Water drips down his smooth jaw, hangs from his hair, his eyebrows, and trickles down the line of his nose.

He brings a hand to my jaw and rubs a thumb over my lips, the forbidden fruit of our arrangement. *Don't you dare kiss me* internally clashes with *Shove your damn tongue down my throat as deep as it will go.*

"J, I need you to know that—"

A phone rings.

Twice.

Camp's.

From his bag I now notice in the middle of the bathroom floor. Which explains why he's here.

It rings again, a loud reminder of real life.

"You should get that," I say, breath shaky.

When it rings again then beeps from a voicemail, he nods as he takes a step back. He looks at me like he's seeing all the way into my soul before dragging a hand down his face. "Yeah," he says.

He opens the shower door, moves to the middle of the bathroom floor where water puddles as he checks his phone. Without saying a word, he peels off his wet clothes and quickly redresses without a hint of what he just did. What we just did. What we almost just did.

Without breathing, I watch every move he makes.

On his way out of the bathroom, he looks over his shoulder, to where I'm still standing in the middle of the shower, water bouncing off the glass around me as my heart bangs in my chest.

He opens his mouth, but seems to think better of it, because instead of saying anything, he picks his wet clothes up from the floor and he's gone.

Eighteen

"Gladdys," I say, rubbing my forehead as I study her lace-trimmed, floral dress and the crucifix that hangs from a gold chain to the center of her chest. "It wasn't supposed to happen. I was going to do it by myself, you know? I'm a modern woman, I can . . ." I pause, lowering my voice. "Masturbate."

I pace across the concrete floor.

"But then he was there. Like the universe knew I couldn't do this without him or something. And, you know, I knew he would know what to do. As much as he drives me crazy, leave it to him to deliver some kind of-of-of erotic water experience in my time of need." I let out a breath, eyes going to Scotty who's filing her nails on the other side of the window, leaning casually, ignorant to my spiraling. "Then—and this is exactly what I didn't want to happen—I thought he was going to kiss me. And, now hear me out, but, it's like, I wanted that. Which"—I laugh maniacally—"just proves my point!"

I pause, feeling myself turning hysterical on the eighty-two-year-old deceased woman, and take a calming breath.

"Then there's this other guy, which, he's basically a mascot for everything I haven't accomplished in my life. And his sidekick, Irma, who won't coddle me because I'm *old*." I bite a fingernail, looking back at Gladdys. "I guess I'm just wondering if it gets any easier. Like . . . how am I forty and feel like I have no clue or control over anything that's happening? I want out of my marriage but can't escape it. I want a career, but I'm not good enough for it. I want my kids to think I'm a good mom, but half the time they don't see me . . ." My voice trails off with Scotty's knock on the glass, the usual five fingers waving on one hand as she adjusts her Dolly Parton T-shirt with the other.

I lift my chin in response.

"I'm sorry, Gladdys," I say to her dead body. "You probably didn't need to hear all of this, but I appreciate you listening."

I smile at her, briefly wondering what kind of life she lived and stories she would tell should she open her eyes and magically start talking back. Would she scold or congratulate me for letting my husband put a showerhead between my legs and spraying myself until I screamed?

Based on her dress and crucifix, I'd say scold.

I squeeze her lifeless hand before resting her palm over her belly then join Scotty in the witnessing room. Her eyes lift to mine as she continues to drag the file across her nails when I close the door behind me.

Through the speakers "Jolene" starts to play.

"Wanna talk about it?"

"About what?"

She cocks an eyebrow. "Definitely not about you letting Camp give you a showergasm and how conflicted you feel about it."

"The hell, Scotty! You heard that?"

She tilts her head to the small speaker on the wall with a wry smile.

My eyes widen. "Do you always listen?"

She stops filing. "My best friend is having conversations with dead bodies, what do you think?"

I glare at her, dropping into one of the chairs with a heavy sigh. "Reed Simmons is back."

"Oh, shit." She sits next to me. "How is *he*?"

"Too hot to be forty. And a photographer."

She snorts. "Bet Camp loves that."

"I thought he was going to rip his head off last night."

"Isn't this what you wanted?" She waves her hands through the air. "Him to notice you? Him to come home?"

"I did, but I wanted it to be his idea. I wanted him to want to do it, not do it because I said I was leaving. And there's value in follow-through, Scott. Like, he'll take advantage of me forever if I just let this slide and go back on my word." I leave out the fact I heard that on a podcast, but the skeptical look on her face tells me she already knows and does not approve. I sink farther into the couch, feeling like a deflated inner tube and wishing the furniture would swallow me whole. "I just wanted this to end easy, but he's, like, everywhere. Having dinner with us, planning picnics . . ."

"Shower humping you."

"And that," I say dryly. "And it's making me . . . I don't know, confused. Like, why couldn't it always be like this? He went from not caring at all to treating our relationship like it's a sacred mission from God. Like he's always home. Eating. And smiling. And being all . . ."

"Wet."

I scoff.

She sighs, sitting next to me. "You know it's okay to want your marriage to work, right? And who cares if it wasn't his idea. He's there now—he's stepped up to the plate—isn't that what counts?"

I do not tell her that it is *not* what counts. That I shouldn't have to tell him to show up. I don't tell her that I heard once that healthy marriages have balanced dialogue, and one person shouldn't always have to ask. That the reason men often view women as nags is because they are always asking. That the only plate Camp Cannon will ever willingly step up to is home plate.

Instead, I blow out another breath. "Where does that leave me with everything else though? The career? My independent-woman status?"

"Yeah, well, that status is way overrated." She smiles, but it doesn't meet her eyes.

I straighten, take her hand in mine, and am instantly aware that all I ever do is come here and complain about my own life. "You okay?"

She grins; it's forced. "I'm not talking to dead people, if that's what you mean."

"You still dating that guy? What's his name? Mark? Matt?" I'm a terrible friend—they've only been on a handful of dates, but for the life of me I can't remember his name. "Did something happen?"

"Mike," she corrects, rubbing her index finger across her bottom lip. "And he sent me a nude picture of him roller skating. So . . ."

I grimace; she laughs softly, but her eyes are distant.

"So . . . what's going on?"

"It's April."

The pieces fall into place. "God, Scotty. I'm sorry. Zeb . . . I forgot."

She shrugs. "It's not your fault my brother's missing his forty-second birthday because he couldn't stop shoving a stream of shit in his veins."

She's trying to be funny but neither of us laughs.

I do the math; it's been twenty years. We were in college, Zeb died, and Scotty came home and never left. When her heart shattered all those years ago, mine did too.

It's hard enough finding one true friend in life, but a friend that survives the ugliest days and lowest lows? It's a holy grail of relationships. Somehow, in this tiny town in the Blue Ridge Mountains, we found each other and weathered every storm, hand in hand. Sat in the lows with each other while we waited for the highs. Her bringing swear words, me bringing wine. I've seen her worst; she's most certainly seen mine.

I study her, her perfect features, hazel eyes that look like they belong on a cat. I know her as well as she knows me. "Wanna talk about it?"

She shakes her head, smile returning, voice sing-songy to the tune of a children's nursery rhyme. "I want to talk about you and Camp, standing in the shower, f-u-c—"

I bark out a laugh and swat her on the arm. "Go away. This is why I told Gladdys and not you. Pervert." She chuckles. "Either way, I don't know. I'm confused, I guess. About what I want. Who I am. I feel like an out-of-focus photo."

She hooks her arm through mine and drops her head on my shoulder. "We all do, Joo."

"I hate how intertwined we are. Everything feels... impossible."

She hums a sound in understanding but doesn't say anything else. No arguing or trying to convince me otherwise. Scotty sits next to me and simply lets me feel.

"Does everyone masturbate?" I ask.

"The fact you have to ask is disappointing to me, Joo."

"Huh," I say, somehow still shocked by this information. "I feel like you've been keeping secrets."

"You obviously haven't been going through my nightstand," she quips with a cocked eyebrow. "Or reading enough of my monster smut."

I snort, she shrugs, then we both stand.

"I have to go. Ms. Mitchell wants to have a meeting with me about the boys. Again. And then it's the damn library." I roll my eyes, slinging the strap of my purse over my shoulder. "Let's do something. Drinks or dinner or whatever. No corpses."

She nods, smiling as she tugs the sleeves of her blazer—black today—over a shirt with Dolly Parton's smiling face. "A boxing gym just opened in the old warehouses; I'm trying it out. They do a fourteen-day trial. Come with me."

I shake my head with a puff of laughter. Scotty does all things any-day-trial. She never commits, always dabbles. *Keeps me unattached,* she explains.

"Yeah, okay." I wrap my arms around her. "Getting my ass kicked seems on-brand for me right about now."

Nineteen

"June, did you hear that we're thinking about homeschooling next year?"

I blink away from the board book I'm holding and look at Mom One, forcing a smile.

"Umm. I don't know if I heard that. Maybe? Sounds..." I wrack my brain for a feasible lie. "Fun."

Mom Two melts into a puddle in her linen shirt at my response. "Doesn't it? You should totally look into it. I bet the boys would just thrive. We'll spend our days giving our kids a childhood just like *Anne of Green Gables*!"

I look at said boys across the library. Ty is on all fours with a puppet kitten in his mouth, baring his teeth as he growls; Hank is putting books down his pants. Homeschooling these kids would be nothing like *Anne of Green Gables*, everything like *The Hunger Games*, and is absolutely not happening.

"Didn't Anne of Green Gables go to school?" I ask.

Mom One smiles. "You know what we mean."

I do not.

"Hmm. Maybe. I actually might go back to work next year. Well, go to work, period. Last job I had was waitressing in college." I laugh; they look destroyed. "Right, either way, guess it's kind of hard to homeschool if you aren't, you know, home."

Kids approach—I can't remember which of The Moms they belong to—and ask for food. Bags of seaweed appear and crunching ensues.

"June," Mom Two whispers, dramatic, slow, and so serious I have to bite my cheek. "Have you thought about this? Like the ramifications of"—her eyes cut around the room, as if she's expecting to see the FBI watching her—"leaving the home? Not just that, but at your age . . . isn't entering the workforce difficult?"

It takes all my effort to not thump this woman on the nose. I want to tell her I'm forty, not four thousand. That my kids will be fine. That I don't know what *ramifications* there could possibly be. But, when I open my mouth, all I can say is: "Uh."

Mom One is ridiculously wide-eyed. "No offense, June, and we've always thought good for you for keeping up with the boys the way you do, but, leaving them now—where will you find the energy to be with them? When you're done with work, I mean . . . I read a study once . . ."

She keeps talking, but I tune her out as every slow syllable pulls at my skin, my fingernails, and the hairs on my head. My tongue is a heavy and useless thing in my mouth, because I say nothing. I sit there, dumb, staring at The Moms as they tell me about my age, about public schools, about Anne of fucking Green Gables.

"Okay, my little friends, time to come to the carpet!"

Librarian Alice's too-cheery voice stabs my brain along with her outfit. Red, polka-dot dress, hair in four—four—braids, and an arm full of books. The sight of her is a metal-spiked cleat to my throat.

I can't do this.

Not for the sake of childhood literacy.

Not for the sake of being around moms with kids the same age.

Not for the sake of socialization.

Not for anything.

As kids and parents alike scramble across the too-colorful rug and obediently sit *crisscross applesauce,* I shoot to a stand, grabbing Ty's and Hank's hands in mine the second they sit down.

"Where are we going?" Hank asks, eyes wide.

I don't answer. I can't. I'm moving on autopilot with one mission: Get the hell out of here.

On the alphabet-covered carpet, everyone turns to look as I try to step across laps and diaper bags and seaweed snacks. I wince apologetically.

"Going the wrong way, friends." Librarian Alice chuckles as a book is splayed open in her hands, picture of a corduroy teddy bear mocking me from the page.

When I look at her, she smiles with all her teeth.

If I don't get out of this room now, I will die.

"Sorry," I say, just above a whisper. "We have a . . . thing. I forgot."

Her smile stays, but the way the shape moves from crescent to rectangular must mean she's angry.

I take another step.

"June!" Mom One whispers, smiling big. "See you next week?"

I look at them. Their linen, their seaweed, and the toddler that now has its head shoved under one of their shirts, nursing, shining a spotlight on everything I'm not.

"No."

Like well-practiced synchronized swimmers, their smiles drop, eyes narrow, and mouths form perfect O's.

"I've aged out."

When they look completely perplexed, the first genuine smile I've ever had in this place curls my lips.

With a sweet, "Good luck with homeschooling," I turn away from them, tugging the boys' arms as I walk. It's exactly fourteen steps to the door. When the April air slaps my skin, I inhale it in gulps. Taking breaths like they are both my first and last.

Ty and Hank stare at me, speechless, faces filled with confused shock.

"So." I look at them, switch my purse between shoulders, and put my hands on my hips. "I hate that damn place."

At the confession, Hank barks out a laugh. "Mama said a bad word."

"You hate the library?" Ty asks, astonished, looking from me to the glass doors of the building then back to me. "I thought grown-ups loved the library."

I laugh softly. "Yeah, well, I don't. Librarian Alice scares me."

They both giggle.

"Let's go to the park instead, shall we?"

When they shout *hooray!* and take off running to the minivan, I feel a fleeting pang of guilt. I know the library is good for them—every poster in the room tells me so—but still, I smile. I've never once done something so brazen in motherhood.

When we get to the park, free of The Moms doing everything right and Librarian Alice being creepy and happy, it's easily Today's Best.

Twenty

I should know by now that anytime I leave the house something disastrous is going to happen. I'm more stupid than I give myself credit for, because the scene in front of me stops me cold.

I drop the bags of groceries and my purse at the front door, unable to move.

My camera bag has been dumped on the kitchen table, gear scattered across it. Thor is sprawled beneath it . . . Chewing?

Chewing.

I scramble across the room, letting out an audible, "No!" as I reach him.

On my hands and knees, I pry a roll of film out of his mouth. Gnawed beyond recognition, I can't tell if it was used or unused.

"Jesus, Thor! What the . . . ?"

Then I hear it, the rest of the scene. The boys, laughing and banging things around.

I dart to a stand. They're standing on chairs. At the stove. With a pot of boiling water. And my coffee canister of shot film.

Dumping.

"NO!" I shout, sprinting to them. I turn off the burner, repeating "No!" in a half-desperate cry, half wail of disbelief.

Because—No! My whole life plan of escaping this disaster is on these rolls of film.

No! Any hope of me being good at something is on these rolls of film.

No! Any chance of these kids seeing me as anything but nothing is on those rolls of film.

No! No! No!

"We're making soup!" Ty declares with a grin, stirring a spoon in the pot. With. My. Film.

I nod, slack-jawed, throat pinched. This is not good.

3-2-1.

3-2-1.

I want to scream like a banshee, but I don't. Mostly because I cannot breathe, much less trust myself not to spit the list of swear words that's dancing on the tip of my tongue.

"Where is your sister?" I ask through gritted teeth.

"In the shower," Hank says, tongue pinched between his lips as he focuses on squeezing a juice box into the "soup."

At this, my sanity shatters.

"No!" I shout, yanking the juice from his hands, tossing it in the trash. "What are you two doing? This is my stuff. My things. Mine!" I snatch the pot off the stove and take it to the sink, dropping it with a clatter. "You don't just-just-just—boil people's things! Do you have any idea how hard I worked on all this?" I look around the counter, my film scattered about as my blood pressure soars to new heights. "How would you feel if I started boiling all your toys? Huh? Huh?"

I glare at them, feeling manic, and both their eyes swell with tears. My kids look at me the way they look at Ms. Mitchell, and it crushes me.

"I'm sorry, Mama!" Hank says, lip trembling as the spoon drops from his hand to the floor. "We were just playing. It was Ty's idea."

Ty starts to cry. "No, it wasn't!"

As they wail, I wilt. Kneeling, I pull them to me. They sob and apologize through short breaths; I *shhhh* softly, repeat *it's okay*, as I rub their backs. It's as much for them as it is for me. They acted like four-year-olds, and so did I.

Finally, less their hiccupish breaths, they're calm, laying on my lap.

"Okay," I start, stroking their hair. "One, I love you more than I love that film."

Their cheeks move against my palms as they nod.

"Two." I pause, making sure I choose my words both wisely and free of expletives. "Never cook my things again."

Another silent nod, and my fingers slip through their penny-red hair.

"And three . . ." My voice trails off as a million thoughts dance around me where I sit on the scratched wood floors that have dents, boards swollen from water damage, and claw marks.

I wonder if Camp and his sister ever sat with his mom on the floor like this when he was a kid.

How many more times I'll do it with the boys.

When the last time it happened with Lyra was.

The noise of the podcasts blur together in a cacophony of advice. Like one continuous string tied in a loop.

Your kids will never see who you are if you don't make them. Let yourself be someone different—the opposite of who you are. Reinvent yourself. Focus on the big picture. Don't let them get away with it.

I squeeze my eyes shut.

"What's three?" Hank's head pops up, little face looking at me. His freckles could be a connect-the-dot puzzle making the lines of him.

"Three," I start, scrunching my nose, looking around the room. "Is—"

"Mom?!" Lyra's voice says from the doorway. She pauses drying her hair with a towel as her eyes widen at the disastrous kitchen. "What happened here?"

"You took a shower," I deadpan.

"Mom, I had no—" I wave her words away.

"Ly, it's fine. It's fine." I stand up, helping the boys do the same. "But we have to get this cleaned up." I move to the counter, inspect the film.

I haven't had much extra time, but when I have, I've been shooting anything and everything.

I photographed the lake I've swam in every summer of my life and the streets I grew up on. The school. Local neighborhoods.

Camp's games, documenting the crowd and the players. Capturing Camp as he helps the pitchers warm up, slinging a ball so hard and fast it's like he was never even injured and laughing as he swats one of the players with his glove.

Despite what Irma and Reed told me, I've been shooting landscapes, desperate to prove them wrong. Desperate to show them that this *is* what I'm made for. I've gone to state parks and scenic drive pull-offs. I've followed tourists and found the secret spots nobody knows about but the locals.

Rolls and rolls of film that I've been working my ass off on, waiting to be developed—waiting to reveal my destiny and reveal if I'm good at anything or nothing—now sit mostly ruined.

I collect the rolls, lay them out across the counter, and I'm flooded with relief. Sharpie-labeled rolls that I shot at local state parks—my last-ditch effort at proving to Irma I am a landscape photographer—are untouched. That means all the probably destroyed film was just the nonsense I did for fun.

A relieved exhale gushes out of me. "Okay, this is all okay."

Then, an idea . . .

"You know"—I hold up a roll of film toward Lyra and the boys—"I took a photography class in college where we shot experimental film."

As if planned, their heads all tilt in confused unison.

I laugh.

"We took rolls of film and, well, destroyed them, for lack of a better word." I think of that class, the quirky teacher, and all the ruined film. We used lighters, stamps, bleach. Anything that didn't make sense, we took it to film. Sometimes making something amazing, sometimes wrecking entire rolls. Sure, these are rolls I shot because I loved them, but nobody else will. Whether we destroy them or create something beautiful, it doesn't matter at this point. "We even made film soup."

When the boys' eyes widen as big as the grins that follow, we get to work . . . with Lyra. We boil water, drop canisters into mason jars, and start mixing concoctions. Dish soap. Vinegar. Lemon juice. Food coloring. SpaghettiOs per Hank's request, and lighter fluid per Ty's. Lyra dumps soda over one. I use rosé . . . before pouring myself a generous glass.

In the midst of the mess, we turn on music, dancing around the kitchen as we mix ingredients, and I order pizza.

Lyra and I lean on the counter, watching the boys as they pour a little bit of everything into the last jar.

"What are you doing all this for?" she asks, studying me. "The photography? You haven't shot, well, as long as I can remember. And now, it's like, you can't stop."

I look at her—her dad's replica and biggest fan—and debate what to say. How to answer. How to soften the blow that's coming after forty-seven days. How to lie.

"I'm trying to work." Her eyebrows shoot to the ceiling, and I chuckle softly. "I want to work, I mean. The boys will be in school full-time next year, and you'll be gone . . . I can't just sit here all day and watch Thor eat the furniture."

She laughs, studying the boys then me as I take a sip of my wine.

"I don't know what I thought I'd do with a degree in visual arts—don't tell Grandpa I said that—but I'm . . . trying to figure it out."

"What kind of photos do you like to take?"

Her question strikes me. *Like*. It's such a simple word—four letters strung together and used repeatedly every day—but its context makes it feel radical. *What kind of pictures do I like to take?*

"Hmm," I say, slight hum to my voice, just enough rosé in my blood to let me speak without filter. "I like stupid stuff—nothing. Photos that tell a story without actually showing the big picture—details. But those aren't good for anything. Not really. In college I started taking landscape photos—I like those too. I think." I chew the inside of my lips before I take another sip of wine. "Have you thought of what you want to go to school for? I know your heart is set on App State like Dad, but have you thought of majors or anything?"

She sighs, dropping her head back. Purple hair hanging down her back. "Doesn't it seem weird that teenagers are allowed to make that big of a decision? We can't even vote!"

I chuckle. "Well, if it makes you feel any better. I don't think adults know how to make that kind of decision either. I'm forty and still trying to figure out what I want to be when I grow up."

She looks at me like I'm silly, popping one shoulder as she says, "You already know, Mom."

She's so sure in her comment. Like it's obvious. Like she knows something I absolutely do not. Before I can ask what she means, she moves toward the boys, who are still maniacally souping. "Put one of Dad's beers in that one."

At the fridge, she pops a cap off a brown bottle—way more expert-like than I'm happy with—at the same time the delivery guy rings the doorbell. In the middle of a messy kitchen, with what is likely most of the film I've shot in the last weeks destroyed in jars, Today's Best happens in grocery store–bought clothes while eating greasy pizza right out of the box.

When Camp comes home, he doesn't bother to hide his surprise as he looks at the chaos of the house.

He slips his cleats off at the door, strolls over to where we're sitting on the floor, and drops next to me. Hand on my back, he leans toward me, just an inch—expression faltering when he realizes what he's doing—stilling before he pulls back. I recognize the familiarity of it; Camp was going to kiss me the way a husband kisses a wife at the end of a long day. He smiles, it's forced.

"I miss a party?" he asks, grabbing a slice and not looking directly at me.

Lyra wipes her mouth. "Mom taught us about photography," she says around her next bite. "It's pretty cool."

Twenty-One

With forty-six days left in our fake happy marriage, life is mostly the same.

Mostly.

I still wake up, take the boys to school, and mutter at the dog. Still do the laundry and scrub pots. Still run in and out of meetings at the high school as we finalize details for prom and start making plans for graduation. More than once I consider asking Lynn about her divorce—to comfort her or seek advice in my own situation—but every time my mouth opens, there are no words. As real as it is, I can't say it.

Other than no longer going to the library and spending more time with my camera, the most glaring change is Camp. He keeps coming home for dinner. Being around. Paying attention. Smiling. Resting his hand—briefly—on the small of my back when he walks by. Helping put the kids to bed. Saying things like, "Your mama's the best."

He's everywhere.

Bothering me.

Annoying me.

I don't know if I want to laugh or cry.

Every night, we go into our room where he still sleeps on the floor, but in these recent nights, I lie on the edge of the bed, look down at him, and we talk. He asks me about my day, what I'm shooting, and I ask him about baseball and the complex.

Camp goes back to being the person who knows me better than anyone. And it aches. Because I know it won't last. It's just pretend. A life built on a white lie of him being home.

Today, he's post-run, post-shower, post-coffee slurping when I hand the information to him about Lyra's career exploration field trip. For the first time ever, I don't read a single detail. They could be going to a gas station as much as a gynecologist—I'm free of responsibility.

"Good luck!" I call over my shoulder on my way out. Translation: I hope you crash and burn.

It's petty, but I want him to fail. I want him to be tired from the chaos of it or stressed by one of the kids doing something they aren't supposed to. I don't think he's ever once gone on one of Lyra's field trips in all her years of school.

I drop the boys off at preschool. Ms. Mitchell glowers at me from her spot on the sidewalk as I drive the gauntlet of car line, but the smile I give in return is genuine.

Nothing will dull my excitement as I drive straight to Resort 765—the fancy resort and spa that sits high on a hill overlooking Lake Ledger.

I park the minivan, so happy my feet barely touch the ground as I move toward the entrance, gift certificate Scotty gave me in hand.

All the while, unbeknownst to anyone around me, up the entirety of my ass lays a string. A string that's purple and connected to the rest of my bathing suit. Yes, on my shopping spree weeks ago as I pulled clothes off the rack in the name of self-reinvention and showing some skin, I bought a thong bathing suit.

Now, standing in the lobby covered in shiny, white marble tiles and an excessive amount of gold-detailed crown molding and columns, the flowy dress I'm wearing in a building I fit into as well as a whore in church, I thoroughly regret my choices.

When I'm called into my massage appointment, I try to walk like it's not the most uncomfortable situation of my life. Like me, in a fancy resort spa, with a string up my ass, is just another day in the life.

As the masseuse, a stocky woman named Gretel, begins to knead my back with the force of a Mack truck, knots of tension melt away. I let out a guttural moan as she presses her thick thumbs into my shoulders.

"Oh my God!" My face flattens against the U-shaped opening. "This is amazing."

She presses harder.

"My husband is on a field trip. Can you imagine?"

Silence.

"I mean, he's involved with the school, but not like that, and"—I grunt as she pushes harder—"I just want him to see what I'm dealing with. You know what I mean?"

When I laugh, her hand stills, thumb resting on my skin. Just when I think she's about to speak, she reapplies pressure, her hardest yet, and effectively shuts me up.

An hour later, I emerge both relaxed and incredibly sore and send Scotty a selfie of me in a luxurious thick white robe, blissful smile on my face, and sipping a glass of champagne at nine thirty on a school day. The caption: *I had no idea burning bodies had these perks.*

Scotty: *If one of them leaves me a hot single guy, I'm not sharing. Enjoy.*

I snort a laugh, take another sip of my champagne, and make my way toward the pool.

Outside, it's gorgeous, and like the rest of the building it's covered in white tile and gold accents, but now there's the added bonus of the views. Lake Ledger sits below the tiled deck of the pool like a piece of blue sea glass in the midst of tall trees. Across from where I stand, a rock face drops to the water. Beyond that, miles and miles of rolling hills. The Blue Ridge Mountains are covered in trees every shade of green.

Even for April, the air is warm. The smells of spring's first flowers along with the fresh scent of the trees flood my nostrils. *Home*, is all I can think. *It smells like home.*

At my lounge chair, robe cinched around my waist, it's my moment of reckoning. Seconds of shallow breaths and knowing that, once I untie this robe, it's just me and my ass and anyone that wants to walk up to the pool. Which, granted, on a weekday morning in early April, there's nobody but me, but that doesn't stop me from thinking they might come, these fictitious hordes of rich people that need pool time on a seventy-five-degree morning. They might show up and stare at my potatoesque mom body and throw dollars at me. Not because they like what they see, but because they want me to get dressed.

No.

I can do this. I *will* do this.

Reinvent yourself. Be someone different. Bolder. Brighter. Better! Give yourself a chance to be You 2.0.

Podcast-fueled, I take those words to heart. June Cannon might be reserved and scared, but June Cannon who hangs out at a fancy resort doesn't give two shits about who sees her in a thong.

Today, I'm June 2.0, and June 2.0 wants to show off her new bathing suit and lumpy bum.

With that lie, I tip my glass of champagne straight to the sky, downing it in a single gulp, and hold the empty glass up to the waiter across the pool—a balding man in a crisp white shirt and black tie—signaling my need for a refill.

I squeeze my eyes shut, mutter, "Don't be a scared bitch," my version of a pep talk, and rip the robe off. Before it hits the ground, I launch myself onto the tan woven lounge chair in an almost belly flop motion. No grace, all grunts, lying with my face down until my new champagne is delivered, which I down again quickly.

I'm alcohol-lubricated enough to relax slightly. When an older couple arrives, taking chairs across the pool from me, I don't panic. To the contrary, I pull wireless earbuds out of my purse and turn on some music—moody and acoustic—tapping my toes and closing my eyes. A song plays, lyrics about not changing a thing, and like I can't seem to prevent in these recent weeks, a slideshow starts. My mind travels in a dozen directions.

When I dropped my film off at the lab—souped and otherwise—a landscape photo on the wall caught my eye, holding me captive. It was a canyon from out west; I could tell by the dusty, barren land and the depth of the chasm. I thought about Irma's words, telling me a photograph should make you feel something. And I did; looking at the image, I felt how big the world was. How much I don't know. But it's what I didn't feel that struck me. I didn't feel compelled to make an image anything like that. Didn't get a thrill from the idea of leaving home and shooting that.

Then Lyra's question echoed: *What do you like taking pictures of?* I thought of my day at the lake, the tired mom with the kids. I never showed anyone, but out of every perfect image I captured that day, my favorite was the shot of them—blurry sticks in the water. It just felt like motherhood. Out of focus. Lonely. Lost. An ethereal kind of beauty that pulls at the viewer for no reason other than, *I get it. I've been there.* A ghost story of who we were and are becoming.

When the song switches to a love ballad my mind jumps to . . . Reed? He represents everything I don't have in a partner. Emotion. Concern. Depth. Understanding. He's artistic and free and looks at me like I'm something new. Something interesting. Everything I'm not. My life not lived.

But then, Camp. Camp. One word meaning a million.

Every option feels impossible. Stay. Go. Reed. Camp. Photography. Motherhood. It's like I'm living in a weird in-between. A sort of midlife purgatory with no exit strategy.

It's only after my waiter, Stan as I learn his name is, sets another glass of champagne down, that I leave the rabbit hole of my thoughts to notice more people at one end of the pool. A lot of people, maybe fifty of them. I shrink slightly into myself, like a turtle trying to suck in all its limbs. Except, I'm not a turtle and my limbs have nowhere to go.

I have nowhere to go.

So—to hell with them. Propped on my forearms, I pull my shoulders back and pop my buns up a little higher. Whatever they are doing here, the view of me is included.

Scotty: *Are you in your suit showing the richies all your ASSets?*

I snort a laugh, opening the camera app, pulling my earbuds out, and holding the phone so I can send her a picture.

When it's only my face filling the screen, I lift my arm higher, working for an angle to get my face *and* rump. If anyone will appreciate this, it's Scotty.

I lift my arm higher . . . almost.

Almost.

Thumb on the shutter button.

"Mom?!"

At the word shouted in groaned disbelief, my head whips around at the same time my phone slips out of my hand. There stands Lyra—hands covering her mouth—and every single one of her friends. And Nick. And most of their parents. Looking at me. My bathing suit. What's missing from my bathing suit. Gawking.

"L-L-Lyra," I stutter, rolling over clumsily as fire swallows my neck, my face, and my entire body. I stumble to stand, fumbling to grab the robe from the back of the lawn chair, the word *fuck* scrolling through my mind on repeat like a song on a scratched CD. I manage to stand, but the robe slips from my hands.

I'm so flustered, so humiliated, I bend over to get it, ass to the crowd, which I now realize is Lyra's field trip, because I see Camp, who has pushed his way to the front of the group and is standing next to our daughter.

And her friends.

And their parents.

And her teachers.

"June?"

And while there's the same disbelief in his voice as Lyra had, that bastard is also amused as hell. Clear as day, lips pressed between his teeth, his stupid mustache twitches so much he has to bring a hand up to cover his mouth to hide it all. But I see it, his brown eyes filled with glittery joy, saying, *I'll be laughing about this for the rest of my life.*

I mentally flip him the bird.

"I can explain this," I say, half choking as I finally get the robe around my body, hiding myself, my ghost-white cheeks, contemplating throwing myself in the pool and taking a deep breath until I drown.

"Scotty gave me a gift card—and-and—"

A few of the kids chuckle.

And parents.

And the teachers.

Lyra groans.

Again.

"You know what, Mom? I don't even want to know." She glares at me, and her eyes rake down my now-robed body as her face turns a fiery red. "I'm going to go wash my eyes with bleach in the bathroom."

She storms off, friends scurrying after her as she circles the fancy pool, bumping into Stan—an innocent bystander—without apologizing.

"I didn't know Coach C's wife was hiding all that every time she came to one of our games," one of the boys says from the crowd, whistling.

I groan from behind my hands, now covering my face as a fresh wave of chuckles ripple across the group.

It's when someone says, "Lyra's mom's a MILF," that I make an audible groan-grunt-shriek noise. The call of a dying animal.

"Okay, okay, okay. My wife isn't the reason we're here." Camp points at who I assume is the manager that's been giving them a tour, lifting his chin. "Can we please move this along?"

She nods, tight-lipped, clipboard hugged to her blouse-covered chest with judgmental disgust in her eyes as she says, "Let's go see the water sport rental shack, shall we?"

The crowd of everyone I know files away, me smiling with the strength of a dying bug at each person who insists on making eye contact, and I pray for death. Slow, fast. I'd prefer either to living through this. June Cannon, the star in her very own shitshow.

When Camp looks at me again, his smile is so unnervingly big it nearly cracks his face. "J, J, J." He whistles. "Aren't you full of surprises." He crosses his arms over his chest, shaking his head.

I smack his bicep.

"Don't *J, J, J*, me, Camp. Did you just see Lyra? I've scarred her for life!" I cry. "She's never going to talk to me again!"

He laughs. Loud.

"You're laughing?!" My eyes widen. "Can you imagine if you would have found your mom in a bathing suit—like this—in front of all your friends?"

He stops laughing, playful look in his eyes as he unfolds his arms, leans in close. "One," he starts, "don't bring my mama into this. And two"—he reaches around and pinches my bottom, making me yelp—"my mama doesn't have an ass like that, J."

My mouth drops open, palms land on his chest, and I push him away with a grunt.

"Are you *flirting* with me right now?! While my life is unravelling!"

He shrugs, casual. Unaffected. Scrubbing his knuckles across his stupid mustache. "What do you think I'm doin'?"

"I think you're not helping the situation," I shriek, arms in the air.

He laughs, lifts his chin, then says, "Can't wait to discuss it over dinner, *sweetheart.*" With a wink, he strolls away, whistling, leaving me humiliated in an expensive robe and too-tiny bathing suit.

Twenty-Two

"Lyra, I'm so sorry. Seriously. I didn't read the paper or didn't remember that's where your class was going or-or-or." I set my fork down, trying to find better words to apologize over dinner.

She rolls her eyes, filling a fork with mashed potatoes. "I do *not* want to talk about it."

I nod. "Okay, well, I get that, it's just, I really need you to know that when Scotty gave me the gift certificate, I never dreamed that it would be the same—"

Lyra drops her fork, folding her hands on the table. "Why do you even have that suit?"

"What suit?" Hank asks.

"The one that shows her entire butt," Lyra snaps, not pulling her eyes off mine.

The boys scream, and Camp, my steadfast dinner guest, chimes in with an out of character, stern-voiced, "Boys. Lyra. Enough."

I let out a breath. "Okay, one it didn't show my entire butt," I lie. "And two, I bought it because . . . I don't know why . . . There was this podcast about moms dressing differently. Being-being-being different. I just wanted to do something . . . different. Crazy, I guess."

"Well, you sure nailed that one," she mutters, picking up her fork again, raking her food across the plate.

When I open my mouth to respond, it's Camp that speaks. "Let's do Today's Best, huh? Boys? You start." As the boys start talking about terrorizing the girls in their class, I give Camp a relieved smile, which he returns with a quick wink. An unexpected lifeline.

Pretend, I tell myself. *We are pretending.*

"Your turn, Mama," Ty says.

"Hm," I say, swallowing a bite of my salad. "Definitely the massage I got. You, Lyra?"

"Leaving the resort," she says with an eye roll. "Dad?"

He leans back in his chair, scrubs his knuckles across his mustache, and says, "I'd say showin' up to the pool at the resort."

When Lyra groans, despite myself, I laugh.

"Ms. Mitchell says we're bad kids," Hank tells me as I tuck him in. "Rotten and can't be saved."

I fill my cheeks with air and release it with a puff. "That's not true." I pinch the blankets tightly down the length of his little torso. "You are . . . spirited. And sometimes you make choices that are less than ideal . . . like the spitballs. And the lighters. And unscrewing the wheels of her chair."

"What about the permanent marker mustaches?"

I laugh under my breath, kissing Hank on the head before moving to Ty's bed. "*And* the mustaches. But you aren't bad. That's not nice of a teacher to say something like that to a kid." I pause, deciding that *not nice* is the nicest thing I'd call that witch. "And maybe she was having a bad day when she said that."

Why do I keep defending this woman?

Ty nods, folding his arms over his spaceship-covered blanket. "She said you can't control us because Daddy was a baseball player, and you think the rules don't apply to you."

My eyes narrow.

"Okay, you know what." I kiss Ty on the head, forcing my instant shot of anger aside. "That's not true either. Dad playing baseball has nothing to do with this. We just need . . ." My gaze moves from Ty in his bed to Hank in his. "Practice. You know, nobody knows how to be a parent. This is the first time I've ever had twin four-year-olds, I'm still figuring out how to make you stop with the mustaches and the lighters."

They both giggle, warming my whole body like heat from a bed of coals. Because, as much as I feel like I have no idea what I'm doing, these kids, these two red-headed boys that are pieces of me—extensions of who I am—are *not* bad. Even on days I think they might be, I know they aren't. They are good. The best parts of me.

And the wildest.

Even as hard as some of the parts of life have been, I can't imagine ever changing any of it if it meant these two wouldn't be here with me now.

"I'm glad you're my mama," Ty says with a yawn.

"Me too," Hank echoes, curling on his side.

My heart expands to the point of pressing bone.

"Me too."

Camp finds me in the laundry room, sorting clothes and pulling a deadly collection of objects out of the boys' pockets.

He leans a hip on the dryer, hooking one bare foot across the other as he folds his arms over his chest. Lopsided smile on his lips.

I cut my eyes to him, pulling an arrowhead out of Hank's shorts. "Don't start with me, Camp."

He chuckles. "Wouldn't dream of it."

My hand in Lyra's jean jacket, I feel the edge of a plastic bag and pull it out. Four squares of what looks like some sort of fruit snack. I open the bag, smelling. The scent, candy sweet, is also skunky. I hold it up to Camp, my eyebrows pinched. "What the hell is this?"

He scrubs his knuckles across his mustache. "Looks like edibles."

"Edibles?"

"Edibles."

I scoff. "I heard what you said, Camp. What the hell is she doing with them?"

He laughs under his breath. "I'm assumin' getting stoned."

"Getting stoned?" I ask in a whisper-hiss.

"Gettin'—"

"I swear to God, Camp, I'll cut you with this arrowhead if you repeat me one more time." I pick up the dagger-shaped stone I just pulled out of Hank's pocket. "How are you so calm? Our daughter has drugs. Probably because I mentally scarred her today at the pool. And you're, just"—I gesture to his calm stance against the dryer—"standing there?!"

Camp chuckles again, wordlessly taking the bag from my hand. He moves methodically, looking at me—studying me like he's weighing his options—then opens it, takes one of the gummy squares out, and pops it in his mouth like a piece of popcorn.

"You're eating one?" I whisper-shriek, looking over my shoulder toward the empty house. "What the hell, Camp?! You don't know where these came from. They could be laced with fentanyl! You could die!"

At this, he drops his head back and laughs, loud enough he could wake the boys.

"I'm 99 percent sure they came from Danny Griffen, who probably stole them from his dad, who makes them in his garage."

"Billy makes edibles?" I ask, whisper-shrieking again, picturing the guy we went to high school with doing such a thing. And, even all these years later, it seems pretty on-brand for him considering he got sent to the principal's office regularly for smoking weed in the bathroom. And supplying the entire high school with it.

Including Camp.

And me.

He pulls another one out, proffering it to me, which I scoff at.

"You don't have to take it, J." He pauses with a slight shrug. "But it might make you tellin' me about where you bought that bathin' suit easier."

When he clicks his tongue, I flip him the middle finger and glare at the blue cube in his palm.

"What about the kids?"

Am I really considering this?

"The boys are in bed and Lyra is gone. Studyin' at Kimber's. What is she gonna do anyway—yell at us for stealin' *her* edibles?"

I blow out a breath, knowing from every angle this is an irresponsible thing to do.

Yet, like a big red button that says Don't Push, it's devilishly tempting. I know I shouldn't. Know this drug-laced piece of candy is off-limits. I'm a mother. I have two kids that were told they were bad and a daughter that currently hates me because her friends saw my ass. I'm in a fake happy marriage with my husband, who is now smiling in a very real happy kind of way, offering me some kind of marijuana candy and a high I haven't felt since I was in college. And, dammit, as much as I don't want to do it—know I shouldn't do it—I want to.

Nostrils flaring, I yank the gummy out of his hand and toss it in my mouth, the taste of berries and weed nipping at my taste buds.

When I say, "I hate you," he grins.

Twenty-Three

On the front porch, sitting in the porch swing with chipped white paint, I'm stoned. We both are.

"Remember that time Scotty ran all those thongs up the flagpole?" Camp asks, laughing loud as his arm drapes around the back of the swing, the streetlight painting the lines of his profile.

I match his laugh until tears drip down my face.

"I thought the ROTC instructor was going to kill her. He was so pissed. I think in detention she had to write an apology letter to the United States of America for disrespecting the flag."

"God," he says, chuckling. "I forgot that part."

Every muscle in my body is relaxed, and every thought in my mind is flowing out of my mouth like a tube on a lazy river as we tell stupid stories about ourselves that are old enough to be in history books.

Headlights shine in our eyes as Lyra's sedan pulls into the driveway.

Panic-seized, I grip Camp's knee.

"She can't see us like this!" I hiss. "High on her drugs!"

"Shhh!" he manages through a snorted laugh. "God, J. Stay quiet and she won't know."

Out of her car, across the yard, and up the steps, she looks at us, stack of books under one arm.

"Hey, Lyra!" I shout. Then wince.

"Hi," she says, drawling out the word as she looks from me to her dad. "What are you two doing out here?"

"Chillin'," Camp says, southern drawl thick and as if *chillin'* is at all part of his vocabulary.

Her eyebrows pinch, and she tucks a strand of hair—back to pink—behind her ear, gaze floating over to me.

"Chillin'?" she asks, confused. "That's weird."

Unfortunately for me, the words in my lazy river of a mouth keep flowing. "Lyra," I say, "you can't do drugs, so we ate them."

Her eyes widen, jaw drops. "You're *stoned*?" she asks, voice shrill.

"Your mom wasn't supposed to tell you that," Camp starts, knuckles scrubbing across his mustache. "But yes."

And that's all it takes for the loudest cackle of my life to come out of my mouth and fly into the night air. When Camp joins me, both of us laugh until we wheeze. Until we forget what we're laughing about. Until Lyra, who is standing dumbfounded, mutters something about my bathing suit, her parents being stoned on edibles that don't belong to her, and storms into the house.

"You're probably grounded for this!" Camp shouts through the screen door, fresh laughter swelling out of both of us when she yells a response we can't understand.

Laughter exhausted, we fall quiet, staring off as the swing sways at a gentle cadence.

"How do you think this happened?"

I look at him. "The edibles?"

He smiles, but it doesn't meet his eyes. "Us. The fallin' apart."

I drop my head on the back of the swing—his arm—and close my eyes. My heartbeat, a steady *badum* in my chest.

It wasn't because I got pregnant with Lyra. As unexpected as it was and as much as it altered the course of my entire life, we were still happy. Even though things were hard, we were broke but good.

It came next. The hard parts after.

Camp reads my silence, my thoughts falling into the pockets of the story we never talk about. Nobody ever talks about.

He bends his elbow as he wraps his arm around my shoulders.

"The lost ones?"

The lost ones, that's what he's always called them. There were two. One early, one late. *Sorry, June,* the doctor had said . . .

When my nose and eyes start to burn, I clear my throat. We never spent much time talking about it, and there's no need to start now, especially while we're edible-stoned and pretending to be something we aren't.

"Life just happens, Camp. I don't think there's any one moment, ya know?"

Whether I'm deflecting or not, there's still truth to my words.

"Death by a thousand cuts," he says, gaze straight ahead.

"Death by a thousand cuts," I echo, realizing it was a slow burn of me going from June to Mom to nothing in between.

"I should have seen it."

"Hmm," I say, both of us turning our heads to face each other. "We're both to blame, Camp. I felt so bad when you got injured. Got cut from the team and lost your dream."

The swing stills.

His hand, his familiar palm, is on my face, pulling my forehead to his. "*You* were the dream, June. Baseball was just a bonus."

And I feel it now, how easy it would be to just fall into him. Love him to forever and back like I always thought I would. Believe that things would be different if we tried again. Believe he'd keep showing up for dinners and planning picnics. But I know he wouldn't. I would stop chasing any other version of myself, and he would fall back into letting me.

Another hand finds my face; his palms become a frame, boxing in a picture of me. Our stare is one I feel in my throat, my eyelids, and deep in my belly. He moves closer, his lips just over mine, and the breath from his nose and the slightest brush from his mustache tickles my skin. Alone on the porch, we're soul-scraped and stoned.

"I want to kiss you," he says, low.

I hesitate, searching his eyes like crystal balls that can tell the future.

Wishing I could see what this is, where it leads, and what to do.

I open my mouth; a phone dings.

His eyes close; the moment shatters.

Camp's hands drop from my face to slide his phone out of his pocket.

"Dammit," he mutters, fingers swiping the screen before bringing the phone up to his ear. He looks at me. "Guess the bus driver for—Dani. Hey . . . yeah, just read it." He chuckles softly, running his fingers through his hair. "They all go to that Chinese place or something?" He pauses, nodding. Eyes crinkling as he smiles before his face goes serious. "Right. No, Jack might be able to do it if we can't find anyone, it's still two days away, can't they take some Pepto?" Another pause.

I tune out the rest of his words, my insides twisting. We can't even have a moment—whatever we were having—without something. Dani. Work. Chinese food.

He's still talking when I stand up from the swing.

"Hey, hold on, Dani—J?" I pause in the doorway and look at him. "I'll be just a minute. Bus drivers have a stomach bug or something—nobody can drive the softball team to the tournament Saturday."

He laughs, and I'm quiet; the sound dies on his lips.

"This won't take long."

I wish that were true.

"It never does."

"J—"

I don't let him finish. I step inside and let the screen door snap closed behind me.

He'll never change. He'll always pick something else. Maybe he wanted to kiss me, but he also wants everything else.

In the bedroom, vibrating with emotions that have nowhere to go, I grab my phone.

Me: *Still up for trying that boxing gym?*

Scotty: *Uh-oh. Campy piss you off?*

Me: *Ignoring you.*

Scotty: *Class at 6 tomorrow night. That work?*

Me: *I'll be there.*

By the time Camp comes in, I'm already in bed, and the mattress shifts as he sits at my feet.

"June?" he whispers.

I listen to him breathing in the dark and wait for him to make his next move. To tell me he's sorry or say something to convince me I'm reading this all wrong. To try to kiss me again or apologize seven thousand times. Something. Anything.

Instead, he sleeps on the floor; I sleep on the bed.

Twenty-Four

What felt like hurt in the dark reveals itself as anger in the morning light.

Campy did, in fact, piss me off.

I refuse to talk to him. Refuse to think of him. Refuse to acknowledge the way he so easily answered his phone and left me hanging—left us hanging.

For every person sacrificing, there's someone that isn't, that never will.

This is all a mirage. Fake, like we decided it would be.

I can't even blame him—though I do—he's doing exactly what I asked him to: being nice in front of the kids, showing up, and being chatty.

Camp is doing what I wanted, and I hate him for it.

Other than the mishap in the shower, everything has gone according to plan.

And as for the shower, I know now it was clearly a mistake. Or a dream. A very *wet* dream.

And him asking to kiss me? That was the drug candy.

There's no other explanation. Because if there was, why on earth would he take that call in the middle of the moment?

A car honks and I remember I'm driving.

With an apologetic wave, I turn up the radio, voices from the latest podcast filling the speakers.

THE PERFECT MOM PODCAST WITH ABBIGAIL BUCHANAN

EPISODE 261: The Art of the Pivot with Greg Brownwell

My fingers tap an agitated beat against the steering wheel as Abbigail introduces the guest, his book, but I can't focus. I can barely hear over the blood pumping through me.

When I pass through town, by Irma's gallery, Reed's Harley, and every other spot that triggers me, I turn the volume up.

> **Abbigail:** Alright, so, Greg, you're a bit of an anomaly. A doctor that goes by his first name and spends more time on a surfboard than in an office.

Greg: Sounds right.

[Light laughter.]

Abbigail: I love that. Well, I don't want to keep you from the waves out there in California, so let's jump into it. Your book, *Stop Building Dams and Go with the Flow*—which, love that title by the way—is all about pivoting with life's ebbs and flows. If you had to summarize the central point, what would it be?

Greg: Ahh, yeah, okay. Cramming three hundred pages into a short paragraph, no pressure. [Light laughter.] In all seriousness, here's the takeaway: We make choices, form opinions, draw lines in the sand for our future self, but life changes—including us and other people in it—and we should constantly reevaluate. Allow.

Abbigail: Allow?

Greg: Allow. Allow ourselves to reconsider. To move the lines in the sand. To change our minds. To pivot. There's an art to it. Sometimes we think, "Oh, if I change my mind, people will think I'm wishy-washy," but if it's done right, you'll come out happier and won't care. I've watched thousands of waves in my life, and none of them care what the last one did. They go where they go. And the sand on the beach doesn't resist it, it changes, and it's beautiful just the same. At the same time, I've watched people—surfers and swimmers alike—try to fight it, try to be a kind of dam against it, but there's no fighting it. Water always wins, and life will too if we don't adjust.

I glare at the radio.

Abbigail: Okay, so can you give the mamas listening an example of how this relates to their lives? How is it applicable?

Greg: Sure. Maybe when you have a baby—even before you have a baby—you think, "I'm going to be the kind of mom that only feeds my kid organic whole foods," but then the baby becomes a kid, and suddenly the only food they will eat is a shit-filled chicken nugget. Do you stay the mom you thought you'd be—feeding only organic food that your kid won't eat—or do you pivot and give them chicken nuggets? Neither is wrong, of course. Sure, the organic option is better for the kid, but if they aren't eating and every meal is a battle, is it really worth it? Is it really even better?

Abbigail: Oh, gosh, I feel that example in my bones as I have two of my own very picky eaters here at home.

Greg: Right? I'd say most parents end up with at least one. And this thought process can be applied to our adult relationships too. When we get married or meet our partners, we are one person. But life changes us—waves against the sand—and what we think relationships will look like often doesn't match up. We need to allow ourselves to adjust expectations. To change our minds about what's working. To look at our life, ask ourselves what we need now, not what we needed five, ten, fifteen years ago, and go with it. We can either go with the flow and make purposeful adjustments or build dams and block progress.

Abbigail: Pivot.

Greg: Exactly.

"No!" I shout, slamming the podcast off.

The weight of a boulder crushes my chest. Like Greg the stupid surfing doctor did that interview just to torment me in my Goldfish crumb–covered minivan.

Pivot?

I scoff.

Yes, Camp has made an effort, but I'm not some kind of pushover. It's too late for *adjusting expectations* and *purposeful adjustments*. There are lessons to be learned. Big-picture things. Heads must roll.

By the time I park next to Scotty's old Bronco, anger is rolling off me like Greg's Pacific Ocean waves.

I get out of the minivan and slam the door, locking it, only to realize I don't have my bag or water bottle, and unlock it. Muttering as I gather my things, dropping them all in the middle of the parking lot, muttering some more.

To hell with Camp. And Greg. And the whole damn state of California.

Blowing out a breath, I face the building in front of me. Kudzu vines stretch across the old brick and around a door propped open with a rock. Loud music pounds through the air, and a neon sign in the shape of a pair of boxing gloves hangs in the window. Fight Club. *Of course.*

I need this, I realize. I need to punch myself back to reality.

Scotty appears at the entrance, my athletic opposite. Where I'm wearing black cotton leggings and an oversized T-shirt, she's in red spandex shorts and a crop top with her hair in a short French braid and looking like she belongs to an actual fight club.

I smile; she doesn't.

"Everything okay?" I ask, looking over her shoulder at the bodies moving around bags and a ring. Shoulders bounce, fists fly.

She bounces on the balls of her feet, gloves tucked under her arm, distracted. She looks how I feel.

"Fine, yeah. Sorry. Just, you know. Fight club?" She laughs ironically, but it's forced. She's not telling me something. "How cliché, right?" She hands me a clipboard with paperwork. "Fill this out and then we can go in." She pauses, her eyes darting around the parking lot. "You tell Camp you were coming?"

I snort. "No. He's doing some kind of *team building* thing with the coaches"—I roll my eyes—"and Lyra's watching the boys. He's being—"

"It's fine." She cuts me off, bouncing in place again.

When she catches me watching the movement, she stops.

"You roasting coffee beans again?" I ask, stilling my pen on the paper as I recall that weird phase of hers. "I haven't seen you this jacked up since you were drinking all that caffeine."

She looks away. "You'll see."

I shake my head, sign the last form—a waiver that says I won't sue them if I die—and walk inside. That's when I see. All of them.

"Sonofabitch."

"June Cannon?" a familiar face says, blocking my view as he steps in front of me while also shocking the hell out of me.

Though I want to rip heads off, the smile I give is genuine.

"Ford Callahan?" I ask, incredulous, giving him a hug, now completely understanding Scotty's bizarre behavior. A grade ahead of us in high school, star football player, current police officer . . . and, once upon a time, Scotty's brother's best friend and her not-boyfriend boyfriend.

"I heard you were back in town. And a cop. It's been too long," I say, taking him in, smile overtaking my face despite that just over his shoulder, Camp is jovially throwing punches as all his coaches gather around him. And Dani. *Team building.*

Ford grins. "It has."

He, like every other man in this stupid town, has aged like a vampire. His hair is buzzed short, and his ageless baby face is now covered with a slight scruff of beard. His contagious smile covers his face—dimples and all—and his dark blue eyes shine. I've learned there are two kinds of police officers: those that eat the donuts, and those that do not. Judging by the way his athletic shorts hang, his T-shirt clings, and his forearms flex when he breathes, Ford Callahan does *not* eat the donuts.

My eyes cut to Scotty; she gives me a tense eye roll. She sees Ford is hot and is pissed about it.

"Way too long." He glances at Scotty. "We should all get together. For old times' sake, you know? At the lake or something. Grab a drink. Catch up."

My eyes shift from Ford—slowly—to Scotty.

Before I can say anything, she lets out the loudest laugh I've ever heard, making the people immediately by us stop what they're doing and look. Ford and I both stare at her as she laughs like a crazy person until tears drip down her face. As abruptly as she starts, she stops, jerking her chin back and looking at Ford. "Shit on a shovel, Ford, you're serious," she says, venom in her voice. She steps toward him, a fraction of an inch from them touching, eyes locked with his. "I would rather eat a maggot-filled asshole out of a corpse than catch up with you."

My mouth opens, stunned, but she grabs my hand and jerks us away, leaving Ford gaping as we march toward someone wearing a shirt labeled Trainer.

"Before I come unglued about Camp being here," I say, stumbling as she drags me across the gym, "please know you handled that like shit, and I'm going to force you to talk about it at some point in the future."

"Go fuck a showerhead," she spits at me at the same time we approach the trainer. His square chin jerks back, eyes wide. Leave it to Scotty to shock the meatball-shaped meathead covered in ink.

"We're here to learn to kick some ass," she tells him, matter-of-fact, eyes one shade shy of red. If she wasn't my best friend, I'd be scared shitless.

"Okay," he drawls with a slight chuckle, rubbing a mangled-knuckled hand over his shaved head.

He launches into an overview about what we will be doing, but my attention goes to Camp, bouncing around with boxing gloves with his coaches. A trainer stands in the corner, demonstrating a move, then they all repeat it. Laughing. *Team building.*

I want to puke.

While I was having a minivan meltdown minutes ago over our situation, he's... fine. Completely unaffected. Whether Camp and I are together or not has absolutely no impact on his happiness, and it raises my temperature by fiery degrees.

I would just love to hear Surfer Greg's thoughts on this. No, I decide, I would not.

Camp spots me from the ring he's in and shock covers his face for a split second before he smiles and waves.

Fake. So damn fake.

While he's looking at me, Dani playfully punches the side of his head with a big red boxing glove, and his attention instantly snaps back to her and her too-swishy ponytail.

My eyes cut to Scotty. As the muscled meatball talks about the importance of warming up, she's glaring at Ford.

We're both powder kegs ready to explode for very different reasons. But maybe not. She hates Ford; I hate Camp.

"Yeah, so listen," I say, cutting off the safety speech, and peeling my shirt off so I'm in a sports bra like Scotty, ignoring the fact my boobs look nowhere near as perky as hers. "We don't need five minutes of jump rope, and I signed a waiver that said I won't sue you if I die. I don't want a warm-up; I need to beat the hell out of something. Let's start there."

A smirk tugs at Scotty's lips. "What she said."

I don't know how long we've been punching the bags, but I'm quite sure all the pent-up anger I'm harboring would allow me to do it forever. The gloves are hot as ovens around my hands, my shoulders scream with every swing, and sweat is dripping into every crevice, but I don't care. I'd hit this bag until my hands fell off and I die of dehydration if they'd let me.

Then Camp's there, next to me, watching every hit as he drinks from his water bottle.

"Didn't expect to see y'all here," he says with his stupid drawl. "Scotty."

She grunts from the bag next to me but doesn't stop the heavy blows she lands on it.

"You and Dani seem to be having fun," I say, breathless as I throw another punch. And another.

He snorts next to me. "We are." I cut my eyes to the stupid smirk that's on his stupid face under his stupid mustache. "You jealous?"

Yep.

As fast as the word pops in my brain, I do what I need to: I take Surfer Greg's advice and pivot. Literally. I spin from facing my bag to facing him and deliver a gloved hook straight to his jaw, sending his water bottle flying to the ground, spilling across the floor.

The shocked look on Camp's face is there as fast as it's gone, then it's amusement in his eyes as he straightens, rubs a palm on his cheek, and stares at me.

I punch him again.

His amusement turns to a laugh.

The sound is gasoline to my red-hot rage.

"Asshole," I mutter.

When I pull my arm back again, sending a red glove shooting toward his face, he blocks it and grabs my wrist with his hand, stopping me with his strength.

My breath is fast and shallow as I glare at him, standing calm and amused. Like seeing me so wound up is the best thing ever.

"Whoa! Whoa! Whoa!" a voice says from behind me. "Sparring only happens in the designated areas, folks."

"Sorry," Camp says, not taking his eyes off mine. "My wife here was just *pretendin'*."

His emphasis sends a thousand needles into my bones. I jerk my arm out of his grasp and meet the trainer's narrowed eyes as his chin jerks back. "Pretending? That looked like a real hook to me."

"Yes, well . . ." I wipe the sweat on my brow with my sweatier forearm before dropping my gloved hands by my sides, eyes going back to Camp. "Sometimes *pretending* makes things confusing, and we forget the real reason we are doing things, and that people always show their true colors when nobody else is around."

Camp steps closer. "Oh, really? Because I thought when people ask for *pretend* that's exactly what they want and nothin' else matters because they've already made up their mind, regardless of what is or isn't or what other people do or do not want."

"Okay," the meatball says, dragging the word out as he eyes us both. "Not sure what any of that means, but no sparring unless you're in the designated area. Got it?"

I roll my eyes, nod, and resume trying to kill the red bag hanging in front of me.

"June, listen—"

A whistle blows from across the gym from the middle of the ring and silences whatever lie Camp was going to say.

"Anyone want to do a sparring demo against Ford? He's professionally trained and will be demonstra—"

"Me!" Scotty shouts from next to me. "I'll do it."

My eyes widen, but she doesn't look at me. She marches toward the ring in the center of the gym, tattoos on her spine peeking out from the bottom of her shirt. She looks like she's about to burn the whole place to the ground.

Ford pauses as he adjusts his gloves, gaze locked on her as she approaches. Tension thickens with her every step.

She slinks between the ropes of the ring, punching the tops of her gloves against each other like she's done this a thousand times, she and Ford staring at each other as we all move to the sidelines.

"Hey, June!" Dani whispers as she steps next to me, eyebrows wiggling like this is the best thing ever. "Camp didn't mention you were coming. It's fun, right?" She grins; it irritates me.

Something in this room turns me into a psycho, because I hear myself say, "Camp's married. To me." Dani's grin crashes, mouth dropping. "Just so you know."

She looks like a kid who got caught with her hand in the cookie jar but says nothing.

Ha!

Jack steps up to her other side, oblivious. "Hey, June."

I flick him a quick smile, then revert my focus back to my best friend, who, according to the tingly feeling on the back of my neck, is about to do something completely unhinged.

The trainer—a dark-haired man slightly less meatballish but just as muscled as the trainer that was talking to us earlier—starts addressing the room, demonstrating some movements. Behind him, Ford leans toward Scotty. His mouth moves as he quietly says something to her I can't make out. She tenses. Looks at me.

I dip my chin, eyebrows raised.

Like I've just given her some kind of green light, her arm pulls back before snapping forward, landing a heavy blow to the side of Ford's face.

Then another.

And another.

Easily weighing forty pounds more than her, he does nothing to stop her, fight back, or move.

Ford stands and takes the hits like he deserves them.

A wave of hushed mumbles sweeps through the crowd as we watch. The shocked trainer spins around, steps in front of Scotty and pushes her back. "Hey!" he snaps. "Hey! Cool it or you're out! You hear me?"

Scotty's chest rises and falls, her breath audible and face red.

"I'm done anyway," she says, not looking away from Ford.

The gym is silent as she undoes her gloves and drops them in the middle of the ring before slipping out between the ropes and taking long strides toward the door, picking up her duffle without even stopping.

I turn to follow her, and Camp grabs my arm, eyes pleading with a question he hasn't asked.

Big picture, big picture, big picture.

Dani, Jack, and a couple of the other coaches chuckle about Scotty's performance. "Hell hath no fury like a woman scorned," one of them says with a laugh.

I don't bother explaining the scorning. How Scotty's brother died and Ford took off like a thief in the night. There's no point.

Without saying a word, I snatch my arm from Camp's grip, grab my bag, and chase Scotty to the parking lot where I find her already at her Bronco, drinking her water in gulps.

I lean against my minivan, squint at the sinking sun, and let the silence hang. Each of us processing the level of crazy we just displayed.

"That escalated quickly," I finally say without looking at her.

She laughs under her breath. "I haven't seen him in years. It's like I couldn't control my reaction. Like my fists *needed* to pound his face."

Silence.

A car parks next to us, and a group of chattering teen boys get out and walk toward the gym, oblivious to the pissed off middle-aged women stewing next to them.

"If it makes you feel any better," I finally say, "I know the feeling. And I live with Camp."

She lets out another soft laugh, takes a long sip of her water, then looks at me.

"You gonna go all podcast on me and make me talk about it?" she asks, pulling the keys out of her bag.

"Me?" I bring a hand to my chest in feigned offense. "I would never."

In the driver's seats of our vehicles, we roll the windows down, angling our heads so we can see each other.

"What'd Ford say to you up there to turn you into a rabid dog?" I ask.

She drops the side of her head on her steering wheel. "He apologized."

I consider saying something funny, but the look on her face tells me she won't laugh, so I stay quiet.

"I listened to a podcast with an idiot from California that says it's okay to change our minds about things."

She snorts, sitting upright again and shifting the Bronco into reverse. "Let me know how that works out for you, Joo."

I tell myself I don't know what that means, but when I open my mouth to argue, she's already peeling out of the parking lot.

Twenty-Five

Instead of a set of prints in a leatherbound portfolio, I carry my laptop containing digital files to my latest meeting with Irma.

We sit around a raw-edged, wood slabbed table made by a local craftsman in the front of the gallery, computer open. I suck in a sharp breath and hold it as I click on the file titled *Landscapes*.

"There aren't many, but I went to different areas from last time. I think these will be more to your liking."

She eyes me over the top of her glasses as I click on the first thumbnail.

"You shot more landscapes," she mutters. "Too stubborn for your own good."

I force a smile, the four cups of coffee I had this morning seemingly hitting me all at once as my jittery fingers struggle to get the file open.

"Uhh . . . umm. Well . . ." As the files load, I clear my throat, pick at skin on a cuticle until it starts to bleed, then wipe it on my black slacks. "I thought maybe I gave you the wrong impression last time. Of my skills, I mean."

Her eyes narrow as the image fills the screen. Shot during golden hour, the hills of the Blue Ridge Mountains spread out for miles and miles into the horizon, orange glow filling the sky, painting green leaves yellow. I grin. It's perfect.

Irma looks at me over the black rim of her glasses, annoyed.

My grin flips and stomach plummets.

I click to the next one. A river. The next, a rock face. A waterfall. An empty dock on Lake Ledger.

With every click, her hard expression is steadfast, her silence deafening.

Finally, I can't take her disappointment.

"You can click," I mutter, leaving my position from next to her.

Click.

Click.

Click.

She stops, looks at me over the top of the computer, making me realize I'm pacing.

I still.

Swallow.

Smile weakly.

She clicks again.

"There's another file on here. *Nonsense.* What is it?"

She doesn't wait for me to answer before I hear a click.

I laugh softly. "Ah, those aren't anything. Just stuff I shoot for fun."

I'm behind her again, looking down at the computer over her shoulder. Despite my warning, the first image loads.

I barely gave these photos a glance when I got them. There was no point. The experimental rolls that Thor tried to eat, and the boys tried to cook, were just for me. Souped, scratched, and scorched. Rolls I shot with unorthodox angles and no regard for technical rules. Photos I made because it's what I like.

As the first image fills the screen, it's with an explosion of color. Lots of it.

The image is of a chain-link fence—the one from the baseball field—with sun flare shooting through the linked squares, bursting in the frame. The players are there, but because of the light and the focus, they are blurry blobs on the field. Layered over the image and the perfect golden rays, there's a bright pink drop dripping across the image. The film soup effect. The mess of motherhood overlapping days spent at a baseball field.

And together, it's all there. A photo and a tangible memory. An image that feels like life—like so many of my Today's Bests.

"Ah," she comments, knowing look covering her features as she moves to the next image. "Tell me about these, June Cannon."

I laugh at her use of my full name.

"Not much to tell," I say, looking at the screen. "The woman that owns the florist in town always puts her favorite flowers outside. These—I don't know what they are—were beautiful, but kind of lonely." In the photo, there's a large rack but one lone colorful bouquet. This one didn't get impacted by the souping, but the colors are nostalgic. An old love story. I shrug. "Anyway, I was just on a walk and . . ."

"It spoke to you," Irma finishes for me, almost amused.

I nod; she clicks to another image. It's a double exposure; the first image is the baseball team in the dugout, the second is the people in the stands—their families and friends. Same blobs of color distorting it just enough to make it interesting—make it art.

The next one, the kids playing at the lake, where I shot them from the ledge, making them look like ghosts.

"And this one? What does it make you feel?"

I think of the young mom crying. How lonely she felt. How beautiful the day and lake had been, but despite that beauty she—I—wept.

"Lost," I admit.

She looks at me, blinks several times, then returns her focus to the screen.

She continues, going through the images of every familiar aspect of my life—every detail that I've seen a million times: the little downtown, Life on the Ledge mural, the lake with the morning light dancing off the surface, Scotty's crematorium, a bar lined with beer at the brewery, the water tower. But they're different. Colorful. *More.* Reality but not. Nostalgic. Light leaks rip across some of the photos, sucking me in. It embarrasses me how much I feel every shot in every part of me. How I look at them and see something beautiful, knowing nobody else will.

My chest aches like I've had my heart broken. I love them so much it makes me sad.

She clicks through them all, pausing occasionally to look at me before going to the next one. Silent the entire time, glasses perched on the tip of her nose, she's unreadable. Stoic as she studies the screen.

Again, she pauses, and we look together. The wild card of every roll of film—the final frame. It's the one Lyra took of Camp and I at the picnic. His arm is around me; I'm leaning against him. His smile is big and lopsided, mine is easy. *Pretending*. Down the image, there's a streak of light, like a tail of a comet, then black covers a quarter of the screen. Final frames are just like that, never knowing what will show up or get left out. As if the camera gets to decide what matters.

"What do you feel when you look at these?" she asks, tone firm as she clicks to the next image.

I think of what Reed said. How the right photo would change me. Change the rhythm of my heartbeat, the organization of my DNA.

I study the screen. It's a shot of long shadows, stretched in the afternoon light. Waves of color from souping mix with stretched lines. My hand holding Ty's, his holding Hank's, his holding Lyra's. The four of us standing in the middle of the sidewalk after a walk. It was a warm day; the ants were hungry little bastards when we went to the park. Hank got a skinned knee, Lyra mostly ignored us listening to music in her earbuds, only pulling them out to ask what was for dinner. We aren't in the picture—no faces or feet or hands—but the shadows are there. Us in the frame—there but not.

"Life," I finally say, fizziness popping in my veins. "I feel life when I look at these. It's messy, imperfect . . . faded even. It's how you might feel at the end of the day. The best days and the worst ones, all blurred together. And even though the colors are too loud in some of them—out of place almost—that's also life. Expectations not matching reality. Love and little details."

She nods, thoughtful, pulling her glasses off her nose and letting them hang from the beaded chain around her neck.

She hates them. That's the only reason why she would be such a statue.

"But, you know, this file is just-just-just nothing. Experimental. *Nonsense*. I mean, you should have seen the dog. And my kids! Obviously not as polished as the—"

"Enough!" She holds up a hand. "Dear Lord, don't argue yourself out of your passion, June. They are perfect if you'll let them be. Artists have such a way of ruining a good thing. I knew a writer once who did the same damn thing." She chuckles, shaking her head. "They are *good*. You should be proud. You weren't made to photograph waterfalls and desert vistas; you were made for this." She taps the screen with her fingertip. "For life. For messy. I felt every image. Tasted the ice cream, felt the warmth of the sun"—she presses the back arrow a couple times, stopping at an image—"and every shot of this subject?" She raises her eyebrows.

I'm dizzy at her words. Faint even. I open and close my mouth—twice—no word seeming good enough to say. Because Irma freaking London likes my photos, *my* photos, and my dream isn't lost. It's different, not gone. And the face on the screen . . .

A motorcycle rumbles through the open door, signaling Reed's arrival as he parks his bike.

"Thank you, Irma." I look back at the screen. "Seriously."

She smiles, lifting a piece of paper off the table.

"We're having a gallery show," she says at the same time Reed walks through the open doorway, easy smile on his face as he strolls to where we're sitting. "I want you in it. It's only two weeks away, but"—she hands me a business card for Piedmont Printers—"you tell them I sent you; they'll get it done."

"A gallery show?" I ask, stunned.

Her eyes narrow as she huffs a breath. "Can you not hear things the first time? I said a gallery show," she snips. "Can you handle it?"

Reed leans over Irma, his intoxicating scent invading my senses as he starts scrolling through the images on my computer. I nod, dumb from the surrealness of what's happening. "Yes, of course. Right. Sorry. I can handle it."

"These are good, June," Reed says, looking over his shoulder at me between frames and clicks. "Damn good. You soup these?"

I think of Hank and Ty literally declaring *soup!* when I found them in the kitchen and a laugh puffs out of me. "Yes."

"Raw but happy." He stops on an image of Camp—the same one Irma stopped on earlier. "Well, maybe not this one."

"Why not that one?" Irma asks.

Reed looks at me, eyebrow cocked.

My face heats. "That's my husband."

"And an ass," Reed chimes in, amused smile tugging at his lips.

"Ah. Well, a good photo—a real one—never tells a lie."

"You're always here," I say to Reed, both of us leaning against my minivan parked on the street. "What's the deal? How do you know Irma?"

It's sunny; the light makes his eyes so bright and flecked in shades of blue it's hard not to get lost in them.

He looks away, rubbing his forehead, as if deciding how to answer. Or if he will.

He lets out a heavy exhale. "She knew my dad."

I pause, consider her album of photos.

"Like . . . *knew* your dad?" I ask, eyes wide.

He snorts a laugh, and it's an answer without words. They were lovers. It explains how she ended up in Ledger.

I have so many more questions, but all I can manage is: "Whoa."

I glance toward the gallery. Through the windows, Irma adjusts frames on the wall then stops to talk to a customer, laughing as she points to the wall and sweeps a hand through her short hair. "What happened? Your mom . . . ?"

"Knew," he fills in. "She loved my dad enough to accept he had fallen in love with Irma. It was . . . weird." He laughs softly at the shocked expression on my face.

"When?"

"Hmm." He lifts his scruff-covered chin toward the sky, thinking. "Maybe fifteen years ago. They met—my dad was a writer, you know?" The words Irma had used, *I knew a writer once,* flutter through me. "Anyway, they met on some assignment. He was writing, she was shooting." He shrugs. "I was pissed for a while; my mom was hurt. But now, I've been in and out of love, I get it. We can't always control it. Who we love, who we quit. When it happens, what we tolerate. Kinda like a photo, you know? We can shoot with a vision, but ultimately, we're at the mercy of everything cooperating with us. Light, movement, space . . ." His voice trails off, eyes to the sky for a beat before continuing. "Anyway, I wanted to meet her. So, one day, I did. I was doing a stint in California; she came to a local gallery. I showed up, introduced myself, and became . . . friends."

"Friends?" I ask, skeptical.

He laughs. "Yes, June, *friends.* I'm not *that* bad."

I look at him, unable to pull my eyes away. Casual grey T-shirt molded to his chest, jeans slung low, lips always on the brink of a smile, saying the words I didn't know a man knew how to articulate. New. Mysterious. Everything that Camp isn't.

"June Cannon, I think you're staring at me," he teases.

Heat envelops my skin, and I blink away, laughing slightly. "You're just . . . different. I don't know. Different." I brave eye contact, redirecting the conversation. "So your dad loved Irma, Irma loved your dad. Then what?"

He scrubs a hand across his jaw. "When he died, my mom was sitting next to him."

I nod. Not seeing the full picture but seeing enough of it.

"You have time for a coffee?" he asks.

Yes. I want to say yes. Desperately. I want to sit with Reed and listen to his smooth voice tell me stories of the last twenty-two years of his life and ask me questions that make me feel like I matter. I slip out my phone, check the time; I have two hours until I have to get the boys. That's plenty of time to get lost in all of him.

Yet, when I open my mouth to agree, I hear myself say, "I can't." Then, "Kids."

And though Reed smiles, his eyes say something else. That he sees my lie.

With a knuckled tap on the roof of the van, he steps away. "Well, I guess I'll see you when you claim your space in the gallery."

When I nod, he strolls away, leaving regret-filled knots in my belly the entire drive home.

Twenty-six

Mave and Dustin Cannon are the most enthusiastic wavers I've ever met.

They're always waiting when we arrive, like they have tracking devices on us, waving on the front porch as we come into view. Arms overhead, palms wide, it's nearly a fitness routine. When we leave, it's the same—waving until we disappear.

Today is no different.

As Camp parks the minivan, their smiles are wide and waves in full force from the porch.

"Mama!" Camp says with a big smile and open arms as he closes the door to the minivan and walks to his mom.

"You've been a stranger, Camp Cannon," she says without heat, walking down the steps and giving her son a hug. "Think you can build some fancy athletic center and leave your mama and daddy in the dust?"

He laughs, palm to his chest. "I would never."

Camp's parents live on a ten-acre farm on the edge of Ledger, which they bought right after we purchased the house from them. The property is beautiful with a small established orchard, rock-bottom creek, and open fields that back up to thick woods. And while Ledger isn't a fancy place, land is expensive. Dustin was a lineman for the electric company, and Mave worked at the post office—prices what they are, it's hard to believe they were able to afford such a perfect slice of paradise. The definition of blue collar, and they made it work.

The year they bought it, Dustin and Camp didn't talk for months. Camp never told me why—just said his dad was a "royal pain in my ass"—but eventually, it worked itself out, and they are as close to best friends as a dad and son can be.

The home on the property is a small ranch of white wood siding and black shutters with a large wraparound porch. In the backyard there's a chicken coop, a couple goats, and a huge garden filled with flowers and vegetables.

While Dustin is mostly quiet and reserved, Mave's a boisterous kind of woman whose face only knows how to smile. She loves flannel, wearing a candy-apple red one today that brightens her already rosy cheeks, and her blonde-white hair hangs down her back in a loose braid under a wide straw hat.

She loves to bake—cookies especially—and often jokes she only does it to lick the batter off the spoon. She also loves to host the kinds of parties that involve friends coming over, drinking wine, and feature a guest that's selling something. "*When you shop from someone's living room, how can it be a bad deal?*" she always asks.

In high school, more than once I was visiting while women pored over plastic containers, make-up, or some other kind of product that I just had to *see it to believe it.*

"You look pretty, Junie!" Mave says, token smile on her face as she wraps her arms around me, her vanilla scent hugging me as much as her body.

I smile. "I wore a clean shirt, just for you, Mave."

She chuckles, brown eyes twinkling as she squeezes my arms and pulls away. "We forget how big of a difference that makes sometimes."

Dustin gives me a hug, smelling like hay from the goats and smoke from the cigarettes he sneaks in the barn that everybody knows about but pretends they don't. Lines carve into his face as he smiles. "This guy taking care of you alright, June?" he asks in a molasses-thick southern drawl.

I look at Camp, who returns his smile easily—like we haven't been avoiding each other like the plague since that night on the porch and the boxing that followed—then to his dad. "Debatable."

"Now, Daddy," Camp interjects, matching his dad's drawl. "J here loves to pretend all kinds of things, don't ya, darlin'? Hard to know what she thinks some days."

Sonofabitch.

Like his parents aren't standing there, we glare at each other.

A shrieked, "Nan!" cuts the air as the boys attack Mave in hugs, and I blink away from him, silence hanging between us in an awkward kind of way.

Dustin looks from me to Camp before letting out a small grunt and greeting Lyra. "Now what kind of hair we got today, young lady?"

Lyra laughs as they stroll toward the house, Camp and I trailing behind.

"You had fun the other night."

My head whips toward him.

"On the porch," he adds, bending over to snap a piece of the calf-high grass we're walking through and slipping it between his lips. "That was fun."

I say nothing, irritated as I watch the grass bobble on his lips as his mouth moves.

"And then I got a call for work, and you shut down."

"What is this?" I demand. "You're talking about this *now*?"

"I've always loved you more than baseball."

Camp's words are as direct as they are shocking, and they steal the breath right out of my lungs.

"But when Dani called," he continues, green blade dancing, "you just shut down. Ran. And, you have to know, J, it's my job. I have to work. But I'm tryin' here. And—"

"Stop. Whatever this is, stop." I look around at the beautiful property, the laughing kids as they climb the steps of the porch. Too juxtaposed to the anger I'm feeling to make sense. I don't know if I want to cry or scream. "It's too late, Camp. You choose work. Always. Every damn time. And, I get it, you've been home for dinner for a few weeks. But I just want you to pick me—us—because it's what you want. Not because it's what I'm asking. Just-just-just . . ." I stop, his eyes searching mine. "God!" I shout, louder than I intend, both of us looking toward his parents, satisfied when we don't see a reaction. I take a breath. "Let's not do this."

"Fine."

"Fine."

"But"—my head drops back with a groan as he continues—"you need to know, you don't know everythin', J, and one of these days you're gonna have to stop bein' so damn stubborn."

When my jaw drops, he jogs to the porch.

"Tell me what's new, Junie," Mave says, setting a plate of sugar cookies on the frosted-glass patio table.

"Hmm. You know, same ol'," I tell her, pouring us each a glass of rosé before I drop into a seat. The smell of warming charcoal fills the air as I take my first sip, the wine bringing my tastebuds to life with its crisp sweetness and warming my throat as I swallow.

She takes a seat next to me and adjusts her straw hat. My gaze wanders until I find Camp. He's with Dustin and the kids at the chicken coop, throwing handfuls of cracked corn into the grass as they laugh.

"What about you?" I ask, grabbing a cookie from the plate and taking a bite.

"Just the usual—Oh!" Her relaxed smile turns to a wide-eyed look of excitement as she waves her hands through the air. "I'm hosting a sex party."

I choke on my cookie.

"I know!" She giggles, and a rooster crows in the background. "I'm so progressive. You should have seen Dustin's face when I brought it up." She wriggles her eyebrows. "I think he's excited. But Donna Rollerson sells it, do you remember her?"

"The minister's wife?" I ask, incredulous.

Mave's eyebrows raise. "That's the one. Anyway, she got into selling the goods—only to married people to align with her husband's preaching—but she does singles parties behind his back."

She smiles with wide eyes, like, *can you believe this hot piece of gossip?*

I nod, dumb. "That's great," I say, though I can't wrap my brain around any of this. Donna Rollerson trafficking dildos and God knows what else to the women of Ledger, all of which probably know how to masturbate and have deliberately been keeping that secret from me. I'm both shocked and annoyed by this information.

Her gaze is steady, watching me over the rim of her glass as she takes a sip of wine and punctuates it with a dramatic *ahh*. She's not my mother, but I've known her long enough to read her as well as she reads me.

I frown.

"Camp told you."

"Whatever do you mean, Junie?" she asks, too sweet to be convincing.

My nostrils flare.

"Are you two having sex?"

I answer her question by way of drinking my entire glass of wine, refilling it to the brim, and drinking as much of the fresh glass as it takes to make my throat feel like it's been lit on fire.

"I'll take that as a no."

I scoff.

"I warned you about this," she presses, pursing her lips and making my eyes roll. "When you got pregnant, I said, 'Junie, people are going to warn you about diaper rashes and all the ridiculous rules around car seats, but nobody ever tells you about the rest. The part where you focus on them and forget about yourself and the other parent. Don't let yourself run ragged for the sake of everyone else and forget about your husband.'" Her face makes a kind of told-you-so look, and I consider throwing my wineglass at her. "Do you remember that?"

She doesn't pause long enough for me to answer.

"And now here we are. You didn't listen. And now I'll say it all again: When a man and woman stop having physical connections, there's too much tension for anything else to work!"

"Oh, really?" I ask, rosé-pissed-off enough to speak my mind. "Camp gets to live his best life—anywhere but at home—and I'm supposed to, what? Just roam around the house naked until he decides to show up? Pretend nothing else matters?" She opens her mouth to say something, but this time I keep talking, louder still.

"And, what about him forgetting about *me*, Mave? How about that piece? Where's that damn pep talk?"

I chug the rest of my wine. She studies me, her eyes moving like she's working out some kind of mathematical equation in her head. A squeal from across the yard floats toward us and I look at the kids then watch Camp across the yard, knocking on a fence post while his dad chuckles next to him. When his eyes hook with mine, they hold a beat before he looks away.

He wasn't wrong, I have been avoiding him since the night on the porch. I didn't tell him about my photos. About Irma's approval or the show. Not knowing what to say, my current plan is to remain silent. Forever.

Mave and I sit, the tension between us calming as we watch the kids play, Hank riding Ty like a cowboy.

"Camp's a lot like his dad." She sets her glass down, and her expression is softer than it had been. "He never wanted me to worry. Just did things without talking about them."

I scoff. "Sounds familiar."

"Before I went to work as a mail lady, I found out Dustin had been working two jobs. That proud sonofabitch." My eyes widen at the same time she shakes her head with a chuckle. "He worked for the electric company; we didn't have a lot of extras. Camp wanted to play on some fancy, travel baseball team, and it was expensive. I needed a new car." She shrugs, shakes her head. "He said he was playing poker with friends every Friday—which, I can be honest now, I wanted to kill him for. We didn't have money for poker!" A smile pulls at her lips as she relives days gone by. "Anyway, I found out he picked up a shift doing night maintenance and janitorial work at the old bottle factory on the edge of town. Dustin spent Friday nights cleaning toilets so we wouldn't have to do without."

The look on her face is filled with so much love and adoration, it instantly makes me . . . pissed. Because, though Dustin may have made these quiet sacrifices, based on the clay-covered cleats I'm constantly picking up, Camp has not.

She shakes her head, patting my knee. "Either way, they're a proud bunch. I know you're frustrated—and I can't say I blame you—but you should know, June, with these men, they work hard but love harder. I'd bet money Camp has his reasons. A method to his madness."

I rub a hand across my forehead, pulse quickening at what she's implying. *He's right, I'm wrong.*

"Everything that happens in our house is so one-sided, Mave. Camp has lived his dreams—*lives* them. He played baseball. *Plays* baseball. Helped design a whole damn complex! And I've done nothing. Nothing! And-and-and he can't even be bothered to come home unless I tell him it's over?" I scoff. "It's not about money. We're fine. He bought that stupid house without even talking to me!" Her expression falters and I wince. "Sorry," I mumble, letting out a heavy sigh. "I just—he's not a partner! I sacrifice, he doesn't know the word. He's not working another job, he's just . . . gone."

I close my eyes and drop my head back on my chair as hers scrapes across the stones of the patio. Muck boots shuffle until the sliding glass door into their house opens then closes a minute later.

"Here," she says, handing me a thick manila envelope as she returns to her seat. "Take a look, when you have time. It might help."

"Please tell me this isn't something sex party-related," I say dryly as I start to pry open the metal clasp.

Camp and his dad make their way toward us across the yard, and Mave's hand grabs my arm. "Not now."

My eyes meet hers, trying to read what she's not saying. Her expression gives nothing away, but I relent, dropping the envelope into my purse along with the conversation. Me complaining only to have her defend her son will get us nowhere.

"Mama, come look!" Hank calls from across the yard.

Wine in hand, I tilt my head in an invitation for Mave to join me. She smiles. When I stand, she does too. Our quiet truce.

"So, Mave," I say, stepping into the grass. "Tell me about this ridiculous party."

She giggles. "I knew you'd ask!" She wiggles her fingers in the air, eyes sparkling as we start to walk. "Donna was telling me about these beads that people put up their bottoms. And—"

"Mave!" I shout, twisting my face in shocked disgust.

"Don't *Mave* me, Junie. She also has these oils"—she takes a hefty sip of her wine—"now wait until you hear this!"

As she tells me every kinky thing she's never known about, as weird as it is, I spend the rest of the afternoon laughing.

Twenty-Seven

After lunch, after the laughing over Mave's sex party, and in the quiet of the drive home, I decide I hate everyone and everything.

It's not menstrual—I checked the calendar—it's Camp.

It's pretending to be happy but not knowing what's real or not. Our whole arrangement is turning me into a crazy person. A lunatic one meltdown away from a padded cell.

It's the tone everyone uses. Like I'm irrational for wanting a partner. A. Partner. I don't want him to do it all, I just want him to help. To *want* to help.

It's Mave, defending him like he's some kind of heroic war veteran.

I was polite for lunch, but now that I'm home, fury wraps around me like shrink-wrap and makes me lash out like a child.

I stomp.

Slam cabinets.

Snap at the kids.

Glare at the dog.

And Camp?

Camp I want to shove into Scotty's cremator and watch him burn to ashes.

When Lyra leaves to meet friends at the coffee shop, I take a shower, failing to scrub the idea of him off my skin.

Instead, I find myself replaying Mave's words, rolling my eyes, and muttering, "they work hard but love harder," and gagging at the sentiment.

In the bedroom, wrapped in a towel, I could climb the walls.

"You ready to talk?" Camp asks, startling me with his presence as he closes the bedroom door.

I scoff.

"Otherwise we're gonna have to replace all the doors you're slammin'."

I ignore him.

"I'm tryin' here, J. Like hell. My schedule can't just change in a blink. I'm workin' on it—so it does get better. It *will*. But you can't just not tell me somethin's wrong for years then drop it on me and expect it to get better in an instant."

"How?" I snap, gripping the knot of my towel with one hand. "You know what—don't tell me. Like you always do, don't tell me and just surprise me with some big decision that I have no say in. Your mom seems to be just fine with that!"

"Jungle Rules," he says, stepping toward me.

My eyes narrow. "What?"

"Jungle Rules. We did it when I played for the Copperheads in Charlotte. When the players got restless with the coaches, they called Jungle Rules, and we could say whatever we wanted—air our grievances—without repercussions."

"No!" I snap. "I'm not playing some stupid baseball game."

"So you'd rather stomp around like a damn lunatic?"

My chest rises and falls in sharp breaths. I nearly grind my teeth to dust as I glare at him.

"I hate your mustache," I blurt.

His eyes widen as he touches his upper lip with his finger. "*What*?"

"You heard me. And I think your barefoot shoes are pretentious." He stills; I grip the knot holding my towel tighter in place, feeling a jolt of courage. "I hate that—that even though you're barely here, you're the fun parent, and the kids don't like me. Lyra always wants to talk to you. I hate that-that-that you act like a few weeks of you showing up fixes years of you not being here."

"I hate your meatloaf," he snaps, shoulders tense. "It's gross."

My jaw drops. "It's *what*?"

"And your music. It's depressin'."

"Excuse me, Norah Jones is iconic!" I argue, my eyes popping out of their sockets. "Coming from the guy who listens to music associated with dirt color, that's real rich, Camp."

"If you'd listen to the Joe Stamm Band, you'd get it!" he shouts, incredulous.

"You slurp your coffee—it's unnerving."

He gasps. "I hate how you drive. It's too slow."

"Oh!" I laugh a loud, cold *ha*. "Says the guy who turns off his truck at every damn red light!"

He steps closer to me, his face as furious as I've felt all day. "I hate your underwear."

"My underwear?"

"Yes," he snaps. "They fit like parachutes."

Asshole.

I grind my teeth.

"I hate you say yes to everyone but me."

He steps closer, and I step back, eyes not leaving his.

"I hate that you smile at Reed Simmons."

I still, shallow breaths puffing through my anger. "I hate that Dani smiles at *you*."

"I hate how bad I want to touch you."

"I hate that you got me off in the shower."

With that, the look in his eyes starts to burn with the heat of a blue flame, and my traitorous bitch of a body matches it.

A step forward.

A step back.

Our dance until my back hits the wall.

Nowhere to escape him, rage fuels the rhythm of my heart.

"I hate that I can't kiss you."

My nostrils flare. "I hate that you *ever* kissed me."

"I hate that towel."

His voice is lower now, and his jaw clenches so severely I expect to see bone pop through skin.

Palm to his chest, I shove with a grunt. He doesn't budge. I grip the knot of my towel, push my toes into the hardwood floor, unable to move anywhere except sliding inches up the wall.

He steps forward, fully pushing the front of him against the front of me.

And I feel it.

There.

Him.

Hard.

His eyes drop to my mouth as his hips pin me to the wall . . . and rock.

"And I hate that you do this to me."

I shove into his chest.

Again.

He goes nowhere.

Again.

"I hate that you do *nothing* to me."

He smirks; I squirm.

Without warning—without permission—Camp puts his mouth on mine.

We still—his mustache-covered lip scratching against mine.

He pulls back.

I push into him with another grunt. "*Nothing.*"

The intensity of his gaze seems to generate an actual temperature.

He pulls his hand from the wall, slips it into the opening of my towel, and traces the bare-skinned line over my hip.

To my inner thigh.

Up.

Fingers between my legs, he knows my lie. Feels it on his fingertips. The truth serum of my body that's currently betraying me.

"Nothin'?" he asks, word drawling like sandpaper across my skin, gaze steady, fingers moving.

Swirling.

Toying.

I shake my head, less convincing as my hips buck against his hand, needy and greedy.

He kisses me again, borderline aggressive, only to pull back fast.

"Nothin'?" he repeats, his face less than an inch from mine.

I shake my head, but the lie feels as heavy as my eyelids.

His fingers slip inside me. Hook. Move.

"Nothing," I grit out, more breathy than combative.

His tongue drags down my neck. Down the divot between my collarbones. Across the knuckles of my fingers gripping the towel. And, sweeping the towel open as he lowers himself to his knees, to the spot above my belly button. Sucking, biting, licking every inch of my body's real estate.

All the while: His. Fingers. Keep. Working.

Orgasm building, I fight it. I refuse. I will not let this feel good. But, dammit, I'm so close I can feel a scream building in my toes.

His mouth on my inner thigh, pushing me closer with the way his lips, tongue, and mustache drag against my skin and match the evil rhythm of his hand.

My teeth clench. "Camp, I—"

"Daddy." Hank's squeaky voice comes at the same time he pushes the door open. My hands slap over my own mouth.

Camp must have superhuman reflexes because his free hand shoots out, preventing the door from opening more than inches.

"Daddy? Why are you on the floor?" Hank asks through the crack of the opening, my eyes widening in horror.

Camp's fingers slow but don't stop. "Fixin' an outlet. What's up?"

"Can you come play?" Hank asks, oblivious where he stands in the hall that the *outlet* Daddy is fixing is the spot right between my thighs.

"Later." Camp's eyes go from the crack in the door to lock with mine. Which are watering. Because he won't stop moving his blessed fingers. "Y'all play on your tablets."

"Yeah!" Hank yells as he runs away from our bedroom. "Ty! We can play on our tablets!"

Camp pushes the door shut; I'm panting.

Like our kid wasn't just here, his tongue is back on my inner thigh. "Camp, please," I hiss. He kisses the spot his fingers have been so skillfully torturing. His tongue as warm and wet as I am.

"Dammit, Camp," I grit out, dropping my hands to his head and running my fingers through his hair. I hate how hard it is to breathe. How good every single touch he gives me feels. That his mouth can unravel me like a thread.

He pulls back—slightly—his chin and lower lip not moving from my most sensitive spot. He looks up at me, lids heavy, and slips both his hands around the backs of my thighs.

"Nothin'?" He smirks and it's hot and I hate him.

And when I don't argue, it's like it's what he was waiting for.

He bites; I choke. Then he grips the towel I'm only barely holding onto and yanks it off, rendering me naked.

In the daylight.

In a forty-year-old body.

His hand leaves the spot it's been working, earning another whimper from my lips, and his mouth travels up.

Across my lived-in belly.

Around my soft chest.

Up the side of my neck.

When he's standing again, he kisses me.

As much as I know I shouldn't—I let him. I kiss him back, letting myself love the way his lips and tongue and stupid mustache feel against me. Letting myself remember the familiar flavor of me and him.

I claw at his shirt, peeling it over his head, revealing his body.

His unchanged perfection amplifies my own self-consciousness. I shrink.

With one arm, I cover my breasts—the ones that changed with more pregnancies than babies—and suck in my belly.

He sees my insecurity and pulls my hands away.

"I hate how good you look," I whisper as he cups my face.

"I hate that I've let you believe you *don't* look good," he says.

We stare, breaths falling into sync with one another.

"Is this pretend?" I ask, needing to know. Needing him to tell me one way or the other.

"You tell me."

And then, before I can say anything, my husband kisses me—deep—like he's trying to drown in the entirety of me. Of us. And I kiss him back. Not forced. Not out of habit or obligation or pretending I'm happy. I kiss Camp Cannon like the feeling of his tongue on mine is the only thing I'll ever need in this life.

His hands drop from my face.

To my neck.

My chest.

His thumbs brushing across my nipples then drop to the curve of my waist.

When his hands drop to my hips, he guides me—naked—across the room with his mouth fused to mine.

We drop to the bed—the one we haven't slept in together in weeks. I'm on my back, he's between my legs.

Every move we make—our mouths, our hands, our hips, our breaths—is carnal. Frantic. Heated. Chasing the same glorious thing.

My hands fumble down his chest, his slight dusting of hair tickling my fingertips, until I'm in his pants and the warmth of his flesh fills my palm. So hard my mouth waters.

He swears against my skin.

My hips lift from the bed, legs hook around his waist.

"I've missed you, J. *This*." He kisses a line across my jaw.

Maybe it's the pending orgasm or maybe it's the realization that I've missed this too—him—but a lump forms in my throat, making it impossible for me to respond.

I nod, blinking back tears, and he moves to stand. Thumbs in his waistband, he—

"Dad!" Ty shouts. "Wi-Fi's not working!" Our eyes fly to the doorway, where he's standing, door wide open, nose scrunched as he stares at his tablet and pounds an angry finger on the screen.

I do the only thing I can think of: I scream. *Loud.*

Ty's head jerks up.

I scramble crawl across the bed—naked—until I land on the floor with a *thud,* hiding myself with the bed.

He tilts his four-year-old head to the side. "What are you doing?"

"Mom's sick," Camp says, covering his mouth with a fist with one hand and adjusting the situation in his pants with the other.

"Where are your clothes?"

"In the washer," I say at the same time Camp says, "She lost them."

I shove my palms so hard into my eyes I see stars.

SHIT!

Instead of attempting to salvage any piece of my dignity, I lie down on the floor. Out of sight.

A real-life *Naked and Afraid*.

"C'mon, Ty," Camp says. "Let's go to the livin' room and see if we can get the Wi-Fi fixed before I head out."

My head pops up. "Head out?"

Camp stops in the doorway, shirt slipping down his torso as he gestures for Ty to go ahead. "Yeah, sorry. I thought I told you. These next few weeks are goin' to be crazy." He leans against the doorjamb. "Short meetin' this afternoon to get everythin' planned out and outline the week. The damn ceremony comes with a million fires to put out . . ." His voice trails off, lost in thought.

I nod, pulling a blanket off the bed to wrap around myself as I stand.

"Right. That makes sense."

It makes sense, yet a pit forms in my stomach. Because it's Sunday afternoon, and he's leaving. The complex is a huge deal and so important, but also . . . that's been the story of our lives these last years. *Everything* is important. Everything except me.

"Hey"—he crosses the room to where I'm standing, lost in doubts, and lifts my chin with his knuckles—"I'll just be an hour or so. And I want to finish what we started."

He kisses my forehead. I bite my cheek to hide my smile.

"Okay."

"Dad!" Ty shouts from the living room.

"Go," I tell him. "I have to find my *lost clothes* anyway."

He kisses me again, then he's gone.

For dinner, I make meatloaf—a new recipe—grinning like an idiot the entire time I cook.

Right until I clear the last dish off the table, including Camp's empty one because he didn't make it home. Instead, a text: *sorry it's a madhouse running behind tournament schedules are a beast and lights aren't working in an entire hallway what a headache*

I put his leftover plate in the fridge and make his bed on the floor.

When he comes in, late, he whispers my name. I pretend not to hear.

I also pretend not to be crying.

Twenty-eight

The only person I tell about the gallery show is Scotty. After Camp left me naked in a blanket and forgot to come home for four hours last week, "Come to my gallery show" were the last words I wanted to say to him.

And with the kids, it's a complex tapestry of excuses. I want them to see me trying something new—set the example that there's a way to be brave at any age—but I also can't bear the idea of failing in front of them. I can't compare to Camp—to a dad that played major league baseball and is the unofficial prince of the town. A few photographs in a small gallery in a small town seems so . . . small. If I'm good enough—if I don't get laughed out of Ledger—I'll tell them. I'll show them the work I made. The work they unknowingly made with me.

Scotty helps dress me: my new jeans, her expensive heels, my black top, her purple blazer. Her style and mine, a collaboration of us.

At the gallery, through the propped-open door, to the small section that contains my collection of twenty canvases, all exploding with unexpected color, I pause. Take it in. Feel it swirl and swell, in my palms, my throat, the space between my shoulder blades, and my knees. Pride.

"They fit together," Irma says stepping next to me, radiant in a red, flowy top.

I nod. "They do. And I like the name."

"Ah," she says, looking at the same placard I am, LOVE AND LITTLE DETAILS written across it. "Seemed fitting." She smiles, squeezes my arm. "Now, get some champagne. First people are arriving. Try to have fun with it, June Cannon. Take the compliments. Pose for the pictures. Let your family gush over you." She runs her fingers through her short hair. "It's the only way these stuffy things are fun."

With a laugh, she's gone, greeting the guests, leaving me with my photos and a split-second regret of wishing there would be family to gush over me.

"You're making us look bad, June," a smooth voice says. *Reed.*

I laugh with a shake of my head. Taking him in. Clothes tailored to his body. A suit sans the tie. Eyes swallowing me whole. Too sexy to be fair. The sight of Reed Simmons nearly knocks the wind out of me as he hands me a glass of champagne.

"You're a liar, Reed Simmons. But my photographs thank you."

"Ah." He lifts his chin, blue eyes calculated. "I didn't even notice those."

He's playing a game. A temporary Casanova in a small town, and I shouldn't let him—I'm married. But, for a night I'm in sexy heels and wearing make-up in front of art I created. Nobody screaming mom. No dog drooling on my lap. No husband leaving me naked in the name of high school athletics.

"Careful, Reed." I tip my glass of champagne toward him. "That mouth of yours has been known to get us in trouble."

It's the closest I've come to flirting with someone other than Camp in twenty-five years and it tiptoes the line of completely wonderful and downright wrong.

He scrapes his teeth across his bottom lip, raking me over with his gaze before shaking his head with a breathy laugh that settles somewhere low in my belly.

I know in the seconds of our heated silence, the sexual tension pulling at every curve of my bones, this is how it starts. An affair. Someone sees another in a way nobody else does. Fills in the fractures that have spread across the surface, wedging their way in with bedroom eyes and fuck-me words. The need to be seen, feel wanted. An itch begging to be scratched, and someone willing to drag fingernails down the skin.

I blink away; we fall quiet. Staring at a photo of Lake Ledger.

Sun bright, amplified by a burst from a light leak, fatefully cutting the image in a way that interpretation decides if it's art or trash. I hadn't planned it to look this way—it was Hank. He yanked the camera out of my bag, asked, *What's this button do?* And, before I could respond, the back popped open, partially exposing the roll. Most were destroyed, but the ones that survived were magic.

"Reed," Irma calls from across the gallery, next to where WOMEN OF THE EARTH are on display, waving her hand through the air with an eager-faced couple beside her.

With a dip of his chin, he's gone, long strides across the room, and I down my champagne.

Like a floodgate opens, the people arrive. The small gallery fills, low music drowned out by conversations and laughter. Their faces are a mixture of tight-lipped almost-frowns of the highest echelon of art perusers to rosy-cheeked smiles of people just here for the wine. Most I know, some I don't.

What feels awkward at first turns into comfortable chaos. The first "How did you make this photo?" shocks me, but the dozenth time, the process rolls off my tongue.

The film soup.

The light leaks.

The prisms.

The tilt-shift lens.

And though the smile is on my face, it becomes my entire personality. Happy. Fulfilled. After seventeen years of being only one thing, proof that I can be more. A mom, *and*.

When I hear, "Look at this bitch, painting the sky in rainbows," it pulls a loud laugh right out of me.

Scotty walks up looking so perfectly her: Chocolate hair in sexy waves, Norah Jones shirt under a pink blazer, and a glass of champagne over her head as she shimmies through the crowd.

I wrap my arms around her, some of my own champagne spilling with our too-big movements. "You came!"

"Of course I came!" she cries, looking around. "This is badass, Joo."

She steps to a photo, one of long shadows on the baseball field. There are no faces, but it's easy to imagine them.

"Where's Camp? I bet he's losing his damn mind." She scans the crowd, bringing her glass to her lips.

"Right . . . I didn't tell him."

Her eyes widen. "The hell? Why not?"

The volume of her voice makes me flinch. "God, Scotty. Shhh!" I grab her arm, pulling her to me. "Because-because-because I don't know why. Because I'm mad at him. And-and-and because this isn't a big deal."

We both look around the room, jam-packed, and the dozen people huddled around my photos. Her look, a silent *this is a big fucking deal, you dumb bitch*, I dismiss with a wave of my hand.

"Since when are you Team Camp?" I ask, annoyance thumping against my sternum.

She scoffs, sliding her phone out of her pocket to take photos of my photos. "I'm team *you*, June. And, don't bite my head off, but I feel like you're looking at this all wrong. Has Camp dropped the ball the last few years? Abso-fucking-lutely. But you are so definitive. Like, you think the only way to make a change, to do all this"—she gestures around the room—"is by abandoning everything else. You're allowed to be more than one thing. Hell, you can be a dozen things if you want. A million! Just because you got knocked up doesn't mean you have to be a martyr. It's like you smothered part of yourself because you shit out a human or three."

She shrugs, takes a sip of her champagne. Nonchalant and arrogant as she snaps another picture.

"It's not that easy, Scott. It's . . ."

She waves my words away, pushing me to stand in front of my display, pointing the phone at me. I smile wide, bend a knee to point a toe midair, and hold my champagne over my head, resuming my annoyed stance when she's done.

"Complicated, I know," she finishes for me, hooking her arm through mine. "I'm just saying, life isn't black and white. There's so much color." She drops her head on my shoulder, facing a portrait of kids licking ice cream cones, covered in shades of pinks and blues. "And judging by these, you already know that."

I drop the side of my head against hers. "I hate how well you know me."

"I know you don't."

I snort a laugh then we fall quiet, sipping champagne among the murmur of voices and soft music playing as we stare at the wall in front of us.

"So. Ford Callahan."

She digs her elbow into my ribs. "For taking such good photos, you're kind of a bitch."

"I know I'm not," I mock, slipping my arm out of hers to face her. "But seriously, is your plan to hate him forever or what?"

"Depends," she says, raking her nails through her hair with one hand as she brings her glass to her lips with the other.

"On?"

"On if you're going to keep up this stupid charade with Camp."

I groan, annoyed with her typical deflective answer when it comes to anything about her, as a roar of laughter bubbles up from across the gallery. Both our gazes float to the source: A small group of people circled around Reed as he tells a story, animated with his hands. His eyes are so bright, even across the room in the low light they shine like two blue suns on his face.

"Oh, shit," Scotty says when recognition strikes. Reed nods in our direction, giving a slight wave without breaking the spell he's cast on the crowd around him.

"Mhm," I say with a mouth full of champagne.

She clinks her glass to mine. "Bet he has a huge dick."

When I choke, she cackles, then takes another photo.

Scotty leaves, the crowd thins, and, high on adrenaline or champagne or both, I check my phone for the first time all night.

My high plummets: twelve missed calls and eight unread texts.

Camp: *hank fell taking him to the hospital call me*

Camp: *At the hospital waiting for doc*

Camp: *J call me*

I don't read the rest, rushing toward the door, heart pounding, I dial Camp.

Hospital?

Hurt?

A million and one scenarios run through my mind within the seconds it takes for his phone to ring then go to voicemail.

Me: *On my way.*

"Irma, I have to go," I say, breathless as I cross the room. "My son—he's hurt or something."

Her eyes widen as she pulls the glasses from her face. "Go. Yes."

"I'm sorry. I'll come get these tomorrow. Or however this protocol is—I-I just—" Tears line my eyes, and panic constricts my throat as I fish through my bag for my keys.

She shakes her head. "No need. Someone bought them."

"What?" I ask, freezing for a split second with keys in hand.

"All of them. Go."

I nod, unable to compute what she's saying, and run.

Twenty-nine

"Hank. Honey, are you okay?" My heels click loudly across the tiled hospital floor as I hurry into his room. Breathless.

"I tried to hide in the kitchen cabinet with the wineglasses," he says with a small smile. His red hair sticks up in forty-two directions as his small body lays in a bed under a blue blanket. His face, so pale it's almost yellow, makes his freckles stand out like floating stars on his face. Across his forehead, eight stitches hold together an angry gash.

"Oh gosh, kid. I guess we never covered not crawling into wineglass cabinets in our list of house rules." I let out a relieved and watery laugh as I run my fingers gently through his hair.

I glance around the tiny hospital room. Ty and Lyra are on a sofa, blanket draped over them as they sleep, poster above them of a beach scene. Camp's in a chair, next to the bed, holding a picture book. *The Going to Bed Book* by Sandra Boynton. If I wasn't so terrified, I'd laugh—Hank's favorite.

Camp's jaw pops, shoulders tense—collar of his shirt smeared with blood—as he studies me, taking in my clothes, my face. The short attention I gave my reflection in the rearview mirror showed mascara that I rarely wear smudging under my eyes like a cracked-out raccoon.

"Camp, I'm so sorry—I had my phone on silent—I came as soon as I saw. I tried calling," I explain, keeping my voice low enough not to wake Ty and Lyra.

He nods, forearms resting on the hospital bed as he looks me over.

"I was with Scotty," I say, half lying. Hating myself for it. Looking down at my clothes, hers and mine, all of which feel ridiculous in the moment, and shrink into my own selfishness. I was in a gallery with photos—flirting with Reed—while Hank's head was being sliced open. And I know how these things are, an inch in either direction, and this could have been so much worse.

He nods, squeezing Hank's arm. "Hey, buddy, Mom and I are goin' to go in the hall and let you rest a few minutes. Doctor should be in real soon, and then we can go home."

Hank smiles, takes the book from him and starts flipping through the pages. Mouthing the words we all know by heart.

We click the door closed behind us and step into the hall. The lights are dim and buzz overhead. A couple nurses check clipboards and give courteous smiles as they walk by.

"God, Camp," I say with a heavy exhale, dropping my forehead to the wall, my body trembling. "I-I-I'm so sorry. I should have been there. I should have never gone out. I-I-I mean, thank God you were there. Or Lyra. Or someone." I'm crying now, fully. Sobs of relief, regret, and guilt. "I'm sorry. I know it's not enough, but—how could I do this? Like what kind of mother needs twelve missed calls?"

His palm finds my back, and it's an instant comfort. Making me cry harder. His grounding touch one I didn't know I needed.

He pulls me to him, familiar arms around me, rubbing circles across my back. Hushing softly into my ear until my sobs against his chest turn to hiccups then normal breaths.

I push away from him, wiping my eyes, laughing softly. "I look like a mess."

"You're beautiful."

I lean my forehead against his chest before snapping my head back. "Your face!"

He rubs a hand across his now-bare upper lip, color flushing his cheeks.

"Yeah." He clears his throat. "I thought a change would be good. Shut Jack up."

He's handsome, devastatingly so, as he holds me, shy look on his face.

I slip my arms around his waist, drop my cheek to his chest, and let the soothing sound of his pulse melt me into him.

"What did you and Scotty do?" he asks, depth of his voice vibrating from his body to mine.

"We went to the art gallery. They had a show." I keep my cheek pressed against him as my half-truth gnaws through me.

His chest rises and falls in our silence.

"You have fun?"

The answer is one that's too big and complex for words. I had fun . . . but Hank got hurt. I did something big . . . but he'll never know that. I loved being someone else . . . but missed all of this.

"I did," I finally say, thinking of Scotty's annoyingly perceptive, *You can be more than one thing, Joo.* "Maybe sometime we co—"

"Mr. and Mrs. Cannon?" The doctor approaches with a white coat and black hair. His friendly face smiles as he reaches for the handle to Hank's room. "Let's get you folks home."

With tight smiles and nods, we follow him into the room, all my unsaid words left in the hall.

Thirty

I TWIST THE FINAL section of Lyra's blue hair, slide the bobby pin out of my mouth, and pin it into place on top of her head. I meet her smile in the reflection of the mirror.

"Prom perfect."

Still in an oversized T-shirt and her face make-up free, she turns her head side to side to examine my work. "Prom perfect," she agrees.

It's a nothing moment, sitting in her bedroom. Just a Friday afternoon. Just another dance after years of them. But there's an enormity to it. Like gravity is amplified by a thousand and pulls down on me.

Because it's not nothing.

It's not just another dance.

It's her senior prom. Another reminder that our time together—her needing me—is fleeting.

She used to beg me to play with my hair and cover my face with ridiculous shades of pink make-up, and now I feel the swing of the pendulum approaching. I'll be begging her soon. Hell, maybe it's already happened, and I'm living in denial. Maybe she doesn't even need me right now. My eyes burn with the thought.

"Mom," she says, making me blink. "You have that look on your face."

I shake my head, meeting her eyes in the mirror. "What look?"

She snorts. "Like you're about to get weird and weepy."

I smack her arm playfully. "I would never."

She pulls her make-up out, sorting out various pencils and eye-shadow palettes. I could leave, let her do the rest on her own, but I can't. I'm glued to the edge of the bed, watching her transform from little girl to a woman right before my eyes.

"So," I finally say, "how are things with Nick?"

Her cheeks flush instantly. Since I caught them in her bedroom, his presence around our house has been almost professional. More than once, I've heard Lyra ask if he wanted to go study in her bedroom, and every single time he tells her he thinks our dining room table is more comfortable.

I dated a high school boy once; I know this is a bald-faced lie. But I admire the respect—and restraint.

She stills, the black eyeliner in her ring-covered fingers hovering just above her skin, and her eyes hook with mine in the mirror. "He's . . . umm . . ." She sets the eyeliner down, turns to look at me, face filling with something like fear. "I trust him. Not to hurt me. I trust him the way you trust Dad."

"Ah," I say with a slow nod, hearing the unspoken, *I trust him enough to have sex with him.*

I look out the window, branches of a newly blooming, pink crepe myrtle blowing softly in the breeze, and wish there were adequate words to get me through this conversation. As much as I want to scream *DON'T DO IT!* my mouth won't let it happen.

"It changes things," I tell her as she turns back to the mirror. "This . . . trust . . . it's a big deal. And it changes things. Makes saying goodbye harder." She moves to the other eye, dragging a thick, black line across her eyelid. "Just—you should know that. Before . . . the trust. And how to be safe about it. All of it."

She turns to face me, thick, cat-eyed lines covering both lids.

"I know, Mom." She shrugs. "But he's going to App State too. So we'll be just like you and Dad, you know?" She grins, and my heart feels like it's made of glass and being thrown on the floor. "No goodbyes required. I mean, look how happy you guys turned out. Loving to forever and back and all that mushy stuff."

"Right." I force a smile but can barely get a full breath. *Look how happy you guys turned out.* I stand, flustered. "I'll let you finish getting ready then. Your dad should be back from dropping the boys off at Nan's. I need to start getting ready. Just, if you need me—for anything—holler."

She nods, opening a compact of blush, flicking me a smile before coating a brush with pink powder.

"Mom?"

I turn from the doorway, pausing to look at her.

"Thanks."

Lyra's dress matches her hair, and as ridiculous as that sounds, as much as we will someday look at photos and laugh about this colorful hair phase she's in, she's stunning. When she comes out of her bedroom, I feel the enormity of it. Her in this moment. I've been so consumed with my own unravelling—my own dreams that slipped through the cracks—I forgot she's just stepping into her own.

Raising my camera to my eye, I capture her. Her smiling. Laughing. Rolling her eyes. Waving me away.

I've blinked, spent the years wishing for days to be easier, faster . . . and now here it is. Months shy of eighteen. Months shy of leaving me. The baby I never expected—never dreamed of ever having—as necessary to my survival as oxygen.

Blue hair, blue dress, beaming smile.

"Mom, stop crying," she says with a laugh when I pull the camera away from my face, revealing wet eyes.

Camp walks in, already dressed in his suit. With his freshly shaven face, I fight the urge to reach my fingers up and trace the lines of his skin and slopes of his lips. He's more handsome than the day we fell in love, two teenagers with bad skin and not a clue what love was. More handsome than the day he stepped on the pitcher's mound with a Copperheads jersey on his back, too cocky for his own good, me screaming from the sidelines. More handsome than the day we married, a random Tuesday between away games, me eight months pregnant, him holding my hands so tightly I thought my bones would break.

He gives me a lopsided grin before turning to Lyra, his expression morphing. He's just as awestruck and proud as I am.

I wipe my eyes, blink back the tears that I'll let fall the second she's gone, and busy myself straightening Camp's already straight tie. "Tell me the plan again," I say, just to have something to listen to. Just to make the moment last a little longer.

"I'm going to Kimber's and we're all riding together. We rented a limo. Well, her boyfriend's dad rented a limo—Dyllan." Kimber has a boyfriend; apparently the divorce didn't flip her sexuality as easily as she thought. "Then we're going to that place on the lake for dinner before all getting to prom. Yes—Nick too." She pauses, grins, then continues. "Anyway, then we'll be there. Which, I mean, it's kind of annoying prom and graduation have to be in the old gym when the brand-new, shiny one is sitting untouched, but I get it, nostalgia and all for you old farts." She laughs, sorting through her sequin-covered clutch.

Camp laughs. "We aren't that old. And it's the last big event there. Next year's kids get shiny new."

"Your claim to fame, Dad." She swats him playfully on the arm.

"And after?" I ask. "What's the plan after? No drinking, I hope. Or driving. Or drugs."

"Way to ruin my night," she deadpans.

"Jerk." I stick my tongue out at her, wrapping her in a hug. "I'm serious. I was seventeen once . . ."

"Stop talking," she says, slipping her shoes on—gold heels with an ankle strap. "I don't need to hear what you and Dad did when you were seventeen—I saw you on the porch the other night. That was enough damage. We are staying at Syd's family lake house for the weekend—with parents." She pauses, grins. "And I'm not a cliché."

While most proms happen on Saturdays, like everything else in Ledger, we have to do it differently. School is out for Friday and Monday, giving everyone a long weekend. Prom happens Friday, and she'll be at the lake until Monday. My mind reels with all the scenarios that could happen in those days apart.

"Ignore your mom. We trust you." Camp drapes an arm over my shoulder, smelling like him.

She laughs, stands tall at the door with arms out. "How do I look?"

My tears fall early, straight down my face in two steady rivers. A bigness forms in my chest that makes it so hard to breathe I wonder if I might die. All I can say: "Perfect."

Lyra used to do ballet, dancing in little tutus, sometimes falling before scrambling back up to twirl, tiny-toothed grin on her face the whole time. Now here she is. A woman in a gown. Stunning. My little girl gone, never coming back, replaced by this version of her. Shedding one skin just to reveal another.

Camp squeezes my shoulder. He's thinking what I'm thinking: *Look at the masterpiece we made.*

"Stop crying, Mom," Lyra says as she hugs me, not understanding how it feels to watch a piece of herself go off on their own.

To house parties where there will be boys and beer and bad ideas, praying they don't fuck it all up. Praying they make the right choice. Hear the right voice in their ear guiding them. Praying they know what they need to know to make it in a world that's so big and loud.

Praying. Praying. Praying.

"I'll drop you off at Kimber's on my way to the school," Camp says, pointing to his truck.

Too soon, she's out of my arms, and I'm wiping my eyes as she awkwardly teeters down the sidewalk in her heels.

"Love you!" I shout.

She laughs. "I'll see you in two hours, Mom."

Camp looks at me, grinning, pointing a thumb over his shoulder. "We did a lot wrong, J, but we got that one right."

I nod, wiping the last of my tears as I lean on the edge of the open door, watching her lift her dress as she gets into his truck. "We did."

My eyes meet Camp's, our history pulling like the tight stitches of a baseball, tying us together.

"See ya tonight, J."

"See ya tonight," I echo as my head drops to the edge of the door.

He strolls down the sidewalk, climbs into his old truck, and Lyra instantly laughs in the passenger seat at something he says—her hero—before they disappear down the street.

I sniff, pull out my phone and text Mave to make sure the boys haven't driven her crazy or sacrificed one of her pets, to which she responds, *These angels would never!* Followed by a photo of them baking cookies. Then another one: *Don't forget to take advantage of a kid-free house, if you know what I mean.*

I snort but slip my phone into my pocket without responding.

Heading to the bathroom to make myself look less cry puffed, I stop at a photo. A snapshot of us. The boys were babies, just shy of one, and Lyra is holding them both, smiling proud, as Camp's tongue hangs out of his mustached mouth as I cheese a smile.

I study him, tracing his lines with my finger.

Since Hank's accident, there's been a shift with us. Not intimate—no sex or kissing or touching or . . . *showering*. But an ease in our interactions. He's been home when he can be, and I've accepted he won't always be. Expect it.

But here's the belief I can't shake, the shadow that clings to everything that he does: It won't last. He chased his dream of being a baseball player until he couldn't. Then it was state championships. Now it's the sports complex. In just a week, it will be finished. The dedication gala will be here then gone. This year's baseball season will end in the following weeks, depending on how the state tournament goes.

In twenty-six days, Lyra will graduate, then it will be nothing. Just us. Just me. And I know, deep in my marrow, I won't be enough. Not for Camp Cannon. Not for the man that is both a dreamer *and* chaser.

And, even more, I can't shake the voice in my head that tells me if I let this be good enough, I'm holding myself back.

Not following through.

Not showing the kids I can be something bigger than they see.

I'll go down in history as a woman that picked up shoes and shuttled kids around in a minivan. I won't be the woman who worked to be appreciated. The woman who reinvented herself. The woman who demanded more.

In the bathroom, staring at the mirror, I splash water on my face.

Every podcast I've ever listened to seems to be blasting in my ears at full volume.

Is it fair that men get to chase their dreams while women don't? For every person sacrificing, there is someone that isn't. That never will. Reinvent yourself. Be someone different. We aren't making lasting changes if we cave the moment the skies start to clear. By caving, you are saying a little bit today is better than a lot forever. It's big picture vs. little details in these situations. Allow ourselves to reconsider. To move the lines in the sand. To change our minds. To pivot. There's an art to it.

I press my palms against my ears, trying to quiet all the noise. I can't think.

With another splash of water, I meet my own eyes.

A different voice comes into play—Irma's. "It seems you have a fan," she had said when I returned to the gallery the day after the show.

"Who?" I asked in disbelief, staring at the sold stickers that were tacked onto the placards of every single canvas.

She shrugged her slender shoulders, knowing smile tugging at her thin lips. "They want to remain anonymous."

Anonymous? I had thought. The word filled out, flattened, and stretched like bubbles in a lava lamp. Why would anyone pay thousands of dollars for photos I created? Not of perfect landscapes but of . . . life. Loud and colorful and messy snippets of life. Love and little details.

I've wracked my brain, but all I can think: Someone out there sees me. Whether they know it or not, them buying something I made, they know me. They see me in a way my kids don't, Camp doesn't . . . and now that I know that piece of me exists, I can't let it go. I refuse.

Scotty said I can be two things, but what I can't get past is how to be two things when Camp's things come first. Always. His dreams. His goals. His life I try to fit into.

And the kids . . . I know I'm to blame for that. For pouring myself into them and leaving no room for anything else. It was my survival mechanism, in a way. A way to heal—however misguided—from the hard parts in between. Whether I meant to or not, Scotty was right—damn her—between loss and heartache and sleepless nights, I became a martyr.

"Shut up," I shout to the voices in my head, making me feel even crazier.

I start the shower and let out a long breath as I reach my hand into the hot stream of water. These are tomorrow's worries. Tonight is for Lyra and for fun and for music too loud and punch served from bowls.

Peeling off my clothes, I step in, letting the water scald my skin, drown the noise.

Eyes closed, I open them, chuckling to myself as I look at the showerhead, knowing damn well I'll never look at that thing the same way. And I think of Camp, him in the shower with me, knowing exactly what my body needed even when I didn't.

Could I do it on my own? Does it make me some kind of sex-crazed maniac if I do it again?

It does, I decide.

But, as I slide the showerhead out of the holder, I also decide . . . I don't care.

Minutes later, I find out I don't need Camp for *everything*.

Though it's his hands and mouth I imagine the entire time.

Thirty-one

During my reinventive shopping spree, I splurged on a way-too-expensive, jewel-toned, green dress, and the fact I don't cringe at myself when I look in the mirror tells me it was money well spent. High in the neck, strappy across the back, and making my body look almost like it's never housed other humans, it's sexy in an "I'm forty with a kid here" kind of way.

In the parking lot of the gym, I check the minivan mirror. My bangs are softer now, swept to the side instead of boldly jagged across my forehead like a madwoman's scarlet letter. The rest of my hair is down in loose waves.

If Scotty were here, I have no doubt she would tell me I'm fucking hot.

I make my way toward the old gym. I've been here seemingly hundreds of times since I've graduated—roamed these halls volunteering to help with committees and events over the years—but this is the first prom I've returned to. The last one I attended being twenty-two years ago with me on Camp's arm, both of us crowned prom royalty. We were young, in love, and for a night, king and queen.

Outside, two colleagues of Camp's check tickets, and we exchange greetings as waves of music blast out at us every time the doors open and close.

I smooth my dress.

Take a breath.

Step inside.

And, though it's not my prom and the kids aren't my friends, it's like stepping through a wormhole.

A strobe light whips beams across the walls, floor, and ceiling of the old gym. After the committee selected the theme, "Kickin' It Old School," we took every detail back in time. Strips of '90s color-block fabric cover the walls and hide the pushed-in bleachers. Turquoise, pink, and black accents scatter across the place, taking me back.

On one wall, photos of events showcase all the proms before. Big-haired queens from the '80s, dapper group photos from the '50s. There are snapshots and articles on basketball games, community voting, and fundraisers. The entire history of Ledger summed up in printed rectangles of life in this gym.

The dresses have gotten shorter and the music worse, but it's a scene so familiar I taste it in my mouth. The quiet kids are on the sideline, sitting nervously next to dates they don't know how to talk to, as they watch their bolder counterparts who are already dancing with heads dropped back and arms over head. And, though it's just starting, a pile of abandoned heels and strappy sandals line the dance floor, half the girls already barefoot.

Including Lyra.

Scanning the room for Camp, my eyes catch hers as she dances with friends. I lift my hand in a wave, and she sticks her tongue out at me, hips shimmying.

"We did it, June," Lynn, Kimber's mom, says as she approaches with an exasperated smile and fitted floral dress. "Now to just survive tonight."

I laugh. "Hard part's over, Lynn. And look how much they love the photo booth." I point across the room at a line of kids waiting to get photos snapped with oversized '90s props. When I suggested it in one of the committee meetings, I got pushback that nobody would use it because everyone has a phone. I knew it would be a hit.

"Maybe all the stress was worth it." She reaches behind her head to pull her hair into a messy bun. "It's hot as hell in here."

"Teenage hormones," I say, pouring us two cups of punch. "They're a life force."

She chuckles, taking a cup from me.

"I hope it's spiked." She takes a sip, frowns. "Damn."

I laugh.

Lynn and I, along with other parents, spent hours upon hours planning tonight. From the decorations to the DJ to the invitations. In our hours together, I tried asking her about the divorce, but every time I chickened out. I either couldn't bring myself to say the word or didn't want to know the truth.

"Lyra told me about you and Dean. I'm so sorry."

She smiles in a way that makes her mouth frown shaped. Sad-like. "Yeah. Me too."

There's an awkward silence as we sip our punch and watch the kids dance.

"Marriage is hard, right?"

She cackles. "Damn hard. And Dean . . ." She shrugs. "We just grew up and grew into two different people, I guess. Like we live on separate planets. And"—she nudges me, eyebrows raised—"he stopped looking at me like that a long time ago."

I follow the direction of her gaze—eyes landing on Camp—at the same time she turns her attention to one of the supervising teachers that approaches and whispers something in her ear. "Alcohol in the parking lot," she says over her shoulder, downing her punch like a shot of whiskey before disappearing through the crowd and out the doors, two male teachers on her heels.

I laugh under my breath, but my eyes stay locked with Camp's as he strolls toward me.

"Mrs. Cannon. I'd say that dress is goin' to cause some problems now that these impressionable young men know what's hidin' under it."

My cheeks flush as a smirk angles across his face.

"Yes, well. It's the risk you take when you decide to wear an overpriced string up your ass out in public on any given school day."

He laughs under his breath, bumping his shoulder against mine. "You look beautiful, J."

Heat races up my neck, burning my ears and drying my mouth. I drink the entire cup of punch I'm holding. The darkness is a blessed thing for hiding every emotion my fair complexion can't.

"So," he says.

"So," I repeat.

"You here with anyone?"

I look at him.

"Are you here with anyone?" I echo, seemingly unable to form my own words.

His fingers interlace with mine, unexpected and abrupt. I stare at them, the lifelines of him and me having no clear beginning or end.

"I am," he says. "If she'll have me."

"She'll think about it," I say, coy, knowing he's just playing. Pretending.

He grins, squeezes my hand, and we're quiet as we look to the dance floor and the teens that fill it.

I can't decide if it was just yesterday or three hundred years ago that I was in their place. Wondering where time goes. How to make it pause or stretch a minute a little longer.

They are so ridiculous as they dance, yet so beautifully free. Untouched by the worries of the grown-up world. All that exists for them is possibility and hope and tonight.

"Alright, folks." The DJ's overly animated voice cuts through the air. "Let's find out who our Ledger prom royalty is tonight." The kids scream and clap as he plays a short clip of dramatic music, and they gather around the small stage he's on, standing next to Gus Chambers, the principal.

Camp's hand drops mine as he joins in the applause, and my palm tingles with the absence of him, but I follow suit, clapping with everyone else, attention going to the stage.

"Your Ledger High School Senior Prom King is..."—drum roll music plays—"Nick Raymonds!" The DJ shouts along with the roared response from the crowd.

I find Lyra in the mix of bodies, hearts in her eyes as she watches Nick emerge from the crowd and the principal positions a gaudy crown on his head. He smiles—at her—his mouth slightly too big for his face.

She loves him. I can see that now. Maybe not a deep love, but I see it on her face; she loves him the way teenagers do. In a true kind of way that consumes every moment of her day. Every breath, every thought, blinding her from the possibility of it not lasting forever. The way only a seventeen-year-old girl can love: with every fiber of their being.

I trust him the way you trust Dad.

I look at Camp, his hands cupped around his mouth as he shouts some baseball nickname at Nick. Watching him, smiling so big, everything I think I know rips to shreds inside of me. Where we started, where we are. I'm so confused. About everything. Who I am, how I feel, what I want.

And still, I clap. Forcing myself to be here now.

"And let's get this king a queen, shall we?" More dramatic music plays as the gym riles up before silencing. The anticipation is palpable as Gus opens the next envelope and shows the DJ. "Your queen of Ledger, Miss Lyra Cannon!" he booms, gym wailing again.

Camp cups his hands around his mouth again, this time it's for a loud "Woo! That's my girl!"

I clap next to him. Fresh swell of tears lining my mascaraed eyes. She shimmies through the crowd—blue hair, blue dress—wide smile turning shy when she looks at Nick, the just as gaudy but daintier crown being set on her head. Spotlight on the two of them, she shines like a star. Like whatever is brighter than a star.

I see it as I watch her, all these years later, she's my parallel line. A girl loving a boy, trusting him easy, believing in an unknown next.

She whispers something in Nick's ear, he grins, nods, then she says something to the DJ who gives a thumbs-up and leans toward his mic.

"Alright, folks, looks like we've got some generational royalty here tonight. Twenty-two years ago in this very room, it seems, Lyra's parents were also crowned Ledger's prom king and queen." My stomach drops as the entire gymnasium falls silent, turning to look at us. Camp stills next to me. "And Queen Lyra requests their presence on the dance floor."

I gape at Camp, mouthing *no*! but he just grins, says, "Don't be a scaredy cat, J," and once again takes my hand in his, this time dragging me to the dance floor with long strides, fist bumping players and students as we pass.

Lyra says something else to the DJ, laughing as she grabs Nick's hand and drags him next to us. My annoyed glare morphs to a smile when the music plays the first familiar notes of The Outfield's "Your Love." The same song Camp and I danced to when we were the ones being crowned all those years ago.

Why should we be the only ones that get a song? I had asked before demanding the DJ play something upbeat.

"How did you know?" I ask Lyra over the music.

"Dad!" she shouts, already bouncing to the beat.

I stare at Camp, surrounded by the baseball players he's coached for years, including Nick, dancing like idiots, singing into the invisible microphones of their hands.

Lyra takes my hands in hers, and I do the same. Dancing and laughing. Twirling with teenagers, like a teenager. The woman I am, the girl I was.

Like a bird formation that happens because of instinct, a circle forms, Camp and I pushed to the center. Nick sets his crown on Camp's head, Lyra puts hers on mine. I laugh, so does he. They're crooked; we don't adjust them.

The teachers, the parents—all the people I've known before I knew who I even was, there with the same ridiculous smiles as us. Bouncing, singing, laughing loud. *Kickin' it old school.*

Kids at heart with our kids embodied.

Camp grabs me and twirls me, crooning out one last line about losing love tonight then stills. Standing in Camp's arms, he holds me too close and too serious for all the playful chaos around us.

We stand like that—his arms around my waist, mine around his neck—barely swaying as everyone around us body bumps and shouts.

He bends slightly and brings his mouth close to my ear. "Don't leave me, June."

Four words, and my knees buckle and stomach drops. The huge gym becomes a coffin formed by a truth I can't run from: I don't want to. I want to love Camp to forever and back like I thought I would when I stood on a stage with a cheap crown next to him.

I can't tell him that; I need air.

Pulling away from him, I find Lyra and force a smile as I set the crown on her head. "Congrats, Queen."

She grins but doesn't stop dancing.

With trembling hands, I push through the crowd, scared I might vomit.

"June!" Camp shouts, trapped in the mob on the dance floor, movements already changing to match the rhythm of the next song.

I don't look back; I don't stop.

I slip behind a wall of fabric.

Down a hall.

Pushing on the first door I find, I stagger inside. A damn closet for athletic equipment.

I don't care, I go in. I need a minute. A breath. Some sort of sign on what I'm supposed to do with my life.

"June," Camp calls from the hall, pushing the door open, letting a sliver of light cover the basketballs and football pads before he steps inside and closes the door, stealing the light and the oxygen. The smell of rubber balls and old sweat fills the stuffy air.

"Sorry. I just needed a minute." I sniff. "With jockstraps."

He puffs out a laugh, finding me in the dark with his hands as the music from the gym vibrates the walls.

He cups his hands around my face, presses his thumbs against the pulse points beneath my jaw. "Jungle Rules."

The scratchy whisper of his voice drips through me like warm honey, and I don't hesitate.

"I'm scared this won't last. That you'll find the next big dream, and we'll be back to where we started."

"No, June—"

"And I'll disappear again. I'll be invisible for the rest of my life because-because-because you're you, and-and-and-and everyone loves you."

"Do you?"

"Do I what?"

He steps closer.

All of him touching all of me.

"Do you love me?"

Muffled voices approach the door. "Dude, I gotta piss." Someone laughs. Another voice—a chaperone. "Not back here, boys. Out."

Feet shuffle away; an upbeat song fills the silence.

"I love you enough to cry when you don't come home." He stills, not even breathing. "And I love you enough to-to-to feel like I'm going crazy when I'm not with you. And, when I imagine life without you it feels . . . terrifying. Like I have no idea how to do that. I love you enough that not telling you every thought I'm having makes me sick. Enough that I agonize daily over if I should call this whole thing off and take whatever crumbs of time you're willing to give me." I blow out a breath, my body vibrating with emotions—including anger. Because, damn him for doing this to me. For making me feel all this. My eyes burn, my next words strained: "Dammit, Camp. I love you enough that when I see you laughing in a boxing ring with another woman it makes me punch you in the face. So, yeah, I guess you could say I love you."

With the final words of my confession, his mouth is on mine, holding my breath and thoughts captive with every swipe of his tongue and pull of his teeth.

My back hits the door. His hand slides from my face.

Down the line of my neck.

The curve of my breast.

My waist.

My hip.

"I need to feel you, J."

Mouth open, I nod.

"Say it," he says as he rubs his nose against my cheek. "I need to hear it."

"Yes. Same. I need to feel you. I want to. Now." It's all choppy, my words and my breaths. My fingers are in his hair, scratching his scalp, and he moans into my mouth.

Hem of my dress in his hands, he lifts it until the fabric is bunched around my waist.

A lick on my neck; I whimper.

Fumble with his belt.

His hands stop at the bare skin of my hips. Bare skin of everything.

"Where are your panties?" he asks, voice hot against my skin.

"Home." I made the decision to not wear them immediately after I made myself scream in the shower.

The confession makes us both move with more urgency. Breathe faster and harder.

Hands roaming my bare skin, he bites my shoulder; I yelp.

I unbutton his pants; he moans.

And he's there, between my thighs.

All he says: "Christ."

His mouth is back on mine, and the way he kisses me—tongue moving and teeth biting—is something as unfamiliar as it is feral.

I hook a leg around his waist, the heel of my shoe digs into him. With a nudge, he's inside of me, stretching me until my cry fills the small space.

He pulls back, pausing, refilling with a strangled breath and hard slam.

Again.

And *again*.

My foot finds a shelf, toes pressing onto the edge, balls rolling off the side and bouncing around our feet. His now free hands grip my hips. Fingertips digging as his hips keep moving—his grunts and my moans falling into the rhythm of the music permeating the walls.

Pushing my back against the wall for leverage, my hips chase his.

"God, J, you feel good."

I can't make words. Not as he repeats the motion, not as he takes one hand and wraps a fistful of my hair into it and pulls. Hard enough it hurts in the most delightful kind of way. I know Camp's brand of sex, and this is absolutely not it. It's hot and it's rough and it's everything he's never given me before. Everything I didn't know I wanted.

I grind into him; he hits something deep. New. Making me scream every time he slams into it.

"You're soaked," he grits out between thrusts, fingers so deep in my skin I might bruise; I hope I do. "You're perfect."

I whimper my way toward an invisible edge, pushing my foot harder against the shelf.

Equipment falls around us, balls bouncing. Mouths fused, we laugh into each other.

"Camp . . ." I gasp through clenched teeth as his hips roll like waves in an ocean. It's smooth and rhythmic and sends an extreme surge of pleasure ripping from the base of my spine to the back of my throat. Fast, fierce, and fucking fantastic.

One.

Two.

Three.

Four pumps into me later, Camp comes right along with me, emptying fully with muttered curses and shallow breaths. Our gasps and soft laughs paired with the music of prom form the hottest post-sex soundtrack of my life.

When our clothes are back in place and our breathing back to normal, the remnants of what we just did stays slick between my thighs, no panties to catch it. A filthy memento I very much like.

He grins; I kiss his mouth before he can open the door.

"I love you," I say, breathless. "But when did you learn to move like that?"

He tugs the door open, light revealing a flush on his face and the crookedness of his tie. "If history is any indication," he starts, free hand reaching around to my ass and giving it a squeeze. "I'd say the same time you started goin' without panties to the senior prom, J."

The laugh that comes out of my mouth is ridiculously girlish and giddy, and I kiss him again, so long I feel like my lips have spent the last twenty minutes in a vacuum cleaner. When I pull away, we're both smiling, and with my hand in his, we make our way back to the prom and the two hundred teens and parents who have no idea what we just did.

"Where've y'all been?" Lyra shouts over the rim of her punch, a sheen of sweat on her skin from dancing.

"A walk," I lie, the same time Camp says, "Makin' out in the bathroom."

I laugh, Lyra doesn't. "Probably stealing my friends' edibles too."

"We still need to punish you for that," I tell her, trying to hide my satisfied smile.

She rolls her eyes, taking another sip of punch. "What happened to your hair?"

I run a hand over it, feeling how disheveled it must look. "Um, right. It was windy." I look at Camp; he offers no help. "On the walk. It was windy."

Face twisted, she shudders. "I don't want to know."

Camp drapes an arm around my shoulders. "Your mom can't keep her hands off me."

I slap his chest with a laugh as she groans. "Gross."

Nick walks up, big smile as he fist-bumps Camp. "Coach. Mrs. Cannon."

"Nick, please. June. Or at least Mrs. Coach."

He relaxes but Lyra rolls her eyes. "Ignore her, I think they've been making out."

I mock offense but say nothing. Because, who cares? I want Lyra to see me as something other than a mom—other than a doormat for everyone else in my life—but it had never occurred to me until right now that that might also be a wife that loves her husband. That there's something to be said for being an independent woman as much as there is for a woman that loves a man deeply, despite his flaws. Despite hers.

"Dance?" Lyra asks Nick. I see it in the way he looks at her; he loves her the same way she loves him, and my heart swells. Whatever they decide to do, they'll learn together—at least for now. Maybe longer.

When they head toward the dance floor, I grab his arm. His serious expression matching mine.

"She trusts you," I say.

He nods. Like he knows. His eyes flick to Camp's then back to mine. "She told me she wouldn't be with me if she didn't feel the same way you felt about Coach. And him about you. She trusts you too." He pauses, hesitating, and courage fills his eyes. "And I love her."

The innocent look on his face and the enormity of his words pinch my throat. I nod, release his arm.

"Hurt her and I'll bench you for playoffs," Camp says, tone playful.

Lyra calls Nick's name, I dip my chin, and he's gone.

I lean against Camp. "There she goes."

"There she goes."

And the rest of the night goes like that—Camp and I either right by each other or stealing knowing looks when we aren't. Looks that say, *I know what those hips are capable of* are met with *I know you're not wearin' any panties*. But the looks I feel the most, the ones that feel like they are getting into my bloodstream and changing what I'm made of and how my body operates are the ones where he's telling me he loves me.

After dancing and laughing and giving Lyra and her friends one too many hugs goodnight, Camp and I come home.

I sleep in the bed; he does too.

Thirty-two

On Saturday, we fuck.

Thirty-Three

"Still fits you like a glove, J," Camp says with an easy grin and mussed hair as he makes eggs-in-a-basket. He's in sweatpants and a Ledger T-shirt, I'm in his high school baseball jersey. Which, despite the curves I didn't have when we were teens, still hangs to my thighs. I was in the closet, digging through my drawers for something to wear, and when it caught my eye, I couldn't not put it on. It's been years since it's seen the light of day, and the light of this Sunday morning seemed perfect.

I cradle a mug of coffee in my hands as I lean against the counter next to him, blowing the steam as the dog sprawls across the floor at our bare feet.

I chuckle with a playful eye roll. "A very worn glove."

With the hand not holding the spatula, he tucks a piece of my wild hair behind my ear and kisses my nose then takes his time as his eyes go from my head to my toes, turning my belly to the warm gooey center of a cinnamon roll. "Still looks good."

I shake my head, taking a sip of my coffee as he refocuses his attention on breakfast.

One look in the mirror this morning and I laughed. I look like Medusa if she had a post-sexathon glow and red hair. But I don't care. The kids are still gone, the house is quiet, and after yesterday—and last night—Camp looks so perfect in the kitchen making breakfast, I don't care what I look like. I want to jump inside him and never come out.

"Remember that thing we used to do when I was still playin' baseball?" he asks, turning the stove off and pulling a plate out of the cabinet. "When I'd been gone and only had a couple days in town and we had so much to catch up on?"

I laugh against the rim of my mug. "Twenty Confessions?" I take a sip. "Where I would tell you actual things that were happening in my life, and you told me, like, three important things and then all the kinds of sex you imagined us having."

He does a kind of half snort, half laugh as he slides our breakfast from the pan to the plate. "That sounds about right." He sets the plate in front of me with two forks before leaning against the counter. "Let's play. Tell me what I don't know."

It's simple, maybe stupid, but seven million butterflies flutter through me as he takes a bite of his food, yolk dripping from his fork and onto his faintly stubble-covered chin. He laughs as he wipes it off then takes a sip of his coffee. It's familiar and it's a freefall.

He raises his eyebrows, as if reminding me I need to answer. "Right. Okay." I set my mug down and cut into the toast and egg. "The boys' teacher might be the actual spawn of Satan."

He barks out a laugh as I take my first bite then stabs his fork into the food again. "Not news. What else?"

"Hm. Okay. I think Lyra and Nick might be having sex soon."

His face twists. "Not allowed. Ever. Next."

I chuckle and take another sip of my coffee. Typical dad response.

"Fine. Scotty—I don't know. Something seems off with her. And of course she won't talk about it, but"—I blow out a breath—"she's alone and—the way she went off on Ford . . ." I shake my head. "I worry. She dates complete morons, lives in that lonely apartment above the crematorium, and deflects like she's been professionally trained. I don't know what's in her head."

He nods, sets his fork down, and picks up his mug. "You think it's about Zeb?" he asks.

I shrug. "I think it's about everything."

I take another bite, he sips his coffee, and we let that hang in silence.

When he picks up his fork again, he says, "Tell me about photography. How's it goin'?"

I want to lie, deflect Scotty-style, but I can't. Not to him. Not here in this kitchen in his jersey eating breakfast. Not with him looking at me the way he is.

"I actually had a show." I pause, clear my throat, take a sip of coffee. "At the gallery."

The guilt of the confession is so heavy I can't look at him, but out of the corner of my eye, I see that he's holding his forkful of food midair, unmoving. I pick at something on the counter.

"Really?" he asks, tone surprisingly neutral.

I nod.

"And how did that go?"

"Good," I say, still not looking at him. "Really good actually. Someone bought every single piece."

He sets his fork—still filled with food—down on the plate. "Why didn't you tell me?"

I brave a look at him, my eyes burning with tears a blink away from falling. "I-I-I was mad at you. And-and I thought maybe I wasn't good enough. Or something. I don't know. It was the night Hank got hurt. And then I felt guilty. And-and-and—"

"J," he says, expression softer than I expect or deserve when he cuts me off. He brushes another rogue hair from my face then wraps a palm around my neck while his thumb rubs the line of my jaw. "I would have been there—I wish I would have known—but I'm proud of you. And you are good enough, no matter what you do. You're better than good."

A lone tear of guilt drops down my face and he watches it. My throat hurts too bad to talk, so I nod.

I'm glad he knows, but I feel like a monster. How could I have not invited him? Not even told him?

"I'm sorry," I say, letting out a shaky breath as he brushes his knuckles under my chin. "That I didn't tell you."

"Don't apologize. But someone bought every piece?" Curiosity fills his face. "Who?"

"That's the weird thing," I say with a sniff. "They wanted to remain anonymous. I have no idea why, but they bought everything. For a lot of money."

His lips twitch as he fights a smile. "You have some kind of secret admirer I need to know about?"

I snort-laugh, snaking my arms around his waist and dropping the side of my head to the crook of his neck. He runs his fingers through my hair. "Ha. Ha. I do *not* think so. It sounds stupid, but it felt good. I don't know . . . special. That someone would do that. Would want to buy photos I took."

"Oh, really?" There's a playfulness to his voice. "Now *you're* a secret admirer of your secret admirer? Do I need to be worried, *wife*?"

This time, my laugh is loud.

"Maybe. But only if he's old and rich." He wraps his arms around me, the food and coffee abandoned on the counter as we tilt our heads to face each other. Our smiles mirrored. "It's your turn. What's new?"

"I was thinkin' about what I could do with you on the counter."

I snort. "That's not how this works. Tell me something."

He takes a step that pivots me so my back is pinned to the counter.

"I met a girl with wild red hair and I'm gonna marry her."

I fail to hide my smile. "Old news, Camp Cannon."

His hands drop to my hips and travel up, under his jersey and on my body; his mouth finds mine.

He kisses me, pulls away enough to say, "I got a job as the athletic director at the high school," and kisses me again. "Oh! And I helped design a new sports complex, and I need a date to the gala. Apparently, I have to be there."

"You're still terrible at this," I half say, half laugh as his mouth stays close to mine.

My hands travel across his skin under his shirt, lifting it halfway up his torso until I see his boomerang-shaped birthmark. I trace it—twice—and he stills. Our playfulness on pause. I want to kiss it. Lick it.

"To forever and back," he says as my fingers dance across his skin.

I hum a soft noise in response, looking back at him—feeling so beautifully content—and poke a single finger into his ribs and make him laugh.

He tickles me in retaliation, making me laugh harder, before squeezing my hips and lifting me onto the counter.

"Lookey here, I got you on the counter," he says with a sly grin as he spreads my legs so he's standing between them.

I laugh with an exhale, the space between us, though barely there, feeling too big. Too far. Like he might disappear if I don't get closer.

"You got me on the counter." I trace the crooked line of his nose and the cupid's bow of his lips with my finger before slipping my hands around his neck. "Now what?"

"Now"—he wraps his hands around my knees and slides his palms up my bare thighs, sending a radiating ache through me; without him asking, my body scoots closer toward the edge—"I'm gonna slide inside you and make you scream my name in the middle of this kitchen with the dog watchin'."

Said dog is splayed across the floor and snoring. And, because it's the only thing I seem to be able to do today, I smile like an idiot.

"That's weird," I tell him, doing nothing to stop him as he slides my panties off.

"Don't care," he says, not breaking eye contact when he drops his pants.

I don't argue. Instead, I wrap my legs around his waist.

He kisses me, tasting like breakfast, and I feel my heart exploding with every beat. Not from the sex we're about to have or that we've already had, but from him being here. From everything else. The laughing. The talking. The eggs in a damn basket. From us being us.

I pull back from his mouth—just far enough so I can speak. "You're Today's Best."

His smile is true; his eyes are bright. "So are you."

Mouth to mouth, tongue to tongue, hands on my hips and with a push of his own, he's in me, turning us into a tangled mess of breathing and grinding and giggles, until—true to Camp's word—I scream his name and the dog barks.

And there, in the middle of the kitchen on a Sunday morning, I fall in love with my husband all over again.

Thirty-four

Our weekend alone is the calm before the storm. With the complex dedication—the big fundraising gala event—and Lyra's graduation, if life wasn't hectic before, it is now.

Me at meetings for graduation ceremony preparations and carting the boys around.

Lyra taking finals and finishing the last of her scholarship applications.

Camp scrambling between baseball practice, games, putting out last-minute fires for the dedication, and finalizing the schedule of hosted games and tournaments for the summer and fall.

Even though we're passing ships all day, we're still in bed—together—at night.

My camera is always with me, coming out in the in-between moments.

Life feels like I've always imagined it should. Busy but full.

I know quieter days are coming. I'll have more time for photography and can figure out my next steps. When the busyness dies down, I can chase my dreams and keep all this. For the first time I see that maybe life can be both.

"What are you going to do when the complex is done, Dad?" Lyra asks as she scoops chicken and rice onto her plate.

His eyes narrow as he chews his food, wiping his mouth. "What do you mean?"

"You're always chasing the next big thing." She chuckles at her very accurate observation, causing me to unintentionally go still.

Camp's eyes go from Lyra's slowly to mine. He clears his throat. Seemingly trying to choose his words carefully. "Jack has his sights set on nationals next year. Probably have a good shot. Last few years it's gone to teams in Florida and Ohio, but I think it could be our year."

Nationals?

A longer season.

More away games.

His dreams, not mine.

"Nationals?" My voice is a whisper as I feel everything from the last days slipping through my fingers.

"He says he thinks the team has a shot," he says, eyes steady on me as he speaks.

I nod, blankly. All I can think: I knew this wouldn't last.

"The assistant coach setting the big goals?" Lyra teases with a grin, ignorant to the implications of what he's just said, popping a spoonful of food into her mouth. "Losing your mojo, old man."

"Watch this!" Ty shouts, catapulting a spoonful of food into the air that Thor catches with a slobbery lick.

Hank's voice is somehow louder. "Let me try!"

Using his hand instead of spoon before I can stop him, chicken and rice landing on the floor with a splat.

The familiar feeling tickles my spine. The walls close in. Camp laughs with a shake of his head at the mess as Lyra rolls her eyes. Calls them gross. Says something about not being able to wait to move out to get away from them.

It's muffled.

Happening around me.

3-2-1.

3-2-1.

Another lob of food into Thor's mouth.

My ears ring.

I can't breathe.

"Boys!" I snap, dropping my fork on my plate and jerking to a stand, making my chair fall to the floor. "Why does every dinner have to turn into a damn circus?"

An immediate silence falls across the table, and the only sound is Thor licking up rice from the floor.

"Sorry, Mama," Hank says in a quiet voice.

"Yeah, well, if you were so sorry you'd stop throwing food everywhere. No wonder Ms. Mitchell is losing her mind with you two!" I want to take the words back as soon as they are out, but instead, I glare at them both—watery lines in their eyes—before storming to the kitchen.

Camp follows me, quiet as I take aggressive pulls of paper towels from the roll.

"You okay?" he asks, putting his hand on my forearm, which I jerk away.

"Fine," I snap.

"You seem upset. I'll talk to them about feedin' the dog at the table. I know it's—"

"It's nothing, Camp. It's fine. It's typical. It's all typical."

He stares at me. "If this is about—"

"It's about nothing." I pull my shoulders back and force a smile I don't feel. "It's fine."

At the table, I drop to the floor, beginning to wipe the rice and slobber up, the burn of tears that want to shoot out of my face burning like lava behind my eyes.

Camp is chasing the next big thing.

That isn't me.

Camp is home now, but it won't last.

The last few days become fool's gold disguised as something real, and I was the fool too blind to see it for what it was: fake. A fairy-tale ending in a mere seventeen days.

"I know it's last minute, but, J, I was wonderin' if you'd want to give the welcomin' speech at the gala? You know this town as well as anyone—the school."

I look up at him, wondering if I've heard him wrong. The eager look on his face lets me know I heard him just fine.

As I scrub dog slobber and rice.

As my world crumbles around me.

Camp wants me to give a speech about the very thing I would like to burn to the fucking ground.

I open my mouth, snap it shut.

Again.

And again.

Finally, my voice works. "I think Lyra should do it. It would mean more coming from a student. And she would have no problem gushing over the great Camp Cannon." I look from him to her as I stand, soiled paper towels scooped in my hands, face hot. With a tight smile I add, "Be good practice for graduation."

The boys stare at their plates, Camp nods slightly, and Lyra says in a soft voice, "Sure, Mom."

Without saying another word, I carry the mess to the trash can, grab the keys to the minivan off the hook, and walk out the door.

I drive without direction or destination. I drive until I spot a vacant parking lot of a dilapidated gas station on the edge of town and park. Busted windows, a broken door, and overrun with weeds and garbage, it's an actual representation of my life.

I park, then cry. I weep for every single thing that's wrong in my life.

When my face is dry and throat raw, raindrops start to fall on the windshield with collective splats, like God knows I have more misery to purge.

I stare at them, trying to count every drop.

A blue light strobes through the rain and I squint to make out a police car parking next to me. *Great.* The door opens, closes, and a blurry blob makes its way toward me and taps at my window.

I wipe my eyes and roll it down.

"Ford?" I say with a slight laugh.

He returns the smile, surprised, no doubt expecting naked teens or a drug deal. "June." He chuckles, popping open an umbrella over himself and the down window of the minivan. He looks at the empty passenger seat and into the empty back. "Didn't expect to see you. The hell you doing out here?"

"Ah, you know, just your everyday desperate-housewife nervous breakdown in the middle of a storm." Thunder rolls as if I planned it, and we both laugh. "I'm fine, just needed a break from . . . everything. Then the storm."

He's quiet, takes a breath, looks into the rain and shifts his weight.

"So, uh, how's Camp?"

I snort a laugh. "That's not who you want to ask about."

He raises his eyebrows; I do the same, daring him to deny it.

A breath puffs out of him and the expression on his face lets me know I've read him like a book.

"I'll help," I tease, lowering my voice. "'June, I'm wondering how Scotty is.' To which I would respond, 'Slightly insane and taking no prisoners, so figure out what it is you want before you try to crack that shell, or she'll go full-blown Mike Tyson on your ass again.'"

He laughs softly, adjusting his grip on the umbrella as he rests his free hand on the holster of his gun. His gaze shifts down the rainy road. The lights from his car strobe against the side of the minivan, reflection bouncing off the side mirror and the million droplets around us.

"She hate me?" he asks, looking at the ground where puddles are forming around his black shoes.

I sigh, trying to answer that landmine of a question. "When Zeb died—the way he died—it broke her, Ford. You don't come back from that easily. Hell, you took twenty years." We exchange a look, and I think back to all those years ago, Scotty devastated, trying to make sense of it all. Blaming everyone. Especially Ford. "And Scotty is Scotty. You've been gone for a while"—the rain starts to fall harder—"which I'd love to hear about in less soggy circumstances. But she . . . if you want to talk to her, it's going to take work. You have to decide. I'm her best friend, the closest thing to family she has in this world, and she barely talks to me about it. It's just . . . messy."

He grunts, nods, scrubs a hand on the angle of his scruff-covered jaw. "Everything okay with Camp?"

"Ha!" I bark out. "That's . . . also messy."

"Ah." His phone rings, knowing look on his face as he slips it out of his pocket. He waves it toward me. "Gotta take this. Drive safe, June."

I smile, roll up my window, and watch him hustle through the rain to his car.

Then, with only one place to go, I turn the windshield wipers on, cue up a podcast, and start the drive home.

THE PERFECT MOM PODCAST WITH ABBIGAIL BUCHANAN

EPISODE 212: Quieting the Noise in a Loud World with guest Erin Gaves

Abbigail: Alright, mamas, we have guest Erin Gaves in today, author of *Shut the Hell Up! A Guide to Silencing the Noise in a World with Too Many Microphones*. And, I can be honest, I'm as much excited as I am nervous to jump into it today. Welcome to the microphone, Erin. [Chuckles.]

Erin: Thanks so much for having me, Abbigail. I'll apologize before we start, I mean no offense toward your mic.

[Both laugh.]

Abbigail: Okay, I'm ready for it. So, even though I'm one of the people with a microphone like you call out in your book, I actually agree so much with your messaging. Can you tell us a little bit about why you wrote this book?

Erin: Absolutely. I've always been pretty transparent with my journey, so I won't shy away from the personal details here. My husband and I didn't have a ton of money, but it was important to us that I stay home. So we budgeted, cash envelopes and all, [chuckles in understanding] and we made it work. I never had fancy things, but we had what we needed. We were so dang happy. Then, one day, it's like social media just blew up. I didn't know what was happening in my kids' classrooms if I wasn't in this online group or what the band schedule was at our favorite restaurant if I wasn't following their page. So, I did what everyone did, I got online. I had accounts. I followed and shared. And while nothing changed at home—absolutely nothing—I suddenly felt extreme dissatisfaction in my life.

Abbigail: Mm. Can you give an example? I know we've all felt this, but I'd love to know your experience.

Erin: Oh gosh, of course. And I could give you a million, but the one that stands out to me the most was about a couch. We had this couch that was so comfortable. We saved and saved because I wanted a new couch, and we got it, it had these reclining ends and huge puffy cushions the kids were obsessed with. Anyway, I get this couch—chocolate brown—and we all love it, right? Then, the internet shows up. And this couch that I loved I suddenly think is hideous. Like, it's dark and dated and not light and sleek. And I'm devastated. Like I go on and on and on about what a mistake it was. All because some stranger on the internet posted photos of a couch that I never would have thought about otherwise. I was literally influenced by strangers to hate what I had just loved. And that's how it started for me: a stupid couch, and it just got worse from there. I'd take a vacation but was never quite as happy because people were taking other vacations. Better ones. Buying better cars. Educating their kids differently. Going on fancy date nights. I was influenced—repeatedly—to buy and do things that made others happy. Others that knew nothing about me. Others that I knew nothing about! I was basing my life choices off the choices of people that were total strangers.

Then, one night I listened to this podcast from a mom that never let her kids inside, and they never wore shoes unless they were going out in public. Cited facts on how kids used to be this way and how much happier they were. How much healthier. Summer was coming, and I thought, this all makes sense. This is what I'm going to do.

On the first day, it was fun—novel. I sat outside with them, read books. Ate watermelon. Made a fort. The whole bit. The next day was not great. An hour outside without shoes and we were all pretty miserable. But I kept going, because follow-through. Because studies and someone else was doing it and they were so happy. By the end of the second day, all three of my kids went to bed crying, one of them had ringworm, and I had a sunburn.

Abbigail: Oh no!

Erin: Right? So, I guess, all that to say, I tried to be someone I'm not. I like museums. I like libraries. I like AC and shoes. And seeing someone else do it differently made me feel like I was doing something wrong. Like I had a problem I didn't even know I was having. I got defensive, felt inadequate, and tried to fit in a box that wasn't me-sized. But with all the noise, it's so easy to forget that there's more than one way to do just about anything. There's no one way to have a happy life.

I wring my hands around the steering wheel, instantly irritated. *I cannot relate.*

My decisions have never been rash. Influenced. I've had problems, and podcasts show up with solutions. They don't *make* the problems. I'm not manufacturing any of this.

> **Abbigail:** I'm sure I am not alone in my confession here, but, been there. [Groans in embarrassment.] Like, so many times. Now the question I've been dreading but I want to just rip the Band-Aid off . . . why don't you share your thoughts on podcasts?

> **Erin:** [Exaggerated sigh followed by a laugh.] I promise it's not that bad. I actually like podcasts.

I smile, validated. "See!" I say to the empty minivan.

Erin: BUT! I think they need to come with the same label as, say, a bottle of vodka: Please listen responsibly. [Chuckles.] Because, yes, a lot of the people we listen to on podcasts are often experts—therapists, counselors, doctors, you know, whatever—but they aren't experts on *us*, on our unique situations. If you're having marriage issues, and someone on a podcast gives a blanketed piece of advice, like, say, "If you're always arguing, go on more dates." Something like that. Well, what if your spouse has a problem with drinking or pornography or is abusive—going on more dates isn't the answer there, right? Or, what if it's not so severe, what if the suggestion is go on more dates, but you are going through financial hardships and literally can't afford more dates. All of the sudden you might think there's no saving your marriage because you can't afford the solution.

Abbigail: So context matters?

Erin: Context absolutely matters. You can apply this to every scenario. Parenting techniques. Dieting. Clothing. Gosh, even back to the stupid couch, right? The post I saw that said this was the couch to have was a single woman with no kids and a ton of money, yet I completely disregarded those details. I just thought: If she has that couch, her house looks like that, and she's *so* happy, I need that couch. Nothing else mattered. And it's not just one person, it's millions. Everyone has a platform.

Abbigail: And a microphone.

Erin: [Chuckles.] And a microphone.

Abbigail: So, what do we do? How do we combat all the noise?

Erin: Yeah, so that's tricky, right? It's the modern world, technology is here to stay. I can't tell the future, of course, but I can't imagine social media shrinking away either. So the most obvious choice is to unplug, but that's not always realistic. I would just say, for every feed we scroll, every expert we listen to, every time we compare what someone else has to what we don't, observe what's happening.

Why do we care? Are we really that unhappy? Do we really need more advice or do we just, you know, need to have a real conversation and listen to our gut? [Pause.] A lot of us already have the people that matter most—who know us best—willing to help and listen, but we ignore them . . . I'll make it simple. When we want to read a book, we look at reviews—often there are thousands of them—from perfect strangers. We don't know them, they don't know us, but we let them dictate what we are going to read. Why? Why do we care so much about what books people we don't know read versus the people that know us best?

I slam my hand against the power knob, silencing Erin. I scoff. Smack the steering wheel. Scoff again. Because, where does she get off? Like—what does she even know about anything? She's probably just jealous because she's not an expert! Looking for a quick buck so she can buy that stupid couch!

I listen to the people around me. *Do I listen to the people around me?*

I think of Scotty and I on the couch of Happy Endings as I bitch and moan and she tries to help. Think of Mave and her damn cookies, telling me how I've been reading Camp all wrong.

I blow out a heavy breath, roll the window down, and let the cool air and raindrops fly into the opening and slap my skin doing nothing to ease the tension that's seized my entire body. I can't explain it. How defensive I am from the podcast. How stripped bare. It's as though every word spoken was for the sole purpose to attack me.

What's worse, I can't shake the feeling that, even though things weren't perfect between me and Camp, even though I was drowning in the monotony of my life, maybe I messed everything up. Went about the solution entirely wrong. Acted without context.

When I get home, the house is dark and quiet, and when I join Camp in bed that night, it's without touching him, without talking to him, and without trusting a single thought I have.

Thirty-Five

"I'll be honest, June, I didn't expect your call," Reed says with a smirk as he adjusts the camera on the tripod.

A nervous laugh puffs out of me from the stool I'm sitting on, trying to forget I'm naked underneath the white sheet that's wrapped around my shoulders. "Yeah, well, I didn't expect to make the call."

The two days since my minivan meltdown have been filled with tension. Though Camp and I have slept in the bed together, we haven't talked. He wakes up, goes for a run, and goes to work; I take care of the kids and feed the dog.

More than once, I've caught him looking like he wants to say something; more than once he never has. Last night at dinner, Camp and I were silent while the kids were oblivious, rattling on and on about end of the school year excitement around the kitchen table.

The same kitchen table Camp bent me over a mere week ago during our whole-house screw-fest.

A bubble of bliss, popped.

The words from the podcast have clawed at me. If I accepted what they meant—that I'd been too cavalier to trust strangers that knew nothing about me—it would mean one thing: I've been a fool.

After nearly two days of agitation, when I read the note saying the boys got red cards in class, it pushed me over the edge; I called Reed out of desperation.

Desperate to escape everything. To be anyone but myself.

"If the offer still stands, let's do the photos," I told him. "But if you do anything funny, I'll knock you out. Scotty took me to a boxing class."

Reed laughed, said, "I wouldn't dream of it," and texted me a time.

So here I am. Mostly nude and posing for a photo on a Tuesday night with Reed Simmons.

He lifts his head from behind the viewfinder, smile turning serious. "Wanna talk about it?"

I shrug, the sheet shifting across my bare skin. "I accidentally spent my life chasing Camp Cannon only to have him never chase me."

He laughs under his breath, switching out the lens on his camera, stance wide as he studies me. He opens his mouth to say something but closes it as though he changed his mind.

"What?"

He presses his lips in a tight line, hesitating. "It's just that, every single time I've seen him since I've been back, and the way he doesn't hesitate to let me know how he feels about me, makes me think otherwise."

"You've seen him once, that's hardly a shock."

He snorts a laugh.

"Either way." I pull at a thread on the sheet. "I just can't spend my life like this, you know? Like-like-like my life might be half over, and what, the rest of it is just going to be me haunting a house he picked out while I wait for him to come home from baseball practice?" I scoff. "He said he was working on being home more, but do you know what he said last night?" I shoot a hand into the air as my voice rises. "He wants to win nationals next year! Nationals, Reed! That's the opposite of being home more." He says nothing. "And, you know, for some reason somebody bought all the pieces I had at the show. Someone saw me—or at least what I was capable of—and, what? I just shut that down so Camp can keep playing baseball?" I make a groan-grunt-shout sound. Reed has the nerve to look amused. "Why are you smiling like that? Like this is at all funny. My marriage is falling apart, and I'm naked under a sheet with public enemy number one."

"What would you do if I tried to kiss you right now?" he asks, tone matter-of-fact. Like a businessman bartering a deal.

I suck in a sharp breath and tighten the sheet around my chest. "Scream. Why?"

He chuckles, putting a lens in a case. "Then I'm not the enemy—and I'm not going to try to kiss you."

Part of me is offended by this fact, but more so, I'm relieved. Reed—smokin' hot Reed—is talking to me like the friends we used to be. The heat his gaze had at the gallery show has been replaced by a concerned warmth. A dynamic shifted.

"Why didn't your marriages work?" I ask, watching him as he moves from his camera to the large, white light boxes in the corners of the studio, angling them toward me.

"My wives would probably say I chased them until I didn't. Work has always been it for me. The thing that lights me on a fire that burns constantly. When things get hard, I shake it up by buying a new lens, going somewhere else to gain perspective. But relationships?" He shakes his head as he pulls a backdrop down. "You're there. Stuck. Nowhere to run but to each other to figure it out."

I blow out a breath. "That's the damn truth."

He steps next to me, looking at the gear scattered around the room, assessing.

"Will you get married again? Is it worth it? The love then loss?"

"Way I see it, there are three questions anyone should ask themselves before they get married: Can I imagine my life with this person? Is my life better with this person? Is having this person worth giving up any other thing in my life?"

He pauses, slipping his fingers to the top of the sheet, laughing at the glare I give him. "I got it, June, your chest is off-limits, and you aren't sleeping with me. Your terms were clear when you shouted them through the phone."

I soften, just slightly, and he works the sheet so it's draped across my chest but leaves my entire back open, spinning me around so my back is toward the camera.

"Anyway," he continues, "those are the same three questions you should ask when you get divorced. For me"—he shrugs—"it's always been three yeses when it starts and three nos when it ends."

I consider this, his questions, my answers. Camp. Reed not being able to stay in a relationship because he constantly wants something else. Something more. He positions me, facing away from the camera, bare back exposed, sheet draped.

"Listen, and here's the last thing I'll say about it. You broke my heart when you were with him in high school. I loved you the way someone that age thinks they love someone they can't have. But we wouldn't have worked—I know that—not now that I see what you have. The kids, the house, the dog that's bigger than your kids in the photos." He smiles, but it doesn't meet his eyes. "And Camp. I get it, maybe more than most, that people don't always see the truth, what happens in relationships behind closed doors. But that man"—he shakes his head—"whether he knows it or you know it or whatever, is the one chasing you. I think maybe you have some image in your head of what's happening and aren't willing to see what's real. What's right in front of you." I say nothing as he positions himself behind his camera. "But as for me, I chase what I want and leave when it isn't—I don't think that's who you are, June. Relationships are about sacrifice. Some are big and loud, but some aren't. Some are so quiet they go unnoticed. A subtle bending to fit—tilt your chin down. Look over your shoulder."

He snaps a series of photos as I follow his posing instructions. "Do you talk to him? Like, really talk to him?"

I jerk my head toward him, chin tucked at my shoulder, eyes narrow.

He laughs again, blue eyes dancing, dark hair disheveled. "I'll take that as a no—go back to sitting the way you were, less angry. Right, like that. Close your eyes." I do as he says and hear another click of the shutter. "My guess is you approach him like you did shooting landscape photography. Hellbent on doing one thing, hard-pressed to see there was something different and better for you. Not that I'm defending the asshole, but how do you expect him to meet you halfway if you don't tell him how?"

I scoff. "I talk."

Do I talk?

I told him I wanted a divorce. That I hated his mustache. That he never helped around the house. That he's always gone.

But . . .

I've never told him how hard dinner routines are for me. How hard it is for me to take time for myself because of how much he works. Plays. How I always sit the bench to baseball.

Why?

Another click of the shutter then Reed switches out his lenses. Does something with the lights.

Because I want him to just know. Because I don't want him to blame me when he's unhappy. Because, according to Camp, I'm *damn stubborn.*

Do we really need more advice or do we just, you know, need to have a real conversation and listen to our gut? The words from last night's podcast burn like acid in my ears.

The realization sinks heavy in my gut. I've always just wanted him to know, but a bigger part of me didn't want him to blame me for his unhappiness when I asked him not to do something or told him how hard it all was. Somewhere along the way, I decided I'd be unhappy enough for all of us and spare him. Only, instead of it working out like that, we're over.

When he told me about playing toward hosting nationals next year. Adding more tournaments to the lineup . . . I didn't ask him not to, I snapped.

How the hell did it take Reed Simmons photographing me in a sheet to realize this?

"Okay, we're going to take one more series but this ti—"

"You're right," I blurt. "I never told him. Any of it. Like-like as far back as I remember." It all flashes before my eyes. Me not telling him I didn't want to stay home. That I didn't want to buy his parents' house. That the absence of the *lost ones* gnawed a gaping hole in me. That finding out I was having twins at thirty-six years old was borderline catastrophic. "I mean, he was a blind moron that didn't pick up on the cues of me digging my own grave, but-but-but." I drop my head back with a groan of realization.

"That bad?" he asks, puffing out a laugh as he moves from behind his camera until he's standing next to me.

I blink, thinking of everything I haven't said in my over two decades with Camp, and groan again. "Where do I even begin? And what if he doesn't want to listen?"

He rests his hands on my bare shoulders, gentle look in his eyes. "That asshole?" He grins and rubs his palms down my arms before dropping his hands by his side. "I have a feeling you'll figure it out. You'll do something or he'll do something . . . where there's a will, there's a way. I've watched you two—he'll listen."

I playfully place my palms on his cheeks, pinching the sheet to my sides under my armpits as I squeeze his face, laughing as I say, "Thank you. Seriously. For all of this. If I didn't have a marriage to fix, I'd kiss you, Reed Simmons."

His head turns slightly, eyes cutting toward the open door to the gallery before snapping back to me. In that split second, his expression changes. Framed by my hands, his smile turns sly. In a movement so quick—so abrupt—Reed moves his face toward me until his mouth is so close to mine his lips brush against my skin when he talks.

"Sorry, Junie," he whispers. "I can't resist."

Before I can move, before I can do anything, he kisses me—fast. His lips are on mine then off before I can register what's happening. There's no passion or tongue or feeling. When he pulls back, my eyes are wide, my heart has stopped, and he has a shit-eating grin as he cocks his head to the side and looks back toward the door.

I grip the sheet around me, speechless. *What the actual fuck?*

"Oh, hey, Camp," he says coolly. "Didn't see ya there."

What?

I turn my head, and then I see him. Camp. Standing in the doorway of the gallery—straight line of sight to what he thinks he just saw—with a bouquet of wildflowers hanging sadly by his side and his eyes filled with hurt.

It hits like a live bomb detonating behind my ribs.

No!

"Camp!"

Driven by an instant shot of adrenaline, I push into Reed's chest with one hand—who stumbles back with a smug chuckle—grip the sheet around my chest with the other, and pounce to a stand, nearly tripping as I stumble out of the studio, down the short hall, and into the gallery after him.

"Camp!" I shout, desperate. "Wait! It's not what you think!"

He's already leaving, and he doesn't stop. Doesn't even turn to look at me. Every shout of his name only seems to make him move faster toward his truck parked in the lot across the street. He ignores every beg, eating up the sidewalk and street in long angry strides. I'm run-stumbling as fast as the sheet will let me—stepping over the abandoned bouquet in the doorway.

"Camp!" I shout again, in the middle of the street as he slams the door of his truck.

"No!" I hitch the fabric high on my chest as I run to him. "Camp!" I smack on his driver's side window. "Camp! It's not what you think!"

For the first time he looks at me, and when his eyes meet mine through the glass, they're red and wet. The pain on his face squeezes all the air from my lungs.

"Camp!" I cry again. "Camp!" I'm screaming now. My throat burns as tears pour down my face and I slap the window like a madwoman. "It's not what you think!"

But he doesn't stop. He doesn't roll the window down. And worse, I know he doesn't believe me.

He looks away, shifts the gear, and leaves me crying his name in the middle of Main Street, wearing a sheet and watching him go.

"Didn't even punch me this time, and I had ya naked," Reed observes—like my life isn't unravelling in front of him—because of him—easily leaning in the open doorway of the gallery.

I storm past him with a sniff. "You're a special kind of fucked up, Reed. Why the hell did you do that?" I retrieve my clothes from the studio, sniveling as I fumble with my bra and pull my shirt over my head, not caring it's inside out.

"You're not going to like my answer," he says, watching me get dressed like a lunatic as he leans in the studio doorway. "But I just wanted to get a reaction."

My head whips toward him from where I'm crouched and struggling to tie my shoe. "Are you kidding me?" I ask with an incredulous shout. "This is my life—my marriage! And you just *wanted to get a reaction*?"

He squints and presses his lips together, as if he's thinking about what I've said. "Yes." He grins. "And I also thought it would be good for you."

Again, his words shock me to the point of paralysis. "*Good* for me? You're insane, you know that? Like-like-like, completely mental. How was this good for me?"

I scramble to find my purse, fishing for my keys. "You *and* him," he says, like it's obvious, rubbing his chin. "You can't talk to him, and now you don't have a choice. You either talk to him or you lose him."

I scoff, finally finding my keys. "So you're some kind of delusional cupid now?"

He answers with a proud smile, and I groan, picking up my sweater as I shove by him again. This time he follows me through the gallery.

"You gonna chase Camp Cannon around forever, Junie?" he teases.

I ignore him, only stopping in the middle of the street when he shouts, "June?" I glance at him as I push the button on my keys to unlock the minivan. "Note on the flowers says, 'I'm done.'"

He's done?

I stare at the note between Reed's fingers, not able to comprehend any of it.

I jam my palms in my eyes, let out a loud groan, then hurry to get into the van.

What the hell did I just do?

Thirty-Six

"Camp, please," I beg.

He's tossing clothes in a suitcase, storming around the room. Face red. Collar of his Ledger Lake Trout polo shirt up on one side, down on the other. He looks like he just survived a trip through a spin cycle.

"It's not what you think. I know it looked bad. I know it did. It was just a photo. Platonic."

"Platonic?" he spits out as he throws a shirt in the suitcase. "You were wearing a fuckin' sheet. Kissing. Him."

"Because I think he might be psychotic. Or-or-or delusional. It was because of you. He-he-he—we were talking about you and—"

He drops his head back and lets out an ice-cold laugh, his gaze hard when he looks at me. "You got one pass with this, June. One. And you used it twenty-two years ago. You want Reed? Go get him. Maybe that's what all this is"—he gestures a hand through the air between us—"you want out of this marriage so you can go fuck whoever you want."

My jaw drops. "No! Camp. I know I messed up. I should have told you about the portrait and Reed, but nothing happened. Nothing. Well, it did, but you saw that. It was nothing—him being an ass. Or helping." Camp pins me with a look. "No, not helping. He said that. I-I-I was just so mad at you. And things were good, but then you said you were focused on nationals. And-and-and he made me realize that I haven't been talking, not really. I-I—"

He throws a wad of socks at the suitcase, pushing past me to the bathroom. "Ah! I see, Reed's a therapist now?"

I'm on his heels, desperation leaking into my voice. "No, that's not what I mean." I squeeze my eyes closed. I'm failing. He's leaving.

He grabs his toothbrush, storms back to the bedroom. "Camp, you aren't listening."

He slings a duffle over one shoulder and rolls the suitcase out of the bedroom.

I catch him in the living room, grab his arm. "Camp, please."

He stares at our contact, like me touching him is the most unfamiliar thing that could happen to him. Like it's a snake. Like he hates it and me.

Finally, he looks at me, eyes so filled with hurt it shatters my soul into seven million pieces.

Out of his pocket, he pulls a piece of paper. North Carolina Separation Agreement across the top.

My stomach drops to the floor.

"Camp—"

"You tell Lyra whatever you want, I'll be at my parents."

I look at the paper, all the lines I had filled in months ago, but now, his name is scribbled on the signature line at the bottom.

"Tell me what?"

No.

Lyra walks in, looking between the two of us. The paper on the table.

Nononono.

"Nothing, it's just that your—"

"What's this? Where are you going, Dad? The gala is in two days . . ." She picks up the paper, eyes narrowing as she reads. Camp and I quiet, telling tears falling down my face. "A separation?" she whispers, paper slipping from her hands to the floor.

I open my mouth only to say nothing.

"Mom, what did you do?" she demands.

"Wha-what?"

"I know this wasn't Dad, he wouldn't just leave," she shouts, running to his side.

He wraps his arm around her shoulders.

"Your mom and I just need a break. I'm goin' to Nan and Papa's for a couple nights. No big deal," Camp tells her.

"It's a mistake. A misunderstanding, Ly," I start, hating how lame every word feels. How small. "I just, you know, it is my fault. I was just so young when I had you, and then I lost myself—then the boys came and . . ."

"What?" she snaps. "You don't want Dad *or* us?"

"Lyra!" I cry. "No, that's not what I meant."

"All that stuff about trusting Nick the way you trust Dad was a lie?" she shouts, hurt filling her voice. "Everything you said. I believed you and it was bullshit!" she spits, making my chest burn. She looks at Camp, desperate. "I'm coming with you."

I cover my face with my hands, trying to hide my own hurt. Wanting to vanish.

"Lyra, stop." He sets his duffle bag down, hands on her shoulders as he looks straight at her. "This isn't about you, it's your mom and me. And it's not her fault. Not all of it. That's what makes relationships so tricky—two hearts tryin' to fall into a rhythm that sometimes gets a bit off." His eyes float to mine. "Sometimes they fall out of sync. But I'm just goin' to Nan's for a couple of nights. I'll see you at school. At the gala in two nights." He hugs her, tight, and kisses her on the forehead as she starts to cry.

As her world and mine and his as we know it crumples.

With a dinosaur roar and the whoosh of an airplane, the boys storm into the room, stopping abruptly at the sight of Camp's suitcase. "Where are you going, Daddy?"

He ruffles their hair, scoops them up with forced monster sounds, and says, "On a work trip, I'll be back soon."

Then it happens in slow motion—all of it. The hugs. Lyra's tears. Him opening the door, looking at me, and watching me shatter.

He shuffles down the sidewalk.

Into his truck.

Gone.

Lyra storms to her bedroom as the boys ask for a snack at the same time they throw the ball to Thor.

I barely even notice when it knocks a glass of water off the table and shards of glass scatter across the floor.

It's the same kind of absence as I've had for the last years—me dealing with chaos alone—only this time, I feel it tenfold.

Thirty-Seven

"You look like shit."

My attempt at giving Scotty a glare as I walk into Happy Endings only results in more ugly crying. Instead, I lean into her, sobbing loudly against her too-perky Taylor Swift T-shirt.

"I fucked up, Scotty," I stutter out, not lifting my face from her chest. Taylor Swift's voice belts out the lyrics to "Love Story" around us and I cry harder. "I can only imagine what he thinks happened with Reed, but it was nothing. And-and-and Lyra thinks I'm the worst."

My sniffles and shallow breaths push me to the cusp of hyperventilating.

Scotty smooths my hair and takes my hand in hers. "I want to show you something."

She leads me through the cozy witnessing room into the sterile cremation room in silence.

I pause, somehow more gutted than I was a second earlier, and bring a hand to my gaping mouth. Tears falling faster as I take in the woman, peaceful and quiet, somewhere around my age. Could be younger or older. In all my years coming in this room, I've never once been with someone so young. So real.

"You've been coming in here since—"

"I know how long it's been," I snap, cutting her off with my echoing voice.

She studies me, expression unwavering.

Ten years. A whole decade of me harboring the hurts that started with *the lost ones.*

"I've listened to every conversation you've ever had—I know you've never said it outright, but I've seen it, Joo. The guilt you've carried, the blame. The way you tried to, I don't know, fix it by changing every piece of you." I stare at the woman in the casket as intensely as I feel Scotty staring at me. "And, regardless of how different our unique shades of fucked up are, I know just as well as you how hard it is. To carry it alone."

I glance at her, hating the hurt of it all and how right she is.

I take a step closer to the casket and stare at the beautiful woman, wishing she'd just open her eyes and walk right out of the room.

She's blonde, thin, by all appearances, healthy. Wearing a yellow sundress and a turquoise necklace. There's a beaded friendship bracelet around her wrist and a simple gold band on her finger. Gone just the same.

"Name's Katie. She had a brain aneurysm. Out of nowhere, the husband said. The kids found her on the kitchen floor," Scotty fills in the blanks. "Forty-two."

Me in a year and a half. I picture it. The boys six, Lyra just coming into her own. Missing it. Camp on a ballfield. Them without me.

"Some days I'd give anything to have your troubles, Joo."

At the confession, I look at her. Seeing my best friend—beautiful and confident and fiercely independent—through a new lens. For one of the few times in our three-decade-long friendship, there's a deep sadness in her eyes.

When I open my mouth, she shakes her head. "Not today."

I blow a breath, steadying myself. "I talk to them because they don't judge me."

"They are the least judgmental group I know," she says, lighter than before, taking my hand in hers as she stands next to me.

"I didn't talk to Camp, I see that. Part of it was because I loved him—love him. I wanted him to be happy. Wanted Lyra to be happy. And-and-and when"—I pause, unable to say the words—"I didn't want to bring him down with me, you know?" She nods; I sniff. "And I just thought if he really loved me—if we were really so good together—he would have just known. Like I shouldn't have to say it all." A fresh shot of tears pour down my face. "Now . . . now it's too late. I never told him how hard it all was. He's gone and Lyra hates me." Another wave of garbled sounds and sniffles erupts out of me.

She gives me a tissue.

"It's not too late," she says, matter-of-fact. "You're still here, Joo. There's always time if you're here and they are too. Talk to him. To Lyra. They might judge you, but they might listen. Say something back you need to hear. Make changes before it's too late."

I look at her, knowing that last line is not just for me, it's for her too.

Another nod.

Wipe of my cheeks.

Slow exhale.

"Can I have a minute in here?"

She squeezes my hand before releasing it. "Always."

When the door clicks closed, I study Katie's face—fair skinned and beautiful and wonder if I ever met her. If her kids would have been friends with mine. If in mere weeks, she might have a kid that's graduating too.

Instead of sitting on the chair to word vomit like I usually do, I drop to the concrete floor. It's cool beneath the skin of my thighs and cheek as I splay out on my belly like a starfish, my pulse ricocheting between the floor and the boundary of my skin.

My own mortality clings to me between breaths. If I knew I would be where she was in two years—what would I do? What dreams would I chase?

I think of the boys, destroying the house.

The dog, destroying everything.

Lyra, hair colors like a mood ring, mouth like a whip, lighting up every room she walks into.

And Camp. Catching every dream he chases, no matter how big.

A tap on the window lifts my head. Scotty's familiar five-minute warning signal accompanied by eyebrows raised high on her head.

I nod but stand, not needing any more time.

I look at Katie, the friendship bracelet that was probably made by a kid, and grief undulates through me like the hills I've grown up in. "I'm sorry you won't see what's next."

Out of the room, I wrap my arms around Scotty. "I never talked to you because I didn't want to bother you, and you're a bossy bitch when you're right," I say into her hair, making her vibrate with a laugh against me. As I pull away, I add, "And sometimes, I feel guilty complaining about the kids and a husband. Like I'm rubbing salt in the wound or something."

"You got the family, Joo," she says, smoothing my hair with a serious look on her face. "But I got the better personality and looks. Nobody has it all."

I snort a laugh, hugging her again, tighter this time. "You can always talk to me, you know?"

"I know. But go fix your own shit, first."

Thirty-Eight

The five minutes it takes Lyra to make it from her classroom to the front office where I checked her out early drags on for eleven years.

Does she know it's me waiting? Is this purposeful torture? Did she skip school?

I pace the familiar laminate floor, every worst-case scenario playing through my head.

"Mom?"

I jump, mid-pace, hand to my heart. "Lyra."

She holds her palms out, a *What the hell do you want?* expression on her face.

Right.

"Sorry, right. I want to, um, show you something." I tilt my head toward the parking lot. "You left this morning before I could talk to you."

She hitches her bag on her shoulder, blinks, then pushes passed me to the double glass doors of the school, opening it just enough for her to disappear into the sliver of brightness outside before it closes behind her.

In the car, it's silence.

At the ice cream shop, it's silence.

Sitting on the bench along Main Street . . . more silence.

"Here," I say, handing her a cup of ice cream as I take the first bite of my own.

She eyes it, me, then takes it without a word, breeze blowing her blue hair.

"I never wanted kids," I say, licking my spoon, watching a car whiz by us. "At least I never thought about it much—I don't know if I ever told you that. I thought your dad would play baseball, and I would, I don't know, tell stories with my camera. I liked shooting weird things—street signs, odd-angled portraits, trash, chairs . . . I didn't think anyone would ever get it, but I loved it. In college, I pivoted to something more serious. Landscape photography."

I laugh softly, imagining my old self as a ghost. Lyra's silent, gaze blankly ahead, ice cream untouched in her hands.

"I fell in love with your dad right in that diner." I point across the street to Paul's Pancake Shack. Green vinyl seats seemingly unchanged. Frozen in time. "He took me there on our first date. A breakfast. I always loved breakfast dates." My throat pinches with nostalgia, and I have to swallow through it before I can speak again. "He said to me, 'June Downin', I think you're the most beautiful girl in the world to eat pancakes, and I never want to eat them without you.' And I just knew that Saturday morning, with that rich southern drawl of his voice, I would love that boy all the way to forever and back. And I told him that too. I said, 'Camp Cannon, I'll love you all the way to forever if you keep feeding me pancakes.' And he laughed. Then he said, 'To forever, huh? What about back?' And it was stupid, but I played along. Pretending I had to think about it. Finally, I said, 'You feed me pancakes, I'll love you to forever and back.' And that was just . . . it."

For the first time she looks at me, features softening, just slightly.

"When he got the scholarship to go to App, it was a no brainer I'd go there. They had a good art department, and he'd be there. It was the easiest choice of my life. Our senior year, he got called up to the minor leagues." I laugh, remembering when he got the phone call. How damn happy he was—we both were. "It was perfect. He would go play; I'd figure out my career path. Maybe even photograph the cities he was playing in. I started looking at different photojournalism opportunities. Worked on building my portfolio as I waited tables."

"Then you got pregnant and your life was ruined," Lyra says, voice flat.

I start to argue, tell her that's not true, but close my mouth. I look at her, fire in her eyes, clenching the ice cream tight in her slender fingers.

"I did and it was."

She didn't expect my brutal honesty because her eyes widen to the size of baseballs, and I chuckle under my breath.

"At least life as I knew it. The life I had imagined for myself." I take another bite of my ice cream. "But I thought your dad would figure out his baseball career then I'd be able to figure out mine. When he got pulled up to the majors, we knew that was it. I waited again. His dream was so much bigger than mine." I pause, lick my empty spoon. "I was living with my parents"—I shoot her a *that was a nightmare* look that makes her *almost* smile—"but I just knew that was it. Him out on that mound—it's what he was made for, Ly. Then he got hurt and his contract didn't get extended..." My voice trails off as the memories rush in.

"I felt so bad for him. It's a devastating thing to watch someone you love lose their dream—have their heart broken. So when he said we'd saved enough money to buy his parents' house, move back home and me stay home with you, I didn't say a word. I did it because I wanted to make him happy after baseball was gone. I put my camera and dreams in a tub in the garage, sealed it like a tomb. Focused wholly on you. They were good years."

I pause, studying her, wondering how much to tell her. How much she's ready for.

"I had two miscarriages," I tell her, my first time saying the word in years. "Lost two siblings that you'll never know."

A semi screeches by, and I tilt my head toward the sky, letting the sun warm my eyelids. I imagine them today sitting with us. They'd be thirteen and ten. Camp's *lost ones*.

"And I blamed myself. Because it was my body. Because I wasn't sure I wanted more kids. Because, selfishly, I wanted time to pursue my own interests."

I pause, breathing through the tears that crack my voice. There's not a 3-2-1 in the world that can save me from the pain, so I sit through it and let it singe my heart.

"The first one happened a week after I found out I was pregnant, you were little, four. The second one was worse—in my second trimester. I was already starting to show. We had told all of our friends and family. 'Sorry, June, we can't find a heartbeat,' the doctor said."

She stills next to me, but I can't look at her. Not as I force myself to breathe. Not as every memory that fills my mind feels like a fever dream.

Camp wasn't with me; he was coaching—out of town at a tournament. I didn't tell him until he got home the next day. They won the state championship; I lost our baby. I couldn't get in to have the surgery until the following Monday, and for three days I carried the dead baby around in my hollowed-out insides feeling like a walking wasteland.

He came home, smiling wide with a trophy in his hand as he swung the door open and stepped inside. I was his opposite: bloodshot eyes, breakfast wine, a disheveled pile on the couch next to Lyra watching TV—a documentary about dolphins. I remember it because one gave birth to a stillborn, and it showed the mother dolphin nudging the dead baby with its nose, desperate for it to start swimming. Seemingly out of nowhere, I started sobbing, and Lyra looked at me like I was crazy.

What's wrong? Camp asked, dropping the trophy on the floor as he scrambled to me.

I lost the baby. My voice was flat, like I wasn't even in my own body.

For the first time—the only time in our lives together other than when he peeled away from the art gallery—Camp dropped to his knees and cried.

I did the same, consumed with grief and guilt. Grief, because I lost another baby. Another life I imagined growing side by side with Lyra. With me.

But the guilt? The guilt was almost worse. I didn't know if I even wanted more kids, and I was convinced my doubtful thinking led to what happened. Like I willed this tragedy into fruition simply by being a tired and overwhelmed woman. And even worse, maybe this meant I was never meant to be a mom at all. Maybe Lyra being here was a fluke. The loss was a sign of my inadequacy as a parent.

In my grief-stricken state, the thirteen- and ten-year-old kids that would have been here today were gone because of me.

Next to me, Lyra takes the first bite of her ice cream.

"It's a weird thing," I confess when I can speak again. "They aren't people you've met, yet somehow, you know them. These little heartbeats deep in your belly that have a whole life ahead of them—God, do you know them. Even though they aren't, they so tangibly are."

I pause, but not to cry. This time it's to take a full breath. The relief from my confession is so instant that it feels a bit like a magic trick. Like, me telling someone all this was all I've ever needed, and it's enough to make me want to cry again.

"After that," I say, "I poured myself into you. Being the mom you needed. Fueled by guilt or grief or whatever it was. I wouldn't have any more kids, but I'd be a good mom to you. And your dad had coaching, started playing on the softball team. He was happy, I was lost. I never told him. Figured I'd find my way. 'These things take time,' the doctor told me. So I started listening to podcasts, I started . . ." *Visiting dead bodies at Scotty's.* Nope. Not ready to unleash that level of crazy on my kid. "Anyway, I just needed a little more time to sort it all out. I told myself when you started high school, I'd take time to do something for myself. My timeline in the sand until—"

"The boys," she finishes for me.

I nod, laugh softly, and take another bite of ice cream as three cars drive by.

"Camp got busier with baseball, and I resented him for that, I think. He was so happy, doing something he loved. Setting goals and chasing them. State championships, the complex, and if he says he wants nationals next year, mark my words he'll have that title. And Lyra, I need you to hear everything I'm saying." I turn to face her, setting my ice cream on the bench between us. "People tell you about potty training and sleepless nights, but they don't tell you how fucking hard being a mom is." Her eyebrows shoot to the sky at my language, but I don't apologize or stop. "About the slow drain that happens if you aren't careful. How you exchange who you are for a different version of yourself without even knowing. Somewhere between dinners and homework and car lines, you forget yourself. And, somehow, despite how hard and thankless it all feels, when you lie in bed at night, you still worry. You still wonder, did I do good enough today? Did I love these little people enough? Encourage them to be nice people and treat others fairly? Do they know how valuable they are? How much I love them?"

I don't wipe the tears that fall like raindrops down my face. Instead, I pick up my ice cream, take another bite, and watch another truck whiz by.

"And somewhere between all these little people we chase, we forget about our marriage. It gets shaved away if we aren't mindful. If we don't tend to it like a garden. Your dad got busy . . . and I let him. Until I was so far gone I didn't know how to fix it. I just needed to feel like myself again. Just needed a break. But, instead of handling it, I made a mess."

"Is that why you showed the entire senior class your ass in that ridiculous bathing suit?"

Despite my tear-streaked face, I let out a watery laugh. "I guess so, yes."

For the first time, Lyra smiles. "A warning would have been nice."

I shake my head, scrape the bottom of my cup for the last drops of now-melted ice cream.

"I do love you, Ly. And your brothers. And your dad. Life is just . . . messy. None of this is your fault. Or his. Sometimes"—I shrug—"people break."

She finishes her last bites of ice cream, then we stand, arms hooked as we walk toward the minivan.

"Sorry about the miscarriages, Mom."

I lean my head on hers as we walk. "Me too."

"So, you and Nick?" I ask as we drop our ice cream cups in a trash can and I unlock the van. "How was prom . . . and everything . . . ?"

She smiles and her cheeks go pink. "Not the same as your night in the tent with Dad, if that's what you mean."

They did not have sex.

She sees the relief on my face, laughs again. "I trust him, but"—she shrugs—"the time wasn't right." She pauses as she opens the door. "And, I'll tell you when it happens."

Deep in my belly: butterflies. Not because she didn't have sex, but because she'll tell me. Because she doesn't hate me. Just . . . because.

In the driver's seat with a weight lifted, my phone dings, and I slide it out of my pocket, hopeful it's Camp.

Hope dies; I groan as I read.

Ms. Mitchell: *Mrs. Cannon, your unruly children have disrupted my class for the last time. Please come see me today at 3.*

I mutter under my breath, hammering away at the keys, rewriting it twice to remove all the swear words. Settling on, *I'll be there.*

"Everything okay?" Lyra asks.

I back out of the parking space. "I'm about to make up for all the words I haven't said."

Thirty-Nine

I settle in a kid-sized seat across from Ms. Mitchell, the boys on either side of me, faces covered in temporary tattoos, as her too-pungent perfume wafts across her desk toward us. Behind us, Lyra sneezes—no doubt from the scent—crammed into a miniature desk of her own.

"As you can imagine, this is not acceptable." Ms. Mitchell gestures to the boys, thick pink fingernails like arrows pointing at each of them.

"Right, well, they are temporary . . ."

"Every student!" she shouts, all of us jumping.

"That's a lot of tattoos," I say, looking down at each of them, making them soften. "Where'd you get that kind of cash?"

When Hank snorts a laugh, Ms. Mitchell sucks in an appalled breath. "You think this is funny?" she demands. "That's part of the problem. You have boys with no regard for rules—for discipline! Just because they have a big-shot father doesn't mean they can get away with this. Bad apples, both of them, with nobody to show them—"

"Enough!" I snap, eyes leeched onto hers. "Lyra," I say without looking away from the witch across the desk. "Take the boys in the hall and wait please."

The boys jerk to a stand, the three of them all but running toward the door. When they are out, I wait for hushed voices to move down the hall before I speak again.

"Do you have kids, Ms. Mitchell?"

She cocks her head, busying herself with the hem of the sleeve of her shirt. "Not that it's any of your business, but no."

"Ah," I say, pausing. "Kids are hard. Twins are harder. Great—an adventure—but God it's a pain. Two of everything. The good *and* the bad. Two hugs, two diapers. Two smiles, two screaming hungry mouths. Blah, blah, blah." I blow out an overly exaggerated breath. "I couldn't nurse them, not the way I could with Lyra. It was too hard. My body hurt. And my *nipples*!" I drop my head back with a booming laugh as her eyes widen. "Those puppies scabbed right over they were so raw. Scabbed right to my shirt." I cup my hands around my chest and squeeze to emphasize my point. The look of horror plastered across her face pleases me way more than it should. "So I went to my pediatrician with two-week-old babies in two clunky car seats. I was crying, they were screaming. I said, 'I'm struggling to nurse, I think they need formula.' And do you know what he said to me?" I pause, but not long enough for her to answer. "He said, 'June, if you give these kids formula, they will have a lower IQ than everyone else in their grade level. They won't perform as well.' I was the oldest mom in that pediatrician's office that day, and God—I had never felt more like a failure in my life." I think of me, oversized T-shirt, bags under my eyes, hair unbrushed. Then I think of the library moms, the guilt I felt every time they nursed in front of me, reminding me of everything I wasn't. "I told him I'd try harder, but on the way home, all of us screaming, I stopped at the grocery store to get formula because I was about to lose my ever-loving mind if I didn't do something."

Ms. Mitchell opens her mouth to speak, but I talk over her. Again.

"Every time something goes wrong, I think of that conversation. Every time I see a woman nurse my chest tightens with guilt—even all these years later. Every note you send home, every red card they get, every condescending text message. I think, *'My boys aren't listening—are causing so much destruction—because I fed them sub-par formula as babies.'* I become that scared mom in a pediatrician's office all over again. Desperate to be good enough but being told I'm not."

Again, she tries to speak, again I cut her off. This time, I stand from my small chair, hands on the edge of her desk, towering over her, my copper braid falling over my shoulder. She leans back. "But here's what I'm wondering. If they are so damaged by my inadequacy, why the hell are they able to find a way to put tattoos on the face of every child in a classroom with someone as intelligent as you in charge?" I click my tongue, small smile tugging at my lips. "Seems pretty damn smart to me. Genius, even."

"Ms. Cannon," she replies in a huff, mouth coming to a pucker. "If you are implying that—"

"It's *Mrs.* Cannon," I correct. A jolt of confidence firing up my spine. "And I'm *telling* you, learn to control your classroom and maybe my *bad apples* won't be able to ink up the faces of the entire four-year-old population of Ledger. Or maybe the board needs to hear how little their teachers think of the students in this district."

Her eye twitches as my words linger between us. With a grin, I tap my knuckles on her desk, turning to leave. At the slightly cracked door, one hand on the handle already, I look back at her. "And, Ms. Mitchell?" She lifts her chin. "Camp Cannon has done more for this town than you ever will. Keep his name out of your damn mouth."

One, two, three beats of my heart later, she says: "Understood."

I slip out of the room, the door closing with a *click*.

In the hall, I freeze.

And then, like an athlete winning the gold at the Olympics, I have a pantomimed freak out. Trembling with adrenaline, my hands shoot into the air, legs run in place, and face does a full-blown silent scream over what I just did.

I defended my kids' honor and told off a teacher. Like a badass. Like Scotty would have done.

A door closes at the end of the hall, making me still, straighten, and come back to the adult body I live in.

Wait.

The hall is empty.

The door to the next classroom swings open and Lyra and the boys come barreling out, shouting and punching fists in the air.

"Way to go, Mom!" Lyra yells, smacking my hand in the air.

"You told her, Mama!" Ty shouts as he hugs my leg while Hank screams, "We ain't bad apples!" with his hands in angry fists over his head.

I stare at them. Judging by their shouts, hugs, and terrible dance moves, not only did they hear me, they're proud.

A loud laugh pours out of my mouth and bounces down the hall. I pull my shoulders back, brushing invisible dust off of them. "Oh, that? That was nothing."

"Seriously, Mom, the look on her face!" Lyra says, nearly doubling over with a laugh. "I wish we had a camera!"

As we climb a short staircase of four steps, she repeats the whole conversation and makes the boys howl with her voices.

For the first time in a very long time, maybe ever, I am two things at once: me and a mom. Like I'm not lost or hidden or covered up, I'm just there . . . waiting to be given space to breathe. Like the bad days and the second guessing and the formula-filled bottles didn't ruin everything. *Them.*

"Hey," I say, buckling the boys into the back of the van as Lyra drops in the front seat. "How did you guys get into that classroom next door? Or even know to go in there to listen? That should have been locked."

"Dad," Hank says, eating a stale Goldfish from the cupholder of his booster seat.

"Dad?" My eyes meet Lyra's in the rearview mirror.

She shrugs, reaching under her seat. "He said Ms. Mitchell sent him a message, too, but when he heard you in there he figured you had it handled."

"Did he hear everything?" I ask as I get into the driver's seat.

"You mean the part where you told her to keep his name out of her mouth?" She cocks an eyebrow, sliding an envelope from beneath the seat. "Oh, yeah he did." She grins, looking down at the folder in her hands. "What's this?" She passes it to me, and I squint, thinking.

Mave.

The envelope she gave me last time we visited.

"Nothing." I take it from her, slipping it back into my purse. "Just old papers from Nan. Must have fallen out."

"Where now, Mama?"

I blow a gush of air through my lips with sputtering puffs. Debating.

"Wanna go see your dad and how the complex looks?"

Forty

I've been to the baseball field of the complex and around a couple of the other fields when I was taking pictures, but I haven't been into the building in at least a month. The automatic door opens, the severity of the chemical-filled smell of "new" has been replaced by a too-strong concoction of Pine-Sol and Clorox.

In the center of the small atrium, a sculpture made by the high school welding class forms a metallic mass of various balls and athletic equipment.

"Cool," Lyra says, dragging her fingers across the seemingly floating laces of a metal football.

"Cool," I echo, slowly taking in the rest of the space.

The once bare walls are now covered in team photos and trophy cases.

The boys take off running down a hall toward Camp's office, screaming like cowboys, Lyra and I wandering behind. A photo of eighteen-year-old Camp playing baseball catches my eye, and I still. So young, yet still so similar.

"Mom," Lyra calls from the hall. "Did you do this?"

Next to her, I'm stunned dumb. Because yes, I did.

A large photo fills the space of a cleat-footed runner, sprinting to first base, dust flying up. For the shot, I used a slow shutter speed, focusing on the base itself. So, while the base is in focus, the legs and feet running by are a blur. And, due to the recipe of soup the boys made that night—heavy on the dish soap and food coloring—turquoise droplets explode across it. The coloring makes a viewer wonder if it was taken yesterday or forty years ago. Relatable, nostalgic, pure.

I nod, tracing the gold plate under the photograph: *Time Flies, June Cannon.*

"And this?" she asks, voice leaking with something unnamable as she looks at the next one.

I laugh under my breath, nod again. "I did."

Looking down the hall, I see it—every photo I had on display at the art gallery is here on the walls of the complex. "I shot all of these," I whisper to nobody. "Camp bought them."

"Mom, these are awesome. Why didn't you tell us?"

I shrug, not able to find words. He knew I had a show. Bought all the pieces. Hung them in this place, for everyone to see.

"And a plaque too?" Lyra whistles as I move to stand next to her and she reads the words: "Collection of art shot by local photographer June Cannon, capturing the joy and magic of Ledger, North Carolina in her collection LOVE AND LITTLE DETAILS."

A baseball-sized lump forms in my throat as I read and reread it. I force myself away toward his office where the boys are already on the floor wrestling, the room otherwise empty.

"Hey, June."

I look up; Jack's there, rapping on the propped-open door, brown shaggy hair hanging from beneath his Lake Trout cap. "Camp just went out to the new gym before heading out to practice with the team. You wanna come with?"

"Hey, Jack." I smile, gesturing for the kids to go. "Sounds good, I'll be right behind."

The kids walk into the hall, Jack standing back. "Bet you're ready for the change of pace next year, huh? I know Camp is." He shakes his head with a whistle. "I don't know how he does it all."

My confusion is written on my face because he follows up with, "The coaching?"

The coaching?

I nod. "The coaching, right . . ."

"I mean, we were stunned, but leave it to Camp, right? Kinda like Mary Poppins the way he floats in here, fixes things, then on to bigger and better things . . ." He laughs, as though he's said something funny. The boys shriek, and his expression morphs to a silent *Get it?* to which I smile too big with all my teeth showing. Because no, I don't *get it*. "Or scarier things."

"Right. You mean the national championship and the tournaments or . . . ?"

"I can only hope!" He scrubs a palm across his jaw. "Don't pressure me!" With a final grin, he flicks a two-finger salute from his cap in my direction before spinning on his heels. His long strides eat up the hall as he playfully swats at the boys when he catches them, and they disappear toward the new gym.

What the hell was that?

In Camp's office, I try to fit the pieces together as I plop into the chair at his desk, black leather-like material sucking me in. His inbox is open on the computer and my eyes flick to the screen. The unexpected name on the top stops my heart. *Reed.*

The subject: *nice nose.*

I'd laugh if I didn't feel like my insides were being swallowed by quicksand.

My gaze goes to the hall—empty. I shouldn't—it's unread—but I click to open it.

>Camp,
>
>
>We both know she made her choice a long time ago. Lucky for you, she has terrible taste.
>
>
>I haven't sent these to her yet. I figured making you live a lifetime with my mark on your face was suffering enough.

That girl will chase you forever, make sure you chase back.

I'd say take care, but we both know I wouldn't mean it.

-R

PS: I kissed her to piss you off. Judging by your tantrum, it worked. You're still the asshole.

I hover the mouse over the files—there are three—absorbing the words on the screen as well as a too-wet sponge on a spill. Nothing makes sense. My photos. This email.

The hall is still empty.

I suck in a breath, click, and close my eyes for the split second it takes to load.

When I open them, it's there: my silhouette, soft, filled with a serene shot of Lake Ledger, but instead of moody tones, it's vivid and colorful. It looks altered in some way . . . then I realize: I shot this image. He used one of my photos along with his. The file name: *Lake Ledger Sweetheart.*

The next one, file name *June Multiplied*, features the same silhouette, but this one is filled with the kids . . . and Thor. The boys are sitting on Lyra's lap, Thor's head on Hank's knee. They're laughing. I took the photo one afternoon sitting on the front porch. It's weird on first glance, my bare back framing my kids' faces in, but somehow, Reed did it. Made it work. Hand to my mouth, I laugh in disbelief, click to the next one.

The image makes fresh tears fall.

The silhouette is slightly different; I'm smiling but my eyes are closed. I'm guessing it was an in-between shot, or, knowing Reed, he had a plan. And there, layered with me, is Camp. Actually, Camp and me. The photo Lyra took at the picnic. File name: *June in Love*.

I trace the lines of the photo with my fingers. Me. Me and Camp. What was it Scotty had said? *You can be more than one thing, June. Hell, you can be a million things.*

She was right; of course she was. I see it in every picture on the screen. Me and this town. My kids. Camp. My photos.

I pluck a tissue from the box, wipe my eyes, close out the images.

I pick up a frame on his desk. A family photo of the five of us from a year or two ago, taken in the dugout of one of his games. I smile at us, set it down, grab another one—it's new. A gold frame, just me in the center. Champagne over my head, smile on my face with a toe kicked up. The picture of me that Scotty took at the gallery. *Of course.* Team Camp from the beginning.

I slide my phone out of my pocket.

Me: *You told Camp about my gallery show.*

Instead of a response, it's a series of screenshots of the conversation from that night.

Scotty: *Your wife is a pain in the ass*

[picture of me]

Camp: *Ive noticed are all those hers*

Scotty: *God, learn punctuation. They are and she's kind of amazing.*

[two more pictures]

Camp: *Buy them all will ya send me a total and tell the gallery Ill drop a check off tomorrow*

He went to the gallery? Of course he did. I think of him in the kitchen that perfect Sunday morning, laughing about a secret admirer buying my photos. It was him. All along, it was him.

Camp*: if dbag reed is there knee him in the nuts*

I snort out a laugh despite the knots permanently tying themselves in my stomach.

Scotty: *Green isn't your best color, Campy.*

"J." A voice pulls me from the screen of my phone. *Camp.*

I stand, sliding my phone into my pocket.

"Hey. Sorry." I clear my throat, swiping at my cheeks one last time. Too-long silence weighing two tons as I stand. "You saw my photos. You know about my photos." I laugh, nervous. Then, finally, "You have my photos."

He glances down the hall, a bold image of the crowd in the stands clear from his open office door. Arms folded over his chest, his expression is guarded as his jaw pops with a tension so visceral I feel it across the room. "Looks that way."

"I think that's nepotism." I shoot for a joke and settle with tragic. I wince, clear my throat, and try again with, "Jack seems—"

"Daddy," the boys shout together, tackling his legs. Lyra jogs up, red-faced and hinging at the waist, hands on her knees as she gasps for air.

"God, Dad," she pants. "You're hard to track down, and this place is too big."

He smiles, but it doesn't meet his eyes. "Sorry, tyin' up loose ends for tomorrow night. Y'all wanna ride the Gator out to the field with me?" The boys yell, loving any excuse to ride the school's UTV, and Lyra nods, still trying to catch her breath.

He tilts his head down the hall, signaling them to head that way, and grabs his ball glove off the chair, slapping it against his outer thigh twice. "You comin'?" he asks, devoid of emotion.

"Uh, no, I don't think so." I force a tight smile. "I have some errands to run. Maybe just bring them home after."

He nods, turns to leave.

"Camp," I call; he turns in response, eyes bouncing between mine. "Sorry."

"For what?"

I shrug, look around his desk, the walls of the hall through the windows of his office. My photographs. "Everything."

He nods, studies me, then says, "Me too."

Without a second look, he leaves.

Forty-one

My pulse rams in my throat as I fumble with the long-forgotten folder Lyra found.

Seat slid back, there's enough space between my body and steering wheel and I dump the contents—all papers—onto my lap.

The first few pieces are newspaper clippings, dating all the way back to high school. Camp setting records. Camp getting a full-ride scholarship to App State. A clipping from *Virginia Beach News*, him on the minor league team. Him at Charlotte, in the majors. His injury. Camp's whole baseball career pinched between my fingers in typed words and black-and-white photos.

A notecard slips out, then a handwritten letter. Camp's familiar handwriting with too-slanted t's and upright l's.

Mama,

I know you're mad and think I'm throwing away a dream for nothing. But I'm telling you—and Daddy if he'll read this—she didn't ask me to do this, but I need to. Baseball is baseball. A ball, glove, and fancy stick. But June? She's been the center of it all since I was a kid without a clue. I did what I came to do—pitched a game in the majors. Pitched a good season. And yes, they want me. But to what end? A life on the road, away from them?

I won't do it.

She can never know, she'd hate herself. Probably even hate me. But I'm not going back. I'm coming home. To her and Lyra. You've always told me to chase my dreams, and I always have. But you've also told me some dreams change, and we have to change with them.

And I know Daddy's mad about the money. He's too proud for his own good. You spent a life sacrificing so I never had to—I bought the house, paid what I paid, so you can have the farm you've always wanted. You carried mail you never cared about, and he worked all those hours so I could someday write this letter. I'm not taking the money back—if he wants to go the rest of his life without talking to me, it's worth it.

Love ya, Mama. Daddy too.

Camp

The world stops spinning with the next paper. An offer letter for another season with the Charlotte Copperheads. Camp's arm healed. He *quit* baseball; he wasn't cut. For me. Overpaid for his parents' house so they could afford the farm they love. Without telling me.

That stubborn, stupid asshole.

I throw the letter in the passenger seat, swipe the tears, and point my minivan toward the gallery.

"My husband bought my photographs," I say, spine stiff as I face Irma from my chair.

She sips tea from a bright pink mug, eyes narrowing before she presses her mouth to a tight line. Assessing.

"If I say yes?"

I concentrate on my hands in my lap. Picking invisible lint off my jeans. "Then I guess I'm wondering how that went. You met him."

She eyes me, takes another sip of her tea before setting it down. "Reed's dad was the one that didn't love me back. At least not as much as I loved him."

I don't react, not surprised by the confession. She either doesn't notice or doesn't care because she continues without prompt. "I met him in Utah. He was a writer. Dabbled in all kinds of freelance stuff. He was a mixed bag: half free spirit, half deep roots." She smiles a fond shape. "Anyway, we met. I was photographing the national parks; he was writing an article about planning a summer trip to the same spots. So we partnered up, spent the summer together. His kids were grown, out, and his marriage had gone stale, and I was alone and had an affliction for scandalous romances."

My jaw drops and she laughs, waving a hand through the air. "I am what I am, June. Can't fault a woman for that."

And there, despite how unorthodox her choices, I admire the hell out of her. She is who she is. Her choices are hers. The opposite of me.

"Anyway, it just happened. I fell in love with him that summer between dusty canyons and dried-up creek beds. He loved me too. The kind of way love stories try to describe. All consuming."

"What happened?" I ask, taking my first sip of tea, chamomile with honey out of a handmade mug—warm as it slides to my belly.

"The summer ended like summers always do. He came home, but we made a plan—I'd come back here. He was going to tell his wife, and we'd be together. Travel as a writer-photographer duo."

I nod, her gaze goes to the window where a couple walks by. She studies their movements until they wander out of sight.

"We did just that, but when I saw him with her, I knew we were over. She's beautiful, Reed's mom, but that's not what struck me, it was the way they loved each other. Ruthlessly. He told her he'd been with someone else, and she was devastated. Then, she just forgave him." She snaps her fingers. "Just like that. Said she knew she hadn't been doing her part in the marriage, and she wasn't surprised he looked elsewhere for what she wasn't giving. When he told me—the look of admiration in his eyes when he repeated her words—there was no competing. It was like watching someone fall back in love."

"You left?"

She nods. "I left. Travelled for shoots like I always had, met Reed. His dad, Rocky was his name, never travelled again. He wrote local pieces for small newspapers and magazines about the Blue Ridge Mountains. It was for her, I know that. He never wanted to stray that far again—wouldn't let himself." She takes another sip of tea. "I know now I wouldn't have fit, you know? He was more roots than I ever was, but now"—she gestures around the gallery—"here I am, roots of my own, just growing a little later than most."

"Did you come back for him?"

She shrugs. "I knew I wouldn't be with him, but, maybe in a way. I got tired of the travel. Of keeping up with the change in technology. The hustle." She shakes her head slightly. "I figured if he was happy here, I would be too. Not with him, but kind of." She pauses for a beat. "I had lots of lovers, but he's the only one I ever loved like that."

I sag back into my seat, eyes going to the somber trail photo she made because of him.

"Shooting the world, I've learned some love stories are just like that. They end without happily ever after, just after. There for a blip of time, something that happens so another thing can. A heartbreak designed for the heal. People change. People *don't* change." Her bright eyes search mine as she lifts her cup again and we sit in silence. She sips her tea; I digest her words.

"What does this have to do with Camp?"

"Ah." She smiles. "Well, he came in here, introduced himself, handed me the check, and then there was one photo he just stared at."

My eyebrows pinch. "Which one?"

"It was a shot of the lake. Blurry people in the water—kids. *The Lost Ones*, I believe you'd titled it."

At this, a fresh shot of emotion rips through me and burns my face.

"Did he say anything?"

She pauses and takes another sip, moving so slowly it's like she's trying to torture me.

"Well, he stood there for a while, just staring, and finally I went over to him. I said, 'She's talented,' and he agreed. Then he said, 'I didn't know it was so hard.'"

My mouth opens but my voice doesn't follow.

"And, I'll admit, I was confused," she continues, "but I just stood there, waiting for him to say more. Eventually he did. He said, 'She was lost and I never knew. Not really. Or maybe I did but didn't want to see it. I thought I'd give her space, thought she'd come back around. I kept waiting and waiting to be invited, and now she's done all this, and I'm not supposed to even know.'"

When she takes another sip of tea, I feel my thousandth first tear of the day fall, and I don't have the energy to fight it or wipe it. I let my sadness stain my skin.

"Then he looked at every photo you shot, studied them like he wanted to memorize every little detail. And I saw on his face what I saw years ago on Rocky's: He was a husband falling in love with his wife all over again."

When she's done, I'm crying. Fully. Every single thing I thought I've known about my husband shatters. I see Camp anew. Like a Polaroid picture finally developing fully. Camp getting cut from the team even though I was so sure his arm looked good. Camp insisting on us living in that house. Camp seeing my art. Years of me bending in silence only to see that he's been doing the same, me never knowing. Balloons flying in different directions just needing a hand to hold them together.

Without realizing it, I've stood and started walking toward the door.

"June?"

I turn toward Irma as she crosses the room until she's next to me, startling me out of my daze with a paper in hand.

"*Travel North Carolina Magazine* is looking for a photographer to capture small towns around the state in a 'unique and inspiring way,'" she says, pausing as I read:

> Photographer needed to capture the quaint glory of North Carolina small towns, including festivals, dive bars, local residents, nooks and crannies, and secret gems. One town will be featured per month. Expectation is candidate can travel to one North Carolina town per month. Compensation covers all travel expenses and negotiated fee per article.

I blink as I look at her, swiping the tears from my cheeks. "I don't know, Irma. Am I even good enough for something like this?"

She chuckles softly, running her fingers across her short hair.

"You aren't Ansel Adams, and you aren't Irma London, but you're June *freaking* Cannon. Of course you are."

Forty-two

The drive home from Irma's is as blurry as the colors that fly by the windows. It's as though my world has been flipped. My entire reality changed.

I listened to a podcast once, it was a night after the boys fought me to sleep and Lyra and I had struggled with a science project—something about batteries and wires I couldn't figure out for the life of me. I was so mad at Camp that night, for letting me be there alone, drowning in motherhood. The frenzied monotony of it all.

Then the podcast—one on struggling marriages—said, "it always takes two people to get to where you are." That line made me even more angry; I was doing everything and him nothing. One person was to blame, I felt that truth at a cellular level, and it was him.

Now, remembering that night from two or three years ago, I almost laugh. Because though I was drowning, Lyra and I also giggled at how hard the project was. We both declared we had to be missing pieces. And Thor, just a puppy then, fell asleep in bed with Hank. I took a photo which now hangs in the living room. It was a hard night, but not as bad as it felt. Not anymore with the rose-colored glasses of hindsight putting it into perspective.

By the time Camp got home from his away baseball game, I was exhausted from the day and everything that had to be done the next that screamed at me in the silence of the house. I couldn't shut it off—the worrying, the overthinking, the need to get everything done and be the one to do it all the time. When he asked, "How was your night?" it turned my blood to ice. I was furious at his ignorance.

How was my night? I could have punched him in the throat for asking such an asinine question.

"Fine," I responded, not elaborating. Not explaining how I got my ass handed to me by the concept of electricity or twin two-year-olds that only operated in chaos mode.

Looking back now, yes, he was gone late. But through his eyes, he saw a clean kitchen, a finished project on the kitchen table, and heard the word *fine*. He had no way to know how *not* fine it all felt in that moment.

In the van's Bluetooth, I call Mave.

"Hello, June!" she chirps through the speakers, her smile evident from her tone. "To what do I owe the pleasure?"

"You should have told me, Mave."

Silence.

"About baseball. The house. I've-I've worried and resented and . . ."

Tears threaten to fall, but I refuse them. I'm sick of crying. Sick of countdowns I've lost track of.

"Ah," her voice softens. "Took you long enough."

"Well, you know, what's a few more weeks on top of the decades already wasted?" I say dryly, flipping my turn signal on as I switch lanes.

"If you would have known, what would you have changed?"

I'm silent.

"Exactly," she answers for me. "You don't know. You might be in this same situation because you'd be mad the other way. Marriage is just hard, Junie. If it wasn't this, it would have been something else. Maybe if you would have known, you wouldn't have been wounded for the same reasons, but you might still be wounded. We can't hide from struggle."

She's not wrong and it's extremely annoying. I wring my hands around the steering wheel, and she hears what I don't say, her tone softening when she speaks again.

"Junie, he loves you, but we're flawed people loving other flawed people. It's all work, never easy. None of us knowing how to do it right." A timer goes off in the background.

"Cookies?" I ask.

She chuckles. "You know me so well."

I hear the oven door open and close followed by the clamber of the pan onto the stovetop.

"So what do I do?" I ask, feeling suddenly vulnerable. "Now that I know, what do I do? Just-just-just—what?"

She chuckles. "Well, I'd start with the sex, but that's just me."

The first thing I do when I get home is throw the separation agreement away. If we are doing this, really ending our marriage, it's after a levelheaded conversation. I don't care if he wrote *I'm done* in the card with the flowers. I'm not, at least not this way. Not without a fight.

Plus, who agrees to a separation with flowers?

Now, after everything, I realize that while my heart was in the right place of knowing something needed a change, my head was absolutely not. Things felt dire, I went nuts.

I make dinner. It's another new meatloaf recipe—this one with barbecue sauce—as an olive branch to undo some of the mess I've made. An apology in the form of ground beef and chopped onions.

When Camp brings the kids home, I'll invite him to stay, and we can talk. Really talk. Starting with Reed. Which, if he's read Reed's email, maybe won't be so bad.

The door opens; Thor barks.

Hank barrels in first.

Then Ty.

Then Lyra.

Then . . . nobody.

"Where's your dad?" I ask, holding the fifth plate midair above his usual spot at the table.

Lyra pauses, looks at the table then the plate in my hand.

"Umm. He dropped us off at my car, I drove us home. He's got stuff to finish at the complex, something about the seating for the gala. And the sound system, or something . . ." Her voice fades as I deflate like flat tire with disappointment.

"Of course, right." I clear my throat. "Boys, wash up and let's eat."

Then we're around the table like we always are, Camp's absence not abnormal but much more obvious than usual. His empty chair a symbol of everything I've wrecked. Every sacrifice he's made that he never told me about, that I've never noticed.

More than once, I catch Lyra looking at me then the empty seat.

"Today's Best!" Hank shouts. "Mama telling Ms. Mitchell off."

I snort a laugh.

"Same. I bet we can get away with anything now," Ty says, earning a glare from me that makes him add, "or not."

"Lyra?"

She grins, blue hair framing her face, Camp's brown eyes looking back at me. "Ice cream with Mom."

I smile, fill my fork with meatloaf, and say, "Me too."

After dinner, after the boys are in bed and the kitchen is clean, I stand in the middle of the living room and a quiet so deep I feel it in the pit of my stomach. The sound I always long for hurts my ears. Even Thor is silent, sleeping on his bed.

It's as though I'm getting a glimpse into my future. Lyra leaving. The house emptying. Camp and the dog gone. Me alone. The house, a shell. Camp's trophies, Lyra's shoes, the dog bowl. Artifacts of a life that's suddenly finite.

"Whatcha doin'?" Lyra walks in and stands next to me in an oversized Ledger Lake Trout T-shirt and reading glasses.

"Contemplating life."

A laugh rumbles in her chest as she leans into me and wraps her arms around my waist. Head on my shoulder she stares at the same photos on the wall I do.

"Are you and Dad really getting a divorce?"

"Hmm," I say, hating the sound of the word. "I don't know."

"Do you still love him?"

"With my whole heart, Ly."

Then we're quiet, looking at the pictures that show pieces of who we used to be and who we are now. Our entire evolution in small frames.

"What are you still doing up?" I finally ask her.

She straightens with a heavy sigh. "I'm working on this speech for the gala—and I suck. I can't think of a word to say."

"What are you writing your speech about for graduation?"

"My hero." She grins.

Of course. Camp, no doubt, will make for an easy speech topic.

"You could use the same one, maybe? I mean, your dad is the evil genius behind the whole operation."

Her eyebrows pinch then her expression changes, as if understanding. "Yeah, I don't think that would fit."

I nod again, consider the situation. The gala. Camp's work on this complex for years, all leading to this. Him asking me to speak, me turning him down. Guilt grips my chest.

What if . . . ?

"You think Nick's still awake?"

"Yeah . . ." she says, skeptical as she adjusts the glasses on her face. "Why?"

"Get your notebook," I tell her, "And your phone. I have an idea."

Forty-Three

Years of plans, fundraising, and meetings have all led to this. The complex is here. A dream for the school and the town alike, due in large part to Camp.

It's been three grueling days since the fiasco at the studio—three days of him staying at his parents' and me realizing how wrong I've been. About damn near everything. This can't be how it all ends. I refuse.

Pulling back the thick green curtain, I peek my head around to search for him in the crowded room. Round tables with white tablecloths are scattered around the center of the dimly lit banquet room and topped with wineglasses, votive candles in bubbled glass jars, and water pitchers. Along the perimeter, rectangular tables are covered with baskets and gift certificates, familiar faces walking along them placing bids for the silent auction items.

Across the ceiling: strings of lights. Thousands of little bulbs hang in the air and look like the starriest sky there ever was.

It's packed, and, for lack of a better word, incredible.

All these people, many of whom I've known since I was a kid—some even childhood friends of my parents—all here because Camp had an idea and ran with it. I don't know if I've ever once told him how impressive that is.

Finally, I find him. He's laughing as he shakes a hand—Greg, the cross-country coach—then only making it another step before someone else stops him. Easy smile on his lips, he's devastatingly handsome in his suit. His face is clean-shaven, his clothes tailored to his lean body.

He entertains every single person that stops him. Patient and smiling easy, his face is filled with genuine gratitude. As he slowly makes his way through the crowd, toward a table, I see him so differently. Through the eyes of all these people as they beeline toward him. Every single person here loves him.

And he picked me.

He sits, looks around the room, takes a sip of champagne, then checks his phone. His knee starts bouncing rapidly—he's anxious. Someone takes a seat next to him, he puts his phone away, takes another sip, and quickly falls into another conversation.

"Mom?" Lyra whispers.

I turn to her, smile. "Hey!" I whisper back. "You get it finished?"

She nods, grinning. "Barely. You got your speech ready?"

I laugh a breathy *ha!* sound. "Something like that." I hold up a paper, covered in my scribbled thoughts. "This might be one of those *fly by the seat of my pants* situations."

Gus walks by, giving me a quick hug before a whispered, "Show time!"

Lyra makes an excited noise, making me laugh as she grabs my arm.

Gus takes the stage, standing behind the mic, welcoming the crowd.

I can't focus on a single thing he says.

Last night when Lyra told me she was struggling to come up what to say, I knew this was it. My chance to apologize. To see the other side of Camp that Mave, Irma, and Scotty all knew, but I refused to look for.

I made a promise to myself as I laid in bed last night: No more strangers with microphones. These women that know me, they are the ones I'll sit with. Listen to. Let tell me hard truths from here on out.

"Alright, folks," Gus says as the lights dim further. "We have a fun evening ahead to celebrate this monumental accomplishment." He pauses, waits for the stragglers to settle in their seats. "Ledger has been described as both Americana and sleepy, the lake our only claim to fame. That's all we have to offer, or so I've heard." A few chuckles from the crowd. "But we've always been a team. Our community. The kids that fill these fields after school and on the weekend. The parents that shuffle kids around, coaches that work tirelessly to help them succeed." Another pause and look around the room. "And we most certainly wouldn't be here tonight if it wasn't for our very own athletic director and baseball legend, Camp Cannon!"

At the applause, I can't stop the grin that overtakes my face, stealing another peek at Camp, smiling humbly and waving slightly around the room. Hating the attention but accepting the appreciation.

Gus chuckles behind the mic. "While I could go on and on what this complex—and Camp—have done for our community, I have someone much more qualified than myself." He extends his hands out to the side. "Let's welcome Camp's much better half, June Cannon."

Gus's eyes meet mine across the stage as he claps along with the audience, and I freeze. "Mom, go!" Lyra says in a strained whisper, pushing me.

Dizzy with nerves, I take my first step from behind the curtain, feeling myself flush, smoothing the shirt I'm wearing—Camp's high school baseball jersey—and adjusting my fitted pencil skirt before crossing the stage to my spot behind the microphone.

At the podium, I gesture playfully for the crowd to stop. "Y'all sure know how to make a girl feel welcome."

I laugh, nervous, and pause, my eyes latching onto Camp's, which are stunned.

"Gosh, so many familiar faces when I look around this room. Feels a little surreal, right?" I begin, heads nodding in the crowd. "A lot of us have called Ledger home forever. Some of y'all might be a little like me and never imagined that twenty-two years after leaving this town you'd somehow call it home. Somehow be standing right in the spot where it started for a lot of us. We were so smart then, weren't we? I mean, at least I was. Teenage June was smart the way all teenagers are: obnoxiously so." A wave of laughs ripples through the crowd. "At eighteen, I knew everything I was going to do. Couldn't imagine a life where my dreams wouldn't work out." I pause again, finding Camp's eyes. When his lips tug to a small smile, mine do the same. I look down at the paper, my well-crafted speech, and abandon it, folding it in half. When I speak again, it's directly to him. "Hi, Camp." I lift my fingers from the podium in a half wave. *Hi,* he mouths. I blow out a shaky breath. "What y'all might not know, is that in two weeks, Camp and I . . ." My words trail off as I think about this looming date that's been stamped on my timeline and how utterly crazy I've been. Camp's eyebrows raise; I lean close to the mic for dramatic effect. ". . .have a daughter graduating." He smiles wide. "And watching her these past months has been a bit like travelling back in time. Reliving my own history—for better or worse—as I watch her just begin hers. It's almost as if every single event—every thought and dream and idea—has been brought to the surface.

"For so long, I thought the best way to fly—the only way to fly—was to leave Ledger. And the people in it." I glance around the room. "I got a lot of it wrong then. And now still, really. To err is to be human . . . or something like that." I clear my throat; the room stays quiet. "But, Camp? It's like that man was born knowing a secret the rest of us had to live to learn. He's always known that it takes a team. Always known people thrive *together*. He's known it so well that he decided to build a whole damn complex dedicated to the concept. Teamwork. Leaning on others. Not doing it alone. Asking for help and accepting it when it's given. I guess

I've known that, too, but in the words of my husband, I'm too damn stubborn." More chuckles. "But for all I didn't know when we were young. For all the bad ideas and dreams that never would be, eighteen-year-old June was ahead of her time in some ways . . . she found a boy and fell in love with him, knowing in her gut she'd love him all the way to forever and back."

At this, obnoxious catcalls ring out, and I grin. Across the room, so does Camp.

"But here's the thing," I continue, voice becoming strong and sure. "Dreams and truths are a fickle thing, and a man like Camp Cannon who has dedicated his life to the concept of team—to others—can never just belong to one person. He's too good not to be shared." I glance offstage, give a thumbs-up, and the screen behind me comes to life, a picture of Camp's high school baseball team filling it. I look to Camp; he laughs into his hands. "It started in high school, with this group of boys, and the coach that swore there was something special about him." I bring a hand to my mouth, stage whispering into the mic, "Like I didn't already know that," earning another wave of chuckles.

I click a button on a small controller, new image, Camp in college, playing baseball. "Then App State." Another click, team photo of him the minors in Virginia Beach. "Virginia Beach." Another click, him pitching for Charlotte. Arm pulled back mid-pitch in his deep-red jersey—so at home on the mound that year in the majors. "When Camp got called up to the majors, pitched that first game, I learned to share him with the world. And while Camp did a lot of amazing things in baseball, this is the year he traded one dream for another. Where a tough decision was made for the people in his life." My voice cracks. "His other team."

I pause again, Camp and I staring at each other like we are the only two people in the room. I click the button again, and a photo of Camp in his first athletic director office appears—cluttered and windowless—as he holds baby Lyra. "So we learned to share Camp with the school that brought us up." Another click, a team photo. "A new batch of baseball players." Another click, him drinking beer at the brewery with the softball team, clay-covered jerseys and wide smiles. "A group of men that tell their wives they can't miss a Tuesday night." Another wave of laughs, wives playfully slapping husbands' arms, lifting glasses in solidarity toward one another across the room.

"And now," I click again, and again, and again, images of the completed complex—photos that I took—fill the screen. "Now pieces of Camp Cannon will be shared with any kid that wanders onto these fields. Any parent, grandparent, and great Uncle Vernon that sits on these bleachers. Hearts will break and heal on this grass. Kids will learn what it means to work hard and succeed as often as they'll find what it means to work hard and fail. There will be fights. Noses will break." My eyebrows raise slightly as knowing chuckles bubble up around Camp's table.

"I didn't do half of what I set out to. Didn't make it very far out of Ledger before getting pulled back in. But Camp Cannon . . ." My breathing gets shallow as I click the button, photo filling the screen of me and him, the one Lyra took at the picnic. "Well, I'll love that man as long as everyone else does—all the way to forever and back." From under the podium, I grab a flute of champagne and raise it toward the crowd. "To Camp," I say, "who I love more today than I did when Scotty Armstrong threatened him into asking me out."

And with that, the room roars with claps and calls, glasses lifted, Camp's name on their lips before they drink.

I blink back tears, so does he.

"That's not all, Camp," I tease into the mic before stepping aside as Lyra joins me onstage with quick steps and a Ledger-green dress.

"Dad," she says into the mic. "We couldn't let this night go without hearing from your team. And, since they were so rudely left off the guest list"—more laughs—"here's what they had to say."

I click the button one last time, and a video starts. The first kid, Tommy, smiles wide on the screen revealing a mouth filled with braces.

"Coach, thanks for all you do. Never would have gotten out of that detention without your note."

Laughter bubbles across the crowd, and Lyra and I smile at each other with all our teeth.

It was a last-minute idea to make this video. She and Nick scrambled to get clips recorded and edited right up until this afternoon. This is the first time I'm seeing them all together.

The next boy, Grant, appears.

"Thanks for not benching me when I walked four batters in a row."

Another, Toby: "Thanks for driving me home from every practice when my parents were working."

Billy: "Thanks for believing in me, Coach."

Dyllan: "Thanks for showing up, CC."

"Thanks, Coach."

"We'll miss you, Coach."

What?

"We'll be lost without you; Coach Jack picks the worst music."

Jack? Jack.

Bet you're excited for next year; I know he is.

I freeze. Eyes—slowly—going to Camp.

"Won't be the same without you, Coach. Keep your office door open, we'll need to complain."

"You taught me how to throw a curveball, Coach—I'll never forget it."

Camp is leaving baseball. For me. Us. Again.

My eyes widen, and the room disappears. He nods. His wordless confirmation.

The video goes on until it ends, and the room erupts, snapping me out of my trance. Lyra's elbow digs into my arm as she claps, and I have to force my hands to move. It's a roar around me, nearly two hundred people standing and clapping for the man who is so much bigger than the teams he's played on and the complex he helped build.

"Did you know?" I ask Lyra when we shuffle off stage, whispering while Gus takes the mic again and starts talking about fundraising. "About next year. The coaching?"

She nods. "I found out last night. I guess Dad just told the team. Nick told me."

I squeeze her in a hug. "You did great."

She pulls back, tucks a strand of hair behind my ear. Our roles feeling backward. Her seeming grown.

"Go, Mom."

I nod, squeeze her again, then adjust my skirt before sneaking down the steps and out into the maze of tables and chairs, slipping into the vacant one next to Camp.

"Guess they like you," I whisper in his ear as I sit.

He turns to me, eyes searching mine in the low light.

"Jungle Rules," he whispers.

I take the lapel of his coat in my fingers and smooth a palm over it as an excuse to touch him. "I'm mad that you lied to me about baseball."

"I'm mad you lied to me about everything else."

"I'm mad I lied about everything else."

"I'm not coachin' next year. Not full-time. I'll help with the pitchers. And I'm still the athletic director, so I'll still have to be at games, but not as many."

My eyes search his.

"You don't have to do that." Applause happens around us as Gus finishes his speech. "I don't *want* you to do that."

He chuckles; soft music starts to play. "Yes, you do."

I exhale a laugh. "Fine, yes, I do, but you still don't have to. We can figure something else out."

"I want to. It's been years and . . . it's time. Jack wants it. He's excited, and I'm . . ."

"Old," I tease, letting my hands trace his jaw then dancing across to the bump on his nose. It's intimate feeling, but even though we're in a room full of people, I can't stop myself. "Why didn't you tell me?"

"I wanted to surprise you. You said you were going to the gallery; I went there to tell you." He shakes his head with a chuckle. "That backfired."

I drop my hands to my lap. "Reed did that, I didn't know. It was nothing, I—"

"I know."

"You know?"

"I know. I read the email."

We're quiet, looking at each other, as glasses clink and waves of conversations float by us.

"I'm not pregnant," I blurt.

His chin jerks back, confusion filling his eyes. "Okay, well the vasectomy probably helped with that . . ."

"Stay married to me."

His eyes narrow. "Wha—"

"You told me you thought I wouldn't have married you if I wasn't pregnant with Lyra. But now I'm not pregnant, so propose to me." When he hesitates, confused, I look around the room, filled with everyone we know, desperation forcing me forward. "Fuck it," I mutter, sliding out of my seat and onto the floor. I attempt to kneel with one knee, but my pencil skirt won't allow it. I settle on both knees, people around us noticing. Stopping. Staring.

"Marry me," I say, making nearby conversations stop. Camp stills, eyes wide. "Stay married to me. Let's keep trying. Let's-let's-let's have great sex and eat drugs and grow old together while the boys and the dog destroy our house. In Ledger. Together."

The tables around us are dead quiet now and I feel the weight of their stares and the gravity of the moment. For a split second I regret using the line "eat drugs" but the way Camp's lips twitch makes me think he very much enjoyed it.

He scrubs a hand down the side of his face while I'm still kneeling on the floor with an audience growing and my heart threatening to pound a bruise in my chest.

"Together?" he asks, feigning deep consideration.

"Together."

"To—"

My nostrils flare, and the word quickly turns to a laugh.

His hands cup around my face and, in a room filled with the people that watched us grow into who we are, my husband presses his lips to mine. "I'll stay married the hell out of you, June Cannon," he says against my mouth, pulling me to a stand before kissing me again.

This time when the calls and claps break out around us, it's not for a man, it's for love. For all our Today's Bests that it took to get us here. It's for how hard it is to make it—to keep fighting when it sucks. When it's loud. When it's exhausting. When we keep kicking even though drowning seems so much easier.

Loud music starts and chairs slide around the floor mixing with raucous laughter and conversation that breaks out around us.

"Great speech, June," a voice says. *Dani.*

I smile, leaning into Camp. "Thanks."

And then I see it: her hand in Jack's. Another fabricated story vanishes from my brain, replaced by what's real. She smiles at me, cheeks pink as she catches me looking at their hands. Dani and Jack. Together. She wasn't giggling at Camp—it was Jack.

I am a fucking moron.

Camp's eyebrows raise—he knows. He's known. He watched me act like a jealous psycho, but he'd known all along this was the truth. *Ass.*

"So, Jack," I say, clearing my throat. "Next year, huh? You ready for it?"

He shrugs, boyishly handsome smile on his face. "I mean, it's not like my predecessor was a big deal or anything."

The conversation is easy and brief until they are pulled off into a different direction and Camp guides me out of the crowd.

"You could have told me." He blinks. "About Dani and Jack."

"Ah. And miss the chance to watch you get all hot and bothered with jealousy?" He lands a kiss on my nose. "Where's the fun in that, J?"

My hand in his, he leads me out of the banquet hall, into the atrium.

In front of the metal sculpture, I stop, looking around at what he's help build. The building, my photos.

I bring my fingers to the gold plaque under the one closest, *The Lost Ones*. "Thank you for this."

"They're good, J." He squeezes my hand in his. "*You're* good."

He dusts a kiss on my lips, but it doesn't linger. In an instant we're moving—fast. Camp is swallowing the space down the hall in long strides and a tight grip on my hand, the heels on my feet making it difficult to keep up.

"Where are we going?" I wobble as I step, stumbling in my shoes. "Camp, you're too fast." He only goes faster. "Jesus. Camp, are you listening? Slow down!"

At his office door, he pushes it open, pulls me inside, then locks it closed.

Panting and annoyed, I stare at him, hands on my hips. "What are we doing here?"

Then, he smiles—wolfish—and I get it.

"Way I heard it," he says, stepping close, eyes hot, southern drawl warm honey in my belly. "You asked me for great sex in front of a room of people and it seems pretty ungentlemanly of me not to oblige."

The giggle that starts to form on my lips is swallowed by his mouth on mine. When Camp lifts me onto his desk, I help christen the office of the only man I've ever loved.

Epilogue

Camp's hand squeezes my knee, making me realize it's bouncing. "Sorry," I say, shifting on the bleachers of the stuffy gym, fanning myself with a program.

"Hope that fancy new gym is a few degrees cooler than swampy balls," Scotty says from next to me.

"Ha. Ha," Camp says, adjusting Hank on the bleachers next to him. Over his shoulder, Mave smiles at me, winks, and hands both boys a cookie from her purse.

"You good?" Scotty asks, linking her arm in mine. "This is a big fucking deal."

I wince. "Scott, language. This is a school event, for God's sake."

"Didn't stop me when I was an actual student, not going to let it stop me now."

I roll my eyes but smile. Scotty is Scotty, forever.

Graduation is an event in Ledger. The people just show up, whether they know someone graduating or not.

My parents walk in, home for a few weeks from travelling around Florida, and gesture to seats in the front near my brothers—whom I haven't seen in months. I smile and wave before they sit. I watch them fall into easy conversation with the people next to them, old friends I recognize, like most people in this town are.

"You haven't come by to see your friends lately," Scotty says, now using her program to fan herself while also wafting air from the collar of her shirt—printed with Lyra's face on it. "You good?"

I steal a look at Camp, who's mid-conversation with his dad but shoots me a wink, before looking back to her. "Yeah, I'm good. I don't, uhh, think I'll need them anymore."

Her eyes widen, but she's also smiling. "Really?" She presses her lips together. "Good." Then, "The podcasts?"

"Or the podcasts."

She stops fanning herself, slinging an arm around me.

"Ladies and gentlemen," she shouts, "June Cannon is a real grown-up girl making her own decisions!"

When I smack her arm, she laughs.

"You're happy," she says.

"I'm happy."

We fall into silence as we watch the steady stream of people walk through the door. Stopping for small talk. Hugging family members. Most laughing. Some crying.

Out of uniform, in dark pants and a mint-green polo, in walks Ford.

I stay quiet, but I don't miss the way Scotty reacts. Her eyes on him, tension shoots off her like bolts of lightning in a storm.

"I'm not an asshole like you that finds it necessary to shout personal business, but you know that we need to talk about that, right?"

She resumes fanning herself, like nothing happened. "Nothing to talk about."

"Junie," Mave says from behind me on the bleachers, tapping my shoulder. "Did you tell Scotty about my sex party? It's next week, you know!" She grins, proud, looking over my shoulder to Scotty.

"No, Mave. I didn't—"

"I'll be there, Mavie," Scotty cuts in from beside me, making Mave shimmy her shoulders. "And so will our little Joo. She's sheltered."

When they both giggle, I swat Scotty on the arm.

On the stage set up in the middle of the gym, Gus takes the mic. "Alright, ladies and gentlemen, our graduates will be entering the gymnasium any minute, so if you can please find a seat."

"I'm not sheltered," I whisper-hiss to Scotty as the last people scurry to find seats.

She rolls her eyes and swears under her breath, fanning herself with the program again.

When the school band starts playing instrumental music, Scotty's off my radar. Camp interlaces his fingers in mine, but all I can do is stare at the doorway. Tears forming before the first kid even appears.

Then, he's there: in a hunter-green cap and gown, big smile, and tassel swinging wildly as he walks. Someone's son crosses the threshold to the next chapter of life. A child turns into a man right before our eyes.

The line files out. One after another. One hundred and seventeen ants in a line, marching toward their future. They walk across the back wall of the gym to form a line in the center, walking toward the front and the seats that await them. And then I see her, Lyra, walking with a proud smile. Her hair, for the first time in years, is its natural sandy blonde and hangs down her back.

No longer in control of my body, I release Camp's hand from mine bring my hands to my mouth, standing as I watch her walk. Trying to commit every detail of this moment to memory. Her. Trying to commit *her* to memory.

Lyra used to do this thing where she'd run out onto the playground, getting right to the middle where she would stop. Timid, she'd turn back, searching, almost frantically so. Waiting to see me. For me to wave at her before she'd run out of sight and play.

Now, in this stuffy gymnasium, she's a young woman, walking down a graduation aisle, head high. She knows I'm here, in the bleachers on the sidelines, but she doesn't need to look. Doesn't need to see me. All these years later, the tables have turned. It's me craning my neck to see her and waiting for her wave.

When she pauses. When she turns to look—I'm already waving. The only parent standing, Camp wraps his hand around my leg and squeezes as tears fall straight down my face at the sight of her. She laughs, waves back, then turns toward her seat, me still waving as she goes.

I get it then, why Mave and Dustin always stand and wave at us like idiots when we drive away. Because they know how fleeting it all is. The ache that comes with every goodbye and lingers until the next hello.

I sit, wiping my eyes. Camp's hand finds my knee and the expression on his face lets me know that he feels what I feel. His thumb captures the fresh shot of tears before he kisses my forehead.

"You did good, J," he says.

I sniff. "*We* did."

"We did."

"God, nothing's even happened yet. You two will never survive this whole thing," Scotty groans from next to us.

I dig my elbow into her side, making her grunt, as the assistant principal finishes his welcome speech. "And now, this year's valedictorian address from Miss Lyra Cannon."

Applause fills the gym, Camp cupping his hands around his mouth for a loud, "That's my girl!" Once again, emotion stunts my speech. The lump in my throat prevents me from doing anything but clapping.

Lyra steps up to the podium and unfolds a paper before smiling at the crowd.

"Good afternoon, parents, teachers, and fellow graduates," she starts, slight echo around the packed gym. "Based on my GPA and the fact I'm standing here, I'm officially the smartest person we all know." In her pause, Scotty cackles. "But we all know that's not true." She grins as a soft laugh rolls across the gym. "Sure, I worked hard, have a good GPA, but there are so many other factors that we don't think about. Like, for example, the fact that Stephen Nickols can take a computer apart and put it back together but had no desire to do homework in any class other than science." A few graduates chuckle, punching Stephen in his skinny shoulder while he shoots his arms into the air with a loud *yeah!* "Or, there's Maggie Fisher, who makes the best cookies anyone has ever tasted—after my Nan, of course"—Mave giggles behind me—"but somehow made it through our entire senior year without actually doing a single math problem."

Maggie stands, does a curtsy, and sits back down.

"And, of course, let's not forget the entrepreneurial spirit of Danny Griffen."

Our unknowing edible dealer tips his graduation cap and earns a knowing chuckle from most of the gym, even his dad Billy, especially Camp, and shockingly Scotty. When I shoot her a look, she shrugs.

"All that to say, sometimes the ones that we need to look to, those that know so much more than us and save us over and over again, aren't the ones giving the speeches. They aren't the ones at the top, receiving accolades, they are something else. Something quieter."

I look at Camp, smiling at him as I nudge him.

"Daddy's girl forever," I whisper to him as she continues.

"Sometimes," Lyra continues, "our heroes are standing right in plain sight. Living an ordinary life that we might mistake for simple"—at the word, I look back to Camp, and he nods, squeezing my hand in his—"but that's where we're wrong. Because while some of us are focused on big dreams, perfect GPAs, and graduation speeches, the ones who aren't are far from simple. Some heroes, I've learned, are the ones that sacrifice one thing—many things—to be great at something else—even if it's not showy. Even if nobody notices. Day after day after day, they just do this thing. Sure, I get to stand up here because I worked hard and got good grades, but I'm not the one who people will run to when their computer breaks. Not the one that will be delivering cookies at the end of a hard day. Not the one . . . sorry, Danny, I've got nothing." She laughs, so does he, and so does everyone else.

"In this life, though I've only had practice for seventeen years, I've learned that while the people who stand up here in the spotlight can do amazing things, so do the people that don't. The ones who clap from the sidelines and cheer for everyone else."

She pauses. Gaze searching around, stopping when she finds me.

"Mom," she says, voice cracking as I stand—once again the only one in the gym doing so. "You have spent your life teaching me how to be selfless. How to give and give and give. You give compliments and smiles. You give time. You once gave a peep show to the senior class in a ridiculous bathing suit." I laugh through my tears along with the entire senior class. "Thank you, for showing me that not all heroes wear capes. That the real superstars don't always win awards and get name recognition. Some are just there, loving everyone around them and taking care of the little details that nobody else wants to. The sole reason that others can shine like stars is because people like you create a sky for us to shine in."

I blow her a watery kiss; she clears her throat.

"From my mom, and many of yours, may we learn to be givers, caretakers, and lovers of life. May we be dreamers. May we spend our life working hard but loving harder. Even when life takes from us and crushes us. Even when we mess up. Even when we think nobody sees."

Scotty's hand wraps around mine, her eyes as wet as my own when I look down at her. I can't make fun of her; I can't even breathe.

"Mom, you're my hero. Thank you for being you so I can be me. When I grow up, I want to be just like you. Thank you."

She steps from behind the podium, gives an exaggerated bow, and the gym erupts with applause. Women around the bleachers dab their eyes, but I cry hardest of all. Because there, in front of everyone, my daughter sees me. All of me. All my parts and pieces. A life spent seemingly doing nothing is suddenly validated.

When I sit, Camp pulls me to him. "*Mama's* girl," he whispers in my hair. "Mama's girl."

"We did good," I tell him, wiping my final tears.

"We did good."

On a steadying exhale, I turn to Scotty, who's wiping her own eyes. "Now that I know Scotty has a heart, I guess this adds to the list of things we will be discussing at our next chat."

When she groans, I laugh.

"You know, you could have warned me you were going to get so mushy, you little shit," Scotty says, hooking an arm around Lyra's neck in the parking lot. "I mean, I would have skipped the eyeliner or something."

Lyra laughs, brown eyes sparkling. "Well, you know, had to make it memorable for dear old Mom here."

"Trust me," Camp says, hand finding the small of my back. "You absolutely did. I don't think she's ever cried that much at once. Actually, she might need water."

"Very funny." I smack his chest. "It was beautiful, Lyra. Thank you, I . . ." My voice catches, and she saves me from myself, pulling me into a hug.

"I love you, Mom," she whispers.

I stay quiet out of fear of weeping and instead hold on to her for as long as she lets me. Over her shoulder, my eyes land on a familiar face. A young woman—standing at the edge of a group around a graduate—with a toddler at her feet and a baby in her arms. When she gives me a tired smile, I recognize her from the lake. The one whose tears lead to mine.

I return the smile, her eyes go to Lyra, and something like hope fills her face.

Like maybe it's all worth it.

It's Nick's call to Lyra from somewhere in the crowd that pulls us apart.

"Go," I say. "Have fun with your friends. Your party starts at five, make sure you're there or your entire guest list will start a revolution."

She smiles, gives everyone another round of hugs, then goes to be with Nick. Nick, who she told me last week, she had sex with. She cried when she told me, overwhelmed with emotion, but by the end of our conversation, she was laughing. She trusts him the way I trust Camp.

"Now what, Joo?" Scotty asks.

"Now," I say, squeezing Camp's arm as a smile curves my lips, "I got that job that Irma told me about. One weekend a month we'll travel to somewhere in the state—all expenses paid—and I'll take photos for the magazine."

Hank barrels into me, hugging my knees and making me *oomph!*

"You and Reed should team up," Scotty says, smirking at Camp.

He drops his head back with an incredulous laugh. "You know, Scotty. If I didn't love ya, I'd hate ya."

"Oh, Campy, don't be silly. There's no fun in that."

"Reed is in Colorado for some art show," I tell them before giving Camp a wry smile. "But maybe when he gets back . . ."

He shoots me a look, but his eyes are smiling before he chases the boys across the parking lot, stopping to talk to some fellow teachers and graduates. While Scotty and I stroll arm in arm, her gaze goes somewhere ahead of us.

There, across the parking lot, Ford opens his truck door, eyes locked on Scotty.

"You know, Scott, you told me you'd stop hating Ford if I ended my divorce charade with Camp."

She whips her head toward me, hazel eyes narrowing. "Bitch."

I bark out a laugh.

I open my mouth; she holds up her hand.

"I hate you."

She grins. "I know you don't."

I sigh. "You're right. Unfortunately, I love you like I love Camp and the kids and even Thor."

"To forever and back?"

I drop my head on her shoulder, watching Camp with the boys ahead of us. "And then some."

Acknowledgments

Of the circle of women I'm lucky enough to call friends, we've collectively lost over twenty babies. In silence, we've grieved little people we never got to watch grow up and go do amazing things with their lives. At the time I'm sitting at my computer writing this, I personally would have nine-year-old twins who simply weren't meant to be mine.

If you've felt this kind of loss—the feeling of knowing you're pregnant, seeing your whole life change before your eyes only to have it vanish like smoke with grim words of, *There's no heartbeat,* you know how jarring it is. How it catapults you from one fantasy land of a future with this little person to another one that seems completely joy-barren and void of life.

Yet somehow, we carry on. Somehow, we mourn the babies we never held, never knew though it feels like we did, and live life without them.

Nel's story was difficult for me to write because it was my first one; Birdie's story was difficult because it was sad. But June's story challenged and stretched me in different ways. In her problems—the monotony of the day-to-day, a marriage gone stale for no one person's fault, and a loss that's so common, profound, yet somehow not talked about—it's been the most difficult story for me to write. I wanted to represent her as one of us. Not fantastical. Not fit. Not perfect. I wanted her to be, in the words of Lyra, simple. In June is every mom I know somewhere. Every single woman I've watched get knocked down—whether by miscarriage, illness, marriage struggles, or something else—and somehow carry on.

To my friends: Thank you for being the people I can lean on, so I don't have to ever feel anything in silence. You let my grief, joy, anxiety, and anger exist loudly and without any judgment; I would never be able to do this life without y'all. Specifically to Nicole, who stood by my side in the hospital room the day I found out there were two hearts, but no heartbeats, and Whitney, who sat with her grief right along with me as we somehow found ways to laugh through the pain.

Kevin, Oak, and Vale: thanks for your unwavering support and loving me through every shade of crazy. You are always my favorite part of the day.

To my first readers and biggest cheerleaders: Sonia, Whitney, Morgann, Monique, and Canadian Lindsay. Thank you for your time, your encouragement, and your laughs.

And always, my editors. Victoria Straw who helped me find the story in my ramblings, Kaitlin Slowik who helped me find the right words to tell it, and Melissa Smith who made it ready for the world. Thank you for your patience, knowledge, and for always responding to my obsessive emails.

My cover artist, Elise, who puts up with my endless requests.

Last but not least, to all my readers who make me believe writing one more book might not be a ridiculous idea—I wouldn't be putting words on paper without y'all. I can't wait for y'all to get to know Scotty next!

Ashley Manley is a current writer and former just about everything else. When she isn't stringing words together on her computer, you can find her chasing her kids, reheating her coffee, or dreaming of her next grand adventure under tall trees. While she's lived a little bit of everywhere, North Carolina will always feel like home. To connect with Ashley, visit ashleymanleywrites.com or find her on Instagram @ashleymanleywrites.

Other books by Ashley
Every Beautiful Mile
When Wildflowers Bloom

Life on the Ledge Duet
Forever and Back
Now to Forever (Scotty's book)

Printed in Dunstable, United Kingdom